PENGUIN BOOKS

The Killing House

Chris Mooney is the internationally bestselling author of the Darby McCormick series and the stand-alone thriller *Remembering Sarah*, which was nominated for the Edgar Award for Best Novel. Foreign rights in the Darby McCormick series have sold in over twenty territories. *The Killing House* is the first book featuring former profiler and now the nation's Most Wanted fugitive, Malcolm Fletcher. Mooney lives in Boston, where he is at work on the next Darby McCormick thriller. For more information, visit chrismooneybooks.com and follow him on Twitter and Facebook.

The Killing House

CHRIS MOONEY

PENGUIN BOOKS

PENGUIN BOOKS

Published by the Penguin Group
Penguin Books Ltd, 80 Strand, London WC2R ORL, England
Penguin Group (USA) Inc., 375 Hudson Street, New York, New York 10014, USA
Penguin Group (Canada), 90 Eglinton Avenue East, Suite 700, Toronto, Ontario, Canada M4P 2Y3
(a division of Pearson Penguin Canada Inc.)
Penguin Ireland, 25 St Stephen's Green, Dublin 2, Ireland (a division of Penguin Books Ltd)
Penguin Group (Australia), 250 Camberwell Road, Camberwell, Victoria 3124, Australia
(a division of Pearson Australia Group Pty Ltd)
Penguin Books India Pvt Ltd, 11 Community Centre,
Panchsheel Park, New Delhi – 110 017, India
Penguin Group (NZ), 67 Apollo Drive, Rosedale, Auckland 0632, New Zealand
(a division of Pearson New Zealand Ltd)
Penguin Books (South Africa) (Pty) Ltd, Block D, Rosebank Office Park,
181 Jan Smuts Avenue, Parktown North, Guateng 2193, South Africa

Penguin Books Ltd, Registered Offices: 80 Strand, London WC2R ORL, England

www.penguin.com

First published 2012
002

Set in 12.5/14.75 pt Garamond MT Std
Typeset by Jouve (UK), Milton Keynes
Printed in England by Clays Ltd, St Ives plc

ISBN: 978–0–141–04951–9

www.greenpenguin.co.uk

ALWAYS LEARNING   **PEARSON**

For Darley Anderson
and
Maggie Griffin

He ne'er is crown'd with immortality
Who fears to follow where
Airy voices lead.

— John Keats

You have caused my companions to shun me;
you have made me a thing of horror to them.

— Psalm 88

I
The Resurrection Men

I

Theresa Herrera stumbled out of her bedroom, fighting to keep the scream caged in her throat. Screaming wasn't allowed; that was one of the rules. The first rule she'd been told. The most important one.

Oh my God, dear Jesus in heaven, this isn't happening.

A phone rang. Not the familiar ring of the house phone or the chiming bells of her cell but a new and completely different ringtone – a constant, high-pitched chirp bordering on a screech. She forced her attention away from the bedroom, away from what had happened to her husband, and started running down the long, brightly lit hall, heading for the bedroom off the top of the stairs – her son's bedroom.

Ring.

The bedroom door was open, always, and everything inside was just the way Rico had left it – the posters of Batman and a futuristic soldier called Master Chief hanging on the walls, the shelves crammed with assembled Lego *Star Wars* ships, books and thick encyclopedias containing the histories of superheroes and popular sci-fi characters from movies and video games. The hamper was still full of his dirty clothes, his desk was still crammed with his drawings, and his bureau was still packed with his scruffy and broken toys. Not a single thing had been moved. Missing did not mean dead. There was always a chance. Always.

Ring.

Theresa raced into the bedroom, her attention locked on the red Spiderman quilt. There it was, just as she'd been told: the disposable cell phone. She picked it up, nearly dropping it in her shaking hands. In the strong light coming from the hall she found the TALK button. She punched it with her thumb and brought the phone up, her mind and body swimming with a dizzying mix of excitement and pure terror.

'Rico? Rico, baby, is that you?'

There was no answer. Could he really be alive, or was this some sort of cruel trick? Four years ago, Rico had been asleep right here in this bed while she attended an awards dinner with her husband. As Barry was being showered with praise for providing free psychiatric care to troubled children and teens, someone had used the aluminium ladder he'd left outside to paint the porch, climbed up to the first-floor window, cut the window screen and abducted her sleeping ten-year-old son from his bed. The babysitter, downstairs watching TV and talking to her boyfriend on her brand new iPhone, hadn't seen or heard a thing.

'Rico, it's me. It's Mom.'

No answer. Theresa pressed the TALK button again. Spoke his name again. Then she realized there was no one on the other end of the line. It was dead.

He'll call back, she told herself. Beads of sweat rolled

down her face and the small of her back, her heart was beating fast – much too fast. She was terrified, short of breath and on the verge of throwing up her Big Mac combo dinner. The only thing keeping the food down was hope.

Before Rico's abduction, Theresa had developed a love of true-crime programmes. The Discovery Channel played them around the clock, the cases narrated by veteran detectives and FBI experts. When it came to child abductions, they all gave the same frightening statistic: if a child wasn't found within the first forty-eight hours, the chance of their being found alive dropped to zero.

Hope came from the real-life case of Elizabeth Smart, a fourteen-year-old girl from Salt Lake City, who, like Rico, had been abducted from her bedroom. The Utah teenager was found nine months later – alive. Theresa's nasty, pragmatic side liked to remind her, too much and too often, that nine months wasn't the same as four years. Still, nine months was an incredibly long time to hold out hope, and Elizabeth Smart's parents had never given up. Theresa had drawn courage and strength from their example, and now, after all these long and painful years, her faith was finally about to be rewarded . . . maybe. Possibly.

The phone rang again.

'Rico?'

Ragged breathing on the other end of the line, and then: 'Mom?'

The voice was slightly older, slightly deeper. Rico would be fourteen now; he would be going through puberty.

'Mom, is that really you?'

It was Rico's voice, no question. The nasal tone was still there, along with the slight lisp. She was talking to her son, her baby.

Theresa felt the sting of tears as that nasty, pragmatic side chimed in: *You need proof.*

The photograph, she thought. She'd been shown a photograph of Rico.

And it could have easily been Photoshopped. You need to be sure, Terry, one hundred per cent sure.

How? How can I –

Ask him something only he would know.

Theresa's eyes squeezed shut. She spoke a moment later.

'Rico, honey, when you were six, we had your birthday party at the Build-a-Bear at the mall. We built a bear together. Remember? You dressed it a certain way.'

'Sergeant-General. That's what I called him. Sergeant-General.'

'What did he look like?'

'He wore army fatigues and a military cap. We recorded a message. When you pressed the paw, the recording said, "I'm an army general, ten-hut."'

Theresa covered her mouth to stifle her cry.

'You recorded the message, Mom. Not me.'

It's him. My baby. The tears came, a floodgate of them, raining down her cheeks.

'Are you okay? Tell me you're okay.'

Rico didn't answer. On the other end of the line she thought she heard someone speaking in the background but couldn't be sure.

Theresa caught movement coming from the hall. A shadow moved across the wall and floor, footsteps heading her way.

Then she heard Rico sobbing.

'Don't let them take me back there.'

'Where? Where did they take you, Rico?'

'I can't take it any more. Please, Mom. Please help me. I don't —'

Click and then Rico was gone.

Theresa yanked the phone away from her ear, frantically searching for the redial button. Rico was alive. Her son was alive and she had just spoken to him and he was terrified and possibly in pain and she had —

The phone slipped from her grasp. She went for it, bumping up against a wall shelf. One of the Lego *Star Wars* spaceships fell against the floor and shattered. A scream roared past her lips and she stifled it with her hands as the woman in the fur coat entered Rico's bedroom.

2

The woman's name was Marie Clouzot. Theresa had never met her before – had never *seen* her before, despite Clouzot's intimation that they *had* met, although the Clouzot woman refused to say where or when this introduction had taken place.

This was what Theresa knew for sure: just a few short hours ago she had told Barry she was heading out to the grocery store. Ali Karim, a New York investigator who had agreed to look into Rico's case, had called her earlier in the day to ask if she and Barry would be home that evening. Karim wanted to send over a man who had considerable experience in abduction cases and needed to know if they would be home between six and seven. Theresa said they would. She had spent the remainder of her Friday afternoon cleaning and tidying up the house (except Rico's room; she never touched anything in there) when at the last minute she remembered she was out of coffee.

When Theresa returned at a few minutes past five, Colorado's winter sky already pitch-black and threatening snow, she hadn't seen any cars parked nearby. She pulled into the garage and opened the door leading into the mudroom, balancing a vegetable and cheese tray she'd purchased at the last minute. Offering food to her guest seemed like the polite thing to do, but there was another component to this purchase: the need to impress. To show that she was a good person, that her son was worthy of Karim's time and attention.

Theresa set the tray on the kitchen island, startled when she saw someone sitting in one of the living-room chairs – an older woman bundled in a rich mahogany-coloured mink. *Has to be one of Barry's hospital or charity friends*, Theresa thought, slipping out of her wool coat. Since Rico's abduction, when her husband wasn't burying himself in patient work at his practice, he was devoting the remainder of his free time to all sorts of charity cases. Barry wanted to be anywhere but home. He barely spoke about Rico any more, and she knew he carried a burning resentment at her refusal to get on with her life. He never said anything to this effect, of course. Barry had never been good at confrontation, and he was simply awful at hiding his feelings – he wore them on his face. But he had voiced his displeasure when he found out she had enlisted the services of what he considered to be nothing more than a glorified private investigator to look into Rico's case.

As Theresa approached the living room, her first thought was that Barbara Bush had come to pay the Herrera family a personal visit. The woman had the same mannish look – George Washington in drag. But the woman in the fur coat wasn't as stout as the former first lady, and she had jet-black hair that was stretched back across her scalp and worn in a bun. A black crocodile Hermès Birkin bag rested on her lap.

One thing was immediately clear: the woman's plastic surgeon had screwed her. Her face had been pulled way too tight, giving her that pale, bug-eyed look Theresa had seen on a lot of older women trying to fight off Father Time with a scalpel. And, if that wasn't bad enough, the woman had a smile that seemed to run from ear to ear. Either God almighty Himself had cursed her with it, or she had specifically asked her surgeon to make her look like the Joker.

The woman stood clutching her handbag. She was tall, almost six feet. Her coat was unbuttoned, revealing a sharp charcoal business suit. Lying against the black blouse was a colourful, ornate jewel necklace that was missing several stones.

Why would she wear a broken necklace? Theresa thought, as she introduced herself. The woman wore diamond earrings and a pair of gloves made of thin black leather. *Is she leaving? And where's Barry?*

The woman didn't introduce herself. Theresa said, 'I'm sorry, have we met?'

The woman smiled brightly. 'You don't remember?'

'I'm afraid I don't.' *I* definitely *would have remembered your face*, Theresa thought.

The woman's smile collapsed. 'Marie Clouzot,' she said, but didn't offer a hand. Instead, she reached into her handbag and came back with a photograph, a close-up of Rico. His head had been shaved and his face was incredibly gaunt, like he'd been starved, and he looked so incredibly scared. Theresa felt the blood drain from her face and limbs as the woman began to speak in a warm and loving voice about Rico – how he was still alive and how she had made arrangements for Theresa to speak to him tonight. Then the Clouzot woman started in on the rules. Don't scream. Don't run or fight. Don't try to call the police. Do anything stupid and Rico would vanish for ever.

Theresa opened her mouth, the questions forming on her lips. She couldn't get the words out, overcome with the same overwhelming dread that had filled her the night she'd discovered Rico missing from his bed, the slit *x* in the window screen; with the same awful sense of her existence having been split in two – her former, normal life with her son and now her new life, this purgatory filled with the constant moment-to-moment terror of wondering where her son was, what had happened to him. And now here was this woman saying that Rico was alive, that arrangements had been made for her to talk to him. Tonight. When Theresa managed to speak, all she could produce was a low, guttural cry.

The Clouzot woman tucked the photograph in her jacket pocket and in that same calm and soothing voice told Theresa to relax. Everything would be fine. There was no reason to be afraid. Dr Herrera was waiting for them upstairs, in the master bedroom. The three of them would talk this out.

Theresa had a vague recollection of moving up the stairs, holding on to the banister for support in case her legs gave out. When she entered her bedroom and saw what had happened to her husband, she remembered the rules and managed to choke her scream back. She stumbled out of the bedroom, as Marie Clouzot said a phone had been placed on Rico's bed. He would be calling at any moment.

And he did. Four long and nightmarish years had passed, and Theresa's unwavering faith that Rico was still alive had just been confirmed with a single phone call. Her son was alive, he was being held somewhere, maybe even close by. He was scared and possibly in pain but he *was* alive.

Theresa gripped the edge of Rico's lopsided desk to keep from falling. The room swam in her vision until her gaze settled on the disposable cell phone lying on the floor.

Don't let them take me back there, Rico had said. *I can't take it any more.*

Marie Clouzot slid her gloved hands inside her jacket pockets. 'I know all of this is an incredible shock for you. Just keeping breathing, nice and slow deep breaths, or you'll pass out. Yes, like that . . . Good.' Her voice was patient and calm and so terribly quiet.

'We're going to go back to the bedroom now, Mrs Herrera. Just remember the rules. No screaming. Don't run or, say, try to hurt me so you can call the police. If you do, I'll have to use this.' The woman held up a Taser. A click of a button and an electric arch of light crackled and jumped between two prongs. 'While you're lying disabled on the floor, I'll take my leave, and Rico will disappear down the rabbit hole again, only this time we'll have to kill him.'

We'll kill him. How many people were involved in this? Theresa's mind was on fire, scrambling to think. But she couldn't, she couldn't hold it together any more. She broke down, wailing.

'I don't want to kill him, Mrs Herrera. I really don't. Your son has suffered enough. If you want him to live, we need to go back to your bedroom.'

'Why? Why are you doing this?'

'This is a conversation we need to have in front of your husband.'

'Please,' Theresa said, wiping at her face. 'Please, I'm begging you, whatever this is about – if it's money you want, I can –'

'We need to go back to your bedroom. I'll be right by your side.' The Clouzot woman offered her a hand.

Theresa didn't take it. 'I want to talk to Rico again. I want to –'

'Do you want me to bring you to your son?'

'Yes. Yes, please, I'll do anything just don't . . . hurt him any more.'

The Clouzot woman put a hand on Theresa's shoulder, the tender, gentle way a woman would – *It's okay, honey, everything's going to be okay.*

'I won't hurt him,' Marie Clouzot said. 'Now let's go back to your bedroom and talk to your husband.'

Theresa didn't move. A dim voice whispered that she was in shock. Maybe she was. She hadn't so much as flinched when the hand touched her, and she didn't fight back when the Clouzot woman lifted her to her feet. Theresa felt the woman gently wrap an arm around her. The next thing she knew she was being ushered forward, her legs numb and hollow.

'That's it,' Marie Clouzot said. 'One step at a time.'

3

Theresa stared at the brightly lit hall. It seemed as long as a mile, and incredulously she thought: *This is what a condemned prisoner must feel like when he's being escorted to the electric chair.*

Her legs gave out as she stepped inside the bedroom. She would have fallen had the Clouzot woman not been clutching her arm.

'It's okay,' the Clouzot woman said. 'I know you're scared. Think about Rico – how excited he'll be to see you.'

The lamps on both nightstands had been turned on, giving the room an intimate setting. The shades and curtains were still drawn. Her husband was still dressed in sweatpants and his ratty old grey Yale T-shirt; he still lay spread-eagled on top of the white ruffled coverlet, his wrists tied to the copper-plated headboard and his ankles to the bedposts. He couldn't speak; a strip of duct-tape was fastened across his mouth. He mumbled behind it, glaring at her, his hazel eyes wide with terror.

'Just a few more steps,' Marie Clouzot said. 'That's it, you're doing great.'

The left side of Barry's face was swollen. Had the Clouzot woman hit him, or had it been her partner? At five foot eight, Barry wasn't a big man. *She could have easily dragged him up here by herself,* Theresa thought dimly. Sweat had soaked through Barry's T-shirt and matted what little remained of his greying hair. She saw where the rope had cut his skin. Bright drops of blood dotted the white pillowcases. This morning's bandage was still on his reedy and nearly hairless forearm. She had gone with him to the dermatologist's office. A mole had changed colour. The doctor had taken a biopsy, and Barry had convinced himself that he had stage-four melanoma.

'Almost there,' Marie Clouzot said, edging Theresa closer to the side of the bed.

Seeing the bandage made what was happening *very* real somehow, as did the item that had been left on the nightstand: the heavy cook's knife taken from the kitchen's butcher block, the German Wusthof with the fourteen-inch blade she used to carve the holiday turkeys and hams. It was within arm's reach.

Pick it up, that pragmatic voice screamed at her. *Pick it up and kill her.*

No.

You can do it, Terry. You have to do it.

I can't. They'll kill Rico.

The opportunity had passed. The Clouzot woman had let go of her grip and moved away. Theresa rested her thighs against the edge of the bed to keep from falling, her heart beating so fast she wondered if it was going to explode inside her chest.

Pretend to pass out, that pragmatic voice said.

She'll wait, Theresa answered. *Either that or she'll hit me with the Taser and just walk out.*

You don't know that. Goddamnit, Terry, you have to try something.

Marie Clouzot, standing at the foot of the bed, reached into her handbag and came back with a small digital camcorder, one of those tiny Flip Video models.

'Whenever you're ready, Mrs Herrera.'

'Ready?' Theresa repeated.

'For your confession,' Marie Clouzot said. 'I want you to tell your husband what you did.'

What I did? What is she talking about?

'Don't be shy, Mrs Herrera. You might not remember *me*, but I'm absolutely, positively sure you remember your former life in Philadelphia.'

Theresa felt frozen in place. A new fear bloomed in her stomach, and for a moment it replaced her thoughts of Rico and what was happening – unfolding – right now inside her bedroom.

'Yes,' the Clouzot woman said, and smiled – a bright and joyous Christmas-morning smile. 'You remember now, don't you?'

Theresa swallowed. She didn't know what to say and she had to say something.

'About . . . that. I didn't know what –'

'Don't tell *me*, Mrs Herrera, tell your husband – and look at him when you speak. If you don't, Rico goes bye-bye.'

The Clouzot woman brought up the video camera.

Theresa forced her attention on to Barry. He gawked up at her from the bed, confused and frightened.

Theresa had been married to him for nineteen years, and not once during that time had she ever considered telling him about Philadelphia. The woman who had been born and lived in the Northeast – that person was dead and buried. Speaking about it to anyone, for any reason, wasn't allowed. Theresa had told no one, not even Ali Karim. He could turn over every rock on the planet, and there was no way he would never find out who she really was.

And yet Marie Clouzot knew. She *knew*.

How? How did she find out?

'Tell your husband who you are, and what you did,' Marie Clouzot said. Her left hand held the camera steady as her right hand dipped into her coat pocket and came back with a compact 9-mm. 'I won't ask you again.'

Theresa began to talk – haltingly at first, and then her words gathered steam. Every word she spoke felt like another hot coal stockpiled in her stomach. She got past it by thinking of Rico – Rico alive and waiting for her.

When she finished, Theresa felt a hollow beating inside her chest. She still didn't know who Marie Clouzot was, but she had an idea.

'Is there anything else you'd like to add, Mrs Herrera?'

'Yes.' Theresa's voice sounded far away, and strained. She cleared her throat and, steeling herself, spoke louder.

'I want to apologize to you. As for what . . . happened, I didn't –'

'You have one minute to make your decision.'

Theresa blinked, confused. 'Decision?'

'I want you to pick up that kitchen knife and cut your husband's throat.'

4

Theresa said nothing. She had nothing to say. That pragmatic voice had nothing to say. Her mind felt as vacant as an abandoned house.

Marie Clouzot had to raise her voice over Barry's muffled screams. 'Kill your husband, and I'll bring you to your son. If you don't kill your husband, I'll kill you, and then I'll leave and kill your son. Are you familiar with slow slicing?'

Theresa didn't hear the question, still in shock by what the woman had said: *Cut your husband's throat.*

'Slow slicing is a form of execution developed by the Chinese,' the Clouzot woman said, reaching into her pocket. 'You use a knife to cut away portions of the body over a long period of time. It's death by a thousand cuts.'

'I . . . I can't . . .'

'Can't what, Mrs Herrera?'

'I can't go through with this.'

The Clouzot woman placed the wrinkled snapshot of Rico on Barry's stomach.

'You have fifty-three seconds left to make your decision, Mrs Herrera.'

'I want to help you,' Theresa said. 'Please, let me help you.'

'Forty-nine seconds.'

Barry was screaming, thrashing.

'We can come to some sort of . . . accommodation,' Theresa said. 'Let's talk about this. Let's talk about how I can help –'

'Forty-three seconds.'

Theresa saw her son's frightened gaze staring up from the photograph lying on Barry's stomach, and she saw her son staring at her from the photographs on the walls and bureau – Rico as a baby and as a toddler, each picture showing a boy with a round, brown face and a mop of unruly black hair; a gap-toothed smile and, along the right temple, a strawberry-coloured birth-mark the size of a dime.

'Thirty-nine seconds, Mrs Herrera.'

She stared at the photograph on Barry's stomach. Rico was alive. Her son's life depended on her next decision – a horribly cruel, life-altering decision.

Was her husband's life worth it?

Don't let them take me back there, Rico had said.

'Thirty-seven seconds.'

I can't take it any more. Please, Mom. Please help me.

Theresa grabbed the heavy cook's knife.

Barry screamed from behind the tape. He screamed and thrashed, the rope cutting deeper into his skin. Blood trickled down his wrists.

'You have twenty-two seconds left.'

God forgive me, Theresa thought, turning the knife in her hands, just as a pair of car headlights flashed across the drawn blinds.

5

Malcolm Fletcher parked the Audi at the bottom of the long driveway leading up to an impressive brick-faced Colonial, the home of Dr Bernard Herrera and his wife, Theresa. It was a few minutes past seven, and a light snow had started to fall.

The lights in one of the upstairs rooms winked off. The other windows blazed with light, but he couldn't see inside. The blinds on the windows facing the street had been drawn.

He wondered why. There was no house across the road. Each home in this upscale neighbourhood here in Applewood, Colorado, had been set up on a good amount of acreage, far apart from one another to give the owners a great deal of privacy. Fletcher killed the engine and picked up the leather Dopp kit from the passenger seat.

While he felt reasonably confident that neither Dr Herrera nor his wife would recognize him, Fletcher still needed to exercise caution. With Bin Laden dead, Fletcher had shot to the top slot as the nation's Most Wanted Fugitive – and the most expensive. The reward for his capture was three million dollars.

Fletcher had not undergone any cosmetic surgery to

alter his appearance. Instead, he relied on the tradecraft he'd learned while employed as a federal agent. From the Dopp kit he removed a plastic case holding a pair of blue-tinted contact lenses. Because he was allergic to the materials used to manufacture lenses, he always put them in at the last minute. Then he put on a pair of glasses with tortoiseshell frames.

He checked his appearance in the rearview mirror. His beard was neatly trimmed and his black hair, thick and long, had grown out over the ears. For the past five months he had been living in Key West under one of his aliases and his skin was brown from the sun. With his tan, stylish glasses and coloured contacts, he bore no resemblance to his fugitive photos.

He was, however, the spitting image of the New York licence and passport photographs he carried for Richard Munchel, a self-employed computer-security consultant who occasionally performed work for the global security company Karim Enterprises. Ali Karim had contacted him using the anonymous and encrypted email system they had set up.

Karim had recently agreed to look into the abduction of a ten-year-old boy from Colorado. Four years had passed with no developments reported by the police, and the mother believed her son was still alive. Karim thought that Fletcher's prior experience as a profiler for the FBI's Behavioral Analysis Unit might possibly uncover a new investigative thread to explore, an overlooked angle or piece of evidence. Fletcher agreed, and Karim scanned and then emailed the police reports. Karim, an old friend and trusted ally, had not only provided him with safe harbour on many occasions over the years; he was also one of a handful of people who knew the truth behind Fletcher's fugitive status.

Years ago, while employed as a federal agent, Fletcher had uncovered a classified 'black book' research project involving the Behavioral Analysis Unit. While conducting his own covert investigation, three men were dispatched to his home to make him and the evidence disappear. Fletcher escaped with his life but not the evidence; the FBI had confiscated it from his storage facility. The research project was quickly dismantled, the hospitals shut down, every scrap of paper and piece of evidence collected and destroyed. The FBI's bureaucratic powers, having decided he was a liability, fabricated a story for the press: Malcolm Fletcher had attacked and killed three federal agents who had been sent to his home to arrest him in connection with the murders of several serial killers – cases he had worked on while employed as a profiler.

Fletcher climbed out of the car, pleased to be wearing a suit after these longs months spent under the hot Florida sun. He was a veteran of private schools, where ties and jackets were required, and then later, as a federal agent, he had grown accustomed to good suits and shoes. They were a part of his true identity, the last vestiges of the life he had led before becoming a wanted man.

His attention turned to the area between the right side of the house and the detached two-car garage – the place where someone had used an outside ladder to climb up to the first-floor window and abduct Rico Herrera from his bed. The intruder had not left behind any fingerprints or trace evidence, but police had recovered a man's size-nine trainer impression from the dirt.

Fletcher shut the car door and moved up the driveway.

6

When the Clouzot woman saw the headlights flash across the closed blinds, she shut off the bedroom lights. Theresa didn't put up a fight when the woman grabbed her arm and, with a surprising strength, marched her swiftly across the room to the windows facing the street.

Theresa was standing there now, with her face mashed against the window's crown moulding and the gun's muzzle digging into her left temple, Clouzot behind her. As instructed, Theresa had pulled back the side of the wooden blinds just enough to allow Clouzot to see the driveway.

Theresa could see too. The man who stepped out of the black Audi had long, dark hair and wore a dark overcoat. *This has to be the man Ali Karim said would be coming by tonight to talk about Rico*, she thought. *The man experienced in abduction cases.*

Clouzot leaned in closer. 'Who is he, and what is he doing here?'

So Barry hadn't told her about the investigator – or Ali Karim.

Don't tell her, that pragmatic voice said. *If you do – if you tell her this man is an investigator, that he's here because you hired someone to look into Rico's case – she might panic and decide to kill you.*

Theresa felt Rico watching her from the photographs.

I can't take it any more. Please, Mom. Please help me.

The doorbell rang.

'He's an investigator,' Theresa said. 'I don't know his name.'

'Police? FBI?'

'I don't know. He works for someone else, a man named Ali Karim. Karim owns a security company in New York. Manhattan. I hired him to look into what happened to my son.'

'Why? What did you find?'

'I don't understand.'

'You found something, some piece of evidence.' Clouzot's voice was quiet, almost a whisper, but the calm veneer was gone. The woman was scared. 'Tell me.'

'Nothing. I just –'

'Just what?'

'I . . . I couldn't live with it any more, not knowing what happened to him. To Rico.'

'Did you tell this Karim person your real name?'

'No.'

'What you did back in Philadelphia?'

The doorbell rang again.

'No,' Theresa said. 'No, of course not.'

'Lie to me and your son dies.'

'*I'm telling you the truth. I –*' Theresa cut herself off when she felt the gun muzzle dig deeper into her head.

'Yell at me again,' Clouzot said, 'and I'll kill you.'

'I'm sorry.'

Clouzot said nothing. Theresa blinked the sweat from her eyes. The wooden blinds rattled in her trembling hand.

A moment later she saw the man move away from the front door. Instead of heading to his car, he walked to the top of the driveway and peered inside one of the garage's bay windows.

Theresa felt the woman's rapid breathing against her nape, heard the hitch in her throat when the man turned and made his way back to the house.

'Let go of the blind,' Clouzot said.

Theresa did. Clouzot released her grip and backed away. Theresa didn't dare move.

Two beeps as the woman pressed the keys for a pre-programmed number on her cell and then Clouzot spoke into the phone: 'If you don't hear from me within the next five minutes, take Rico away and kill him.'

Fletcher couldn't see inside the house. The blinds on the nearby windows had been drawn, and the front door, made of solid mahogany, contained no small perimeter windows.

No matter. Both the doctor and his wife were home. Both vehicles were parked in the garage. He rang the doorbell again, about to follow it with repeated knocking, when the heavy door cracked open.

7

When Theresa saw the man standing on her doorstep, she immediately wanted to scream for help – scream as she threw the door wide open and pointed at the sick bitch Clouzot, who was pressed up against the wall only a few feet away, listening. The owner of the black Audi was at least six foot five and as broad-shouldered as a timber beam – the kind of strong and powerful man she imagined could lift a small car or run through a wall without so much as suffering a single scratch.

'Mrs Herrera?' the man asked. He had a foreign accent – British, maybe Australian.

'I'm Theresa Herrera.'

He eyed her suspiciously, and then she remembered how she looked – face and clothes drenched with sweat, hands and limbs trembling.

'I've got that rotten stomach flu that's going around,' she said. 'I take it that was you who rang the doorbell a moment ago.'

The man nodded. 'Ali Karim sent me.'

From the corner of her eye Theresa saw Clouzot's handgun. It was aimed at her, and there was no doubt in Theresa's mind the woman would use it.

If you don't hear from me within the next five minutes, Marie Clouzot had told her partner, *take Rico away and kill him.*

Theresa pressed her face closer to the door's opening and said, 'I'm sorry I didn't answer. When I'm not lying in bed I'm lying on the bathroom floor. I'm afraid now isn't a good time.'

'May I speak to your husband?'

'He's not here.' She remembered he had looked inside the garage and seen both cars. She said, 'He's gone out for the evening with a friend and won't be back until late, I'm afraid.'

The man took off his glasses, the lenses wet with melting snow. He had bright blue eyes.

'My husband,' Theresa said, the words drowning in her throat. She swallowed and started again. 'My husband and I . . . we've decided not to retain Mr Karim's services.'

The man showed no reaction. He glanced past her, inside the foyer. For a moment she thought he was going to push the door open and rush in.

Instead, he said, 'May I ask what changed your mind?'

'Finances.'

The man snapped his attention back to her.

'We simply couldn't afford Mr Karim's fee,' she said. 'The bank denied us a second mortgage – they called only a couple of hours ago. I'm sorry you came all the way out here. Please tell Mr Karim I'll gladly reimburse him for any expenses he's incurred.'

'There's no need.' The man dipped a hand inside his coat, staring at her with an unsettling intensity. It had a hypnotic quality, as though he had somehow entered her head and was listening to her true thoughts.

Then, incredibly, as if he knew what was happening inside her house, his hand came back with a 9-mm handgun.

Theresa stared at it with equal measures of fear and relief. Her expression was hidden from Clouzot. There was no way the woman could see her face – or the man's handgun.

In an act of bravery – *Please, God, please let this work* – Theresa looked sideways, to the corner where the Clouzot woman was hiding. She held her gaze there for a moment as she said, 'Again, I'm sorry for the inconvenience.'

'Have a good night, Mrs Herrera. I hope you feel better.'

The man reached forward, about to grab her or maybe to push the door inward, when the gunshot rang out.

8

Fletcher had caught the palpable relief on Theresa Herrera's face when he removed his sidearm – a SIG SAUER P226, the same reliable and powerful 9-mm weapon used by the Navy's SEAL Team Six. She was staring at it as he placed one foot on the threshold, about to throw the door open, grab the Herrera woman and pull her out when the gunshot erupted from inside the house.

Part of Theresa Herrera's head disappeared, and she slumped to the floor like a puppet whose strings had been cut.

The front door swung inward. Inside the foyer of dim light and crouching behind the door was an older woman dressed in a fur coat. He caught a glimpse of her face, the odd, horse-like grin looking at him from across a 9-mm handgun.

The first shot, fired from less than a foot away, hit him dead centre in the chest.

Fletcher staggered backwards from the sudden impact. He spun awkwardly, tumbling back against the wrought-iron railing. The woman fired again. The round hit him in the abdomen, and he slipped on the snow-covered landing and tumbled down the short set of brick steps.

Fletcher landed face first against the walkway. He immediately rolled on to his side, hissing back the pain, snow stinging his face.

The woman fired again. The shot kicked up a clump of dirt and dead grass dangerously close to his head. Fletcher moved to his back and brought up his weapon, about to fire when the shooter threw the front door shut.

Theresa Herrera's limp arm hung over the threshold. The door hit it and bounced back. Fletcher caught a flash of the dark fur coat retreating down the foyer.

Fletcher staggered to his feet. The lightweight ceramic armour plating woven inside the bulletproof vest had prevented the two rounds from piercing his body, but the impact had cracked at least one rib, sending his muscles into spasms.

The bullet had removed most of Theresa Herrera's head, killing her instantly.

A spent shell caught his attention. Well studied in ballistics, he immediately registered what it was.

A door slammed open from the back of the house. Struggling to breathe, the cold air sharp with the odour of cordite, he stumbled across the front lawn towards the left side of the house – a task made more difficult in his shoes, as they offered no traction in the snow.

One shot. All he needed was one clear shot to take the woman down.

Fletcher stuck close to the side of the house. When it ended, he turned the corner, bringing up his SIG.

The garden, wide and long, was partially lit by the

light shining through the back windows. A back door hung open; it led to a deck of pressure-treated wood. Through the falling snow he saw a clear set of footprints near the deck's bottom step. He followed them across the garden until they vanished inside a black forest of tall pines. In the far distance and glowing like eyes in the night were the windows of a half-dozen homes.

He saw no sign of the woman. Had no idea if she was running or hiding somewhere, waiting for him.

Fletcher might have given pursuit if she didn't already have a good lead on him. In his current physical condition, there was no way he could bridge the gap.

A more practical and urgent consideration, however, made him immediately turn and move back to the front: the police. One or more nearby neighbours had no doubt heard the multiple gunshots and called 911.

The front door hung wide open. Fletcher clutched the railing as he moved up the front steps. Snow blew inside the house, coating the foyer and Theresa Herrera's small, still body in a fine layer of white. She lay face down in a twisted heap on the brown tile. Blood had pooled around her and dripped over the threshold, staining the snow a bright red.

Fletcher dropped to his knees, his ribs screaming in protest, and looked at the entry wound. It was tattooed with black powder. The size of the wound and amount of gunpowder confirmed the gun had been fired from a close distance – a few feet away from the door, to his right. The shooter had stood there, but she couldn't have seen him – couldn't have seen him drawing his weapon. There were no windows installed around the door, no nearby windows that looked on to the front landing. So why had she suddenly panicked and shot Theresa?

Wary of destroying potential latent fingerprints, he used a pen to pick up the casing from the floor. Fletcher dropped it inside one of the small evidence bags he kept tucked inside his back pocket, sealing it shut on his way back to the car.

9

Fletcher backed up and drove away, the car tyres slipping and skidding on the snow until they found purchase. Everywhere he looked he saw home windows bright with light. He caught more than one face pressed against the glass, examining the street for the source of the gunshots. They couldn't see him; he was hidden behind the Audi's tinted windows.

But they could see his car.

During his early years as a fugitive, Fletcher had invested his considerable savings in the stock market. Through careful management, he had amassed a small fortune, which had allowed him to purchase a number of safe houses under the names of various well-crafted identities and corporations. The closest home was in Sturgis, South Dakota – a small ranch house with a private garage holding a Honda Accord.

The townhouse in Chicago, however, had a custom-made Jaguar stored in the small garage. Armoured and bulletproof, the car contained other useful features that would be beneficial during the course of his investigation.

Fletcher cracked open the windows and listened to the cold night.

Two minutes passed with no sirens.

Ten minutes passed and he saw no police cruisers.

The city snowploughs, however, were out in full force, busy clearing the roads. Their numbers suggested a major snowstorm was about to descend upon central Colorado.

It was only when he reached the highway that he allowed himself to turn his attention inward to examine what had happened at the Herrera home.

Fletcher started at the beginning, seeing each frame with remarkable clarity, as though it had been filmed. He ran the movie forward and backward, sometimes pausing to study a particular frame.

He kept wondering if his actions – or lack thereof – had contributed to Theresa Herrera's death.

It was clear the moment the petite woman cracked opened the door that something was wrong. The fringe of her short blonde hair was matted across her damp forehead. Her face was pale, her bloodshot eyes wide with terror. She had dark rings of sweat underneath the arms and collar of her long-sleeved grey T-shirt. *I've got that rotten stomach flu that's going around,* she'd told him.

A logical explanation, and one he might have believed if she hadn't told him the reason why she and her husband had decided to forgo Ali Karim's investigative services at the last minute: *Finances. We simply couldn't afford Mr Karim's fee.*

Karim, Fletcher knew, hadn't charged the Herrera family for his services. He didn't charge anyone.

Karim, a former CIA operative, had left the Agency at a relatively young age. Instead of entering the lucrative private sector, he established his own security company in Midtown Manhattan. Having recently divorced, and with his ex-wife taking their only child, their son, Jason, back to live in her family home in London, Karim put his time and energy into his business.

In less than a decade, he had opened additional offices in several major US cities. Then, with the explosive growth of the Internet during the nineties, Karim's careful and well-timed investments had allowed him to expand his business and purchase several private forensic companies in the United States and abroad. By the dawn of the twenty-first century, Ali Karim was the owner of a global security empire – and one of the nation's richest men. Karim devoted his considerable wealth, talents and resources to providing pro bono investigative services for the victims of crime.

When Theresa Herrera said she couldn't afford Karim's fee, Fletcher thought the woman was trying to warn him – about what, he had no idea. He had drawn his weapon, wanting to be prepared, and he saw her relief before she looked sideways and held her gaze where the shooter was hiding, watching and listening. He was about to grab Theresa Herrera and take her to the safety of his car when the woman in the fur coat fired.

Still, he wondered if there was something he could have done to change the outcome. If he had acted immediately, instead of using the time to remove his sidearm, it was possible that . . . Useless, childish thinking. Theresa Herrera was dead.

Fletcher unbuttoned his shirt. The adrenalin had abated, leaving in its wake a growing pain in his chest and abdomen. He slipped a hand inside his shirt and undid the vest's straps to relieve the pressure.

He gently pressed on his breastbone. Daggers of pain erupted from the left side of his chest; he had cracked at least two ribs.

While breathing was painful, he didn't feel short of breath, dizzy, lethargic – all promising signs that he hadn't suffered a flail chest, a life-threatening medical condition that occurred when part of the rib cage detached from the chest wall.

The next part would be difficult, but he had to do it.

Fletcher took in a slow, deep breath. Sparks of pain exploded through his brain and burned a bright white across his vision, but he fought his way through it. Having suffered such injuries in the past, he knew the importance of taking in the deepest breath possible in order to prevent pneumonia or a partial collapse of lung tissue known as atelectasis.

He took another deep breath and then repeated it again. Again. When he finished, he was flushed, drenched in sweat.

Fletcher took out his smartphone and dialled Karim's private number. A small pause followed as the encryption software scrambled the call, and then Karim's deep and smoky voice erupted on the other end of the line.

'Well, that was bloody quick. I take it you found something good.'

Fletcher managed to speak clearly over the pain.

'Theresa Herrera's dead,' he said, and walked Karim step by step through everything that had happened.

A long silence followed. In his mind's eye Fletcher pictured Karim, a short, round man of Pakistani descent, seated behind the immense glass desk in his private office, leaning back in his chair and smoking one of his foul Italian cigarettes.

'Do you need a doctor?' Karim asked. 'I can get you one, someone discreet.'

'No. I know how to treat this.'

'Do you always wear a bulletproof vest when visiting the home of a grieving family?'

'My lifestyle demands that I live in a constant state of paranoia, Ali. I have to be prepared for any eventuality.'

'What about the husband?'

'I saw no signs of him, but I found two cars in the garage.'

'And the woman who shot you?'

'Just a glimpse,' Fletcher said. 'She's Caucasian, late fifties to early sixties. Black hair pulled back across the scalp. I suspect she's had a facelift.'

'Would you recognize her if you saw her again?'

Fletcher, recalling the woman's distinctive-looking smile, said, 'Absolutely.'

On the other end of the line Fletcher heard the flick of a lighter. A pause as Karim drew on the cigarette, and then he said, 'The police will go through Theresa Herrera's phone records and see my number. Forgive me for asking this, but did you leave behind any evidence?'

'No. I wore gloves the entire time.'

'Witnesses?'

'I don't believe so.'

'Still, you need to do something about your car. Someone might have seen it.'

'I plan on switching it when I reach Chicago.'

'I hope you're not planning on driving there right now. I was watching the Weather Channel in preparation for tomorrow morning's flight. The storm has changed; Colorado is about to get slammed with at least two feet. Best to play it safe and wait it out. You can't afford to get stuck, or in an accident.'

Karim was right. Visibility was poor; Fletcher could barely see the highway.

'It goes without saying that I'd like your assistance on this, Malcolm. That being said, I've put you in an odd and uncomfortable situation. If you need to disappear, I understand.'

Fletcher thought about the shell casing in the evidence bag and said, 'I need a portable mass spectrometer – a new model, and preferably one manufactured in the UK.' British companies were always on the cutting edge of forensics.

'I'll get you one,' Karim said. 'When will you be arriving in Chicago?'

'Let's meet Monday morning, at six.'

'Six it is. Give me the address.'

Fletcher gave it to him.

'If you're going to be late, please call me,' Karim said. 'A dark-skinned man like myself loitering on the streets and holding a big, bulky suitcase – well, we don't need anyone conducting racial-profiling and summoning the police about a possible terror threat, now do we?'

'Paulson won't be driving you?' Boyd Paulson was Karim's personal bodyguard. Born in Dublin, raised in London, the pugnacious former boxer had been attached to Karim since the beginning of time – and rarely let Karim out of his sight, as Karim had been the target of many death threats over the years.

'Boyd is on holiday,' Karim said. 'If you need anything else – anything at all – call me.'

'I will.'

'Malcolm . . . There's nothing you could have done to save her.'

'I'll see you Monday,' Fletcher said, and hung up.

10

When Lisa Alcione turned nineteen, she ran off to Los Angeles with the man she'd later marry, swearing to her parents she'd never return to Morrison, Colorado. She was forced to return once, to attend her mother's funeral. Her husband, Tony, had not joined her. Business obligations.

He's up to no good, her father had told her. *A pig dressed up in a suit is still a pig, Lisa.*

And now here she was, thirty-five and newly divorced, back in Morrison, back to working the front counter of her father's 'family-friendly' motel, with its quick and easy access to the ski slopes. Maybe the family-friendly thing was true thirty years ago, but now the place catered to budget travellers and cost-conscious adulterers from Denver who paid for rooms in cash and registered under false names.

Standing behind the front counter, she watched her father clearing away the snow in his rickety Ford pickup. She'd been here only two months, and there didn't seem to be a moment when dear old dad wasn't reminding her how she had royally screwed up her life. *I told you that good-for-nuthin' had a wandering eye. Guys like Tony, with their Hollywood looks and money, they're always gonna be lookin' to upgrade to a younger, fresher model. Men got options, Lisa.*

Women don't. Sure, the bright ones do, but God didn't bless you with either brains or particularly good looks. You need to get your head out of the clouds and stop dreamin' about some goddamn Prince Charming and settle for someone on your own level.

She'd told her father that Tony had simply wanted out – seven-year itch and all that bullshit. The truth was Tony *had* dumped her for a younger model, a neighbour's 22-year-old Swedish au pair who, incidentally, was three months pregnant with Tony's baby. Dale Alcione would have had a field day with that little nugget of info.

A black car pulled into the lot – an Audi. It drove into the space next to the front office.

Probably another bunch of rich teenagers on their way back from the slopes, looking to spend their Friday night getting wasted or high, she thought. *That or some older guy with a young chippie looking to pork their way through the storm.* The excitement never ended around here.

The car door opened. Not a teenager or some fat old bald guy but a *very* tall and *very* big man dressed in a sharp overcoat. He was alone. When the car door had opened, the interior light clicked on; she saw no one else inside.

The man smiled as he approached the front counter. He had nice teeth and wore a pair of stylish glasses. He had beautiful blue eyes, intense and intelligent. Straightening, she pulled on the edges of her angora crewneck sweater, wanting to show off her figure.

'Good evening,' he said. 'I was hoping you might have a room available.'

Definitely from somewhere overseas, she thought. 'I'm sure I can accommodate you.'

'Thank you so much.'

She told him the rate.

The man took a wad of cash from his pocket.

'I need a licence and a credit card,' she said. 'Security deposits and all of that fun stuff.'

'I'm afraid I've lost my licence.' The man handed her a hundred-dollar bill. 'Will this be enough to cover a security deposit?'

'That'll do it. Just give me a name and address.'

'Ted Parker.'

'Your accent,' she said, typing in his information. 'What is it, British or Australian?'

'Australian, mostly, although I did spend a good number of my formative years in London.'

Something about the man triggered a comparison with one of her favorite actors, Russell Crowe. Maybe it was simply the Australian connection, because this guy certainly didn't talk like Crowe did in his movies, and there was absolutely no physical resemblance. That wasn't a bad thing. Ted Parker was certainly doing just fine in both the looks and the body departments, and he had that same animal magnetism Crowe gave off in his movies, that rugged sense of . . . well, manliness. The kind of testosterone-fuelled alpha male who always won in a bar fight and had his pick of women. A man, she suspected, who knew how to treat a woman right.

'I'm pretty sure the bars and restaurants in the area

are closing down for the night on account of the storm,' she said. 'If you're hungry, I can make you a sandwich. Dale – that's my father, he owns the place – he has some beers in the fridge. Bud cans, nothing fancy. I can bring some on by if you like.'

'That's very kind of you, but I've already eaten this evening.'

Lisa gave him her best smile as she placed the key on the counter.

He paid in cash, thanked her again and left. Lisa watched him all the way to the car, wanting to know more about the mysterious and charismatic Ted Parker, why he made her feel safe.

Fletcher parked around the side of the dingy motel, where his car couldn't be seen from the highway. In a few minutes' time, it would be covered with snow, and no one would recognize it.

He popped the trunk, selected the rucksack and carried it with him to his room. The stale air smelled of bleach and industrial cleaners. He drew the curtains and turned on one of the bedside lamps. Dust swarmed in the cone of light. He suspected the room hadn't been cleaned in weeks.

Not wanting to leave fingerprints, he switched his leather gloves for a pair of latex. He slid the desk chair across the room and wedged it underneath the doorknob to prevent intrusion. He doubted anyone would come inside, but he had to be careful. He hung up his coat and carried the rucksack to a bathroom decorated with salmon-coloured tiles.

Fletcher removed his contacts. Wearing them even for a few short hours irritated his eyes. He put in a few antihistamine drops and turned on the shower to allow the water to warm up. He undressed carefully, his ribs screaming in protest.

One of the rounds had managed to penetrate the vest's Kevlar fabric, lodging itself in the cracked ceramic plating – not surprising, given the short distance from which it had been fired.

Slowly, Fletcher bent down and reached for the tactical knife strapped to his calf. He used it to remove the slug, then pitched the edges between his long fingers and held it up to the cheap fluorescent bulbs mounted above the mirror. It was a 9-mm round, but not one he recognized. His suspicions had been confirmed. He dropped the slug inside an evidence bag and continued to undress.

Standing under the hot water, he examined his chest. The tanned skin above his abdomen and left pectoral was red and swollen, tender to the touch. Encouraged by his steady but painful breathing, he doubted he had suffered any internal injuries. He'd been lucky. If he had been shot with a .44 Magnum or an armour-piercing round, he would have bled to death.

Within a few days' time, the skin would bruise and then fade. The cracked ribs would take at least six weeks to heal. The pain could be managed with ibuprofen.

Dressed in fresh clothing, he removed a Ziploc bag from his rucksack, went outside and packed it with snow. He wedged the chair back underneath the doorknob, propped up the pillows and sat down on the stiff bed. He took out a pad of paper, and with the cold plastic bag placed over his cracked ribs he sketched the face of the woman who'd shot him.

Time passed. Fortunately, there was no need to return to Key West. Before leaving Florida, he had wiped down the rental home and packed his meagre possessions inside the pair of suitcases resting in the Audi's trunk. He had called the woman he'd been seeing, an art-gallery dealer, and told her that he had business in France and didn't believe he would be returning to the States in the foreseeable future. The woman expressed her disappointment. It was a shame, she said; she'd liked the time they had spent together and had hoped their relationship would develop into something more serious.

Fletcher had thought about her during the long drive to Colorado. He wished he could have got to know her better. Stayed a bit longer.

Even if Karim hadn't called, it was time to move on. Fletcher hadn't been caught because he had followed a certain set of rules, the first of which was not staying in one spot for too long. He always had to be on the move, ready to run at a moment's notice. He didn't get too friendly with the locals, he didn't make friends, and he avoided emotional entanglements. He had to lead a compartmentalized life and stay forever vigilant; if he grew, he would make mistakes. No rational person would choose to live this way, but this was his life, and there was nothing he could do to change it. It was what it was.

Fletcher stopped sketching and examined the result. Satisfied, he put the pad and pen aside and then lay down. He stared at a cobweb on the ceiling, wishing he had a bottle of Château Latour to keep him company.

The wind battered the motel room's rickety windows. Fletcher wondered if he would die this way – alone in a motel room of beige frieze carpet, seeing, as his last images, bad watercolour landscapes hung in cheap frames on mustard-coloured walls.

He closed his eyes and, as though he had entered a private screening room, again replayed what had happened at the Herrera home. His attention kept drifting back to Theresa Herrera, kept seeing the woman sprawled across the foyer floor, her limp arm hanging over the threshold.

Malcolm Fletcher did not indulge much in regret. Still, he wished he could have saved the woman's life. Wished he had acted sooner.

11

Fletcher woke early on Saturday, looked out the window and found the snowstorm was still raging. There was no way he could drive today. He paid for a second night and spent the morning inside his motel room working on his netbook. He wrote several pages of notes, ate the protein bars he kept in his rucksack, and used the room's coffee-maker and complimentary packs of coffee.

Under normal driving conditions, it would take him sixteen hours to reach Chicago. But he had to factor in the storm. That would add extra time. He was on the road by early Sunday morning.

He reached Chicago on Monday morning, in the hour before dawn.

While he enjoyed most big cities – their large and fluid populations allowed him to wander without arousing suspicion – he was particularly fond of Chicago, drawn to its cosmopolitan history, its noted architecture and varied nightlife. He especially enjoyed watching the Cubs play at Wrigley Field.

Fletcher had purchased the townhouse for a song when the real-estate bubble burst during the financial crisis of 2007, which was, at least according to some prominent economists, still ongoing. Located in the historic Prairie Avenue District and nestled between multimillion-dollar mansions, the spacious, four-level brick home had been upgraded with modern amenities by the previous owner, who had also invested a considerable amount of money into custom lighting, two marble baths and a dual-zone HVAC system. Two large decks offered sweeping views of the area that had formed the city's cultural and social fabric until the late 1800s.

The gourmet food shops near his townhouse were closed at this hour, as were the chain grocery stores. He would have to make do with the meagre and subpar offerings available at convenience stores. He made two stops and then continued to his destination.

Fletcher turned on to the private, tree-lined parkway. With the Jaguar taking up most of the garage's small space, he had to edge his way carefully inside. He exited the Audi, retrieved the house and car keys from their hidden location, and left the garage through the side door. It was the middle of February; an unforgiving, bitterly cold Chicago wind greeted him as he made his way across the narrow flagstone walkway crusted with a film of ice and hard snow.

He knew no one had accessed the townhouse while he'd been away. He had installed a sophisticated, hidden security system in each of his homes; an email and text message would alert him of any intrusion. The townhouse had remained vacant and quiet. He was safe.

Fletcher entered through the patio-deck door and

stepped into a well-designed and airy kitchen of beige walls and white crown moulding, stainless-steel appliances and rich cherry hardwood floors and units. Several paintings adorned the walls, the only decorations inside the house.

He drew back the curtains and opened the windows to let out the stale air. Stiff and sore from fighting crosswinds during the long drive, he headed upstairs to relax with a long shower.

Now he needed to change his appearance.

Fletcher shaved off his beard and then, using a pair of clippers, cut his hair short to conform to the shape of his head. He opened a cupboard door and surveyed the various salon-quality hair dyes he always kept on hand. He decided to go grey. Half an hour later, the process was complete.

He examined his new appearance in the mirror. He thought he looked like a retired Marine, but one who was still physically capable of battle.

The passports and accompanying documentation he needed were stored in a floor safe inside the master bedroom's walk-in closet. He found the one for Robert Pepin and noted the man's green eyes before slipping the passport, driver's licence and credit cards into the pocket of a pair of pinstriped light grey trousers. He selected a white shirt. Like all of his clothes, it had been custom-made to accommodate his 50-inch chest, large neck and long arms.

Fletcher rolled up the shirt cuffs, put on a dark navy-blue vest and retired to the corner leather armchair to meditate. Twenty minutes later, he blinked awake. Rested, his head clear, he retrieved the notes he had made inside his motel room. He transferred the information to three sheets of paper, tucked them inside a manila folder and headed back downstairs to the kitchen.

The doorbell rang promptly at 6 a.m. Fletcher opened the front door and saw Karim. The man wore a beat-up driving cap that matched the rest of his bargain-basement attire – a threadbare flannel shirt, wrinkled chinos and scuffed burgundy loafers that needed to be resoled.

'You didn't have to dress up on my behalf,' Karim said.

'It's called blending in, Ali. If I dressed like you, I'd draw attention from the neighbours.'

Karim chuckled as he stepped inside the wide marble foyer. Gripped in his hands were a bulky plastic case and a brown shopping bag. He dropped the case on the floor and with a grim smile handed the shopping bag to Fletcher.

Inside was a new bulletproof vest.

'It's a Modular Tactical Vest – the same one used by the Marines,' Karim said, taking off his cap. His hair, as thick as porcupine needles, was still black, but his grey sideburns had turned white. 'Modular PALS webbing, integrated side SAPI pouches and a quick-release system to remove it in case of an emergency. There are also integrated channels for communications wiring.'

'Completely unnecessary, but thank you.'

'It's the least I can do, since this latest errand almost got you killed.'

Fletcher hung Karim's coat and hat in the foyer closet, and then motioned to the hall leading to the kitchen.

Karim was believed to be somewhere in his early sixties, but during the three decades Fletcher had known him the man moved like someone who seemed a moment away from collapsing. He shuffled into the kitchen and groaned as he sat in one of the high-backed chairs arranged around the centre island.

'I believe this is the first time I've ever set foot inside one of your pieds-à-terre,' Karim said. 'Do you spend a lot of time here?'

'When I can.' Fletcher, standing on the opposite side of the kitchen island, picked up the Cafetière and poured coffee into two white mugs.

'That oil painting,' Karim said, pointing to the far wall inside the dining room. 'Why does it look familiar?'

'It's a poor imitation of Monet's *Waterlillies at Giverny*.'

'So why did you buy it?'

'I didn't. I painted it.' Fletcher slid a plate across the black-speckled marble.

'What's this?'

'Breakfast,' Fletcher said. 'More specifically, an omelette.'

Karim prodded it with a fork. 'Why would you put lettuce in an omelette?'

'It's spinach.'

'Same thing.' Karim sighed and took a bite. 'These eggs have no bloody taste.'

'I made yours with egg whites.'

'And here I was, thinking we were friends.'

'The last time we spoke, you were enraged that your physician ordered you to change your diet and lose weight in order to decrease your soaring cholesterol levels.' He glanced at Karim's considerable paunch and added, 'Either you're carrying triplets, which I highly doubt, or nothing has changed.'

Karim picked up his coffee mug. 'Cream?'

'No cream, no sugar. It's coffee, Ali. Not candy.'

'You'll make some lucky man a wonderful wife, Malcolm. You've got the nagging part down.'

Karim put down the cup and pushed aside the plate. Then, in an act of defiance, he lit a cigarette. He had the courtesy, however, to tilt his head back and blow the smoke up at the ceiling.

Fletcher opened a manila folder. 'This is the woman who shot me,' he said, and placed the sketch in front of Karim. 'Do you recognize her?'

'No. I would have remembered seeing a face like that. Is that really her smile?'

Fletcher nodded as he leaned forward and rested his elbows on the counter. 'She grinned at me just before she started shooting,' he said, and picked up his fork. 'I take it you've spoken with the Colorado police.'

'Rather, *they* spoke to *me*. They pulled Theresa's phone records, saw my name and started dialling. I told them the truth – leaving your name out of it, of course.'

Karim flicked cigarette ash on to his plate. 'I also spoke with my contact at the Applewood police station – the homicide detective who referred Theresa Herrera to me. No one saw your face, but two people reported seeing what they believed was a black car with tinted windows leaving the house. No licence plate, thank God.'

'They wouldn't have found anything.' The address listed for the licence belonged to an apartment complex in Queens, New York.

Fletcher forked the last bite of his omelette. 'What about our shooter?'

'The woman in the fur coat? What about her?'

'Did anyone see her?'

'My contact didn't mention anything, and he's involved in the investigation. Then again, he's not looking for her.' Karim inhaled deeply from his cigarette.

'What about the crime scene?' Fletcher asked.

Karim peered at him through the smoke. 'You haven't heard?'

'Heard what?'

'There is no crime scene, Malcolm. The house is gone.'

'I assumed you'd heard it on the news or read about it on the Internet,' Karim said.

Fletcher shook his head. He had taken few breaks on his journey from Colorado to Chicago, and these had been spent processing the information he'd collected, forming possible theories about the Herrera family, the female shooter and what had been occurring inside the house before he showed up.

'What happened?'

'An explosion took down most of Theresa Herrera's house,' Karim said. 'It happened before the police arrived. The shock wave shattered the windows of nearby homes, and the falling debris caused significant property damage. No casualties, thank God, just minor injuries from the exploding glass and the usual trauma one experiences in such things.' Karim flicked his ash on the plate. 'The Applewood police station is small, and since they're ill-equipped to deal with something like this, they called on their brothers in blue in Denver for assistance. The Bureau of Alcohol, Tobacco, Fire-arms and Explosives, incidentally, has a field office in Denver, so they too were summoned.

'The preliminary theory is that the bomb was placed

on the first floor. The blast pattern suggests dynamite. You didn't hear it go off?'

'No,' Fletcher said. 'And I doubt the shooter returned to the house to plant the bomb, so it was detonated either by a timer or remotely by a beeper or a cell phone.'

'Why plant a bomb?'

'To destroy evidence. *Is* there any evidence?'

Karim let loose a dark chuckle. 'The storm dumped almost two feet of snow by the time it tapered off late yesterday afternoon. It's going to be quite some time before the police find anything of value – it will be *weeks* before any information trickles my way.'

'From your source.'

'*Sources*. Now that the ATF is in play, the agent I know there will discreetly send me copies of the reports once they've been filed. The Colorado homicide detective has agreed to keep me in the loop. He knows that, when the time is right, I'll give him the information he needs to make an arrest. These sort of high-profile cases come around once in a lifetime. They can make or break a career.'

'So you intend on pursuing this.'

'Why wouldn't I? I gave my word to Theresa Herrera that I'd look into her son's abduction.'

'And now her murder.'

'And now her murder,' Karim repeated softly. 'There's also a personal reason.'

'Which is?'

'Like you, I don't enjoy loose ends – or mysteries.

I want to find this woman.' Karim tapped a finger against the sketch. 'I want to know what she was doing inside Theresa Herrera's house.'

'And you don't believe Colorado is up to the task.'

Karim shrugged. 'Who's to say? You know how it goes with small-town police departments. The best talent moves on to greener and more lucrative pastures, and what's left behind is more often than not a mid-level offering of people who are constantly being threatened by yet another round of budget cuts, bureaucratic red-tape and superiors who are more concerned about advancing up the career ladder than rolling up their sleeves and doing actual work.'

'Denver is assisting them.'

'But that will last for only so long. Denver has its own problems, and as for the ATF . . . When it comes to bureaucracies, it's been my experience that shit always floats to the top. I saw it happen at the Agency, and I know you witnessed it at the FBI. I've learned not to place my trust in such things.'

Fletcher drank some of his coffee.

'Theresa Herrera told me her husband had gone out that night with a friend. Has he shown up?'

'The police have been unable to locate him,' Karim said. 'At the moment they have him listed as a "person of interest". Until they find him – or what's left of him, if he was inside the house when it exploded – they're obligated to investigate the theory that he planted the bomb, which only benefits us. While they're chasing their straw man, we can pursue this mystery woman who shot you without them looking over our shoulders.'

'What can you tell me about Barry Herrera? I assume you conducted a background check.'

'I always perform a thorough search on anyone looking to hire me.'

'And?'

'He's as clean as a whistle,' Karim said. 'The man was born and raised in Montpelier, Vermont, the only child of Marcus and Samantha Herrera. They both died of cancer – the father in 1978, the mother in 1984. Barry attended the local high school, where he excelled in academics and tennis. Brown offered him a scholarship. He graduated summa cum lade and moved on to the BU School of Medicine, where he picked psychiatry as his field of study. From there he, like many doctors, bounced around various public and private hospitals, working mainly with troubled children. In 1989 he met Theresa Henderson, an office assistant at a privately owned clinic in Raleigh, South Carolina. They married in 1993 and moved to Applewood, Colorado, in 1998, when he accepted a job.'

'And the wife?'

'Unremarkable. Born Theresa King in Danbury, Connecticut. Went to the public school and local college. Moved with a college friend to South Carolina, met Barry Herrera, married.'

'How deep did you dig?'

'As deep as I could,' Karim said. 'A routine background check provides a snapshot – a starting point.

The real treasures, as you well know, are locked behind secured databases scattered all across the Internet. I assigned someone else to do the actual data mining. This person is as good with computers as you are.' Then, with a sly grin, Karim added, 'Maybe even better.'

'Anything jump out?'

'No. Nothing.'

'Financials?'

'Barry made a good living, so the wife stayed at home. They had a reasonable mortgage, which they paid on time every month, along with their credit card and car loans. They invested in their retirement accounts and saved a tidy sum for an emergency. No suspicious payments or withdrawals. They were a boring, upper-middle-class couple living the American dream.'

'Until someone abducted their son.'

'Yes,' Karim said sombrely. 'Until that.'

'Did you meet him?'

'No. I was scheduled to meet him and his wife yesterday at their home. I never spoke to the man on the phone, only his wife. She was the one who initiated contact.'

'Did he share his wife's belief that her son was still alive?'

'She never mentioned anything to the contrary.'

'What did she say about her husband?'

'Just that he was busy. That in the last two years he spent more time away from home, burying himself in his work as a child psychiatrist. What happened to their son put a strain on their marriage. These things often do.'

Karim, Fletcher knew, had first-hand experience with such matters.

For years Karim had maintained a rather bonhomie relationship with his ex-wife, Judith, often travelling to England to share holidays with her extended family, who still welcomed him into the fold. Their son had wanted to attend high school in the States, and at age fifteen moved across the pond to live with his father.

Jason Karim was seventeen years old when he was abducted on his way home from a private Manhattan school. Karim had endured five dreadful, nightmarish days before his son's body turned up in an alley in the Bronx. Karim flew to London to deliver the news to his ex-wife.

Judith blamed him for their son's murder. Jason should never have been allowed to navigate his way through such a dangerous city, especially at night. Karim acquiesced to his ex-wife's wishes to have their son buried in London. But Judith had attended neither the wake nor the service; she'd suffered a breakdown and was now confined to a private hospital paid for by Karim.

Karim still made semi-annual pilgrimages to visit Judith, who had retreated to a cocoon of fantasy, telling doctors that her son was alive, travelling the globe as a hedge-fund manager. Despite medication and therapy, she still regularly picked up the phone, dialled an imaginary number and pretended to speak to her imaginary son, his imaginary wife and her two imaginary grandchildren – a boy named Bradley and a girl named Clare.

Karim had used his personal loss as a turning point. The ghost of Jason Karim was both the inspiration for, and a silent partner in, his father's enterprise of helping fellow victims who called on him for assistance. Each case he solved, each missing child he recovered, provided not only a purpose to his life but also helped him to manage the considerable guilt he dragged like shackles through his days.

'Clearly something has aroused your curiosity,' Karim said. 'Otherwise, you wouldn't have asked me to fly out and personally hand-deliver a portable mass spectrometer.'

Fletcher finished the last of his coffee, thinking about the manila folder in front of him, wondering where he should start.

'Meet me in the dining room,' he said.

13

Fletcher placed the empty cup inside the sink on his way to the foyer.

Mass spectrometry, the method of identifying a substance's chemical composition by separating its gaseous ions, had evolved considerably since its first application in the late 1950s, when it was used to analyse amino acids and peptides. The bulky equipment, which once took up an entire room of a forensics lab, had now been compartmentalized into a single, portable unit that could be carried to crime scenes and used at airports to detect and identify explosives, chemical-warfare agents and environmental toxins.

Fletcher placed the heavy plastic case on the dining-room table. He snapped free the latches and, from the padded foam lining, removed a heavy, rectangular unit, along with a small netbook computer and assorted cables.

As he set up the equipment, Karim hovered close by, peering through his bifocals like an anxious chemistry professor watching a student mixing potentially volatile chemicals.

'Aren't you about due for another cigarette, Ali?'

'What happened to your concern about my health?'

'I value my personal space more. Please, have a seat.' Fletcher retrieved the two evidence bags from his trousers pocket – the spent cartridge and the slug he'd removed from his vest – and placed them on the table. Then he returned to the foyer and opened the closet door.

Sitting on the top shelf were several small plastic toolboxes holding various forensics supplies. It took him a moment to find what he needed.

'This slug,' Karim said as Fletcher entered the dining room. 'It looks like a 9-mm round.'

'It's been modified.'

'How can you tell?'

Fletcher placed the toolbox next to the MS device. 'The cartridge,' he said, pulling out a chair, 'is a wildcat.'

'I'm not well versed in ballistics, so you'll have to explain it to me.'

'The term refers to a cartridge that isn't mass-produced. More specifically, a wildcat is a cartridge that has been modified in some way in order to optimize a certain performance characteristic such as efficiency or power.'

'So it's a home-made round?'

'That was my initial suspicion, but the components show no evidence of shoddy craftsmanship. In fact, it's quite the opposite.' Fletcher opened his toolbox and continued to speak as he collected his items and placed them on the table. 'While the slug contains a manufacturing stamp I don't recognize, given the superior craftsmanship I'm inclined to believe the round was created by someone who specializes in custom-made ammunition.'

'And the mass spectrometer will show you how the gunpowder was modified.'

Fletcher nodded. 'My hope is that it will give us a unique chemical fingerprint, which will allow us to trace the owner – once we've identified the manufacturer.'

Hands covered in latex and the empty cartridge pinched between his fingers, Fletcher rubbed a cotton swab along the inner brass wall to collect the gunpowder residue. Karim came around the table to watch, then, thinking better of it, lit a fresh cigarette, entered the living room and began to pace across the oriental carpet. Sometimes he paused to examine a painting or charcoal drawing, standing in such a way as to keep Fletcher's progress within his line of vision. Then he resumed his pacing.

Twenty minutes and two cigarettes later, Karim noticed that Fletcher was leaning back in his chair.

'What is it?'

Fletcher didn't answer. He propped an elbow on the table's corner, resting his chin on a thumb as he rubbed his index finger across his bottom lip, staring at the computer screen.

Karim marched back into the dining room and, standing behind Fletcher, bent forward to read the results.

The mass spectrometry software had failed to identify the sample.

'I was told these portable units have a limited library,' Karim said. 'I'll have this sample tested in New York. My forensics people are at my lab right now. The mass spectrometer we have there is hooked up to a software library that can identify every —'

'That won't be necessary.'

'You know what this is?'

Fletcher nodded.

'Human ash,' he said.

14

A cool silence enveloped the dining room.

Karim broke it a moment later. 'Someone's cremated remains were packed inside that ammo cartridge.' He spoke slowly, as if having trouble finding the correct words. 'That's what you're telling me.'

Fletcher nodded, his gaze fixed on the computer screen. He didn't doubt his findings. Mixed in with the gunshot's chemical components, its primer residues and organic compounds, were the unmistakable chemical signatures of human ash – phosphate, sodium, calcium, chloride, sulphate, silica, potassium and magnesium.

He read them off one by one for Karim's benefit. Karim, however, still seemed unconvinced.

'The concentration levels of each leave no room for debate,' Fletcher said. 'Minute quantities of beryllium and mercury are also present, as well as –'

'I believe you.' Karim drew heavily on his cigarette. 'Could our lady shooter have loaded the ashes herself?'

'If she had the proper tools and the proper knowledge, yes.'

'I can tell by your tone you don't think she did.'

'You have to know exactly what you're doing or you'll risk a misfire. Why risk it when you can hire a company to do it for you?'

'There's a company that performs this . . . service?'

'I know of only one. It caters to hunting enthusiasts.'

'You mean gun nuts,' Karim said. 'Is this legal?'

'Perfectly legal.'

'Let me guess: this company is based in the South.'

'Alabama, I believe.'

'Of course,' Karim added in a sour tone. While he had a permit to carry a gun, he rarely did. He detested firearms, believed their availability and the ease with which they could be obtained in the United States – through simplistic forms and substandard background checks, especially in the Southern states, where owning a firearm was as common as carrying a wallet – had directly contributed to the country's rapidly rising crime levels. The notion had been firmly cemented in Karim's mind by his son's murder. Jason Karim, after enduring a savage beating, had been shot to death with seven hollow-point rounds.

'So instead of sprinkling Uncle Bobby's ashes at sea, in a garden or what have you,' Karim said, 'you pay to have his cremated remains stuffed inside shotgun shells so you can go out and, what, shoot yourself a Thanksgiving turkey? Then everyone gathered around the holiday table digs in comforted by the idea of having a tiny part of Uncle Bobby digesting in their bellies, is that it?'

'I'm not debating the merits of such a service, Ali. I'm merely telling you it exists.'

Karim examined the ash dangling from his cigarette. He flicked it into his coffee cup and said, 'I'd thought I'd seen everything. The world we live in now . . .'

Karim shook the disgust from his face and looked around the dining room before his gaze settled on a reproduction of Marie-Denise Villers's *Young Woman Drawing*. He stared at the angelic face, at her intense but gentle dark eyes and the golden corkscrew curls dangling across her small shoulders, as though waiting for her to validate his feelings.

'Will the Denver crime lab discover this?'

'Depends on the expertise of the forensics staff,' Fletcher said. 'If someone recognizes the cartridge as a wildcat, he or she may decide to run testing. But they won't find anything.'

'Because the crime scene has been contaminated by the bomb.'

'And the snow. By now it's already washed away the residue needed for testing.' A pause, then Fletcher added, 'You can't extract any DNA from these ashes.'

Karim blinked in surprise at hearing his thought spoken out loud.

'The cremation process destroys the phosphodiester bonds that hold DNA nucleotides together,' Fletcher said. 'All that remain are the chemical signatures listed on the computer screen.'

Karim's cell phone rang. 'Excuse me for a moment,' he said, pulling his BlackBerry from a rumpled pocket.

While Karim conducted a near-silent conversation with the caller on the other end of the line, Fletcher took out his smartphone, connected to the Internet and searched for companies that specialized in placing cremated remains inside ammunition. As he suspected, there was only one such company, and it was based in Alabama. He clicked on the link for the company website.

Sacred Ashes, based in the town of Dunbar and formed by two former game wardens, billed itself as a cost-effective memorial for the outdoors person. Page after page extolled the benefits of using their service – the virtually non-existent ecological footprint compared to interment; the significant savings that would be made by opting out of purchasing traditional funeral services, casket, burial plot, gravestone or urn. One pound of human ash and a payment of $1,500 provided 250 cartridges for either a shotgun or a pistol. The rifle enthusiast had to make do with 100 cartridges. All the ammunition came in standard calibres. An additional payment of $100 provided the mourner with a finished handcrafted ammunition box that was 'mantel-worthy'.

Fletcher was reading through customer testimonials when Karim returned to the line. 'That was my contact in Colorado,' Karim said. 'They found Barry Herrera – or, more specifically, his head.'

'Where?'

'Sitting on a tree limb about half a mile from the blast site.'

'So the husband was either close to the bomb or right on top of it when it went off.'

Karim nodded. 'At least now we know he was inside the house that night.'

'He was alive when the bomb detonated.'

Karim's brow furrowed. 'You told me you didn't see him.'

'I didn't,' Fletcher said. 'When Theresa Herrera answered the door, she was frightened but composed. She wouldn't have been able to maintain her composure if her husband was dead – or if she knew about the bomb.'

'What I don't understand is why the shooter allowed Herrera to answer the door in the first place. Why not just wait for you to leave?'

'I think the answer lies in the sequence of events,' Fletcher said. 'Let's start when I pulled into the driveway. I saw the lights for one of the upstairs bedrooms turn off. The blinds had been drawn – the blinds for all the windows facing the street had been drawn. That happened before I arrived.

'I rang the doorbell twice, and, when no one answered, I went to the garage. I saw both cars and decided to return to the house. I think the shooter was watching me from the bedroom window. The lights were off, it was dark in there, and she could watch me undetected. The shooter saw me coming back and at some point made the decision to escort Theresa Herrera downstairs to send me away.'

'And now we know the husband was inside the house that night.'

'*And* we know the shooter didn't bring the husband downstairs,' Fletcher said. 'I didn't see or hear him. After she killed Theresa Herrera, after she tried to kill me, she fled out the back. I returned to the front and picked up the spent cartridge. Again, I didn't see or hear anything to give me an indication the husband was inside the house.'

'And then you drove away.'

Fletcher nodded. 'I didn't hear the bomb go off, so a significant period of time elapsed before it detonated. When it did, Barry Herrera must have been right on top of it or very close to it, for his head to have been thrown such a distance. That suggests a fixed position. That he couldn't move.'

'You think he was tied up somewhere, maybe the upstairs bedroom?'

'And gagged,' Fletcher said. 'Remember, I didn't hear him.'

'What if he was already dead by that point?'

'The woman in the fur coat was inside the house *before* I arrived. If she had killed the husband, why didn't she also kill the wife? Why wait? And if the husband was already dead, why escort the distraught and terrorized wife downstairs to answer the door? Why take the risk?'

'Because something was in progress when you arrived, and you interrupted it.'

Fletcher nodded. 'Whatever was happening inside the house, whatever this woman in the fur coat had planned, it was important enough to risk allowing Theresa Herrera to answer the door. She wanted to send me on my way so she could get back to it.'

'Only Theresa Herrera warned you with that bit about not being able to afford my fee.'

Fletcher nodded again.

'Then the shooter killed Theresa Herrera, tried to kill you and fled the scene.'

'And after she was a safe distance away, she detonated the bomb,' Fletcher said. 'I don't think she came back with it. Too risky – someone might see her. I think she brought it with her to the house, possibly concealed in something inconspicuous, something that wouldn't arouse any suspicion – a handbag, possibly.'

'It must have been one hell of a big handbag.'

'Bringing a bomb to the house . . . if her goal was simply to kill Theresa Herrera and her husband, she could have driven up to the house, left the bomb at the front door and detonated it from a safe location any time she wanted.'

'Agreed,' Karim said. 'So why use the bomb? To erase evidence?'

'Using a bomb doesn't completely erase evidence. It only makes the pieces of the puzzle more difficult to put together. I think she used it because she couldn't afford to let anyone know what she was doing inside there – she *needed* to hide what she was doing inside the house.'

'What do you think she was trying to hide?'

'That she's done this before,' Fletcher said.

15

'What makes the Herrera family so unique?' Fletcher asked. 'What sets them apart from anyone else?'

'Their missing son,' Karim said. 'Rico.'

Fletcher nodded. 'We know Rico Herrera was abducted from his bedroom while he was sleeping. Four years have passed, and the police have failed to find him or to uncover any new investigative angle or piece of evidence. The trail has gone cold. Dead cold. The mother refuses to give up hope. Maybe she really does believe her son is alive or maybe, on an unconscious level, she knows he's most likely dead and needs the police to find him so she can grieve and move on with her life.'

'It's probably a combination of both,' Karim said. 'Hope is always the last thing to die.'

'We know she's referred to you by your contact in Colorado, the homicide detective who worked her son's case. You ask me to talk to her and her husband. I arrive to find the upstairs bedroom light being turned off. When Theresa Herrera finally answers the door, she's frightened but able to maintain enough composure to concoct a story about suffering from a stomach virus and that her husband is out for the night. She tries to send me away, and we know what happens next.

'These are indisputable facts. We also know the shooter is inside the house before I arrive on the scene, but we don't know why. What is her *reason* for gaining access to the house? I started with that question and operated from the theory that the shooter is somehow connected to Rico Herrera's abduction. If so, why would she decide to visit the family four years later? It certainly wouldn't be to tell them their son is dead.'

'I think you're right,' Karim said. 'If the shooter had told the mother her son was dead, she wouldn't have allowed Theresa Herrera to answer the door. The woman would have been too distraught. Even with a gun pointed at her, she might have risked screaming for help – or chosen to flee the house.'

'So the shooter had leverage, something to make Theresa Herrera cooperate.'

'You think, what, the shooter told Herrera that her son was alive?'

'It would give the shooter the power to force Theresa Herrera to do what she was told.'

'It's possible, sure. But we don't know that was, in fact, what happened.'

'Correct. Let's go back to our original assumption that the shooter is either responsible or somehow connected to Rico Herrera's abduction. If this is true, we're back to the original question: what's the shooter's reason for being there? Not to kill the wife and her husband. If this was simply about killing, she could have done that very easily. We know she gained access to the house, and we know she had a gun. She could have used it at any time, but she didn't. She *made* Theresa Herrera answer the door to send me away.'

'You know what was going on inside the house, don't you?'

'I have a theory.'

'Let's hear it.'

'Our shooter, the woman in the fur coat, planned on abducting one of the parents.'

Surprise bloomed on Karim's face.

Fletcher stood, his ribs screaming in protest, and left the dining room. He entered the kitchen and came back with the manila folder holding the three sheets of notes he had written earlier that morning.

Fletcher resumed his seat and said, 'I conducted some preliminary research and found eight families who have had either a son or a daughter abducted from their house, on their way home from school, from a car – the abduction methods vary. The child vanishes, and after a significant amount of time passes – several months or, in the case of Rico Herrera, several years – one of the parents vanishes, never to be seen or heard from again.'

'And the surviving spouse?'

'Killed inside the house.' Fletcher slid the folder across the table and added, 'They're all unsolved.'

Karim read through the pages. They contained only salient details: the names of the eight families; the names of their missing children and the date and circumstances of their abductions; the date and details involving the murder of the husband or wife followed by those for the husband or wife who vanished after-wards.

'These families are scattered all over the country,' Karim said.

'And there may be more. I only had a day to do the research.'

'Where did you get this information?'

'Articles posted on various newspaper websites,' Fletcher said.

'It's an interesting theory – certainly one that warrants further investigation.'

'There's one other thing.'

Karim glanced up from his reading.

'Theresa Herrera wasn't who she said she was,' Fletcher said.

16

'That can't be . . . that's not possible,' Karim said. 'If what you're saying is true, the person I assigned to do the data mining would have found it.'

'The person you assigned was very thorough. I read the reports.'

'But?'

'I checked Theresa Herrera's medical records on MIB – the Medical Information Bureau,' Fletcher said. 'It's a digital warehouse for the country's medical records.'

'I know what it is,' Karim said softly. 'Insurance companies use it. What did you find?'

'Her social security number doesn't have a match on the MIB.'

'Nothing?'

'Not a single file.'

'Could be a simple clerical error.'

'Or it could have been expunged,' Fletcher said. 'Whatever the reason, it warrants further investigation.'

Karim nodded as he shut the folder.

'There's only one company that specializes in adding cremated remains to ammunition,' Fletcher said. 'Sacred Ashes, based in Dunbar, Alabama.'

He slid his smartphone across the table. Karim looked

at the company website displayed on the phone's screen.

'I'll drive to Alabama,' Fletcher said.

'Why?'

'To look through the company's records.'

'No, I mean why drive when we can fly? We'll take my plane.'

'In case you forgot, I'm a fugitive.'

Karim waved it away. 'What do you have for ID?'

'A passport and driver's licence.'

'Let's see them.'

'The provenance is clean.'

'Always check, Malcolm. Always check.'

'I always do.' To allay Karim's concerns, Fletcher handed over the items for Robert Pepin.

Karim inspected them for several minutes before placing several phone calls to make sure the documentation hadn't been compromised or flagged for review. His final call was to a contact at Interpol. Fletcher had, under his own name, been given an Interpol Red Notice – an international arrest warrant.

'They're clean,' Karim said after he hung up. 'What's your plan once we reach Alabama?'

'Surveillance,' Fletcher said. 'Then I'll break into their company, examine their computers and paper-work, and find our shooter.'

17

Seventeen-year-old Jimmy Weeks saw police lights explode across his rearview mirror.

It wasn't an ordinary cop car. Directly behind him and practically riding his back bumper was a big, black Chevy suburban – an undercover-cop car, he thought. No sirens, just flashing lights installed in the front grille.

Jimmy felt his chest tighten. An inner voice urged him to relax.

You haven't done anything wrong, that voice said. *The cop probably just wants you to move out of the way since you're hogging the lane and driving like an old lady.*

He *was* driving slowly – and with excessive caution. His dad had agreed to hand over the keys for his BMW. In return, Jimmy had agreed to run to the grocery store to pick up a few items needed for 'Wafflepalloza', his father's hip term for the waffle extravaganza he cooked up every Sunday morning in an attempt to get everyone to sit down and spend 'quality family time' together. Completely lame, but Jimmy had to admit the waffles were pretty good.

Jimmy pulled off the main road and banged a right on to Haymarket Street.

The Chevy followed. The flashing lights shut off as it pulled up directly behind him.

'But I haven't done anything wrong,' he mumbled to himself.

And that's why you have nothing to worry about, that inner voice counselled.

But that didn't stop beads of sweat from popping out along his hairline. He parked against the kerb, removed the Velcro-canvas wallet from his back jeans pocket, leaned across the console and opened the glove box. He was fishing out the registration from the piles of papers when the knock came at the window.

The undercover cop was a woman. She wore a bulky black winter parka and a pair of sunglasses with mir-rored lenses. A black knit cap covered her head and ears.

There was something wrong with her face. Like the skin had been stretched too far back. Mrs Dempsey's botched facelift came to mind as Jimmy rolled down the window.

On the heels of that thought came another one: *Why would an undercover cop pull me over?*

Jimmy handed over his licence and registration. The lady cop didn't take them. She held up a leather wallet displaying a heavy gold badge. Beside it and tucked underneath a clear sheet of plastic was an ID with 'FBI' printed across the top in big bold blue letters. The accompanying picture showed a middle-aged woman with black hair worn tight across her scalp. Her name was Marie Clouzot.

FBI. She's a federal agent, oh sweet Jesus.

'Are you the owner of this vehicle, sir?'

Jimmy nodded. Then he said, 'It's my dad's car.'

'Your name?'

'James Weeks. What's – did I do something wrong?'

'Well, Mr Weeks, it seems you're driving a vehicle that was used in the commission of a robbery.'

The heat that spread across Jimmy's face was so intense he thought his skin would melt.

'Several eyewitnesses reported seeing this model of BMW at the pharmacy last night, and they gave us a licence-plate number. *Your* licence-plate number, Mr Weeks.'

Everything came into a sharp and sickening focus – the way her eyes moved behind her sunglasses as she searched his car, her breath steaming in the frigid Pennsylvania air. His lips and jaw trembled as he stammered his way through an explanation.

'There's got to . . . No, that can't be true. This car belongs – it's my dad's car.'

'Where were you yesterday, Mr Weeks?'

Yesterday. He'd had hockey practice after school. After that, he'd spent a few hours doing homework and preparing for Mr Glassman's upcoming ballbuster history test, and then he'd gone over to George Durant's house and played the new *Call of Duty* game until nine or ten – *and* he'd driven there in his mother's shitty Toyota Corolla.

Jimmy told all of this to the FBI agent.

'Where do you live, Mr Weeks?'

'Boynton Street,' he said. 'It's not that far, less than ten minutes.'

'Are your parents at home?'

Jimmy nodded, kept nodding.

'Do you have a cell phone?'

'In my coat pocket,' he said. 'I can call him right now, he'll –'

'Please keep your hands on the wheel, Mr Weeks.'

'Call him. My dad. He'll tell you where I was. I didn't – I wouldn't hold up a drugstore.'

She stared at him from behind her sunglasses.

'I swear to God I'm telling you the truth,' Jimmy said.

'Here's what we're going to do. You're going to get in my car. I'm going to drive you to your house, and we're going to sit down and talk to your parents, see if your story holds up.' She opened his door. 'Make sure you lock your car.'

He did. Agent Clouzot told him to get into the passenger's seat. He did. After she got settled behind the wheel, she asked him for his cell. Jimmy gave it to her. She examined it for a moment before slipping it inside her jacket pocket.

She started the Chevy. Then she took out a pair of plastic handcuffs.

'Please turn around and place your hands behind your back.'

'But I – I haven't done anything wrong.' Jimmy felt the sting of tears. Felt embarrassed and ashamed for acting like such a pussy – especially in front of a woman.

'Mr Weeks, the last person who professed his innocence attacked me while I was driving and almost got me killed. If you're as innocent as you say you are, then you won't mind wearing these until we arrive at your home. It's for your safety, and mine. If you refuse, I'll place you under arrest.'

Jimmy's mouth felt like cotton. He swallowed dryly.

'We can talk to your parents at your house, or you can call them from our federal office. What do you want to do?'

Jimmy, frightened by the idea of being arrested and having to call his parents, turned around in his seat. He stared out of his window and, heart thumping at a frightening and furious clip, placed his hands behind his back.

This is some sort of mix-up, he told himself as the woman tightened the cuffs against his wrists. *I didn't rob a pharmacy. My parents know where I was yesterday. There are at least, what, a dozen witnesses who can tell this agent I was –*

Something sharp pierced his lower thigh. Startled, he swung around in his seat, knocking his head against the side window as a hot and stinging liquid flooded his muscle; FBI Agent Clouzot had stuck a needle into his leg, and her thumb was pressing down on the plunger of a syringe.

He tried to twist away, his shins slamming into the glove box. The woman reached up, grabbed him by the back of the neck and sent his face crashing down against the console separating the two seats.

The impact broke his nose. Jimmy felt it crack, heard the sound boom through his head, certain that bone fragments were flying through his brain. His eyes watered, and blood poured out of his nose and down his throat, and he kicked underneath the glove box. He couldn't move his head; the FBI agent was placing all of her weight down on his neck, like she wanted to snap it. With his face smashed against the console, Jimmy let out a garbled scream, spitting blood against a brown leather sunglasses case.

18

As a federal fugitive, Fletcher no longer had the luxury of commercial flight. In the wake of 9/11, the Transportation Security Administration, the government agency responsible for safe air travel, had been moved under the Department of Homeland Security. His visage, fingerprints, age-progressed photographs and other distinguishing characteristics were stored on its database, which could be accessed easily by any TSA agent or passport official.

The TSA had also implemented a number of security measures designed to stop a terrorist from smuggling a bomb on to a plane. Careful attention was paid to clothing: shoes, coats and belts were checked – and now underwear, thanks to Umar Farouk Abdulmutallab, a young Muslim man who had managed to board a Northwest Airlines flight en route from Amsterdam to Detroit, Michigan, with plastic explosives smuggled inside his pants. Fortunately, the bomb had failed to detonate.

While luggage X-rays, full-body scans and searches amounted to nothing more than theatre – a performance meant to impart a false sense of security to commercial-airline travellers – people who owned a plane or had the financial means to charter one weren't subjected to the same scrutiny. Lobbyists working for the highly lucrative domestic private air-travel industry had thwarted the TSA's attempts to implement similar security measures for people flying by general aviation aircraft. These travellers were allowed to access their planes directly, bypassing all security checkpoints.

Before leaving the townhouse, Fletcher had changed into clothing more suitable for surveillance work. Wearing sunglasses, he pulled a rolling suitcase behind him as he followed Karim across the windy tarmac. In addition to his sidearm and MTV vest, the suitcase contained a wide assortment of tools and equipment.

Fletcher had made no effort to hide anything; Karim had assured him that the suitcase wouldn't be subjected to a search. Karim had also assured him that they could speak safely on the plane. His people swept it for listening devices, always, prior to takeoff.

Karim, Fletcher knew, considered owning a plane a waste of money. His business, however, sometimes required him to fly at a moment's notice. The man had purchased a Cessna Citation, a modest jet compared to the lavish corporate Gulfstream parked near by. A Gulfstream could seat a dozen people comfortably and offered a host of amenities, such as an area for conferences and multiple flatscreen TVs with innumerable entertainment choices.

Karim didn't indulge in such pomp and circumstance. The interior of Karim's Cessna was entirely practical, consisting of six comfortable and spacious tan leather executive seats strategically arranged to maximize space. High-gloss veneer tables bolted to the floor and cabinetry with polished gold accents decorated the cabin, along with a beige carpet that showed no sign of wear.

The pilot stood outside the cockpit door. Karim shook the man's hand and introduced Fletcher as a business associate who would be accompanying him to Alabama. The pilot didn't ask for Fletcher's name or passport, and he didn't ask to search his suitcase. He retreated inside the cockpit, shutting the door behind him.

Blocking the aisle leading to the rear of the plane was a tall, thin woman dressed in a form-fitting black jacket and a matching pencil skirt. A long, side-swept fringe of stark white hair concealed her right eye, its tips hanging like daggers across her cheekbone. All of her hair was white, the sides cut short, the back cropped. Fletcher had seen this type of haircut on a good number of young cosmopolitan women. It complemented her sharp, angular features.

She held out a hand a good arm's length away and said, 'Your coat and suitcase please.'

She was British. Her accent suggested she had been raised and educated in the Midlands – Birmingham, Fletcher suspected.

'There's no need for that,' Karim told her. 'This is Robert Pepin, an old, dear friend and colleague. This is my personal assistant, Emma White.'

Fletcher extended a hand. 'A pleasure to meet you, Miss White.'

She shook his hand and he felt the strength in her grip.

'I'm not anyone's miss,' she said, polite but firm. 'M. As in the letter.'

'Yes. Right,' Karim said. 'Now let's get –'

'I'm sure Mr Pepin won't mind a security search,' she said.

'*I* mind it,' Karim replied. 'Please step aside and let Mr Pepin through.'

The young woman complied but didn't hide her disapproval. Her face, stark and severe in its beauty, expressed clear Teutonic characteristics – pale, almost translucent skin and a thin but strong nose in profile. She had applied a light touch of eyeshadow and lipstick to her porcelain features, but there was nothing delicate about her.

Fletcher moved to the end of the plane and stuffed his suitcase and jacket in the overhead compartment. Knowing he had aroused Emma White's suspicions, he decided to take a seat facing the cockpit so he could keep a close eye on her.

He watched her behind his sunglasses. Emma White – M, as in the letter – reminded him of another woman he'd met several years ago, a Boston-based investigator and forensics expert named Darby McCormick.

The McCormick woman still fascinated him. Much like Emma White, Darby McCormick possessed a distinct and savage beauty. But it was the woman's fierce intellect that had drawn him, and her physical mettle brought to mind comparisons with the legendary female Amazon warriors from Greek mythology. Fletcher wondered – and not for the first time – what it would be like to know Darby McCormick more intimately.

Karim strolled down the aisle, holding a cardboard box stuffed with pastries.

'Would you like one? Coffee?'

'No, thank you,' Fletcher said. He leaned forward in his seat, and in a low voice added: 'You neglected to mention that someone else would be on board.'

'Emma takes over the role as my shadow when Boyd is away. She takes the job quite seriously.' With a conspiratorial grin, Karim added, 'She's quite capable of handling herself.'

I'm sure she is, Fletcher thought. When the young woman offered to relieve him of his belongings, Fletcher had caught sight of fine scars along her callused palm and fingers.

'In case you forgot, Ali, there's a three-million-dollar bounty on my head.'

'You have nothing to worry about. In addition to being stubbornly loyal, M is *very* discreet.'

Fletcher didn't question Karim's conviction; the man had a finely tuned internal Geiger counter for such matters. Still, he marvelled at Karim's ability to trust. With the exception of Karim, Fletcher did not indulge in such sentiment. His survival depended on it.

'And she can help us,' Karim said.

'How?'

'Her knowledge of computers is . . . well, frightening.

She performed the data mining on the Herreras. I'll have her research this company you're going to visit, see what we can find out about the premises.'

Fletcher said nothing. Karim was a meticulous planner; the woman's presence here was no accident. Karim had intended to use her on this from the very start.

'I'd prefer it if you limited our interactions.'

'I'll keep her up front,' Karim said. 'Would you mind if I joined her for the flight? She has some paperwork for me.'

Fletcher shook his head and Karim trudged away.

Fletcher closed his eyes as the plane taxied to the runway. He saw himself standing on the front doorstep of the Herrera home. Felt the falling snow against his hair and neck as he replayed his conversation with Theresa Herrera.

He paused the frame just before she was shot.

The shooter had been standing only a few feet away from Theresa Herrera. The woman in the fur coat could hear them talking but she couldn't *see* him. There were no windows to watch from.

You couldn't see my face.

You couldn't see me drawing my sidearm.

So what made you panic and start to shoot?

19

Marie Clouzot drove through the entrance of the Franklin Grove Cemetery, a maze of looping, hilly roads contained within ten-foot stone walls. She knew where she was going, having scouted the area during a previous visit to Petersburg, Pennsylvania.

She climbed a steep hill on the northeast side of the cemetery and, reaching the top, saw the new silver Cadillac DeVille Statesman hearse parked in the prearranged meeting spot. She pulled behind it, angling her Chevy so Brandon could easily access their latest prize.

They always picked cemeteries to do the exchange. Here, a hearse wouldn't arouse suspicion, and more often than not there were no security cameras watching. Such was the case with Franklin Grove; Brandon had checked with the company in charge of both maintenance and security. The person with whom he'd spoken hadn't found the questions in the least bit odd or suspicious, as Brandon Arkoff was the owner of Washington Memorial Park, one of the finest funeral homes Baltimore, Maryland, had to offer.

The lapels of Brandon's navy-blue suit jacket flapped in the wind as he darted around the hearse, his head turned so she could see only the right side of his face.

Even after all their time together, he was still sensitive about his disfigurement.

Having done this many times before, there was no need to speak. They knew their responsibilities.

Marie moved to the back of the hearse and opened the hatchback. The door swung to the left, blocking the view of anyone who might suddenly appear at the bottom of the hill. No one was standing there, but Brandon always moved as though the police were about to descend on them at any moment. He threw open the Chevy's door, flinching at the sight of the blood on the passenger's seat. It was everywhere, bright and red: smeared against the seat and console, across James Weeks's jeans and the front of his wool coat, on his cut and swollen lips; it had soaked into his long, blond, girlish fringe and dried on his high, smooth forehead peppered with acne.

Brandon shot her a withering look of disapproval.

'I accidentally broke his nose when I pinned his head against the console,' Marie said, fishing the plastic police-grade handcuffs from her jacket pocket.

With a grunt Brandon lifted the limp body out of the passenger's seat, turned and dumped the unconscious teenager on top of the tarp set up next to the coffin they always used – a dark stained timber model with a high-gloss lacquer polish and carved panels of *The Last Supper* fitted on each side. The lid was already open, the edge resting against the hearse's padded ceiling.

Marie secured the cuffs around the boy's ankles. Brandon, kneeling on the hearse's back seat, reached over the headrest and grabbed the teenager underneath the arms. Together they lifted Weeks and moved him inside the coffin – a difficult task, given the tight opening. Weeks's lolling head smacked up against the edges of the lid and coffin. Having been heavily sedated, he made no sound, nor any sign that he had registered pain.

It took a moment to get Weeks settled on his back. His broken nose had started to swell, reducing the blood flow to a trickle. Brandon stuffed the edges of a handkerchief up the boy's nostrils to stem any further bleeding. Marie went to work folding the tarp, careful not to allow any blood to spill.

'How much of the sedative did you give him?'

'All of it,' she said.

'Put the tarp inside the coffin – and your coat and gloves. They're covered in blood.'

She did. Brandon reached up, grabbed the edge of a polished sheet of inlaid wood and swung it down. It clicked in place, hiding James Weeks.

Marie reached inside the coffin with her clean hands and grabbed the small lock resting on the white satin bed lace interior. She pulled back the fabric and locked the bottom half, while Brandon secured the top. Now Dr Stanley Weeks's eldest child was imprisoned inside the coffin's false bottom. Holes had been drilled along the sides; precious Jimmy would have plenty of air for the long drive back to Baltimore.

Marie shut the hatchback. Three minutes of work and it was done.

Brandon joined her outside. 'I'll take care of the Chevy,' he said, winded from the exertion. Stocky for as long as she'd known him, middle age had packed on another thirty pounds; exercise easily fatigued him. 'Take the hearse in case someone saw you.' He opened the back of the Chevy and removed the plastic bucket holding the rags, bleach and paper towels. 'Get going. I need to clean up this goddamn mess.'

Marie shot him an icy stare. She didn't have the time for another argument.

She left without kissing him goodbye.

Marie concentrated on driving. When she reached the highway, she stayed in the slow lane and stuck to the speed limit.

Her thoughts drifted to Brandon. He had always been prone to worry, but what had happened in Colorado had pushed him over the edge.

Brandon hadn't accompanied her to Colorado; he'd been in Baltimore with Rico Herrera. Brandon manned the phone so Rico could talk to his mother. Theresa Herrera was supposed to kill her husband and then disappear. For ever.

But it hadn't worked out that way. Theresa Herrera had employed a New York private investigator to look into the disappearance of her precious little boy, and a man had shown up on her doorstep. Listening to their conversation, Marie had known the man simply wasn't going to skulk away. And he would have insisted on coming into the house – something she couldn't allow to happen. The idea had panicked her, yes, but, as it turned out, her instincts *were* correct. When she threw back the door she saw the man holding a gun, and she shot him. The bomb was to be used only as a last resort, a way of cleaning up a crime scene in case something went horribly wrong. The dynamite, connected to a disposable cell phone and detonated by a single call, was concealed at the roomy bottom of her beautiful Birkin bag. During the course of her many home visits to the parents of missing children, she had never once come close to using it. Nine times out of ten the wife killed the husband, or vice versa. In the two instances when this hadn't happened, she had killed both parents, staging the scene to appear as though they were victims of some sort of domestic squabble. Marie slipped out the door, leaving no evidence, and drove home with no one the wiser.

Brandon had demanded that they postpone the trip to go after James Weeks. It was too soon, he'd said. Marie had tried to soothe his paranoia by reminding him – again – of the facts. The man who had showed up on Theresa's front doorstep, the private investigator or whatever he was, was dead; she'd shot him twice in the chest. She'd fled through the back of the house and disappeared into the woods; nobody had seen her, and no one had followed her. Theresa Herrera was dead and the Birkin bag sitting on the foot of the bed had killed Dr Herrera. There were no survivors, no witnesses. Everything was fine. There was no reason *not* to head to Pennsylvania.

Brandon had wanted the dust to settle. He had wanted to wait at least three months.

Marie had no intention of waiting that long. She intended to take James Weeks, with or without Brandon's help. He had relented, but not without a fight.

Her anger began to soften when her thoughts turned to all the obstacles she and Brandon had overcome. Together.

She needed to show Brandon how much she appreciated him. Maybe order a takeout from that Italian restaurant he loved, then settle down in front of their big LED-screen TV and watch the video she'd taken of Theresa Herrera.

Marie made it to Baltimore in two hours flat.

The building for the defunct printing press had a long, wide bay that could accommodate a tractor-trailer. She pulled inside and parked at the far end. Then she got out and went to work.

Everything was set up and ready when Brandon arrived nearly an hour later, sitting in the passenger seat of a champagne-coloured Toyota Camry. The driver was bundled in a wool navy-blue pea coat. Marie saw the craggy face and thick, bulbous nose, and smiled. Gary Corrigan, tall and in his early fifties, had devoted the past two years to bodybuilding. Whenever Marie hugged him, as she did now, it felt like she was wrapping her arms around a cloth sack stuffed with smooth boulders. Corrigan kissed her on the cheek and then scurried away to leave them to it.

Marie already had the casket gurney pushed up against the back of the hearse. The coffin was too heavy for her to lift by herself. With Brandon's help, they grabbed the bars and pushed the coffin across the gurney's sturdy rollers. He refused her offer to help him carry Jimmy Weeks downstairs.

She followed him, glancing at the small refrigerator set up on a grimy corner desk. She was about to go to it when she remembered she had already tucked the bottle of Gatorade inside her pocket.

Brandon placed the teenager face first against the operating table. The sedative had started to wear off; James Weeks moaned as they removed his clothing. He flinched slightly when the scalpel cut a two-inch incision between his shoulder blades. His eyes fluttered open under the bright operating lights.

While Brandon shaved off the boy's hair with a pair of electric clippers – head lice were a constant problem down here – Marie picked up a flashlight and made her way back towards the stairwell. She moved past it, her trainers whisper-quiet against the concrete floor, and unlocked the door at the far end of the short hall.

Lying near the back of the small room and curled into a foetal position on the concrete floor was a bone-thin teenaged boy dressed in torn jeans and a threadbare T-shirt several sizes too small. Barefoot and shivering, he held up a shaky hand to shield his eyes from the bright beam of light.

The smell, as always, was atrocious. Breathing through her mouth, she moved closer, careful of the slop bucket. When she leaned forward, placing her hands on her knees, the boy didn't try to move away.

'Are you ready to see your mother, Rico?'

20

Rico Herrera broke down, sobbing in relief. Being mildly dehydrated, he could produce only a few tears.

Marie smiled. 'I brought you something to drink,' she said, and placed the bottle of Gatorade on the floor, directly in his line of vision. 'Look.'

She stepped back, shining the beam of the flashlight on the bottle. Rico stared at it. He swallowed dryly several times, but didn't dare move without permission.

'Go ahead, honey. You've suffered enough.'

Rico rolled on to his stomach. Having little food and almost no water for the past three days, he crawled to conserve his strength.

Marie smiled when his grimy, shaky hand clutched the bottle. He nearly cried out in triumph.

Rico cracked open the cap. He had started to roll on to his back when she said, 'You need to sit up and drink it . . . Here, let me help you . . . There, isn't that better? Now drink it slowly, or you'll throw it up . . . That's better. Take your time.'

All the while Rico sipped it, crying, Marie knelt behind him, rubbing his bony back and reassuring him that his mother was waiting upstairs to take him home. When Rico tilted his head back to drain the last of the liquid, she wrapped a rope around his throat.

Rico didn't have the strength to mount a fight. When his arms went limp, she kept twisting the rope. She had to make sure his brain was deprived of oxygen for just a few more seconds.

Marie had no intention of killing him. She just needed him unconscious. Strangling required more effort, but it was much easier than trying to administer an injection. She had tried that with the first few, and every time they saw the needle it triggered some sort of adrenalin reserve. They fought back and screamed. She wanted them to sit still; too much of the sedative in their weakened condition could potentially stop the heart.

Finally, Rico slumped to the floor. She didn't require Brandon's help with this part; she could easily lift Rico herself.

Cradling Rico in her arms, Marie stood and carried him out of the room, the length of rope tapping against her thigh.

21

Gary Corrigan had changed into medical scrubs and wore green neoprene surgical gloves that ran all the way up his forearms. A clear plastic shield protected his face.

Marie placed Rico on the operating table. She removed the rope, along with his clothing, and stepped back to give Corrigan room to work.

Corrigan rubbed a swab of surgical spirit against the crook of Rico Herrera's elbow. Next he inserted the IV, taped the line down and then began scrubbing and washing away the filth and grime covering the teenager's bare chest. Water sluiced over the edges of the operating table and ran into the floor drains.

Next came the Betatine. Corrigan swabbed the iodine-coloured liquid over Rico's chest, picked up a scalpel and made what he called a 'midline incision'. It started at the suprasternal notch and ended at the pubis. Corrigan had studied a new and rapid technique for multiple organ harvesting that allowed the organs to be cooled *in situ* using cold intra-aortic and intraportal infusates. The surgery would take no longer than sixty minutes.

Marie found it difficult to stand still. A fevered rush always gripped her at this stage. There was so much to do, so many decisions to make. She needed to maintain patience and calm in the midst of this exciting yet draining emotional storm.

Harvesting organs to fund their operation had been Brandon's brainchild. He had come up with the idea early on, when their financial resources were extremely limited, back when they were storing the children in the small basement of their home. With the families scattered all over the country, they could afford to take only one child at a time. Driving to a particular state and staying at hotels, the endless days spent watching the family and waiting for the perfect moment to abduct the child and disappear without getting caught – all of this required a significant investment of capital, and it had to be paid in cash because money didn't leave a visible trail.

And the costs didn't end once the child was locked away. There was the constant feeding for months and sometimes years at a time. The vitamins, fruit and vegetables needed to keep the child reasonably healthy. The constant monitoring to make sure the child didn't escape, the unexpected illnesses that always cropped up – colds and stomach flus that required trips to the drugstore; infections that demanded antibiotics. The third child they abducted, Anthony Jacobs, had a life-threatening asthma condition that necessitated using the Internet to purchase enough inhalers to last an entire year.

Then came the return trips to abduct the parent.

More costs, more time spent having to save up money, the maddening and seemingly endless waiting . . . until Brandon told her how they could sell organs to fund their operation. Unbeknownst to her, Brandon had been methodically researching the idea – and he had already made contact with an 'organ broker'. This man was part of a global network consisting of other organ brokers who represented people who either wanted or needed to bypass the traditional organ waiting lists. Buyers were lined up all over the world, and they were willing to pay a premium, in cash – especially for young, healthy organs.

Brandon's idea had proved to be extremely lucrative. They purchased the building of a former printing press, which allowed them to abduct and store *multiple* children and their parents for long periods of time. They paid off the loan for Washington Memorial Park, and Brandon lavished her with gifts. They could afford to do anything they wanted, anything in the world.

Marie inspected the coolers. There were five. Each one would house a separate organ – heart, lungs, liver, kidneys and pancreas. The Custodiol HTK solutions were ready. Everything appeared to be in order.

She glanced at her watch. It was almost noon. She checked Corrigan's progress. Another forty minutes and the harvest would be finished. She could meet the buyers at one thirty. They had flown in last night. Right now they were staying at hotels near the airport, waiting for her call. Marie took out her phone.

Brandon walked back into the room. He joined her and, noticing the phone in her hand, said, 'I already called the buyers.'

'When?'

'After I picked up Corrigan. Once he's finished, you can head to the office. I know you're anxious to get there.'

'What about Ted?' Ted Keller was the funeral home's assistant director.

'I sent Ted home for the day,' Brandon said. 'You'll have the place all to yourself.'

This was Brandon's way of apologizing for being such an idiot to her at the cemetery.

Tears stood in her eyes. Marie remembered her make-up and, not wanting the mascara to run, tilted her head back and blinked them away.

'Thank you.'

She kissed him. Deeply.

Then Marie hugged him fiercely. She could see Corrigan removing Rico's heart.

'I love you.'

'I love you too,' Brandon said. 'Come home as soon as you're done.'

Marie rolled the gurney across the funeral home's basement suite of dull white walls and grey linoleum flooring. The adrenalin rush from the past few hours had departed, leaving in its wake a bone-crushing exhaustion. Still, she felt relaxed. The funeral home was empty, and she had the rest of the afternoon to herself.

The crematorium had three separate ovens. She pushed the gurney up against the middle door. Rico's carcass had been wrapped and stored inside one of the long, cardboard boxes the funeral home used to put corpses awaiting cremation. She opened the door and slid the box inside the chamber. After she locked the door, she ignited the burners. The process would take thirty minutes.

Marie left for her office, aware of a new feeling worming its way through her: sorrow. She felt a sense of loss, always, at this stage. Each death brought her one step closer to the completion of her life's purpose – her life's mission.

Fortunately, she had discovered a way to remember each child and parent. To keep them alive in her heart and mind until the moment she gasped her last, dying breath.

She unlocked the office safe and from the top shelf

removed a large velvet jewellery box. It contained the necklace she'd worn while visiting Theresa Herrera. She never wore it here at work, just at home and when she visited the grieving parents.

The gold necklace was very elaborate, made up of eleven diamonds of various colours, each one a different shape and carat size. There were three empty settings. She wondered where she should put Rico.

The funeral-home business had brought her into contact with a vast array of companies offering specialized services for honouring the dead. The last decade had produced a rush of companies that created certified, high-quality diamonds from cremated remains, or a lock of hair. These lab-created diamonds had the same molecular identity, brilliance, lustre and hardness as the natural stones sold at any posh jewellery store. She had done business with several of these companies over the years, all under different names, and yet each and every time she visited their websites she was overwhelmed by the choice. There were cuts, degrees of clarity and sizes to consider – and colours. She had five to choose from: colourless, blue, red, yellow and green. Which colour was Rico?

The answer came to her immediately: red. It had taken a long time to break his fiery resolve – and that temper! He had fought her at nearly every turn.

Now she had to choose the cut and the clarity. She turned to her computer and logged on to one of the websites. She scrolled through the pages, thinking.

When she couldn't come to a decision, she checked

her watch. Twenty-two minutes had passed. She rose from her chair, and on her way back to the oven ducked inside a room to put on a face shield and apron to protect her from the intense heat.

Opening the crematorium door, she saw Rico's skull in the blaze of fire. She used a T-shaped iron rod to break it down into smaller fragments. She did the same with other, larger bones and then returned to the computer.

An hour passed and she still couldn't come to a decision.

No matter. The inspiration would come to her eventually. When it did, she would fill out the paperwork and put eight ounces of Rico's ashes, along with a money order, into the post. Another packet of ashes would be mailed out to the exciting new company she had just discovered. Sacred Ashes specialized in placing cremated remains inside rifle cartridges, shotgun shells and handgun ammunition, custom-made to any calibre.

Marie carried a 9-mm handgun in her handbag when she visited the parents. Until Colorado, she had never fired it inside a home. She did, however, use it frequently inside the printing press.

The moment she'd discovered Sacred Ashes, the idea of incorporating the cremated remains of her previous guests inside her handgun had struck her with such intensity that she shook for nearly an hour. It was as though she had been granted a dark and magical power to summon the dead from their graves (or, more appropriately, their incinerated ashes, all of which she had kept) to carry out an execution.

And it had given her a power. Approaching the cages with the handgun raised, she could recall, even now, the thrill of watching the look of terror in each parent's eyes as she rattled off the names of the dead loaded in her gun clip. Each time she fired a round, she felt lighter. Better.

Marie had placed three orders, with many more to come. The boxes of ammo were tucked inside the safe.

Marie had one regret: she wished Theresa Herrera had known the name associated with the bullet that had killed her. Wished the woman could have died with the knowledge.

Marie returned to the oven. The bone fragments had cooled. She picked up a long, metal broom with a brush made of high-carbon stainless-steel bristles and hummed a Spanish lullaby as she carefully swept Rico into a steel catcher at the front of the crematorium door. She switched to a normal paintbrush with a wide head to collect the finer fragments and then transferred everything into a crematorium pan.

Marie inspected the debris and, finding no metal, carefully dumped the fragments into a special processor. As the motorized blades pulverized Rico's bones to ash, she decided to honour Rico with a 1.5-carat, emerald-cut red stone. The $25,000 diamond would be the centrepiece of her necklace.

23

Ali Karim's plane touched down at an airport located near the southeastern corner of Alabama. Established in 1941 by the US Army Corps to train additional airport personnel for the Second World War, the Dothan Regional Airport was still used primarily by the military, but it also serviced one major commercial airline carrier and accepted all types of general aviation aircraft.

Airport operations were conducted inside a wide, ranch-shaped building with a brick face and a sloping grey roof. The interior was immaculately clean and accommodated a fair number of local retail and dining options. Fletcher stepped up to the Hertz counter and presented Robert Pepin's driver's licence and credit card to the clerk. Half an hour later he was seated behind the wheel of his rental – a Ford Explorer with its own GPS system. The town of Dunbar was an hour's drive.

He had visited Alabama once, when the FBI's Birmingham field office had asked the Bureau's Behavioral Analysis Unit for assistance in the case of a fifteen-year-old girl who had been abducted from her bike. While reviewing the case details and working up a profile to give to local law enforcement, the girl's mother had confessed to murdering her only child. Her new husband had been lavishing too much attention on his comely stepdaughter. The mother had killed her daughter out of jealousy.

Birmingham acted as the state's cultural capital, and was stocked with historic buildings, museums, botanical gardens, art galleries, ballet companies and symphony orchestras; the town of Dunbar, however, consisted of small, practical homes sprinkled between rambling meadows and dense forests. Despite the bright sunshine, the area had a haunted feel, as though the homes had been deserted. He passed no cars and saw no people.

Sacred Ashes, the company that specialized in adding cremated remains to shotgun and firearm cartridges, operated out of a brown-painted ranch with a sagging front porch. It was nearly identical in size and structure to the handful of ramshackle homes built haphazardly along Old Gracey Road, a long, meandering street carved through a seemingly never-ending maze of brown fields populated with ancient longleaf pines and spruces. The only advertisement for the company came in the form of adhesive gold letters placed on a new black mailbox mounted near the front door. The house contained no garage or carport. A pair of dirt roads wrapped around each side of the house and ended in an ample and currently empty dirt lot covered by a mat of brown pine needles.

Fletcher parked his Ford Escape rental on a trail in the woods where it wouldn't be seen from the main road. He collected the backpack holding his equipment and set off to find a place to conduct surveillance.

The edge of the woods led into a wide-open field of tall yellow grass that bent and swayed in the cooling afternoon wind. Hidden behind a tree, Fletcher unzipped the backpack and pulled out a laser mike. His broken ribs prevented him from lying on his stomach. Wearing a pair of headphones, he sat near an area of thick brush and aimed the laser mike at the windows.

Twenty minutes passed, without any sound or movement of any kind.

Then a phone rang inside the house. The company's answering machine picked up, and a woman with a thick, backwoods accent left a message. She had two sons, and, while both were avid outdoorsmen, they used different firearms. The mother was hoping it was possible to have their daddy's ashes split between shotgun shells and pistol rounds. She wanted to negotiate a price.

Fletcher pulled out his field glasses and studied the back of the house. When he finished, he took out his phone and called Karim, who was waiting inside the plane and helping his assistant, M, as in the letter, research information on Sacred Ashes.

The company had been open for less than a year, Karim said. The two men who had started it had taken out a second mortgage to purchase the 1,200-square-foot ranch home in Dunbar. They had also taken out a sizeable personal loan to buy the ammo supplies and equipment needed to modify gun cartridges. In the light of their debt, the owners had elected not to quit their steady, full-time jobs in Midland City, where both men also lived.

Fletcher thought about the house. At the moment it was empty. And Midland City was over an hour's drive from Dunbar. He wondered if the two owners had elected to take Sunday afternoon off to spend time with their wives or girlfriends.

M; Karim said, had uncovered some useful information concerning the house itself: there was no alarm system, as far as she could tell.

But that doesn't preclude the existence of one – or some other type of security, Fletcher thought. He thanked Karim, hung up and powered off his phone. Field glasses in hand, he searched the area. Assured that he was alone, Fletcher stood and tucked the field glasses into his jacket pocket. Then he tied his backpack to the top of a tree limb. There was no need to bring it with him. The tools he needed were packed inside the tactical belt hidden underneath the bottom edges of his windbreaker. He moved out of his hiding spot and jogged across the field.

Fletcher reached the back door, his broken ribs throbbing. He unzipped his jacket and removed a device that looked like an ordinary smartphone from his tactical belt and moved it around the door's edges. The light remained green, the signal that the house did not contain a security system. He put the device away and snapped on a pair of latex gloves. Using standard lock picks, he opened the door.

Since the house had no basement, the formal living area, shaded by cheap plastic blinds, had been transformed into a workshop. He found the usual assortment of equipment and tools needed to modify wildcat cartridges, all of which were neatly organized according to calibre on a series of metal shelving units resting against the walls. He opened a random box of 9-mm rounds and removed a bullet.

The cartridge was an identical match to the empty one he'd collected in Colorado.

There was one other interesting item in the room: a folding table holding FedEx and UPS mailing envelopes and small cardboard boxes. Two were open. They both contained human ashes sealed inside clear Ziploc bags.

Tucked underneath each box and envelope was a set of three stapled sheets. The first page was a computer form generated by the company website. It contained the requester's contact information, the decedent's information, type of ammo requested, packing and shipping preferences and a box for additional comments. The second sheet was a signed contract agreeing to the type of ammo requested and cost; the third, a copy of the deceased's death certificate.

Fletcher examined the other stapled sheets. Same three pages, same order forms. The buyers were all from Southern states with little or no gun or ammo restrictions. Since the United States Postal Service prohibited the mailing of ammunition or any other item it considered to be 'ORM-D', or 'Other Regulated Materials for Domestic Transport Only', shipping services for Sacred Ashes were performed by UPS and FedEx, as the two private transport companies had no restrictions on shipping firearms or ammunition, provided it complied with the state's particular gun laws.

Fletcher moved inside the kitchen. It was small and held an industrial-sized rubbish bin overflowing with empty beer cans, pizza boxes and fast-food containers. Five quick steps and he entered a sparsely furnished room containing a flat-screen TV propped up on milk crates and a pair of second-hand sofas covered with pillows and blankets. It appeared that the owners slept here during weekends and, possibly, after working late into the night on weekdays, rather than making the hour-long drive back to Midland City.

The adjoining hall, short and dim, led to two bedrooms. The one at the far end was empty, but the other was used as an office. There was only a desk, a cheap, pressboard thing sold at office-supply stores. Its top held a telephone, a laptop and an assortment of opened and unopened mail. The desk's rolling side drawer held hanging file folders.

He removed a portable hard drive the size of a deck of playing cards. After plugging it into the laptop, he slid a CD into the tray. He turned on the laptop. The software on the CD automatically engaged, collecting every scrap of data stored on the laptop's hard drive and writing copies to the portable drive.

Fletcher sat in the chair, about to start rooting through the hanging file folders, when he heard the unmistakable sound of an approaching truck.

24

Fletcher got to his feet. Having encountered such scenarios dozens of times over the course of his life, he felt no sense of danger or unease. It could simply be a passing vehicle. Or, if one or both owners were about to arrive, he could dart back to the bedroom office, quickly gather his things and escape. He would not be seen or caught.

The bedroom across the hall overlooked the front of the house. He pulled back the dusty blinds. A truck was pulling off the main road – a Ford 350 Super Duty painted black and covered in dirt and dried mud. A diesel engine, judging by the sound.

The truck parked round the front. The driver didn't kill the engine. Left it running as he opened the door and got out holding a big, metal toolbox. A rotund older man with a thick white beard: Santa Claus dressed in cheap flannel. He dropped the toolbox on the porch, turned and moved back to the truck.

Fletcher returned to the office. It took him only a few seconds to find the folder holding the company's completed order forms. He removed the thick stack of paper and then checked the rest of the hanging-file folders. Finding nothing else of value, he slid the drawer shut.

He checked the laptop. The software was still running. He leaned back in the chair and rifled through the stapled sheets. Thirty-six completed orders dating back to early March of last year.

Placing the papers on the desk, he leaned forward, pulled up his left trouser leg and removed the Velcro straps securing the portable scanner to his calf. The wand-size cordless device scanned a black-and-white document in two seconds, storing the images on the unit's micro-SD card.

He slid the scanner across the first page, then the next. Within four minutes he had scanned all 108 pages. He had to wait another six minutes for the CD software to finish copying the files to his portable hard drive.

His gear packed up and tucked away, Fletcher left through the back door and jogged across the field to retrieve his backpack from the tree.

Having been condemned to a life of constant vigilance, Fletcher was forced to take every conceivable precaution to make sure he wouldn't be caught. While he had found no evidence to suggest that he had been followed here, he could never entirely dismiss such a possibility. His rental car, locked and parked on the hidden trail in the woods, had been left unattended for the past hour.

Fletcher spent several minutes sweeping the car for listening devices or a GPS-tracking system. Finding it clean, he drove like a man who knew he was being followed. He watched the rearview and side mirrors for any signs of a trail – a task made much simpler by the remote setting and its lack of vehicles – and conducted the normal counter-surveillance measures. Deciding it was safe to return to the airport, he called Karim.

The conversation was brief. Fletcher explained the items he'd recovered. Karim didn't ask any questions and assured him everything he needed was on board the plane. They picked a meeting spot.

An hour later, Fletcher parked his rental car and made his way across the lot. It was half past five and there was still light in the Alabama sky, the February air still pleasantly cool – a much welcome relief after Chicago's frigid temperature and biting winds.

He found Karim waiting near a flagpole in front of a brick-faced building. Only waiting wasn't an accurate description. The man was smoking and pacing at a furious clip, like an expectant father from the time when men weren't allowed in delivery rooms, leaving him to fret while his wife underwent the world's most difficult childbirth. Karim, Fletcher knew, always acted this way at the start of a hunt. He kept fuelling the adrenalin with too much coffee and nicotine.

'Good, you're here,' Karim said. 'I was thinking, this information you recovered –'

'You want Miss White to analyse the data I recovered from the company laptop while you and I sort through the scanned documents. It will save time, and possibly allow us to identify our shooter before the plane lands in Chicago.'

'Either you've developed psychic abilities, or I need to develop a better poker face.'

'You intended to use her from the very start, Ali. That's why you brought her along.'

'I've come to rely heavily on M's talents.'

'That is, of course, your choice. But I won't be joining you on the return flight.'

Karim's expression turned stoic. 'After all our time together, do you honestly believe I'd bring someone into the fold who would put your freedom in danger?'

'No, I don't. But you're not living under the sword of Damocles. A man in my position has to be careful.'

'I know this woman, Malcolm. I trust her as much as I trust you, which is considerably.'

'Be that as it may, the three-million-dollar bounty on my head might change her mind.'

'Your fears are unwarranted. Even if she knew who you really are – and she doesn't – M would never do such a thing. She's incapable of it.'

'"Passion persuades me one way, reason another."'

'I'm sorry, but I forgot to bring along my copy of *Bartlett's Familiar Quotes*.'

'Clearly this woman has cast some sort of spell on you. You should see the way you simper in her presence.'

Karim chuckled as he dropped the last of his cigarette.

'I'm not judging you,' Fletcher said. 'In addition to being attractive, she projects a rather intense magnetism. Your choice of paramours is your business, but I would suggest you exercise caution.'

'Oh, and why's that?'

'Ali, the woman is young enough to be your daughter.'

'That she is,' Karim said, stubbing out the cigarette butt with his heel. 'She is, in fact, my daughter.'

25

'My *adopted* daughter,' Karim said, fetching the crumpled cigarette pack from his shirt pocket. 'My simpering, as you called it, is nothing more than the expression of a proud father.'

Fletcher, taken aback by Karim's admission, said nothing.

During the course of their professional relationship, Karim had made it abundantly clear that he would never remarry, let alone have another child. Burying his son and having to endure the painful mental disintegration of his former wife had banished Karim to a private hell from which few emerged. When he had finally managed to claw his way back to the demands of the living, Karim made the conscious decision to conduct his emotional life from within a fortified prison. He kept people at a distance, and in his private life the handful of women who had aroused his interest had been amputated like a necrotic limb the instant they expressed the wish for a serious emotional connection. Fletcher knew this was partly a coping mechanism but even more an act of self-flagellation. Karim refused to forgive himself for having failed to protect his child.

'When did this happen?'

'The adoption? Officially, when she turned sixteen.'

Karim lit his cigarette. 'No one knows about it. Not even Boyd. I took some rather elaborate and extensive measures to make sure no one could find out. You're not the only one with powerful enemies, Malcolm.'

Clearly there was more to the adoption story, and Karim's connection to a woman who had been born and raised on the other side of the pond. Fletcher's natural investigative instincts prompted him to delve further, but this matter was none of his business, and counter-productive to the issue at hand.

'How long has she been working with you?'

'Since she graduated from university,' Karim said. 'M came to the States and went to work in my IT department. She lasted about a year. She found the work mundane and tedious, and so asked if she could work directly with me. I hired her as my personal assistant. During that time, I noticed that she possessed a certain unique set of skills, which could be invaluable to my . . . side projects.'

'How long?'

'The last two years. M performs all the computer work so it can't be traced back to my company.'

'What's this "M" business?'

Karim shrugged. 'That's what she likes to be called.'

'And she's aware of what you and I do?'

'She's aware of what *I* do, yes. That's how much I trust her, Malcolm. But she doesn't know about you. I would never betray our confidence.'

Fletcher knew this to be true. Karim was a man of his word.

'And I would certainly never do anything that might jeopardize your freedom – *our* freedom, as I'm the one who's aiding and abetting a known fugitive. I have no doubts concerning M. That being said, I should have told you when we were in Chicago. I know the value you put on your privacy. My apologies.'

'How much does she know about the case?'

'She did the data mining on the Herrera family,' Karim said. 'At the moment, her knowledge is limited to the information she recovered from the Internet and various databases. She knows I was in contact with Theresa Herrera regarding her missing son. She also knows about the bombing, but I didn't tell her about your involvement or about the shooter.

'If you allow M to work with us on this – and I think you should, Malcolm – you can control the flow of information, the extent to which she's involved. Or you can work this privately and report back to me. Your choice.'

Fletcher didn't need to think it over; he had already made up his mind. He indicated his intentions by motioning to the airport building, curious as to what made the mysterious M so special – and how the young woman had penetrated Karim's ironclad, wounded heart.

Fletcher preferred reading to be a tactile experience. He didn't want to read the scanned order forms from Sacred Ashes on his netbook computer screen. When he boarded the plane, he headed to the back and plugged the scanner's micro-SD card into Karim's high-speed laser printer. M, seated in the rear of the plane and hunkered over a MacBook Pro laptop, paid him no attention.

That changed when he stepped beside her. She stared intently at him over the top of her MacBook, her body rigid. He noticed her hands gripping the edges of her seat.

Fletcher placed the portable hard drive on the table. She listened attentively as he explained the data he'd collected from the company laptop, what information she should focus on and the tasks he needed her to perform. She punctuated each of his requests with a nod. She didn't speak. When he finished, she didn't have any questions for him.

Inside the bathroom Fletcher took off his sunglasses. He put in his contacts and washed his face and hands. When he returned, he removed a thick stack of papers from the printer tray. There were two copies. He handed one to Karim, who was seated across the aisle from M.

The table where Karim sat held a cheese tray and a pair of long-stemmed glasses set around an opened 1998 bottle of Château Latour à Pomerol. Fletcher offered M a glass. She politely declined without looking up from her MacBook.

Fletcher settled himself in the spacious leather seat across from Karim. As the plane taxied to the runway, Fletcher started reading, slowly, studying the information printed on each sheet. When he reached the last page, he returned to the beginning of the stack. He didn't look up until he had finished his third and final review.

Fletcher grabbed a fresh sheet of paper. He wrote down his instructions and, reaching across the aisle, slid the sheet on to M's table. She glanced at it, nodded once, and then switched her gaze back to her MacBook.

Fletcher glanced at the cockpit door. It was closed.

'It's safe to talk,' Karim said.

'Notice anything?' Fletcher asked, tapping the stack of order forms resting on his lap.

'All the orders were placed by men,' Karim said.

'And none from Colorado.'

'So not only does our lady shooter live in another state, she took steps to conceal her identity.'

Fletcher nodded. 'I noticed one other thing,' he said.

'Just one?' Karim grinned. 'Where?'

'The page containing the agreement order and the liability waiver.' Fletcher removed three earmarked pages from his stack and, pushing the cheese tray aside, placed them on the table. 'These three men from Virginia. Barry Johnson, from Purcellville. Jon Riley, from Leesburg. And Jessie Foster, from Ashburn. Take a look at the signatures. The slope of the writing and the connecting lines used between the letters are similar. The letter "J" is the most telling example. It's identical in each case – and see how the writer connects it to the adjoining letter?' Fletcher pointed for Karim's benefit.

'Bloody hell,' Karim said. 'You're right.'

'All three men placed orders for 9-mm rounds. Johnson placed the first order in November of last year, followed by Riley in December and then Foster last month.'

Karim's brow furrowed. 'So this person used three different names to create three separate orders using, what, three different sets of human ashes?'

'It's a possibility. The name of the deceased is different on each death certificate. I wouldn't put too much stock in the names. Death certificates can easily be doctored using templates readily available on the Internet, and Sacred Ashes only requires a copy of the death certificate. They wouldn't be checking its validity.

'The weight of cremated remains depends on the weight of the individual,' Fletcher continued. 'A 200-pound man, for example, would yield six pounds of human ash. When I entered the house, I saw opened boxes containing roughly a cup of human ashes – about eight ounces. So you would have plenty of leftover remains to use for additional orders.'

Fletcher returned to his stack. Out of the corner of his eye he could see M watching him intently.

'Are you aware of Virginia's gun laws?' he asked Karim.

'I'm not, but I'm assuming they're fairly liberal.'

Fletcher nodded. 'Take a look at this,' he said, and placed three new pages on the table. 'Here are the shipping instructions provided by Johnson, Riley and Foster. They all ordered the same 9-mm rounds, and in each case Sacred Ashes mailed the ammunition to a local firearms dealer for pickup. This would make sense in a state that has restrictions on the type and/or amount of ammunition that can be delivered to a person's home. Virginia, however, has no such restrictions.

'If you took out a map, you'd see these three Virginia towns are close to the Maryland border. And Maryland does have strict ammunition guidelines. If our shooter lives there, all she would have to do is drive to the Virginia dealers and pay their out-of-state FFL-transfer fees.'

'If we contact the dealers and ask to see their records, we may tip off our shooter.'

'You're assuming they keep strict records. Some ask for a licence while others ask for nothing at all. And if our shooter hid her identity from Sacred Ashes, I think it's safe to assume she would have taken similar precautions when picking up her ammunition. Exploring that avenue is a waste of time.'

'What would you suggest?'

Fletcher turned to M, saw that she was already looking at him, waiting, her hands folded on the table.

'The three names I wrote down for you, were you able to find their emails?'

She nodded, her emerald eyes glowing in the Mac-Book screen's light.

'I traced the ISP for each email,' she said. Her tone was neutral, her expression almost phlegmatic. 'All three emails originated from the same place.'

Karim swung round in his chair. 'Where?'

'A house in Maryland,' she said.

26

Jimmy Weeks's eyes fluttered opened to darkness. It swam around him, as impenetrable as a wall. While he couldn't see anything, he could *feel* things, minor sensations that seemed to be calling to him from a great distance, like an orbiting space satellite thousands of miles away relaying vital information to an earth base. He knew he was lying on his left side, on something cold and hard and flat. His knees were tucked against his chest. Something had happened to his back; he felt pain between his shoulder blades, and it seemed to be trying to draw his attention, urging him to investigate.

Had he been in some sort of accident? Was he in a hospital and being given drugs? Or was he drunk? He *did* feel drunk, and a little sick to his stomach. It reminded him of that party at Tim Doherty's house when he'd chugged an entire six-pack of Milwaukee's Best within an hour. Huge mistake. He had got so shitfaced that he could barely stand. After he threw up, Tim had brought him to the basement and put him on a sofa. Jimmy remembered how he'd forced himself to sit up, everything spinning around him. Then, mercifully, he'd passed out.

He didn't feel like he was going to puke. More than anything, he felt tired. He shut his eyes, thinking about the cold trapped in this darkness. Yeah, it was weird, and yes, these tingling sensations crawling all over his body were disturbing, but his brain . . . it was like it had gone on holiday, leaving a fog in its place. A moment later he drifted off into a restless sleep plagued with fevered dreams.

Like any normal person, he suffered from the occasional nightmare. The ones from his youth – involving a faceless alien creature that roamed the house at night and hooked its tentacles on to him and his family and drank their blood – had been replaced by more typical, standard fare: falling from the top of a building or being trapped inside a strange house full of endless halls and ever-changing rooms. His dreams turned really odd once he'd entered his present oh-so wonderful adolescent phase, with its constant bounty of boners that occurred during class for no reason at all, and acne that spread across his face, back and shoulders like the indestructible crabgrass in his parents' lawn. Now his nightmares became more personal, more rooted in reality. The one he was having right now involved a recurring fear: public speaking. Principal Shelly told him it was time to address the students and pulled back the curtain. Jimmy walked on to the auditorium stage, his stomach doing flip-flops, and was immediately greeted with gasps and shrieks. Now came gales of laughter. It was at that moment he realized he wasn't wearing any trousers. Or underwear.

Jimmy resurfaced from the dream, sensing it had been prompted by a real-life event. His mind served up a real memory: showering after last week's hockey game. The coach, a tiny moustached man named Peter Walsh, insisted that his players take a shower after each practice or game. Why, Jimmy didn't know, but the guy stood guard like a cop in the locker room to make sure you did. Jimmy had been standing in the school's big prison-type shower with half a dozen other guys, his buddy Michael Hauptman standing right next to him and soaping up when Haupy nodded with his chin to Jimmy's crotch and said, 'Dude, what's up with your junk?' Jimmy felt cold all over – the same way he felt right now.

As Jimmy's eyes fluttered open again to the darkness, he consulted his brain for an explanation. It failed to provide one, so he moved his right hand up and touched his chest. Bare skin. He felt his knees. Bare skin. He moved his hand round to his back and felt his bare ass. His junk was, in fact, exposed. He wasn't wearing his boxers.

Embarrassment more than terror parted the fog, and he managed to get himself on to all fours. Dizzy and still feeling drunk, he reached out and his fingers got caught in some sort of barrier made of chain link. He grabbed it with both hands and stood. Slowly he turned to his right, feeling the chain link, hearing it rattle. Then the barrier ended and turned to his right. More chain link. He followed it with his fingers and when it ended he felt something cold and hard and rough. Concrete. A concrete wall. He followed it and felt another chain-link barrier.

I'm buck-naked and locked inside a . . . what? What is it?

At that moment his brain returned from its holiday. The fog lifted and memories started to trickle in. Being pulled over by that undercover woman FBI agent, who'd claimed his father's car had been involved in some robbery. Sitting handcuffed in the woman's Chevy SUV, her stabbing him with a needle, and then . . . He couldn't remember what happened next, but none of that mattered. A cop wouldn't inject you with a drug. A cop or an FBI agent wouldn't strip off your clothes and place you in this –

A flashlight was turned on, the bright beam aimed at his face. Jimmy caught a flash of his surroundings before the light blinded him: he was trapped inside a cage made of the same type of chain link people used for fences. For dog kennels.

The flashlight was turned off. He opened his eyes, bright stars burning across his vision. A shuffle of footsteps approached him and he backed up, blinded. He bumped into the concrete wall, his heart quickening as a door creaked open. He heard moaning – at least that's what it sounded like, someone moaning in pain, or fear, or both.

The door shut and the sound disappeared. The darkness surrounded him again, leaving him alone with his terror.

I'm locked inside a chain-link cage. I don't have on any clothes and there's a throbbing pain between my shoulder blades. He reached around his back with both hands, trying to feel the wound. He couldn't reach it, but the smooth skin of his forearms rubbed against his head and felt stubble. He rubbed his hands across his head. No hair, just stubble. His head had been shaved.

Jimmy was too terrified to cry. His mouth opened, making blubbering sounds as his mind decided that now was a good time to play clips from all the horror movies he'd seen over the course of his life. He tried to shut them off, but they kept playing.

What am I going to do?

He thought about the moaning he'd heard a moment ago and his insides turned to water. Then the tears came.

What's going to happen to me?

I don't know, a voice answered. *But you're trapped in here.*

Jimmy hadn't been raised to practise any particular faith. He didn't attend church, and wasn't sure if he believed in God, but he closed his eyes and clasped his hands together and prayed as though his life depended on it — because it did.

II
The Living and the Dead

27

Malcolm Fletcher checked out of his hotel on the evening of his fourth day in Baltimore. He paid using Robert Pepin's American Express gold business card and politely declined the valet's offer to fetch his car from the hotel garage.

Fletcher had parked on the top level, where there were fewer vehicles. He was alone, and he didn't have to worry about security cameras. He opened the trunk and then rooted through his various cases, selecting the items he would need that night with great care.

After he finished, he climbed behind the wheel and started the car.

By the time Karim's plane touched down at Chicago's O'Hare Airport, M had traced the emails and website orders of Barry Johnson, Jon Riley and Jessie Foster all the way back to a residential home in Dickeyville, a small historic village located on the western edge of Baltimore City.

Fletcher had checked M's work himself. There was no question in his mind about the validity of her information. It was rock-solid. Not wanting to waste any time, he left the plane, headed to his car and made the twelve-hour drive to Dickeyville. Karim had called once, to inform him of M's additional research. The three Virginia men were fictitious; they were not residents of the state. The names of the deceased written on the order forms were also false. The death certificates had been forged.

The house in Dickeyville was a single-family, weather-beaten white Colonial. It had been built on the top of a sloping hill on half an acre of land. Trees, shrubs and a waist-high wall made of stone separated the Colonial from the neighbouring homes.

The lights were off, the attached garage empty. Fletcher searched the house using a monocular equipped with thermal imaging. The technology, developed by the British SAS, could pick up heat signatures through walls and floors.

The home was empty. Fletcher decided to wait until he had more information about the house. There was no urgency, no need to rush. He found a hotel located less than seven miles away, checked in and slept. In the morning he collected the supplies he needed for surveillance work.

Fletcher watched the Colonial for three long days. With the exception of the postman, no one approached the house. No one collected the mail. On the evening of his first night and under cover of darkness, he approached the mailbox and examined its contents. No bills or personal correspondence of any kind, just a meagre offering of promotional leaflets, catalogues and other assorted junk mail, all of it addressed to 'current occupant'.

The news hadn't surprised him. Karim, using M's computer skills, had completed a preliminary investigation on the property. The historic Colonial, built in 1870, had last been sold to ABC Property Management, a limited liability corporation owned by Mark Sullivan, of Madison, Wisconsin. The LLC was listed on the utility and property tax bills, all of which were paid through an online banking account set up by a man named Rodger Callahan.

Subsequent data mining on Rodger Callahan and Mark Sullivan revealed an endless web of phone numbers and addresses all across the country that either did not exist, or that belonged to abandoned or foreclosed property. Karim pulled the LLC papers for ABC Property Management that had been filed with the Baltimore Chamber of Commerce. Its business address belonged to a gas station in Madison.

Karim had also pulled, scanned and emailed the Colonial's architectural plans to Fletcher, who memorized the layout during the boring slog of watching the house.

Amongst Karim's information was the technical specification of an important item: the home's alarm system. According to the installation notes, the control panel had been placed inside the basement. There were two security alarm keypads: one mounted near the front door, the other in the master bedroom. Each keypad had a panic button that, when pressed, immediately dispatched police and fire units. Both keypads also came equipped with a speakerphone that allowed the homeowner to communicate directly with emergency personnel.

Tonight Fletcher would bypass the alarm system, enter the house and conduct a thorough search. Then he'd wait inside for someone to return – hopefully the shooter, the woman in the fur coat.

28

Dickeyville consisted of two main roads: Wetheredsville and Pickwick. The historic homes, such as the one at No. 5131 Wetheredsville, the house of Union soldier and Gettysburg flag-waver Billy Ware, had been preserved with remarkable care. Construction for new homes, as well as existing homes requiring modernization, had to meet strict guidelines set by the Dickeyville Community Association in order to maintain the village's historic charm.

Fletcher took Pickwick and snaked his way across the quiet and deserted street. He reached the Colonial, surprised to find the downstairs windows lit. Someone had returned. The driveway was empty, which suggested that the homeowner had parked in the garage.

Fletcher drove past the house. When he reached the end of the street, he turned and made his way to Gwynns Falls. The area, with its numerous urban hiking and biking trails, offered a discreet and direct route to the back of the house.

Fifteen minutes later he drove across a parking lot of compacted dirt. Given the time of night and the cold weather, there were no other cars – or neighbouring homes. He could dress privately. He popped the trunk and stepped out of the car.

Fletcher wore a black, long-sleeved shirt over his bulletproof vest; all of his clothing was black. He took out his tactical belt, buckled it and strapped the nylon gun holster with its spare ammo clip to his thigh. He slipped on a pair of latex gloves, then exchanged his leather ones for a tactical brand made of Kevlar. The fingertips contained no extra material to get in the way of a trigger guard. He shut the trunk and locked the car.

Fletcher buttoned his coat as he made his way across the frozen ground. He didn't need to use his flashlight. The peppering of bright stars provided enough ambient light for him to make out his surroundings. It disappeared once he stepped on to the main trail, but he could see well enough, and he knew where he was going, having already walked this same route twice. Several minutes later, he moved off the main trail and headed up a slope matted with dead leaves and pine needles, the silence occasionally punctuated by the cracks of dried twigs and the crunch of downed branches beneath his boots.

He studied the house using the monocular. Two glowing heat signatures, but only one was moving – the person walking through the ground-floor rooms. The second figure was upstairs and horizontal, lying in one of the first-floor bedrooms facing the garden.

Fletcher watched the figures for the good part of an hour. The person downstairs wandered freely. The person on the first floor didn't move at all.

According to the schematics Karim had sent him,

the alarm system was a standard wireless model that used passive infrared and six glass-break detectors. Fletcher suspected the detectors had been installed on the ground-floor windows. Most homeowners never bothered to install the detectors on the first-floor windows, as they were generally inaccessible.

The back porch had a shingled roof, and there were no lights on the first floor.

Fletcher tucked the monocular back inside his trousers pocket as he moved out from behind the tree, making his way to the garden's picket fence.

29

Fletcher found the latch for the gate, opened it and walked into the garden. There was no need to run. The owner hadn't installed sensor lights here. No one was watching him from the windows, and the neighbours couldn't see him.

The only light came from the porch's sliding glass door. He could see part of the kitchen. Once he reached the bottom of the wooden steps, he could make out the deep mahogany units and the black-and-white-chequered tile floor. He moved to the left side of the porch, grabbed the railing and pulled himself up. Made of pressure-treated wood, the railing was sturdy, and he climbed on to it, got his feet settled, and then stood and grabbed the edge of the porch roof, his broken ribs groaning in protest. They exploded in pain when he jumped and hoisted himself up. It took a moment for the pain to subside. Nothing worse than broken ribs. No treatment, nothing to do but suffer through the pain until they healed.

Now he crept across the roof, his attention locked on the window he couldn't access from the roof, the one for the occupied bedroom. Monocular in hand, he looked through the window and saw the glowing heat signature still lying flat and level. A press of a button and the bright and swirling colours gave way to the green glow of night vision. The filmless micro-channel plate and auto-gated power supply with its reduced halo effect provided remarkably vivid details.

A man lay on top of a twin bed. He was bald and barefoot. He wore trousers and a collared shirt. Fletcher couldn't see the man's face; it was turned away from the window.

The man didn't pose a threat. His hands hung above his head, his wrists were bound to the headboard's spindles with what appeared to be zip ties. Fletcher zoomed in and discovered that that was, in fact, what they were. The man's left shirtsleeve had been loosened and pulled up across the elbow to accommodate an IV needle, which was connected to a hospital-grade piggy-back IV stand holding two bags of fluid.

Fletcher switched back to thermal imaging and turned his attention to the window for the accessible bedroom. No heat signature; the room was unoccupied. He crawled his way to it and then used night vision to examine the window. It contained no glass-break detector or magnetic sensors. The window had a tight seal, and it was locked. He couldn't use his tactical knife to prise the clasp loose. He tucked the monocular away and stripped off his Kevlar gloves, revealing the latex ones he wore underneath. The latex would allow him to handle the tools he needed.

Fletcher placed a suction cup on the thick pane around the window clasp and, glasscutter in hand, went to work. It took him less than a minute to cut through the glass. The suction cup kept the square-shaped section from falling. He pulled it loose, turned and flung it far into the garden. He didn't hear the glass break. He unlocked the clasp and used his tactical knife to open the bottom part of the window. It slid open easily. He went in feet first, stood and eased the window shut.

The bedroom door was open; muted voices came from the hallway. Television voices. A man and woman arguing about how the president was bankrupting the nation with his universal health-care programme. The arguing stopped, and was replaced by a commercial for a new medication to treat erectile dysfunction.

Fletcher entered the hall and turned right, the carpet masking his footsteps. The door to the occupied bedroom was also open. He slid inside the room. The man was still lying on the bed, still unconscious. He appeared to be of Hispanic descent, early twenties, and relatively short in size and stature. Not bald but a shaved head thick with stubble. His jaw hung open, and he was breathing rapidly. The damp skin smelled of soap.

The piggyback IV stand was by the side of the bed facing the window. Fletcher moved to it and read the labels in the dull light: a ten-litre 0.9 per cent normal saline in one bag, the other holding a wide-spectrum antibiotic used to treat severe bacterial infections.

Fletcher pressed two fingers against the man's damp, hot neck. The man did not stir or register the touch. Fletcher tracked time in his head. After a minute passed, he moved his hand away.

The young man had an elevated heart rate, and he seemed to be suffering from a fever.

Fletcher used one of the surgical-spirit prep pads on the nightstand to wipe the screen of his smartphone. He used it again to clean the man's fingers.

Fletcher pressed the fingertips of the man's right hand against the screen, holding them in place as a narrow beam of light scanned them. He wiped the screen and scanned the man's thumb. Then he did the left hand. He sent off the prints to Karim's private email, traded his phone for his sidearm and moved back into the hallway.

30

Fletcher found the stairs easily in the dark.

His movements were slow and smooth as he crept down the carpet runner, listening for movement and watching for shadows. He reached the foot of the stairs, stepped into the roomy kitchen and waited. No sounds, no movement. He walked across the tiles and followed the television voices, his footsteps whisper-quiet against the floor.

Sidled against a wall, he peered around a corner and found a large living room decorated to resemble a pol-itician's lair – burgundy-painted walls and dark leather sofas and club chairs arranged on a sweeping oriental rug; side tables holding crystal ashtrays and coasters. He could see part of a bar, the polished mahogany shelves stocked with top-shelf spirits.

In the room's centre were three faux Chippendale armchairs made of cherrywood. They were arranged around a coffee table. Each chair faced a flat-screen TV above a black marble fireplace crackling with wood. An older Caucasian male sat in the middle chair, watching the TV. Fletcher could see only the back of the man's head, the carefully combed white hair and the left elbow propped on the armrest. The man held his arm at a ninety-degree angle. Gripped in his hand was a hard rubber blue ball. He squeezed it and then relaxed his grip, squeezed and relaxed, all the while watching the television.

Minutes passed and then the man dropped the ball on his lap.

Now his left hand moved to the side table, which held an ashtray and a column of stacked coins. The man pushed the ashtray aside. His longer fingers gripped the top coin, a quarter. He held it in the air, studying his hand for a moment before placing the coin down on another part of the table.

The fingers moved back to the stack and picked up a dime. Again the man studied his hand before placing the dime on top of the quarter.

The man went back to watching the television as he repeated the process again. Again.

Fletcher holstered his SIG. He removed a leather sap, slid around the corner and entered the living room.

The man heard the heavy thump of footsteps. Startled, he jumped to his feet. He was tall and wore a navy-blue suit and a white shirt without a tie. He had half turned when Fletcher raked him hard and fast against the temple with the sap. The man's knees buckled, and he dropped to the floor and lay as still as a clubbed fish.

Fletcher found the remote and shut off the TV. Kneeling, he grabbed the tactical knife strapped behind his calf muscle. A series of quick cuts, no more than a few minutes' work, and the man's clothing lay in a shredded heap on the carpet. He bound the man's wrists and ankles with police-grade FlexiCuffs. Beneath the man's cologne Fletcher caught a subtle yet distinctive medicinal odour.

He scanned the man's fingerprints, stood and left the living room. Having already memorized the home's layout, Fletcher knew the quickest route to the alarm's main control panel in the basement. This he filled with liquid styrofoam, which hardened and immobilized the system. He darted back upstairs, found the security-alarm panel next to the front door and filled it with styrofoam. The remaining alarm panel was upstairs. He would deal with that in a moment. First, he took a moment to examine the surrounding rooms.

The dining-room table was covered with white Irish linen and held six place settings with crystal wine glasses. The man had smartly opened two bottles of Brunello di Montalcino, one of the best and most expensive Italian reds on the market, to allow the wine to breathe. Apparently he was expecting company sometime this evening.

Fletcher took a moment to consider his next course of action.

Returning to the living room, he found the man still unconscious. The left side of his face had started to swell. Fletcher saw a long camelhair overcoat draped over the back of a chair. He examined the coat and the torn clothing on the floor for a moment before rooting through the pockets. They held an iPhone, an elegant black leather billfold and a sterling silver Tiffany key ring. According to the man's Baltimore driver's licence, his name was Gary Corrigan, aged forty-eight. The credit cards had been issued in the same name.

An envelope holding five thousand dollars in greasy hundred-dollar bills was tucked inside the suit-jacket pocket along with a small plastic vial containing half a dozen pink and blue pills. Fletcher tucked the vial and iPhone in his pocket, then dragged Corrigan into the dining room and lifted him into the elegant high-backed chair at the head of the table. Fletcher cut off the Flexi-Cuffs. Then he took out fresh ones and secured the man's wrists and ankles to the armrests and legs.

Fletcher selected two items from the kitchen. One came to rest inside Mr Corrigan's mouth. The other was placed on his dinner plate. The man would see it, even in the gloom.

Back upstairs, Fletcher turned on the bedroom lights. The man tied to the bed did not stir, even when he was searched.

His pockets were empty. No identification. Fletcher studied the face. Karim had emailed him several pictures of Rico Herrera. Herrera had a round-shaped face, a gap between his front teeth and a birthmark along his right temple. The man on the bed had a square face, small and even teeth, and no birthmark. This man wasn't Rico Herrera.

Fletcher moved into the adjoining bathroom. Inside the medicine cabinet he found a surgical-strength bottle of antiseptic. He soaked a facecloth in cold water, returned to the bedroom and placed it on the man's forehead. Then he cut the zip ties. The man's arms flopped against his head. He didn't stir or make a sound. Fletcher laid the man's arms by his sides. The light brown forearms were punctured and bruised by needle marks.

The nightstand drawers contained an assortment of surgical-spirit prep pads, gauze and plasters, packaged IV needles and syringes. He found vials of the narcotic pain medication Demerol mixed in between saline bags. A folding knife was in a bottom drawer.

Fletcher left to explore the room across the hall. The security-alarm keypad glowed from the wall next to the door. He turned on the lights and filled it with liquid styrofoam.

The master bedroom contained a king-sized bed and a pair of nightstands, a lamp on each one. Both nightstands held alarm clocks. One contained a bottle of hand cream, the other a biography of Winston Churchill. A leather club chair sat in a corner. The walls were bare. The bureau did not contain any framed pictures, and he had seen no pictures downstairs. Inside the bureau drawers he found a mix of men's and women's clothing.

Fletcher took in the room, with its Moulin Rouge colours and recycled Louis XIV-style furniture and fabrics: pop Victorian mixed with the taste of a French bordello. A knock-off Gustave Serrurier-Bovy armoire made of rich mahogany stood in a corner. He had seen the original, crafted in 1899 by the late Belgian architect, on display at Paris's Musée d'Orsay.

Fletcher was more interested in the closet door. It

was made of solid wood – the kind of door used primarily on the front or back of a house to prevent intrusion. What made the closet door even more peculiar was the mechanism used to secure it: an electronic lock that required a magnetic keycard.

Gary Corrigan wasn't carrying a magnetic keycard.

Fletcher wondered if the closet contained its own separate security system. He took out his device resembling an ordinary smartphone and moved it around the edges of the closet and the brushed stainless-steel light switch overhead. The green light did not turn red. There was no electronic security. He tucked the device away and snapped open the tactical pouch containing his various lock-picking tools, selecting a heavy circular ring made of aluminium. It housed four powerful magnets that could bypass any electronic lock.

He slipped the ring over the door handle and then, slowly, turned it clockwise, waiting for the magnetic fields to find the metal parts residing inside the electronic lock . . . there. Now a quick twist counterclockwise and the lock clicked back. Fletcher flipped the light switch as he opened the door.

31

Here was a long walk-in closet of recessed lighting and custom-made white shelving, shoe racks and cabinetry. The back held a tall built-in bureau with six drawers. Beside it was another Louis XIV-designed chair, this one covered with ivory linen and with cabriole legs of distressed wood. An antique side table sat next to the chair, its top holding an empty highball glass and a half-empty bottle of Maker's Mark bourbon.

Fletcher turned his attention to some plastic garment bags hanging from steel rods on either side of the closet. There were eleven bags, and the spaces between them were perfectly even. Each bag faced the aisle of light brown carpet, turned at a slight angle so it faced the chair.

He stepped inside. The air was stale and dust swarmed in the cones of light.

Within the clear-plastic bags were clothes belonging to both men and women – complete outfits, the clothing combinations artfully arranged on the hangers as though they were on display for purchase in a store. He found suit jackets draped over shirts with ties and silk scarves. Long-sleeves and short-sleeves and T-shirts paired with chinos and jeans. One bag contained a green hospital smock and scrubs.

The clothes were of various sizes. Sitting underneath

each bag was an odd assortment of well-worn footwear—shoes, trainers, boots, even two worn white clogs. Two pairs of women's shoes were missing heels.

Fletcher inspected a random garment bag. It held a wrinkled linen sports jacket draped over a wrinkled and torn pale blue Oxford-collared shirt. The garment bag next to it contained a pair of men's jeans. The pocket was ripped, the fabric above the knees covered with grime and dried blood. The accompanying white T-shirt, dirty and mangled, had underarms marred with yellow perspiration stains.

He inspected the built-in bureau's six drawers. Each one contained men's and women's jewellery, laid out on black velvet cushions. Some pieces were bent and broken. Others were scratched or missing a small diamond or stone.

Fletcher sat in the chair. The garment bags faced him.

Eleven bags containing mangled and bloody clothing. Eleven bags for eleven victims. The garments were killing souvenirs. Trophies. He looked at the highball glass. Its rim was smeared with red lipstick. The shooter, the woman in the fur coat, had used this glass. She had sat in this chair, sipped her bourbon and stared at the clothing of her victims.

And she had a male partner. She lived with and slept next to a man every day and every night. The man had to be her partner because there was no way she could hide this grisly tableau from him. Fletcher got to his feet, wondering if the pair had designed the killing museum together.

And how did Gary Corrigan fit into this? He wasn't the woman's partner, Fletcher was sure of it. The bedroom's bureau drawers held XXL jockey vests and boxer shorts. Corrigan had been wearing a form-fitting tank-top vest and Calvin Klein briefs, both in a size large.

Fletcher removed Corrigan's iPhone and then reached for the small, boxy forensic unit strapped to his tactical belt. He unspooled a cord and connected the end to the iPhone. The unit's LCD panel came to life and then began the process of extracting the phone's data.

All the clothes in here belonged to adult men and women. He looked at the sleeping figure on the bed.

Who are you? And why are you tied up to this bed?

It was time to speak with Gary Corrigan. Fletcher slid the highball glass inside an evidence bag, about to shut it when he noticed a faint black residue resting at the bottom, a small collection of particles resembling cigarette ashes.

Not cigarettes ashes, Fletcher thought, looking around the closet. The shelves above the hangers were bare. Kneeling, he searched the area behind the shoes. Behind each one he found a sealed plastic bag holding cremated remains. Human ashes.

The forensic unit vibrated against his belt, the signal that it had finished the download. Fletcher removed the cord and examined Corrigan's iPhone as he left the closet.

32

Entering the dining room, Fletcher was pleased to find Gary Corrigan conscious. The man's head bobbed and swayed from side to side, eyes blinking rapidly as he tried to clear away the pain, tried to focus.

Fletcher picked up the small kitchen torch sitting in the centre of the table. A press of a button and the bright blue flame ignited, parting the gloom.

Corrigan sat up, his back ramrod-straight against the chair, his eyes as wide as the saucers decorating the splendid table.

'"By an unfaltering trust, approach thy grave,"' Fletcher said, lighting the first of four candles wedged in delicate crystal blocks. '"Like one who wraps the drapery of his couch, / About him, and lies down to pleasant dreams."'

The man didn't answer – couldn't, even if he had been so inclined, due to the dishcloth stuffed in his mouth.

'The last lines from William Cullen Bryant's poem "Thantopsis",' Fletcher said. He lit the final candle and returned the torch to the table. 'I doubt you're praying to God right now, Mr Corrigan, but at the moment you may lack perspective.'

Corrigan's licence picture showed an older man with

157

a sagging chin and a bloated face. The man strapped to the chair had noticeably different features. In addition to a subtle facelift, he had gained muscle mass. In the flickering candlelight Fletcher could see the thick fibrous muscles flexing and moving beneath the pale skin. Show muscle. Lots of low reps with heavy weights, their bulk and definition aided by steroids. The diminutive size of the man's testicles proved he had been on the juice for quite some time.

Sensing the man's embarrassment at having his genitalia on display, Fletcher pushed the chair up against the table until the lip of the linen tablecloth covered his lap.

Fletcher took the chair next to Corrigan. 'Do you own this house, Mr Corrigan?'

Vigorous shaking of the head: *No, no, no, no.*

'I thought not.' Fletcher picked up a coffee cup painstakingly decorated with hand-painted violets and vines and, turning it over, read the writing printed on the bottom: 'Haviland Limoges. I'd compliment you on your excellent taste, but I suspect you had nothing to do with the purchase. A man who could afford Limoges china and the antique luxuries inside this house certainly wouldn't scrimp on his clothing, would he? Your Hugo Boss suit and Hermès overcoat are clearly knockoffs. You can tell by the inferior stitching.'

Fletcher leaned forward and pulled the cloth from Corrigan's mouth. The man's chest heaved as he sucked in air. Inbetween the rapid breaths Fletcher heard the ticking from the antique grandfather clock sitting in the room's corner. Corrigan glanced at it as he spoke.

'Who are you?' He had a light and airy voice. Educated. 'What do you want?'

'As for who I am, think of me as a borrowed angel – *your* borrowed angel, Mr Corrigan, sent from on high to unburden you of your sins. Now let me explain what I want.

'The path to salvation can be very straight and narrow, but I should warn you, I'm someone who finds dishonesty unspeakably ugly. Please bear that in mind before you answer my questions. If I feel you're lying to me, I'll use this on your fingers.' Fletcher tapped the meat cleaver resting on the man's dinner plate. 'If that doesn't help clarify your priorities, I'll move on to the more sensitive items residing a few inches south of your navel. Do we have an understanding?'

The man nodded, swallowing.

'Good.' Fletcher leaned back in his chair and crossed his legs. He draped his arm on the table, resting his fingers next to the handle of the cleaver. 'We'll start with an easy question. The gentleman tied up in the upstairs bedroom: what's his name?'

Corrigan swallowed. 'Timmy.'

'Does Timmy have a last name?'

'I'm sure he does, but I don't know it.'

'And why, pray tell, is Timmy hooked up to an IV?'

'He's dehydrated. Some sort of stomach flu.'

'He has a number of needle marks on his arms.'

'He's a junkie,' Corrigan said. 'Heroin, I was told.'

'Told by whom? The woman who owns this house?'

'What woman? What are you talking about?'

'The one with the black hair pulled back into a bun. The one with the fur coat. Where is she? What's her name?'

'I don't know anything. This is my first time here.'

Fletcher sighed. 'Does Mr Jenner live here?'

Corrigan went a little pale.

Fletcher held up the man's iPhone. 'I examined the call log,' he said, and then placed the phone on the table. 'Over the past three hours I noticed seven incoming and outgoing calls between you and someone named Jenner. I checked your contacts and saw a listing for Jenner but no first name or address, just a cell-phone number. Enlighten me.'

'I don't know if Jenner is the man's first name or his last.'

'Is this his house?'

'I don't know.' Corrigan stole another glace at the clock. 'Whatever this is about, I've –'

'Why did you tie your patient's hands to the headboard?'

'Jenner did that. He didn't want Timmy to rip the IV out of his arm. I had to get fluids in him. He called me – Jenner – he called and asked that I come over to treat Timmy.'

'You inserted the IV?'

Corrigan paused a beat, considering the question. 'I was a nurse a long time ago.'

'Why did you give it up, Mr Corrigan?'

'It gave me up. Cutbacks. The economy.'

'I see. And when did you give up practising surgery?'

'I don't know what –'

'Your hands reek of chlorhexidine,' Fletcher said. 'You scrubbed your hands in the upstairs bathroom before treating your patient, didn't you?'

'That doesn't mean I'm a surgeon. It's a standard antiseptic cleaner. I use it because –'

'I watched you doing your hand exercises with that rubber-strengthening ball.'

Corrigan grew still, his face shiny with perspiration.

'Then I watched you pick up your little stack of coins and check your hand for tremors. I'm assuming that's why you take these.' Fletcher held up the man's plastic vial of pills. 'One is a betablocker, and so is the other, Propranolol. These are the only two medications that, when used together, decrease surgical tremors and anxiety.'

Corrigan couldn't mask his surprise at being found out.

'If you're not a surgeon, Mr Corrigan, then why are you taking these medications?'

The man didn't answer. Beads of sweat rolled down his face.

Fletcher reached for the cleaver.

'*Was*,' Corrigan said. 'I *was* a surgeon.'

'But you told me you were a nurse.'

Corrigan swallowed. Licked his lips and swallowed again.

'Let's talk about this like two civilized people, okay? I'll tell you everything I know. It's not much, but I'll —'

'You lied to me,' Fletcher said, picking up the meat cleaver as he stood.

33

'*Hold on,*' Corrigan screamed, jerking against his restraints. The dining-room chair tipped back. Its arms banged against the table's underside and the chair rocked forward. '*For the love of Christ just hold on a moment and let me explain!*'

Fletcher rested the tip of the cleaver against the plate. 'Why does Mr Jenner employ a surgeon?'

'Former surgeon. I'm a *former* surgeon.' Corrigan's breathing came hard and fast. 'He employs me to treat people he doesn't want to bring to the hospital. That's all I do, *I swear to God.* Whatever beef you've got with him, it isn't with me, so let's just –'

'What, exactly, is Mr Jenner's business?'

'It's none of mine,' Corrigan said. 'I don't ask questions, I just take care of the medical end of things. He called and told me to come here, and I did. Timmy was already here and tied up to the bed, that's the God's honest truth. Jenner told me to give him the antibiotics, and I did.'

'And Demerol.'

'Yes. Yes, I did. Timmy was going through heroin withdrawal. Jenner wanted him to sleep, so I sedated him with Demerol. Jenner tied him up because he didn't want Timmy getting his hands on it.'

'Dosage?'

'A hundred milligrammes every two to three hours.'

'IM injection or slow IV push?'

'Push,' Corrigan said. 'Who *are* you?'

'Who supplies the medicine, you or Jenner?'

'Jenner. I tell him what I need and he gets it for me.'

'And you're saying Mr Jenner does not own this home.'

'That's right.'

'Who does?'

'I don't know, I swear to Christ –'

'I think you do,' Fletcher said. 'And I think if I apply the right amount of pressure, you'll tell me.'

'How many times do I have to say it? *I. Don't. Know.*'

Fletcher pulled out Corrigan's chair at an angle, exposing the man's right hand.

'*You're asking the wrong man,*' Corrigan howled, squeezing the chair's armrest. '*I'm just a hired hand, I swear to God I'm telling you the truth.*'

Fletcher rested the blade against the man's wrist and said, 'Then tell me the name of the man and woman who own this house.'

'*I don't know! I don't know!*'

Fletcher brought up the cleaver.

The veins in the man's neck stood out like cords of rope as he screamed: '*I'M TELLING YOU THE TRUTH, I SWEAR TO GOD, JESUS IN HEAVEN, I DON'T KNOW WHAT JENNER DOES FOR A LIVING OR WHO OWNS THIS HOUSE OR WHO'S*

COMING OVER TO DINNER, FOR THE LOVE OF GOD PLEASE DON'T HURT ME!'

Fletcher placed the cleaver on the table.

'What time are your dinner guests arriving?'

Corrigan struggled to catch his breath. 'They're not *my* guests,' he said. 'I have no idea what time they're coming.'

Fletcher suspected that was a lie. He suspected that every word Corrigan had spoken was a lie. Given the number of times the man had consulted the grand-father clock, Corrigan was expecting Jenner and/or tonight's guests to be arriving shortly – perhaps within minutes. The man was stalling to save his life.

Fletcher picked up the iPhone and placed it on the doctor's dinner plate.

'What are you doing?'

'We're going to have a conference call with your employer,' Fletcher said.

34

Corrigan stared at his iPhone as though it had suddenly transformed itself into a poisonous snake. Fletcher outlined how the upcoming conversation would be conducted as he removed his own smartphone and, with it, a cord wound into a tight coil. He placed both items on the edge of the table.

'I have five thousand dollars in my suit pocket,' Corrigan said, his eyes brightening with purpose. 'I've also got another fifty grand in cash stored inside a safe at my house.'

Fletcher slid one end of the jack into the iPhone.

'Take me with you and the cash is yours,' Corrigan said.

Fletcher slid the other end of the jack into his own phone.

'*Goddamnit, listen to me!*'

Fletcher pressed the iPhone's on-screen button for the speakerphone.

'I'm begging you,' Corrigan sputtered. 'In the name of God please don't do this.'

'You have nothing to fear, Doctor. I'll be standing right behind you to lend moral support.'

Fletcher slid the chair back up against the table.

'I'm not speaking to him,' Corrigan said.

Fletcher pressed the on-screen button to dial the number.

'Please don't do this.'

On the first ring Fletcher picked up the cleaver.

'Please,' Corrigan whimpered. 'Please, I'll do anything but this.'

Another ring and the line on the other end picked up: 'What's up, Gary?' Jenner had a deep and nasal voice. He sounded nervous.

Corrigan wouldn't answer. Kept his lips clamped shut.

Fletcher pressed the cleaver against the doctor's throat.

'Gary, you there?' Jenner asked.

'I'm here,' Corrigan answered, his voice pinched tight.

'Can this wait?' Jenner asked. 'I'm just about to stop for some gas. I should be there in twenty minutes or so.'

'No.' The doctor cleared his throat, started again. 'No, it can't wait.'

'Is it Santiago? Is the infection under control?'

Corrigan couldn't reply; Fletcher had clamped a hand over the man's mouth.

Corrigan trembled, beads of sweat dripping on to the plate. When he failed to answer Jenner's question, Jenner said, 'Jesus Christ.' Heavy breathing, and when Jenner spoke again, his voice kept rising: 'You said the infection was under control – said we had *nothing* to worry about. What the hell happened?'

Fletcher whispered his instructions into Corrigan's ear.

Jenner waited for an answer. The silence lingered.

'Don't tell me Santiago died,' Jenner said, his tone full of dread. 'Please don't tell me that.'

Fletcher looked at his phone. The software had locked on to Jenner's signal; the man was eighteen miles from the house.

Plenty of time, he thought, and released his grip on the cleaver.

Corrigan said, 'Our patient is doing fine. Are you coming alone?'

A grateful sigh of relief echoed over the speakerphone. 'Jesus, you had me scared there for a moment,' Jenner said. 'How're your hands holding up? You ready for surgery?'

'Are you coming alone?' Corrigan asked again.

'I've got Marcus with me. The others will be arriving around nine or so. Why? What's going on?'

Corrigan couldn't answer the question; Fletcher had terminated the call.

Fletcher came out from behind the chair. 'Your patient, Santiago,' he said, collecting his phone and equipment. 'I want his full name.'

'Nathan,' Corrigan replied, trembling. 'Nathan Santiago.' He fought back tears. 'I'm sorry I lied, but you have to understand –'

'Do you want to save your life, Doctor?'

'God, yes.'

'Rico Herrera. Where is he?'

'I don't know their names.'

'How many others are there?'

'I don't know. I swear to God I'm telling you the truth.'

'You said that last time. Why should I believe you now?'

'Three, I think,' Corrigan said. 'There are three others. At least.'

Are, Fletcher thought. There *are* three others. Present tense. 'They're alive,' he said.

Corrigan nodded, then broke down, sobbing.

'Where?' Fletcher asked.

'Let me go and I'll take you there.'

'Give me an address, and I'll consider it.'

'No. You have to take me with you.'

Fletcher felt a spike of anger. He looked at the cleaver.

'I won't tell you,' Corrigan said. 'You have to take me there.'

Fletcher couldn't take both Corrigan and the man lying upstairs, Nathan Santiago. There wasn't enough time.

'If you don't take me with you,' Corrigan said, 'you'll never find them.'

'And the surgery you're due to perform?'

'I'll explain everything once we arrive at our destination. Then I'll disappear, you have my word. Now hurry up and untie me before –'

Fletcher hit Corrigan in the throat.

The doctor's head whipped back, his face turning a dark crimson as he sucked in air in painful, broken gasps.

The second blow crushed the man's larynx.

Fletcher balled up the dishcloth and stuffed it in the man's mouth. Corrigan bucked and thrashed against his restraints, the cutlery and plates rattling against the table. The FlexiCuffs tying him to the chair had cut through his skin, and he was bleeding. Fletcher picked up the wine bottle, shoved the man's head back and poured the wine into the dishcloth. Corrigan started to choke. Fletcher turned the empty, heavy bottle in his hands and swung it across the man's face, shattering his nose. He swung the bottle again and smashed it against Corrigan's temple.

35

As the doctor started to die, his brain bleeding out from the two blows and his muscles convulsing in protest, Fletcher removed a small, battery-powered audio bug from a tactical pouch. He peeled off the self-adhesive strip and stuck the bug underneath the table. Then he pulled the dishcloth from the man's mouth.

Wine and blood and shattered teeth splashed down across Corrigan's chest, splattering the dinner plate and staining the tablecloth. Fletcher quickly wiped his gloved hands on his black trousers and then opened another pouch and retrieved a small, circular object the size of a pencil eraser. He jerked the doctor's head back and shoved the GPS transmitter past the slick tongue and down the man's throat. To make sure it stayed in the man's stomach, Fletcher stuffed the dishcloth back into Corrigan's mouth.

He left the doctor's iPhone on the table. He made two quick stops, in the living room and kitchen, before heading back upstairs.

Gary Corrigan's patient was no longer on the bed. The nightstand near the window had been overturned, the drawers pulled open; Nathan Santiago, semi-conscious, clawed at them as he lay sprawled against the floor, moaning, his drowsy eyes blinking, trying to focus on the objects blurred by his Demerol haze.

Fletcher darted inside the master bedroom, stepped back inside the walk-in closet and found a hiding spot for a second audio bug. He picked up the evidence bag holding the highball glass on his way out.

Nathan Santiago saw Fletcher approaching and held up a shaky arm to shield his face.

'There's no need to be afraid,' Fletcher said, kneeling. Corrigan's long camelhair overcoat was draped over his arm. He placed it on the floor. 'I'm going to bring you someplace safe. Lie still while I take this out.' Fletcher removed the IV needle and covered the puncture wound with one of the fresh bandages scattered along the carpet. Then he helped the man sit up.

Santiago didn't fight him. Corrigan's roomy overcoat swam over the thin, frail body.

The man clearly couldn't stand on his own, even with assistance. He needed to be carried. Fletcher scooped him into his arms, his broken ribs exploding in pain. He fought his way through it and carried the shivering body out of the bedroom.

During his previous trip to the kitchen, Fletcher had opened the sliding glass door. He moved outside and down the porch steps, then across the dark garden, Santiago was as light and frail as a bird in his arms. He opened the gate and, cradling Santiago against his chest, moved down the leafy slope. He had reached the main trail when he heard the roar of a car engine followed by a peel of tyres.

The trip to the parking lot was prolonged by his injury. Fletcher reached his car, winded, sweating despite the cold air. With a press of a button the Jaguar's lights flashed as the doors unlocked. He laid Santiago across the backseat, folding the man's limp arms across his chest, trying to make him as comfortable as possible.

Fletcher staggered to the trunk. He opened it, placed the evidence bag inside and removed the small leather briefcase holding his netbook. He drove out of the lot and headed back to the house.

36

Having become well acquainted with the neighbour-hood during his surveillance, Fletcher knew a location where he could watch the house without arousing any suspicion.

He plugged his netbook into the cigarette lighter as he drove. The computer, resting on the passenger's seat, booted up quickly. Ten minutes later, as he climbed up the steep hill, the program he needed had been loaded. He pulled over and set the audio bugs to record the conversations they overheard to the hard drive.

Fletcher cut the car lights and slid against the kerb, stopping when he saw the Colonial at the far end of the hill. He had an excellent view of the garage. Its exterior sensor lights had turned on, and he could see the car parked in the driveway.

The monocular aided his view.

The car was a silver Lexus sedan. He couldn't see the plates, not yet. Turning to the passenger's seat, he pressed the computer key for the audio bug tucked underneath the dining-room table. Footsteps clicking across the hardwood floors echoed over the netbook's small speakers.

Faint voices spoke and Fletcher turned up the volume.

'. . . not upstairs,' said a phlegmy male voice. Not Jenner's voice. Jenner had told Corrigan he had a passenger with him, a man named Marcus.

'The sliding glass door in the kitchen is open,' Jenner said. 'He's probably loose somewhere on the trails.'

'Going where?'

'That big parking lot at Gwynns Falls, maybe – no, stay here. We wouldn't make it in time.'

Shoes crunched across broken glass. They had entered the dining room.

'Jesus,' Marcus said.

Jenner said nothing.

'No cop would've done something like this,' Marcus said.

Jenner did not comment.

'The doc say anything about who did this to him?' Marcus asked.

'No.'

The trill of a ringing phone played over the net-book's speakers. Fletcher heard Jenner speaking to the caller. 'I'm here . . . I'm standing in the dining room right now . . . He's dead . . . No. I don't know where he is. This guy must've taken him . . . No, it was open . . . No, just me. Marcus didn't go upstairs, that's your . . . Okay.'

Jenner lapsed into silence. Fletcher checked his rear-view mirror. Nathan Santiago was still unconscious.

'Load the doc into the car,' Jenner said. A new tone in his voice: fear. 'Use a body bag.'

'And take him where?'

'Your place, for now. I'll meet you there later.'

'You're not coming?'

'I've got a few things to do here first. Call Rick on your way, tell him to keep everyone at the hotel.'

'They might as well hop back on their jets and go on home,' Marcus said.

'Get moving – and make sure no one follows you.'

'You think this guy's lurking around?'

'I just don't want to take any chances.'

Over the computer speakers, the footsteps walked away and then faded.

Fletcher called up another program. He switched to the audio bug placed inside the closet, then called up another program and keyed in the alphanumeric serial number for the transmitter he'd placed inside Corrigan's stomach. The transmitter was broadcasting perfectly.

He watched the garage through the monocular, listening to Jenner's heavy breathing inside the closet, the crinkle of plastic as the man touched the garment bags.

'Oh my God, Jesus Christ,' Jenner mumbled to himself.

The garage door opened. Fletcher watched a heavy-set man dart outside – Jenner's companion, the man named Marcus. He got behind the wheel of the Lexus, pulled into the street and then backed into the garage. Fletcher caught the licence plate and committed it to memory.

He turned down the volume on the netbook and called Karim.

'I need a private doctor,' Fletcher said after Karim answered. 'Preferably one in Baltimore.'

'How badly were you injured?'

'Not me. Someone else. His name is Nathan Santiago. I sent his fingerprints to your computer, along with prints for a Baltimore resident and former surgeon named Gary Corrigan.' Fletcher briefed Karim on what had transpired, stopping short when the Lexus pulled out of the garage and drove away in the opposite direction.

He stole a glance at the netbook's screen. The GPS unit inside Corrigan's stomach was still transmitting.

Fletcher had resumed his conversation, nearly finishing it when a black Lincoln town car with tinted windows pulled up alongside the driveway. Another Baltimore plate.

'I need you to run two plate numbers for me,' Fletcher said.

'Go ahead.'

Fletcher read off both numbers.

'Let me get to work on finding you a doctor,' Karim said. 'I'll call you back.'

Seventeen minutes later, the front door opened. A potato-shaped Caucasian man with ruddy jowls stepped out, his leather-gloved hands clutching a white laundry sack. *Jenner*. The man shut the front door, testing the handle to make sure it was locked, and then waddled to the waiting car, the wind lifting the fine grey and white hairs combed over his balding pate.

Jenner dropped the sack into the Lincoln's trunk and

shut it. He didn't get into the passenger's seat; he climbed into the back.

Fletcher slid back in his seat as the Lincoln drove up the hill. He heard it whisk past him a moment later. He readjusted his seat, watching the glowing tail-lights in the side mirror growing dimmer. He started the car and, looking back at the Colonial, saw bright flames jumping from behind the windows. Jenner had set fire to the house.

37

Will Jenner badly wanted a cigarette but he was afraid lighting one would blow up the car. He had spilled gas on his shoes, trousers and overcoat. His hands reeked of it, and fumes filled the Lincoln. He had cracked open his window to help air out the car.

Fortunately, he had recently decided (again) to try to stop smoking and had a blister pack of nicotine gum tucked in his jacket pocket. Shit tasted like burnt pepper, but the important thing was the nicotine. He needed it to help soothe his frayed nerves.

He hadn't told the buyers what had happened. They were waiting at the hotel, three of them – two who had flown in from Texas, the other from California. They had all arrived on private jets paid for by the clients they represented. Jenner had worked with these three men on a number of occasions over the years. They were expecting to be picked up at their hotel and driven to the house in Dickeyville. There, they would go upstairs and inspect the merchandise. Clients paid hundreds of thousands of dollars for the young organs Marie Clouzot and Brandon Arkoff provided, and the buyers always insisted on inspecting the merchandise. They had been burned before in the past, but not by Jenner. They knew him to be a professional, a man of his word, a man who ran things smoothly and didn't make excuses.

Once they had seen the merchandise and had their questions answered, money would be exchanged in cash because wire transfers left a trace that could potentially lead back to him. Then everyone would go downstairs and enjoy a fine meal provided by Clouzot while Arkoff and the surgeon, Corrigan, took the merchandise to a separate facility to harvest the organs. An hour or two would pass before the coolers would arrive at the house. The buyers would be driven to the airport, hop on their private planes and deliver the coolers to their clients, who were standing by and anxiously awaiting the organs that would prolong, if not save, the life of a spouse or child. This schedule had been followed meticulously for the good part of the last decade, without so much as a single wrinkle. Tonight everything had gone to hell in a handcart, and he didn't have a clue as to what had happened back at the Clouzot and Arkoff house.

And Marie Clouzot, who was sitting next to him in the backseat, bundled up in a fur coat and wearing fancy jewels – the only thing she cared about was whether anyone had accessed her bedroom closet. She didn't want to discuss how to handle the buyers. No, she wanted him to go inside that creepy closet of hers and collect the eleven sets of human ashes. Then she ordered him to set fire to her house. The gas cans were inside the garage.

Were Arkoff and Clouzot shutting down their operation? It sure seemed that way.

Would she broach the subject with him? Or would Arkoff do it? He was sitting behind the wheel, a big man who looked like spoiled vanilla pudding poured into a cheap suit. His face had been disfigured from some sort of accident, and whoever had put Humpty Dumpty back together had done a pretty decent job. The raised surgical scars were razor thin and camouflaged by make-up. But there was no amount of make-up in the world that could hide the man's drooping eyelid, the thick scars that were visible on his scalp.

Jenner suspected Arkoff wouldn't say anything. He rarely spoke – at least to him. Jenner dealt exclusively with Clouzot, who also had a frightening appearance from what he suspected was a botched facelift.

Jenner had waited long enough. Turning in his seat, he saw that she was still crying. Her mascara had run, giving her already bizarre features an even more ghoulish appearance.

'Where are we going?'

'To see the children,' she said.

Jenner had no idea where she kept them, had never asked. *Not at the funeral home they owned*, he thought. Arkoff was driving in the opposite direction.

'You have someone to replace Santiago?' Jenner hoped to God she did. Santiago had had a rare blood type, one that had commanded a substantial cash bonus for all the parties involved.

Marie cleared her throat. She touched her colourful diamond necklace, her voice shaking with rage when she spoke.

'Tell me everything Corrigan said. Word for word.'

Fletcher shadowed the Lincoln as it drove north on the Jones Falls Expressway.

He had travelled to Baltimore on a handful of occasions but had never ventured north of the city. Unfamiliar terrain. Not wanting to be surprised, he used the dashboard computer's GPS-navigation system. The screen held a standard map of glowing blue, red and yellow bands representing streets and highways. Names and points of interest were written in white.

Nathan Santiago kept drifting in and out of consciousness. Fletcher had tried to speak to him, but the man hadn't responded.

The Lincoln drove at the speed limit and stayed in one lane. Fletcher watched it from a safe distance.

The Lincoln pulled off the highway, taking the 'Falls Road' exit. If the driver planned on conducting any counter-surveillance manoeuvres, it would be here, in a suburban setting that offered a variety of choices, especially at night.

Jenner stopped speaking when Marie held up her hand. 'You haven't said anything about the man who did this.' She had turned to give him her full attention. She had stopped crying.

'That's because I don't know anything,' Jenner said. 'Corrigan didn't describe him.'

'Did you ask?'

'I didn't get a chance. The guy who was with Corrigan terminated the call. Corrigan couldn't have done it; he was bound to the chair. I hightailed it to the house. You know everything I do.'

'And you're saying that when you went upstairs, the door to my bedroom closet was open.'

Jenner nodded and, thinking about the rows of soiled clothing, swallowed his disgust.

'That's . . . not possible,' Marie said. She was having trouble keeping her anger in check. The look in her eyes reminded him of Grandfather, a mean son of a bitch who would beat the shit out of you until he'd exhausted himself. Guy's kids'd spent more time growing up in hospitals than they had at home.

Jenner shifted in his seat. He'd never felt comfortable around this broad. There was something about her that gave him a queasy feeling he still couldn't put a finger on. His gut sensed something repulsive lurking beneath her patrician features, her dignified air and speech.

'I think we can safely rule out that whoever did this is a cop,' Jenner said. 'A cop wouldn't tie up a guy and kill him – there'd be hell to pay for that, lawsuits up the wazoo, you name it. My first thought was a private investigator, but then you have to ask yourself, what's this guy's agenda? Why call me instead of the police?'

'Did Marcus see what was inside the closet?'

'No, just me.'

'What we do in the privacy of our home is not any of your business.'

'Agreed.'

Marie continued to glare at him, as if wanting him to prove her point.

'How long have we been doing business together? Seven years?'

'Almost eight,' she said.

Even better, Jenner thought. 'Eight years, and we haven't had a single problem. I think I've proven I'm capable of discretion.' He changed the subject. 'We need to talk about Santiago,' he said. 'I still have contacts on the force, people who owe me favours. I'd like to let them in on this, have these guys go and cover the hospitals, see if our merchandise shows up.'

Marie turned and looked back out of her window.

She didn't speak.

38

Fletcher shadowed the Lincoln through a residential area. Traffic was mercifully light.

Far ahead, he saw the Lincoln slow at a four-way stop sign. So far, the driver had failed to perform any counter-surveillance measures.

The Lincoln turned right on West 41st and continued to move at a normal speed. The driver didn't appear to be in a rush to reach his destination.

Fletcher consulted the Jaguar's GPS unit to see where West 41st turned. He quickly memorized the surrounding streets, pulled into the opposite lane and planted his foot hard on the gas, taking the driver in front of him by surprise. He blew past the stop sign and came to a sudden halt against the corner where Falls Road met West 41st.

The Lincoln had two choices: continue straight on West 41st or turn left on to Hickory Avenue, a street about a quarter of a mile long. It offered two left turns, both of which would loop the driver back on to Falls Road.

Fletcher looked out of the passenger's window, at Hickory.

The Lincoln drove by and vanished from his view.

Fletcher pulled away from the kerb and drove straight

ahead, accelerating to the next turn, Weldon. He pulled against the corner kerb and this time cut the lights. Again he looked out of the passenger's window.

The Lincoln passed Weldon and kept driving across Hickory.

Has to be driving to his destination either on Hickory or the next street, West 42nd, Fletcher thought, pulling back on to Falls Road with his lights still off. He accelerated to West 42nd, turned right and drove halfway down a small street lined with identical homes: two-floor boxy structures stacked against each other, white-trim windows, metal or cloth awnings installed over the white front doors. None of the homes contained driveways or carports. Residents parked on the street.

Fletcher pulled against the kerb and waited.

Seconds passed and the Lincoln didn't come.

Fletcher crept to the end of the street, where it turned into Hickory. Straight ahead he found three connected brick buildings. A quick glance to his right and he caught sight of the Lincoln's sagging rear bumper before the car disappeared behind the buildings.

The windows for all three buildings were dark, and there were no outside lights. A sign made of wood had been staked in a small front lawn of dead grass: SCOTT & ALVES CAR DETAILING.

Fletcher switched the GPS to an aerial view and zoomed in on the roofs. The buildings took up the entire block between the end of West 42nd and Weldon Avenue. In the back was a small parking lot surrounded by a vast forest of trees. The Lincoln had nowhere to go. Either this was its destination or the driver had spotted him and was waiting to see what he would do next.

Fletcher decided to wait too. Monocular in hand, he examined the buildings for heat signatures.

Jenner had turned in his seat and was facing Marie, talking to her about how to handle the Santiago situation, when he heard the rumble of a big metal garage door opening. He looked out of the front window as the Lincoln dipped down a ramp, heading for an underground garage belonging to a five- or six-storey brick building.

Brandon Arkoff pulled inside, killed the engine and got out. Jenner followed. The garage bay was wide and cold. It held a single vehicle, an old black Mercedes. The air smelled damp. He spotted some hoses connected to spigots.

Arkoff disappeared behind a glass door at the far end of the garage. A light clicked on and he came back out, holding the door open. Jenner nodded his thanks and stepped inside the concrete stairwell, his foot planted on the first step when he felt something sharp wrapped around his throat. He clutched at it with both hands, his fingertips slicing against the razor wire sawing its way through his neck. As he was pulled back out into the garage, blood – *his* blood – sprayed the walls and glass door. Great warm pools gushed down his chest, his scream lost in his severed throat.

39

The monocular's thermal-imaging technology, while state of the art, couldn't penetrate multiple walls or floors. Fletcher had searched the buildings for nearly half an hour and failed to find a single heat signature, not even a blip of swirling colour from a heating vent or a computer monitor or tower unit. He suspected the buildings were void of actual business.

There are three others. At least, Corrigan had told him.

If Rico Herrera and the other victims were locked somewhere inside one of these buildings, Fletcher couldn't see them – at least not at this angle, seated behind the wheel of his car. He couldn't see the Lincoln either. The car was still parked somewhere in the back, possibly in a garage. Behind the wind he had heard the distinct sound of a garage door opening and closing. He didn't know where they were or what they were doing. He did, however, know he wasn't being watched. There were no heat signatures outside the buildings, which suggested he hadn't been spotted.

Jenner had entered the *back* of the Lincoln. Either the passenger's seat was occupied or the man had to speak with someone sitting in the backseat. Including Jenner and the driver, that left the possibility of two, maybe three additional bodies inside the car – two in the front, three crammed together in the back. A maximum of five men – or four, if the woman in the fur coat was inside the car.

In order to investigate, Fletcher would need to leave his vehicle. That meant leaving Nathan Santiago alone inside the Jaguar. The car doors could be opened only from the outside, and the bulletproof windows had been treated with a special coating that prevented anyone from breaking in – or kicking their way out. Such a risk would have been acceptable if the man lying in the backseat didn't require medical attention.

Fletcher picked up his phone and called Karim. 'Did you locate a doctor?'

'I did,' Karim said. 'But not in Baltimore, I'm afraid.'

'Where?'

'Manhattan. She's already on her way to Cape May, New Jersey. Boyd is driving her. This woman has performed a number of services for me over the years, so you're guaranteed discretion. Santiago will be in good hands – and well protected. How is he?'

'Still sedated.' Fletcher rubbed a finger across his bottom lip as he stared at the dark buildings.

What are you doing in there, Mr Jenner?

'Do you have an office in Baltimore?'

'No, not any more,' Karim said. 'The closest office is in Trenton, New Jersey.'

'I followed the Lincoln.' Fletcher gave Karim his address and then told him about Jenner setting fire to the house in Dickeyville.

'Looks like they're shutting down their operation,' Karim said.

'Corrigan told me there were at least three other victims. They could be somewhere inside these buildings, but I don't see any heat signatures. And I don't want to leave Santiago alone in the car.'

'It will take my people at least two hours to arrive. Baltimore PD would be quicker.'

'Agreed. I'm assuming you've already culled someone from your vast network of contacts.'

'A homicide detective.'

'Is he discreet?'

'He is, and he's good with sharing,' Karim said. 'But to ask him to go inside the buildings and take a look around without a warrant is a tricky business.'

'Tell him you've come across information from a credible source that one or more missing children are being held there. Say "missing children". That will give him probable cause to enter – and it will garner a faster response.'

'Any sign of our lady friend?'

'Not yet.'

Karim gave him the address of the house in Cape May.

'Malcolm, before I let you go, your passenger . . . has he seen you?'

'He's unable to see much of anything in his condition.'

'Make sure he doesn't see your face,' Karim said. 'I can't afford for him to connect you to me.'

40

Marie Clouzot hosed off the blood from William Jenner's body, watching the bright pink swirls circling the drain before disappearing. Her life's work had just disappeared too.

Well, not all of it, she reminded herself. *The clothes are gone, but at least I still have the ashes.*

Knowing this brought a small measure of relief. But the clothes . . . they were irreplaceable. It had taken years of hard work and sacrifice to collect them, and now they were gone. No more wonderfully blissful evenings spent sitting in the chair with her bourbon, no more evenings or weekends spent dressed in the clothes and matching jewellery.

Thinking about it brought on a fresh round of tears. She should have gone back to retrieve the garment bags and the jewellery. Mr Jenner would have offered to help; they could have done it in a single trip.

Brandon had absolutely forbidden it.

We're not driving around with a trunk full of god-damn evidence, he'd said. The evidence needs to be destroyed, he'd said. We're shutting down the operation, Marie. Call Jenner back and tell him to set fire to the house right now or so help me God I'll go in there and do it myself.

She'd said no, of course. Brandon pulled over to the side of the road, leaned over the seat and screamed at her with such ferocity that she thought the car windows would shatter. He had even come close to hitting her. Gripped with a terror she hadn't experienced since her awkward and terribly painful teenage years, she called Jenner back and told him to set fire to the house. Hearing her speak those words had temporarily mollified Brandon – or so she'd thought. When he started in on what they would be doing for the remainder of the night, she decided to send Mr Jenner a text message, telling him to grab the big laundry liner from the master bedroom's wicker basket and use it to collect the ashes.

When Brandon saw Mr Jenner coming out holding the laundry sack, she thought he was going to reach over the seat and strangle her.

Instead, he gripped the steering wheel with both hands, squeezing it. He relaxed his grip when Jenner entered the car. Brandon drove away, but not to the printing press. He wanted to make a point and had taken her here, to the building for the old car detailing service, to send her a message.

Now the garage's interior glass door swung open and Brandon stepped out, lugging a big, rolling suitcase. It held clothes and enough money to start a new life anywhere in the world. Brandon had packed it in advance, in case the day came when they had to drop everything and run. And that day had arrived. This was the message he wanted to deliver to her. It was time to go.

Brandon walked by her without saying a word. She felt an eerie calmness settle over her as he placed the suitcase in the trunk of the Mercedes. Then he worked William Jenner inside a fresh body bag. After he zipped it up, she hosed off the plastic to rinse away any lingering blood.

'I called the hotel and spoke to the brokers,' she said.

Brandon carried Mr Jenner to the Lincoln and dropped him inside the trunk. Marie kept hosing down the floor.

'I told them we ran into a small complication,' she said. 'They agreed to wait two more days. That gives us enough time to –'

Brandon slammed the trunk shut, harder than he had to, and whipped around to face her. 'The man you shot in Colorado? He isn't dead, Marie.'

'Oh yes he is.'

'What happened there is all over the news,' he said. 'I've been reading about it on the Internet. The cops found Theresa Herrera and parts of her husband. That's it, no one else. You realize what that means?'

'It means they haven't found his body yet.'

'He's alive, Marie. He's alive and he somehow followed *you* here and he took –'

'No,' she said. 'You weren't there. I shot him. I saw him go down. He's dead, end of discussion.'

Brandon, not having another fight in him, waved his hands in surrender. 'Okay, fine, he's dead. You killed him, and the cops haven't found his body yet. But you *did* tell me this guy was working for someone else.'

'The man I killed came there alone. No one followed me back to Baltimore.'

'And this guy, in case you've forgotten, was working for Ali Karim, who owns a security company. Rico's mommy hired him to find her son. Maybe it would have ended there if *you* hadn't decided to start shooting.'

Marie dropped the hose.

'You killed one of Karim's employees. What do you think, that he's just going to forget that? Pack up and call it a day?'

'Then where are they? What are they waiting for? They didn't follow us here, you said so yourself.'

'I don't know, Marie. But I do know this much: it's time to leave Baltimore.'

That's what you think, Marie said to herself, and stormed off to the Lincoln. *Don't forget, Brandon, you owe me your life. I'll take away yours before you take away mine.*

41

Each local and state police department was responsible for meeting a certain monthly quota of speeding tickets to line a city's coffers. A highway at night offered patrolmen and state troopers the best opportunity to catch the most fish. Hidden by darkness, patrol vehicles parked on a median strip underneath a bridge could aim their radar guns down a highway without being seen – a problem for most drivers, as their vehicles didn't contain the necessary equipment to detect radar.

Fletcher had installed two highly advanced and illegal items in the Jaguar: a scanner that would alert him to the use of radar guns, and a radar-jamming system. He had both units running as he drove across I-95 North. At his current speed, he would make it to Cape May, New Jersey, in good time.

Movement inside the backseat and then a sleepy voice croaked, 'I'm gonna be sick.'

Karim's warning came back to him: *Don't let him see your face.*

Fletcher pulled into the breakdown lane. It took a moment to decelerate and come to a full stop.

His passenger was yanking hard on the door handle, trying to get out.

'I need to open the door for you,' Fletcher said. 'I

also ask that you close your eyes and keep them closed until I inform you otherwise. You have my word I won't hurt you. You don't have to be afraid of –'

'Yes. Yes, now *please*.'

Fletcher, having already tucked away his sidearm in a seat compartment, stepped out of the car and made his way around to the other side. He opened the door, about to reach inside and help Santiago out, when the young man darted away.

Santiago stumbled barefoot down a slope of dead grass, then cartwheeled and collapsed. Fletcher raced after him, wondering if Santiago were trying to escape. Then he saw the young man push himself up on to all fours and start vomiting.

'Keep your face forward,' Fletcher said. 'Do not turn around and do not look at me.'

'I'm sorry.' Plumes of breath appeared around Santiago's face and evaporated, his bony arms quivering as he vomited again. 'I'm sorry, I couldn't help it.'

'There's no need to apologize. But we need to get moving.'

'Where are you taking me?'

'To a home in New Jersey. A doctor will treat you, and preparations will be made for you to call your parents. Close your eyes and I'll escort you back to the car.'

Santiago pushed himself back on to his knees. 'I don't think I can stand. Can you help me?'

Fletcher helped the young man to his feet. Santiago spun around, and Fletcher caught a wink of metal. Instincts engrained into his muscle memory from years of SEAL training took over; he snatched the man's wrist and gave it a sharp twist. Santiago yelped in pain and surprise, the sound quickly muted when Fletcher gripped his throat and pinned him against the ground. Fletcher saw the weapon – a knife, the small, folding model with a black handle that had been inside the nightstand drawer back at the house.

'Don't hurt me,' Santiago said, his voice thick with tears. 'I'll behave from now on. I'll be a good boy, I promise.'

Don't let him see your face.

Too late, Fletcher thought. He patted down the man's pockets and, finding no other weapons, lifted Santiago to his feet. The young man sucked in air as he rubbed his throat.

'I apologize for hurting you,' Fletcher said. 'Given your experiences with the likes of Mr Jenner and Mr Corrigan, I don't blame you for not trusting me, Mr Santiago. That is your name? Nathan Santiago?'

The young man nodded.

'I don't work for Mr Jenner,' Fletcher said. 'You no longer have to worry about him or anyone else. You're safe, and I'm bringing you someplace safe.'

Fletcher wrapped an arm around Santiago's back. Santiago didn't fight him, and they trudged up the slope.

'How old are you?'

Nathan Santiago had to think about it.

'I don't know.'

'Where are you from?' Fletcher asked.

'Lynn. Lynn, Massachusetts.'

'How long have you been . . . gone?'

Santiago didn't answer, staring at the car with a mounting dread.

'The place where I'm taking you is a short drive away, less than an hour,' Fletcher said. 'When we arrive, a doctor will examine you, and then we'll make arrangements to bring you home.'

Santiago looked up at him. 'Who are you?'

'Someone who helps people such as yourself.'

They had reached the car. Santiago started to tremble.

'There's no reason to be afraid,' Fletcher said. 'This doctor will *not* hurt you. She works with people who –'

'Don't lie to me. Please don't –'

'Listen to me. The doctor is going to examine you, and then we're going to make arrangements to take you home.'

Santiago wouldn't get inside the car. Fletcher thought about telling the young man he could call his parents once he got inside, but it sounded too manipulative, and it was too risky. His parents could still have a standing trace on their home phone.

'Would you feel more comfortable sitting up front?'

Santiago didn't answer. Fletcher opened the passenger's door and kept reassuring Santiago that he was safe. It took some coaxing, but he finally managed to get the young man inside.

Fletcher, settled back behind the wheel, pulled on to the highway.

Nathan Santiago was curled up against his door.

'You're safe,' Fletcher said. 'I won't hurt you.'

Santiago seemed to crumple into himself. Then he began to sob.

'You're safe,' Fletcher said again, and placed a hand on the young man's shoulder. 'No one will hurt you, I promise.'

42

The properties Ali Karim used for safe houses were often lavish affairs — elaborately furnished brownstones, condominiums and townhouses in highly crowded downtown cities; exquisite beach-front properties used as rental homes in tourist spots where there was a constant turnover.

The secluded home in Cape May was no exception. It sat on top of a hill, a Frank Lloyd Wright-inspired contemporary settled among sand dunes overlooking the Delaware Beach. Soft lights glowed from behind the drawn Venetian blinds covering the windows.

Fletcher moved up a steep and curving driveway. Nathan Santiago lay curled asleep on his side.

When the awful wailing had stopped, Fletcher had tried to engage the man in conversation. Santiago, reduced to a childlike blubbering, hadn't answered. He had exhausted himself, and at some point during the drive, aided by the Demerol in his system and, quite possibly, by a sense of overwhelming relief, he had drifted off into a deep sleep. Fletcher had used the time to update Karim.

Motion-sensor lights winked to life when Fletcher reached the top of the driveway, a circular path both wide enough and long enough to accommodate a small fleet of vehicles. The area was empty but not the garage. Its single door was open. Parked in the wide bay was a black BMW with a New York licence plate. The garage was connected to the home by a portico.

The side door for the house's wraparound porch flew open. The man who stepped outside had a misshapen face, crooked nose and cauliflower ears from years of boxing and street brawls – Karim's personal bodyguard and childhood friend, Boyd Paulson. Dressed in his customary dark suit and matching shirt, Paulson jogged down the steps with a curious agility and grace for a man his size. He reminded Fletcher of a retired Lancaster bomber he had once seen displayed at London's Imperial War Museum – a solid and crafty machine that had endured several wars and still possessed the means to carry out one last mission.

Fletcher killed the ignition and exited the car. A harsh ocean wind, coarse with sand, salt and grit, rattled the home's windows, bent and twisted the brush and reeds in the sand dunes.

'Where is he?' Paulson asked.

'Passenger's seat.' Fletcher went to open the car door.

Paulson grabbed his arm. 'Karim doesn't want him to see your face.'

'He already has.'

'Aw, bloody hell.'

'He doesn't know my name, and he's asleep.' Fletcher opened the door. The interior light clicked on. Nathan Santiago didn't stir.

'I'll take him up,' Paulson said.

Santiago moaned as he was lifted, his eyes fluttering

open. Blood had soaked through the left side of his coat. Fletcher looked over the car door and saw more blood smeared against the leather seat.

Paulson darted up the porch steps, speaking over his shoulder: 'Get the door – and you might want to put on your sunglasses.'

Fletcher did and held the door open. Paulson turned sideways and entered a generously sized kitchen of stainless steel, the warm air fragrant with strong coffee – Turkish, most likely, the only kind Karim stocked. A Cafetière with two mugs stood on the small kitchen island. Fletcher followed Paulson across blond hardwood flooring scuffed by shoes. He had to duck under the archway leading into a large living room with modern lighting and cathedral ceilings fashioned with old timber beams. Wood popped and hissed from a fireplace. Behind the pleasant smoky pine he smelled new leather. A glass coffee table, coated with a film of dust, still had a price sticker attached.

Glowing squares of light caught Fletcher's eye. He gave a quick glance to his left, down a short hall and through an open door, where he saw monitors housed inside a surveillance station.

Up a set of stairs with a burgundy runner and then Fletcher trailed Paulson down a hall of fresh white paint and brand-new carpet. Three doors hung open to identical bedrooms: twin beds, oak dressers and reading chairs, everything draped in plastic. The bookcases and unbreakable mirrors had been bolted to the walls.

The hall turned left and led into a master bedroom transformed into a treatment room. The doctor, a slight

Asian woman dressed in a hospital-green smock, stood rigidly by a hospital bed that had been rolled into the centre of the room, the pillow and mattress covered in plastic liners. The other two beds were shrouded with plastic tarps.

The woman's eyes widened when she saw Fletcher. She backed up as he approached, bumping up against the surgical tools arranged on a rolling stainless-steel cart.

Fletcher caught a faint whiff of the woman's perfume, a rare and distinctive scent, and knew who she was: Dr Dara Sin.

Paulson placed Santiago on the bed. Fletcher removed the man's coat. The doctor had already pulled on her latex gloves. The stethoscope draped around her neck swung slightly as she ushered Paulson and Fletcher away from the bed with a wave of her hand. She tore open Santiago's shirt and listened to his heart and checked his pulse.

Santiago's light brown skin was covered with scars new and old, welts, sores and cuts. His arms were swollen from oedema. Fletcher wondered if the young man's fever and decreased level of consciousness had been caused by septic shock, a bacterial infection.

Paulson's cell rang. He moved into the hall.

'Demerol, I was told he was given Demerol,' the doctor barked. 'How much?'

'One hundred milligrammes via a slow IV push. He was also being treated with an aggressive IV fluid therapy and a wide-spectrum antibiotic. Cefazolin. I found Lasix on the nightstand. Twenty-milligramme tablets.'

'Hand me that oxygen tank.'

Fletcher had to walk around a crash cart to reach it. He picked up the tank and placed it near the bed. She strapped the mask across Santiago's face, set the tank's gauge to deliver fifteen litres and darted across the room to shelves packed with medical supplies.

Fletcher discovered the source of the bleeding: a curved and raw ten-inch incision that ran from Santiago's pubic bone and ended just under the bottom of the ribcage, the wound held together by a Frankenstein mess of surgical staples, several of which had torn or were missing.

He must have torn them while vomiting, Fletcher thought. The wound's distinctive horseshoe-shaped pattern told him what surgical procedure had been performed. It also showed signs of infection. The tissue contained within the island of staples was swollen and, oddly, vibrating as though something was trapped beneath it.

The doctor returned carrying an indwelling Foley catheter. She inserted it into his penis, guiding the tube into the bladder. A moment later the bag filled with urine and blood.

Paulson called from the doorway. Fletcher joined the man in the hall.

'That was Karim,' Paulson said in a low voice. 'He wants you to come to Manhattan straightaway. House is cleared out. Use the garage entrance.'

Fletcher felt he should be with Nathan Santiago when he woke up. The man would be confused and frightened by the strange faces.

'She'll take good care of him,' Paulson said. 'Anything he needs, we've got it covered.'

'I'll leave once I know he's stabilized. Tell the doctor to meet me outside.'

Fletcher needed to clean up the blood on his car seat. He couldn't afford to have it seen, should he be pulled over during the drive to Manhattan. An unlikely scenario, but one he still had to consider.

The cabinet underneath the kitchen sink held liquid soap and rolls of kitchen towel but no soft cloths, towels or bucket. He ventured outside to the garage and saw a small green glow of light. It belonged to a security camera mounted in the far-right corner. He walked to the back shelves mounted against the wall and helped himself to a small plastic bucket and a stack of folded micro-fibre cloths.

Outside, on the right-hand side of the garage and in clear view, was a garden hose wrapped around an ornate wrought-iron hanger. After he filled the bucket, he added a dollop of soap and placed the spray nozzle on top of the holder.

Fletcher had finished mopping up most of the blood when he heard the porch door open behind him. Light and hesitant footsteps moved down the steps. The doctor. He dropped the bloody cloth into the bucket, cleaned his hands with a fresh piece of kitchen roll and slipped on his sunglasses before leaning back against his car.

43

Even behind the sunglasses' dark lenses Fletcher could make out the lines etched around the woman's eyes and mouth. The shoulder-length hair, at one time completely black, was now streaked with grey and white, and was brittle. She hadn't zipped up her parka. She wore form-fitting chinos and a white shirt cut especially for her petite frame.

She was about to extend a hand when she suddenly tucked it back into her jacket pocket. Clearly Karim had instructed her to not to introduce herself.

'I understand you wanted to speak to me.'

Fletcher nodded. He caught the distinct scent of her perfume again and in his mind's eye saw the crime-scene photographs: a pregnant woman bound to an oak kitchen chair; her son and daughter, aged sixteen and fourteen, bound to similar chairs, duct tape strapped across their mouths. He saw blood-splatter patterns on white living room walls; gunshot wounds and soiled boot prints left on an oak hardwood floor.

'Do you mind if we speak out here?' she asked. 'I'd like to stretch my legs, and the sea air feels good – unless you're cold.'

'I'm fine, thank you.'

Dr Sin zipped up her jacket and strolled towards

the dunes overlooking the water. Fletcher fell into step with her. He suspected the woman knew who he was; her gaze had lingered too long on his face.

'The man you brought here is in the early stages of septic shock,' she said.

'From the kidney removal.'

Dr Sin stopped walking. She had to crane her neck to look up at him.

'How did you know?'

'The shape and location of the wound,' he said.

'It wasn't done by a butcher. A trained surgeon made that incision.'

'A surgeon was, in fact, treating him.'

'But not in a hospital.'

'No. It was a . . . private setting.'

She digested that for a moment. 'That makes sense,' she said. 'When I removed the staples, I found some-thing . . . well, interesting.'

'Maggots.'

Surprise bloomed on her face. 'You've seen this sort of thing before?'

'Upstairs, when I saw the wound and the way the tis-sue rippled, I suspected maggots since they consume necrotic and infected tissue. It's an effective, low-cost method of cleaning an infected wound.'

She nodded. 'American doctors used this technique in the prison camps during the Second World War. They'd take the infected soldiers out to the latrine area and let flies lay their eggs inside the wounds. Then they'd cover them, and after the maggots ate the infected and dead

207

tissue, you'd have clean and sterile wounds. Some hospitals still use the treatment today. Are you a doctor?'

'No.'

'But clearly you have some sort of medical training.'

'No. What else can you tell me?'

She folded her arms across her chest. 'Here's what I don't understand,' she said, examining the tops of her shoes. 'Using Lasix after a kidney removal is typical, as the drug stimulates kidney function and urine output. Patients who've had a kidney removed are susceptible to infection, so treatment with a wide-spectrum antibiotic is, again, typical. A surgeon or any other reasonably trained medical person would know *not* to administer Demerol to a patient who is clearly showing signs of septic shock – fever, an increased heart rate and tachypnea, which is rapid breathing. Administering Demerol or another type of narcotic to someone in this condition causes decreased blood pressure, which more often than not results in death. Is there anything else you can tell me?'

'I've told you everything I know,' Fletcher said. 'Did he speak to you?'

'No, and I don't think he'll be able to for some time. At the moment, he's stabilized. After I stemmed the bleeding, I flushed the wound with sterile saline and drained off the puss with a surgical drain and a suction bulb, then packed it with sterile gauze and dressed it with a sterile dressing. Now we have to wait and see about the sepsis. I need to bring him to a hospital. I spoke with Mr Karim, and he's going to make arrangements at Sloan-Kettering in Manhattan. I work there. We're going to admit him under a false name. The paperwork will be fudged so no one will find him.'

'When will you move him?'

'In a few hours. He needs to rest, and Mr Karim needs some time to procure the documentation and work out a cover story.'

'Thank you for your time and your efforts, Doctor.'

Fletcher had turned to leave when she said, 'Mr Karim is a good man. I met him while I was living in Brookline – that's in Massachusetts. Three . . . men broke into my house. I was married with two children and pregnant with my third. They tied us up, and after they robbed us, one decided to come back.' She brushed the hair blowing around her face and breathed deeply, holding it for a moment. 'I still don't know how I managed to survive.'

'I'm sorry for your loss.'

'The Boston police never caught the men responsible.' She faced the sea, watching the wind bending the sea grass. 'Mr Karim, however, believed he could find them. He seemed so . . . absolute in his resolve, that I said yes. When I asked him the cost for his services, he baulked. He said he provided pro bono assistance for victims of violence. Then he told me what had happened to his son, Jason.

'Months passed, and then one day Mr Karim showed up and told me that justice had been served. That I wouldn't have to live out the rest of my life wondering if those men would come back for me. To use his words, "The matter had been put to bed." I wanted to know details but he refused to tell me anything – their names, how they had been found. He said it was for my own protection.'

'I don't mean to be rude, Doctor, but I must be leaving.'

'When Mr Karim called and asked me to provide him with some discreet medical service, I was only too grateful to help. He didn't tell me your name, just that he trusted you implicitly. Before he hung up, he mentioned you had worked for him on a number of occasions. You helped Mr Karim find the men who killed my family, didn't you?'

Fletcher did not reply.

'He didn't tell me anything, if that's what you're wondering,' she said. 'When I saw you walk into the room, I had this . . . sense that you recognized me despite the fact we've never met.' A polite smile, and then she added, 'I would have remembered meeting you.'

Then her expression changed, her eyes cursed by the same look he had seen in all victims of violence: that damnable need to know what she'd done to invite this horror into her life. Why she had been chosen.

'Tell me why,' she said, hot-eyed. 'Please.'

Fletcher weighed the question on his cold scales. 'Because they could,' he said.

'It has to be more than that.'

'You lived in a nice home. They envied your possessions. You were available.'

She stared at him, wanting more.

He didn't have anything else to give her.

'Tell me they suffered,' she said. 'At least give me that.'

All three men had died the same way: wrists and ankles manacled and left alone to rot in the decrepit and soggy earthen belly of an abandoned mineshaft where their screams couldn't be heard. Would knowing the details help her heal, or curse her?

'I can assure you, they suffered,' he said.

A moment passed. When he provided no further explanation, the woman nodded, then kept nodding, her head down at the last nod. She stared at the ground as though she had dropped something.

'Thank you,' she said. 'Please take care of yourself.'

Fletcher got back behind the wheel of his car. The doctor continued to stare out at the water – a shell of a woman condemned to living in a grey-filtered daze, alone with a cemetery of memories and the ghosts of her loved ones whispering words she couldn't understand.

44

Marcus De Luca had packed on a considerable amount of weight since the last time Marie had seen him. Short and stocky and cursed with a permanent five o'clock shadow, De Luca now looked like a former prizefighter who'd let himself go to pot. His shirt collar was unbuttoned to accommodate his multiple chins, and fat had crept into the thin, puffy and bruised skin beneath a pair of eyes that looked like raisins pressed into dough. He reeked of menthol cigarettes and dressed with the flair of an Italian mobster, complete with loafers with those god-awful tassels.

Like William Jenner, De Luca was a former Baltimore cop. The two patrolmen had been partners once upon a time. They had served together and, ironically, were about to be buried together.

At the moment, De Luca was sitting comfortably in the passenger's seat of the Lincoln, mopping his brow with a handkerchief. They had just returned from setting fire to Gary Corrigan's home. The former surgeon was now resting in the trunk, on top of the body bag holding William Jenner. De Luca had casually enquired about the second body bag. 'Defective merchandise,' Marie replied, suppressing a smile.

She hit the garage-door opener and backed into the

funeral home's wide loading bay, parking next to the hearse. Marcus De Luca, ever the gentleman, offered to perform the heavy lifting.

Marie held open the door leading to the funeral home's basement level. Since the man had never set foot in there, she had to tell him where to go. 'Take your first left and you'll see the cremation unit.'

Marie stripped out of her coat as she trailed him down the hall. She ducked into a room, threw her jacket over the back of a chair and grabbed an apron on her way out.

'Which one?' De Luca asked, nodding with his chin towards the three separate doors to the ovens.

Marie unlatched the door to the first oven. De Luca swung the body bag off his shoulders and, cradling it in his arms, squatted a little and slid it inside.

'Push him all the way back,' she said. 'That's it, just a bit further . . . Good. Thank you. Are you sure you wouldn't like some help with the last one?'

Marcus waved away the offer. He sucked in air, exhaling with a slight, crackling sound.

'Put the other one in here,' Marie said, and opened the door to the second oven. De Luca nodded and huffed his way back to the Lincoln.

She unlatched the door to the third and last oven but didn't open it.

He came back with the body bag containing William Jenner slung over his shoulder. Since Jenner was considerably fatter, De Luca was grunting and sweating from the exertion.

She grabbed an end of the bag, feeling Jenner's thick ankles beneath the plastic, and placed them inside the oven's entrance. Then she stepped aside to give De Luca some room.

'Same as before,' she said, moving behind him. 'Push it all the way back.'

De Luca ducked his head just underneath the oven's door and gave the bag a good, hard push. Marie removed the concealed .38 snub-nose revolver from her trouser pocket, pressed it against the back of his head and fired.

She threw herself up against his back, using her weight to pin him against the cremation unit as she dropped the gun on to the oven floor. With both hands she grabbed the man's shirt collar and held him tight, his limbs jerking in protest and what was left of his head banging inside the oven as he bled out. She wondered if she'd have enough time for a quick shower. The funeral home had its own living quarters on the top floor; she and Brandon slept there during the week. A quick shower to wash away the smell of gunpowder, a change into something more comfortable and she would be on her way.

Mr De Luca had stopped his death dance. She dragged him over to the remaining oven. Christ, he was heavy. Thank God she had to drag him only a few feet.

Marie loaded him face first into the oven bay, gripping the back of his belt to keep him from falling out. Then she picked him up by the legs and pushed him inside. She was covered in sweat by the time she'd finished.

And she was covered in blood. It was on her hands and forearms, smeared on her apron and nice shoes and splattered across the floor and along the cremation unit itself. She gathered her supplies, cleaned up and threw the bloody rags inside the oven. Then she stripped out of her apron and clothes, threw them inside, fired up the ovens and walked upstairs wearing nothing but her birthday suit.

Showered and dressed in clean clothes, she headed back to the cremation unit. She smashed the bones and brushed out the ashes, collecting everything inside an ordinary plastic rubbish bag. The empty .38 gun cartridge went into her trouser pocket.

Driving away in the Lincoln, Marie carefully paid attention to her side and rearview mirrors, searching to see if anyone was following her. She could feel the brass cartridge digging against her hip.

She had left behind two empty gun cartridges in Colorado. Normally, she would have picked them up, but there hadn't been time – and she assumed the blast would have scattered them to Kingdom Come. She wasn't worried about fingerprints; she had worn gloves as she loaded the bullets. Still, police crime labs could do all sorts of new and tricky things with evidence.

But the police weren't involved – at least not yet. A cop wouldn't have snuck into her house, tied up and then tortured Mr Corrigan. Someone else had done that. Someone had tortured Gary Corrigan for information before escaping with Nathan Santiago.

There were only two plausible scenarios. Either the man she'd shot in Colorado had, through some miracle of God, survived and was hot on her tail, hell-bent on revenge; or maybe the man he worked for, Ali Karim, had done the deed himself. If the mysterious Colorado man was alive, maybe he was working together with his boss on some secret agenda to find and kill her.

Then why didn't he wait for me at the house? Why take Nathan Santiago and run? And how had he — they — found her house?

She had no idea, not even a working theory. The lack of answers made her feel cold all over.

Maybe Brandon was right. Maybe it was time to get out of Dodge while they still had time.

Then her thoughts turned to James Weeks and any idea of leaving vanished.

45

Jimmy Weeks was thinking about water. When he wasn't thinking about it, he was dreaming about it. The only thing he cared about right now was something cold to drink. Yes, it was crazy — bat-shit crazy, given his circumstances — but, for whatever reason, his mind had fixed on it, despite the terror of being locked away in the dark.

Every once in a while he'd hear the big, steel door outside his cage swing open. A moment of darkness would follow and then he'd hear the click of a light switch and the bare bulb would expose the small room, with its concrete walls and floor. Erected on either side of him were two more cages, both empty.

The woman who had pretended to be an FBI agent smiled every time she came to bring him food. The first time she visited, she gave him a plastic Wal-Mart bag holding someone else's clothing: a pair of tight-fitting black sweatpants, wool socks and a big crimson sweatshirt that had the Harvard emblem printed on the front and a tear along the collar.

The food was either hard dinner rolls or Wonder Bread smeared with peanut butter, a bottle of Gatorade or water. He had tried to speak to her, asking her questions, but she simply ignored him. She gave him his food, left and shut the door. There had been no showers, and he hadn't brushed his teeth.

She hadn't hurt him or threatened him in any way – which made sense, because this was nothing more than a cut-and-dry kidnapping. Jimmy had seen enough movies and TV shows to know the procedure: the woman would keep him locked up in here until the time came to bring him to the drop-off point, where he would be traded for some gym bag stuffed full of cash. Do what he was told and everything would be fine.

That inner voice kept disagreeing with him, and it spoke up again now: *You're wrong, Jimmy.*

No, he replied. No, I'm not.

Let's review some key facts, then. Let's start with –

No, I don't want to –

Fact number one: every time she comes in here, she's not wearing a mask. Why would she let you see her face? If she lets you go, she knows the police are going to question you. She knows you've seen her all up close and personal. You can describe her from head to toe. You think she doesn't know that?

Shut up, please, just shut –

And here's fact number two: you're not alone. You know what I'm talking about.

Jimmy forced himself not to think about it, but his mind had this really shitty way of making him see things that he didn't want to see. Every time the heavy door opened, he'd heard someone moaning, the sound near and yet far away at the same time – from a room close by, he thought.

Not just one voice, Jimmy. Several. You're not the only person here.

He hugged his knees to his chest, swallowing.

I know that scares the living shit out of you, but you know as well as I do this isn't a kidnapping. A kidnapper wouldn't lock you naked inside a goddamn dog crate — and then there's the matter of that wound on your back. I don't know what that's about, and I'm not going to bullshit you and say I have the first clue as to what's going on here, but there's one thing I do know, and you need to hear it. And I'm going to keep repeating it until it sinks into your head.

He jumped at the sound of the deadbolt sliding back.

You're going to have to find a way to kill this woman.

A key was moving inside the lock.

You need to escape from this place, Jimmy. If you don't, you're going to die a horrible death down here.

46

Fletcher reached Midtown Manhattan a few minutes shy of 7 a.m., dry-eyed and weary. A cold and milky predawn light had broken across the streets and buildings of Fifth Avenue, the setting of Edith Wharton's Pulitzer Prize-winning novel *The Age of Innocence*. The horse-drawn carriages that had once dominated this area over a century ago had been replaced by hustling delivery vans, taxis and limousines. Joggers, dog-walkers, and early risers off to work paced the streets, while doormen in garish uniforms poised like sentries guarded gold-plated gateways leading to luxury kingdoms owned by the new century's robber barons.

Karim lived and conducted his day-to-day business operations from inside a historic five-floor neo-Italian Renaissance mansion commissioned in 1922 by a wealthy German merchant and designed by one of the city's most prominent architects at the time, C. P. H. Gilbert. Karim did not employ a doorman, driver, maid or chef. With the exception of Boyd Paulson – and now, the mercurial Emma White – Fletcher did not know the names of the employees who worked out of the man's home. Every time Fletcher visited, Karim sent his people to the company's main office in Downtown Manhattan.

Snaking his way towards his destination, Fletcher saw a businessman step over a vagrant passed out in the middle of the pavement. A patrolman directing street traffic turned his back on a young woman repeatedly slapping her child. Seeing the common ugliness on display beyond the Jaguar's tinted glass made him long for a hot shower, followed by an even longer, uninterrupted sleep.

He turned left and drove up the short ramp leading to Karim's private garage. The metal gate was closed. A pair of security cameras watched him.

The gate rose a moment later and Fletcher entered an underground garage. Four high-end luxury vehicles were parked to the far left. Fletcher drove straight on and parked in a space near a set of concrete steps leading up to an elevator. Security cameras, each positioned in a corner, were fixed on the entire area. He knew they had been turned off, as Karim did not want any recorded video footage of a wanted fugitive entering his home.

Fletcher traded his leather gloves for latex. He insisted on wearing them when visiting the man's home. Netbook in hand, he removed the evidence bag from the trunk, stepped inside the elevator and pressed the button for the fourth floor. The doors closed and the ancient piece of machinery, one of the few items Karim had not replaced or updated, waited as if deciding whether or not it wanted to move. Finally, it rose, slowly and unsteadily, the gears creaking.

*

The elevator doors opened to a long hall of cream-coloured walls and a hardwood floor covered by a Turkish rug. Fletcher walked across it, passing by a side table holding stacks of mail and a bouquet of orchids arranged in a vase, and stepped into an anteroom designed to resemble an old English library. The tall space held several leather armchairs and sofas, a pair of antique secretarial desks and folio stands. The book-cases, made of a deep mahogany, stretched from floor to ceiling, the shelves packed with rare first editions.

The elegant room usually smelled of old wood and aged paper. This morning, the pleasant aromas had been spoiled by Karim's cigarette smoke. It drifted in through the cracked-open door to the man's office, a Spartan, oval-shaped room of bare white walls and windows offering a sweeping view of Central Park. Karim, dressed in another one of his threadbare flan-nel shirts, sat behind a bank of flat-screen monitors displayed on a multilevel glass desk.

'Good morning,' he said in a dry, tired voice. 'Would you like coffee? There's an urn in the waiting room, along with some pastries and fruit.'

'No, thank you.'

'Do you want to rest for a bit or do you want to get right to it?'

'Right to it.' Fletcher placed the evidence bag on the desk and said, 'The drinking glass from the closet.'

'I'll have my lab process it for fingerprints this morn-ing, see if we can get a name to match this woman's face. Speaking of which, that wildcat cartridge you found? No fingerprints. Any other presents for me?'

'I also downloaded data from Corrigan's phone, but I haven't had time to examine it.'

Fletcher draped his coat over the back of the chair set up in front of the desk and settled into his seat.

'Let's start with my Baltimore contact,' Karim said. 'I told him I came across information from a credible source that the building you found might contain missing children, and he agreed to take a look.

'The building was empty. No sign of the Lincoln or any other vehicles. There was, however, an under-ground garage. He found hoses and told me the floors and walls were damp. He also said the garage reeked of bleach. No blood – at least none that was visible. He can't call in forensics until he gets more "concrete" information from me.'

Karim inhaled deeply from his cigarette. 'I've got him wiggling on a fishhook. He thinks I'm sitting on something big, asked to speak to my source. He's not going to wait for me. He'll start sniffing around on his own.'

'Who owns the building?'

'Another limited liability company,' Karim said. 'This one is called Crowley Enterprises. David Crowley is listed as the LLC's owner, and the address listed on the documents? Belongs to an undeveloped strip of land in Oregon.'

'And the Baltimore plates I gave you?'

'Both the Lincoln and the Lexus belong to ABC Property Management.'

'The same LLC that owns the house in Dickeyville.'

'Correct. So now we have two LLCs with phoney addresses: ABC Property Management and the one that owns these buildings you found, Crowley Enterprises. Two different lawyers filed the papers – one in Baltimore, the other in San Diego. Going after them is a waste of time – client confidentially and all that. I could use my own lawyers to press them, but the only thing we'd end up with is a physical description of our lady friend – and that's if we're lucky. Besides, I doubt she used her real name.'

'I think she has a male partner,' Fletcher said. 'In addition to the king bed, I found an assortment of men's clothing in the drawers. Someone lives with her.'

'So we're looking at a couple who kill together *and* sleep together.' Karim stifled a yawn. 'How romantic.'

'And we know they employ at least two people – Jenner and his companion, Marcus. Have you spoken with Dr Sin?'

Karim nodded. 'She told me about the missing kidney. What do you think that's –' He cut himself off, looked at Fletcher sharply. 'I didn't divulge the doctor's name to you, and I gave her explicit instructions not to –'

'She didn't tell me,' Fletcher said.

'Did Boyd tell you?'

'No.'

'Then how do you know her name?'

'I recognized her perfume.'

'Her perfume,' Karim repeated.

'You asked for my assistance with her case. The home invasion that killed her —'

'Right, right. I completely forgot you handled that matter.'

'The night I went through her home I found two bottles of Ce Que Femme Veut in the bathroom vanity,' Fletcher said. 'It's quite rare. Last manufactured in 1965.'

'When was that?'

'The night I entered her home? Thursday, 19 October 1994.'

'Your memory is goddamn remarkable.'

Fletcher said nothing.

'There's a name for your kind of memory, did you know that?' Karim said. 'It's called "superior autobiographical memory". A professor of neurobiology at the University of California, Irvine, coined the term. It's very rare, this type of memory. This professor has found only a handful of people who possess this unique intellectual gift. He gave each person he tested a random date and they could go back in time and recall everything they experienced on that day — what meals they ate, the people they spoke to and the content of their conversations. What they read and the television programmes they watched. These people can remember almost every single detail of their lives going back years, the way an ordinary person remembers what happened yesterday, if he or she can remember it at all.'

Fletcher did not share Karim's wide-eyed enthusiasm. He had been born with this type of instant recall. For as long as he could remember, he could pick a date at random, travel back in time and relive any memory as though he were experiencing it in real-time. He remembered everything and forgot nothing.

'Were you able to uncover any information on Nathan Santiago?'

'Yes, I have the information right here.' Karim started to root through various loose sheets and pads of paper. 'I didn't run Santiago's prints yet, thank God. That would have set off a firestorm of questions. Here they are.'

Karim handed him sheets of paper holding printed aged-enhanced photographs of Nathan Santiago. In the photos, the young man had black hair worn in a variety of styles, but the face was identical.

'That's him,' Fletcher said, placing the sheets on the corner of the desk. 'What happened?'

'Nathan Santiago left his three-decker tenement home in downtown Lynn, Massachusetts, to visit a friend who lived four blocks away. The boy vanished into thin air, never to be seen or heard of again – until now.'

'Boy?'

'Teenager,' Karim said. 'He was seventeen when he disappeared, which would make him twenty-five today.'

'He's been missing for eight *years*?'

Karim nodded sombrely. 'There's more,' he said, stubbing out his cigarette in a small and crudely shaped clay ashtray created by a child's hand. Jason Karim, Fletcher knew, had made that for his father.

'Nathan Santiago's mother?' Karim said. 'She vanished too.'

47

Karim reached across the desk and handed Fletcher a thick sheet of paper. It was a colour picture of a round-faced, middle-aged woman with light brown skin and shoulder-length black hair. Her nose was crooked. Fletcher suspected it had been broken one too many times by a husband or boyfriend. The haunted look in her eyes brought to mind Dr Sin, the way the doctor had stared into space, wondering what she had done wrong for such horror to have entered her life.

'Louisa Santiago was a single mother and a nurse,' Karim said. 'She left her job at Boston's Massachusetts General Hospital, and that's the last anyone saw of her. The police found her Honda Civic in Lynn, parked in the lot for the subway stop for Wonderland Station. Husband's not in the picture, as far as I can tell. I won't know anything further until I get copies of the police reports.'

Fletcher continued to stare at the photograph as his attention turned inward, his mind's eye focusing on the eleven garment bags hanging inside the closet. He could recall each item of clothing, the rips and tears, the dried spots of blood. He saw himself turning to the garment bags hanging on the right-hand side – here it was, the second to last bag holding a green hospital smock and matching green scrubs. Sitting below it was a pair of white clogs with scuffed and worn edges.

He told Karim.

'You're sure?'

'They were the only hospital clothes inside the closet,' Fletcher said. 'Did Louisa Santiago disappear before or after her son?'

'After. Nathan Santiago was abducted on the evening of 5 November 2004. The mother, Louisa, vanished four years later, the day before Thanksgiving.'

Fletcher thought back to the research he had conducted inside his Colorado motel room – the names of the eight families who had a child disappear, followed months or years later by a parent. Eight families, and the closet contained eleven garment bags.

'The list of the families I gave you in Chicago,' Fletcher said. 'I didn't include single parents in my preliminary search.'

'I know, which is why I asked M to expand her search.'

His office phone rang. Karim glanced at the caller-ID screen and with a grin said, 'Speak of the devil.'

He answered the call. Karim didn't speak for the first few minutes. He ended the conversation asking M to come straightaway to the house to deliver an evidence bag to the lab.

Karim hung up and said, 'M looked into the medical records of the missing parents on your list. You'll be pleased to know that, in addition to Theresa Herrera, these parents don't have their medical records stored on the Medical Information Bureau's database.'

Karim lit a fresh cigarette with a worn, gold-plated lighter. 'So now we have a connection between Theresa Herrera, Louisa Santiago and the eight married couples on your list. It appears your initial theory was correct – that our lady friend in the fur coat was there to abduct Theresa Herrera.'

Karim leaned back in his seat with a heavy sigh. 'Rico Herrera,' he said. 'Do you think he could still be alive?'

'We'll have to ask Nathan Santiago – the sooner, the better. Dr Sin told me she's bringing him to Manhattan.'

'He'll arrive at Sloan-Kettering between seven and eight this morning. M has the documentation ready for Santiago – driver's licence under another name, corresponding medical insurance, et cetera. That way we can keep Santiago safe and hidden. She has a cover story already worked out. I've managed to procure a doctor who does emergency rounds. This person will be in place when Boyd admits Santiago.'

Fletcher nodded, well aware of Karim's Rolodex of the walking wounded – prior victims of violence he had assisted, people who were all too willing to perform some favour or service to help out a fellow innocent.

'All the bases are covered,' Karim said. 'We haven't discussed Santiago's missing kidney. What do you think that's about?'

'I think our couple is subsidizing their kidnapping operation with the sale of blackmarket organs.'

Fletcher told Karim about Corrigan's vial of pills, how the two medications were used in conjunction to treat hand tremors and alleviate surgical anxiety. How Corrigan had been scheduled to perform surgery – a fact confirmed by Jenner. *How're your hands holding up?* Jenner had asked Corrigan on the phone. *You ready for surgery?*

Then Fletcher told Karim about the ornate dining-room table and the words Jenner had spoken to his companion, Marcus, while inside the house: *Call Rick on your way, tell him to keep everyone at the hotel.*

They might as well hop back on their jets and go on home, Marcus had replied.

'Private or chartered planes aren't subject to the same security as commercial flights, as you well know,' Karim said. 'If people had flown in to collect organs, they would be ushered back to their private jets or chartered planes without having to undergo any searches. They could fly away with their organs properly packed and cooled with no one the wiser.'

'Your Baltimore contact who searched the buildings, did he find any coolers or medical equipment?'

'The buildings were empty. What about the house in Dickeyville?'

'Organ harvesting requires specialized surgical equipment. I didn't see anything.'

'So if Corrigan was telling you the truth – that there

were at least three other victims who were still alive – then he was performing the surgery in another location.'

'Which is all the more reason why we need to speak with Nathan Santiago. These people are shutting down their operation.'

'I understand and share your frustration, Malcolm, but I'm not a magician. I can't wave a wand and make Santiago wake up and start talking. He's near death as it is.'

Fletcher opened his netbook.

'What are you doing?' Karim asked.

'I placed a GPS transmitter inside Corrigan's throat.'

Karim smoked, waited. Fletcher pressed keys and moved a finger across the netbook's track pad. Fletcher stared at the screen, his eyes narrowing in thought. Then he went back to typing.

A moment later, he leaned back in his chair, propped an elbow up on the armrest and rubbed a latex-covered finger across his bottom lip.

'What?' Karim asked.

'The signal is no longer transmitting,' Fletcher said.

48

On the computer screen Fletcher saw the route the transmitter had travelled, where it had stopped broadcasting.

'Malfunction?' Karim asked.

'I don't think so,' Fletcher said. 'It was transmitting perfectly before I left for New Jersey. I need you to look up an address for me: 9611 Washburn Road in Baltimore.'

Karim turned to his keyboard. Typed and clicked the mouse button repeatedly.

'Address is in West Baltimore,' he said.

'Is it a funeral home?'

Karim eyed him curiously. 'How did you know?'

'Does it offer cremation services?'

'Hold on . . . Okay, here's the website. Funeral home is called Washington Memorial Park . . . Yes, it offers cremation services.'

And now we have the reason why the GPS *tracker stopped transmitting its signal,* Fletcher thought. *The device was destroyed when Gary Corrigan's body was cremated.*

'How did you know?' Karim asked again.

'I didn't. The ashes inside the closet made me think of it. To obtain the ammo from Sacred Ashes, you need to be able to *provide* ashes. Someone with access to a crematorium could do it – and easily forge the necessary death certificates.'

'This business of making ammo using human ashes, what do you think that's about? Why does she – or he – do it?'

'Part of their revenge fantasy, I suspect. Does the funeral home's website contain the names of the owner or owners? Photographs?'

'I'm looking right now . . . No. There's nothing listed under the contact page, no names or personal photographs. There are, however, pictures of the facility. It's set in a wooded area, has its own adjoining cemetery.' Karim looked away from the screen and said, 'What if the other victims are somewhere on the grounds, maybe even in the funeral home itself?'

'We won't know until we perform a search.'

Karim glanced at his wristwatch.

'Have your Baltimore contact do it,' Fletcher said. 'If these people are shutting down their operation, we can't afford to waste any time.'

Karim nodded in agreement and reached for his phone. While he conducted his conversation, Fletcher ruminated on the bedroom closet containing the killing shrine.

Eleven garment bags and eleven sets of cremated remains tucked in bags behind the footwear. The highball glass contained a small trace of ash – human, not cigarette, ash. The closet did not smell of cigarette smoke. The woman in the fur coat sprinkled cremated remains in her bourbon and ingested her former victims

as she sat in her chair, staring at the clothing and reliving
. . . what? The kidnapping of the parent? She had also
used the ashes to place three separate orders with a
company that specialized in adding cremated remains to
gun ammunition. She didn't keep the ammo inside the
closet. And what was the reasoning behind the custom-
made ammunition? What purpose did it serve?

Fletcher didn't have an answer, just an idea that led
back to his original theory that all the victims were connected. One thing was clear: the woman in the fur coat
and, possibly, her male partner were motivated by
revenge.

And the children . . . after you harvested their organs you cre-
mated their remains, didn't you? But what did you do with their
ashes?

Karim hung up the phone. 'My contact is going to
look into the funeral home,' he said. 'Now let me tell
you what I found on Gary Corrigan. He has a record.
After he graduated from the University of Maryland
School of Medicine, he completed his residency at
Saint Agnes, also in Baltimore. He stayed on and
worked there as a cardiac surgeon until early 2000,
when a routine audit showed he was shorting patients
their medications, most notably Valium.'

'He must have been using Valium to treat his hand
tremors or surgical anxiety. Or both.'

'You said he was using a beta-blocker and that other
drug.'

'Propranolol,' Fletcher said. 'The medical cocktail is
relatively new.'

'So he tried self-medicating with Valium and got caught. Why not just seek treatment?'

'Because the hospital would have to disclose it or face possible lawsuits. And would you want a surgeon who suffered from hand tremors?'

'Good point,' Karim said. 'In any event, the hospital didn't sweep the matter under the rug. Saint Agnes brought Corrigan up on charges. After his arrest, the medical board revoked his licence to practice. Judge didn't give him any jail time, just fined and ordered mandatory drug counselling. Corrigan entered a rehabilitation unit in Maryland that specializes in addiction within the medical community – drug addiction, from my understanding, is a common and widespread problem. Three months later, he was released.'

'His current occupation?'

'Corrigan worked a variety of odd jobs until early 2001. There's nothing listed after that year. That's when he also stopped paying taxes. IRS never caught up with him.'

'Background?'

'Married in '93, divorced a year later. No kids. Never remarried. Parents are deceased. No siblings. No debt either. House paid in full. That's all I have on him at the moment.' Karim picked up a small remote from his desk and said, 'Now let's see if we can find this Jenner bloke.'

49

Karim pointed the remote at the windows. The light-blocking shades began to lower and the office grew dark.

But not the walls. Made of high-tech plasma screens, they glowed a bright white.

'I found twenty-three men living in Maryland with either the first or last name of Jenner,' Karim said.

Fletcher got to his feet. 'I'm interested in a white male, late forties to early sixties.'

Karim clicked away on his keyboard.

Minutes later, the brightness dissolved away in a series of pixels. Digital pictures started to fill the blackness – three rows of Maryland driver's licences, fifteen in total.

Fletcher found him in the middle of the third row: there was the man he'd seen leave the home in Dickeyville and enter the back of the Lincoln.

Fletcher tapped the licence. Karim enlarged it and the others disappeared.

William S. Jenner was fifty-eight, five foot ten and 220 pounds. He lived in Baltimore, at No. 922 Black Oak Road.

Karim went back to typing and clicking, using the number printed on the Baltimore driver's licence to unlock William Jenner's social-security number, the master key in the digital kingdom. Fletcher entered the anteroom and helped himself to a bowl of fruit set up on the wet bar's polished countertop.

His thoughts turned to Nathan Santiago. Abducted at seventeen and found eight years later, a 25-year-old man with a bony frame and malnourished skin bruised with needle marks, and with a raw and infected horse-shaped incision from a kidney removal.

Eight *years*.

Fletcher recalled the moment when he had pulled back on to the highway, on his way to Karim's home in Cape May. Santiago had collapsed into himself, wailing, refusing to speak. Did he know his mother had also been abducted? Had she been imprisoned with him?

The child is taken first, Fletcher thought. *Years pass as the parents live moment to moment on a bridge suspended between hope and reality — hope that their child might yet still be found alive, while the overwhelming reality suggests that their son or daughter is most likely dead, never to come home.*

Why take the child first?

Psychological torture.

Years pass and then a single parent is abducted, the spouse killed. Why?

Payback.

Revenge.

And what happened to the abducted parent? Was he or she brought to the place where their missing child was being held?

Santiago had been found tied to a bed. He had been

washed and in clean clothing. Why? Was he on display for the dinner guests, the people who had flown in to collect organs? Had Nathan Santiago been scheduled for the operating slab?

Fletcher saw the closet again, with its garment bags and human ashes tucked behind the footwear. The woman in the fur coat and her male partner had erected a private sanctuary inside their killing house. They had collected – so far – eleven garment bags for eleven victims. Eleven adults, and each one had a child who had been abducted. Each child had been missing for years and then a parent was abducted.

Fletcher marvelled at the predation at work here, the cunning sophistication and ruthless patience required to pull off such a feat. The feeling didn't repulse him. As a profiler, he had learned to view deplorable acts as works of art. It was the only way to decipher the meaning behind the brushstrokes.

Karim called for him. Fletcher returned to the office.

'Here's what I found during my initial pass,' Karim said. 'William Jenner worked as a patrolman for the city of Baltimore until early '98, when he and his partner, Marcus De Luca, responded to a 911 call from a woman who said her ex-boyfriend had come to her house and threatened to kill her. The woman later claimed that both cops had raped her.'

Lovely, Fletcher thought.

'Because the woman was mentally ill – a paranoid schizophrenic, according to a doctor's testimony – and because there was no forensic evidence to back up her accusation, the jury dismissed the charges,' Karim said. 'Interestingly, both Jenner and De Luca retired from the force after the trial. Now take a look at this.'

Karim turned back to his computer. William Jenner's licence disappeared from the wall, to be replaced by a silent video clip of a well-dressed newsreader with stylish glasses for Baltimore's ABC2 news. The woman spoke wordlessly for a moment; she was then followed by a video montage of firefighters battling an early-morning blaze.

'That would be William Jenner's house,' Karim said. 'The address matches the one on his licence.'

Fletcher wondered if Jenner had been killed, his body dumped inside his house – or cremated at the funeral home.

'I also checked Gary Corrigan's house,' Karim said. 'That too had been set on fire. There's no doubt our lady shooter and her male friend are closing down shop and getting ready to leave. I need to share this information with my Baltimore contact and make some additional phone calls. Let's reconvene here in, say, two hours. Take a shower and relax.'

Fletcher took his netbook and left the office to collect a fresh set of clothes from the Jaguar. He also retrieved the forensic unit holding the data downloaded from Corrigan's iPhone.

There are three others. At least, Corrigan had told him.

They're alive, Corrigan had said.

If you don't take me with you, you'll never find them.

Fletcher thought of the three homes that had been

set on fire and wished he had taken Corrigan up on his offer.

Fletcher entered Karim's private basement apartment. He did not take a shower, and he did not relax.

The spacious bedroom contained a small desk. He placed the netbook and forensic device on its top and turned on both items. Dust swarmed inside the milky columns of light pouring through the pair of ground-level windows. He could hear the busy Manhattan traffic, the rapid click of shoes and heels moving fast across the pavement, people talking to one another, in person or on phones.

Fletcher connected the forensic device to the netbook. He transferred the data and rubbed the fatigue from his eyes.

Would Nathan Santiago survive his septic infection, or would he die?

Fletcher felt his heart racing. The question had triggered the lizard part of his brain, the prefrontal cortex area housing useless emotions – anxiety, apprehension and fear. Adrenalin coursed through his system, the hormones and neurotransmitters already beginning their savage attack on his central nervous system. Fail to stop it now and his rational mind, already vulnerable in his fatigued state, would gallop away. But fighting it by trying to tighten the reins only fuelled the irrationality, making the brain nearly impossible to control.

Long ago and through much practice, Fletcher had learned how to subvert the disruptive chemical process through transcendental meditation. He didn't have time right now. He needed to see if Corrigan's phone contained any information on the possible whereabouts of Santiago. He shelved his concern for the moment, about to get to work, when there was a knock on the apartment door.

He heard it open and then Emma White spoke to him from the adjoining room.

'Forgive the intrusion,' M said, 'but Mr Karim sent me. He needs you straightaway. He's waiting for you in the garage.'

50

Fletcher stepped out of the elevator, carrying a garbage bag full of laundry, and found Karim pacing near the Jaguar. The man had thrown on his tatty bomber jacket but left it unzipped. Beneath the buttoned flannel shirt Fletcher saw the outline of a bulletproof vest.

Fletcher opened the trunk and tossed the garbage bag inside. Karim stopped pacing.

'My contact at the hospital called me – the one working the ER who was going to get Santiago squared away for us,' Karim said, his voice echoing through the chilly air. 'Boyd hasn't shown up, and he isn't answering his phone. Neither is Dr Sin.

'Boyd's BMW has a tracking unit – all of my company vehicles do – and the signal shows it's still parked at the beach house. His phone also has a GPS chip, and it shows he's still at the house.' Panic had leached colour from Karim's face and there was a visible sheen of sweat on his smooth forehead. 'I don't know about Dr Sin. She doesn't use one of my phones, so I can't locate her through my network.'

Fletcher's mind was already working. 'When I was inside the house, I noticed a security console in one of the first-floor bedrooms.'

'That's the monitoring station for the security

cameras posted in and around the house. I know where you're heading. Yes, it's connected into my network, but I can't access the cameras or whatever videos are stored on the hard drive. The whole bloody thing is offline.

'Malcolm, I know I shouldn't have to ask this, but were you followed?'

'No.' Fletcher, ever vigilant, had made sure no one tailed him to Cape May, New Jersey – or to Karim's home.

'Then they must have found the house some other way,' Karim said.

'What about triangulating Dr Sin's cell signal?'

'I don't have that equipment here. It's under lock and key at a secure location – the police and federal government don't look too kindly on an independent security contractor who can trace a cell signal at whim when they have to obtain court-ordered subpoenas.'

'Are you heading there now?'

'No. I've sent M. I'm going to New Jersey.'

'I'll go.'

'I'm coming with you. I have to be there in case . . .' Karim's voice trailed off. He didn't know what to do with his hands and he had difficulty swallowing.

Fletcher leaned over the trunk to start collecting his tools and weapons. 'Before we leave, you need to check to see if the New Jersey police were called to your home.'

'They weren't; I already checked. Did you check your car for a tracking device?'

'I always do.'

'I'd feel better if we took one of my vehicles,' Karim said. 'I'll drive.'

The black Range Rover had tinted windows and a cream-coloured interior and smelled of new leather. As Karim navigated his way through the morning traffic clogging Midtown, fighting for any opening, Fletcher divided his attention between the windows and the passenger's side mirror, studying the vehicles, watching for any sign of a tail.

'I have people following us, watching for anything suspicious,' Karim said. 'They'll follow us to New Jersey and then my people there will take over – we'll be completely covered. Don't worry, they won't see you.'

Fletcher nodded but still conducted surveillance, memorizing vehicle makes and models.

Karim drove with both hands on the wheel. His BlackBerry sat inside a dashboard cubbyhole. He kept glancing at it.

'You can't call an ambulance,' Fletcher said.

'We're a good hour away – probably more in this traffic. For all I know Boyd and the doctor are clinging to life.'

'You need to consider the evidence.'

'What evidence?'

'Since Boyd and his car are still on the premises, it stands to reason neither he nor the doctor had time to clean up properly. If you call for an ambulance, the paramedics will enter the house and, at the very least, find blood in the treatment room. The police will be summoned. Forensics will be called in to collect blood samples. If Santiago's DNA sample is stored inside CODIS, they'll want to know how blood from a missing seventeen-year-old wound up inside your home.'

Karim threaded his hands through his hair. 'You and your goddamn logic,' he muttered. Then, louder: 'What's that pragmatic brain of yours telling you about how Santiago was located?'

'I can tell you he wasn't wearing a tracking device.'

'You checked his pockets?'

'His pockets were empty.'

'Shoes?'

'He was barefoot,' Fletcher said. 'Tracking units are bulky items. If Santiago was wearing one, I would have found it.'

'Then they must have used something else – something small, something that could have been sewn into Santiago's clothing. Or his skin.'

'His skin?'

'How familiar are you with radio-frequency identification?'

'I know the meat-packing industry uses RFID tags to identify a livestock's herd of origin.'

Karim lit a cigarette. 'Human applications have been devised,' he said, cracking open his window. 'A glass-encapsulated RFID chip slightly larger than a grain of rice can be tucked inside a pocket or sewn into clothing – or, in the case of biometric security, surgically inserted beneath the skin. The Mexican attorney general did that to his senior staff, had a chip implanted in that web of skin between your thumb and index finger. You notice anything like that on Santiago?'

'The man had a number of scars,' Fletcher said. 'If I'm not mistaken, the RFID chip you're referring to is no longer manufactured.'

'You're partly correct. The FDA approved the chips for human use in 2008. Then all these independent medical studies tested the glass-encapsulated chips on dogs and cats. They developed cancerous tumors, and the FDA revoked approval. The company that manufactured it – there was only one – went into bankruptcy, but then they received a godsend when the Indian government started a project to take every citizen's fingerprints and iris scans, and store them on these tiny RFID chips so they could be identified.'

'And the range of these chips?'

'A couple of miles,' Karim said. 'All you need is a special antennae hooked up to a computer that has the right software. If you weren't followed, Malcolm, then Santiago had to have been tagged with one of these RFID chips or some other type of hidden tracking device that emitted a signal powerful enough to allow his captors to pinpoint his location. It's the only conceivable scenario.'

And one I failed to consider, Fletcher thought.

Karim propped an elbow on the door and massaged his forehead. In the silence that ensued, Fletcher contemplated what might have happened in Cape May. He surmised that Nathan Santiago had been removed from the premises. The question facing him was, had the woman and her partner decided to remain behind – or had they left people behind? They employed the services of at least two men: William Jenner and Marcus De Luca. Jenner's home had been torched, but Fletcher couldn't assume that either Jenner or his partner were dead. Were the former Baltimore patrolmen waiting at the Cape May house?

Fletcher considered tactics. Tall brush and scrub cedar bordered the driveway; even in daylight, the area would provide plenty of hiding spots where he could watch. With the downtown area a quarter of a mile away, an outside gunshot would sound no louder than a firecracker in the harsh ocean wind.

Shooting, however, would be foolish. Karim equipped all of his vehicles, even his personal ones, with bullet-proof windows and special armour that could withstand a bomb.

'How do you do it?' Karim asked.

'Do what?'

'Unplug yourself from your emotions.'

'I'm not *uncaring*, Ali.'

'Looking at you – hearing you – I don't get a sense that you're . . . well, feeling anything.'

Fletcher didn't answer.

They drove in silence.

'Mathematics,' Fletcher said.

'I beg your pardon?'

'The human body is nothing more than a complex energy system. It has a finite amount of resources.

Focusing energy into endless speculation is a waste of time and, worse, a drain on mental resources. Better to channel my focus on the upcoming task.'

'Malcolm,' Karim said, drawing out the word, curls of smoke drifting from his nostrils, 'there are times when I truly envy you.'

51

Fletcher insisted on making the final approach to the house alone. When he exited the car, he wanted Jenner, De Luca and whoever else was waiting in the house to think he'd come alone.

Karim's Cape May home was on Whitney Avenue, a road that curved around a tall, sand-dusted hill upon which sat the house. It turned on to Greenview, the street that ran parallel to Whitney. Because of the narrow roads and the dangerous curve, street parking wasn't allowed.

Fletcher took Greenview. Only one other home was near by, and both sides of the street were empty of vehicles. He drove where the road curved around a rocky shore and pulled onto Whitney. He saw no cars parked anywhere nearby. Fletcher drove past the driveway entrance for Karim's home and continued straight ahead, looking for someone in a parked car and watching the beach house. He found no parked cars or people.

The small downtown area consisted of boutique stores, coffee houses, bistros and restaurants. The area was relatively quiet, given the winter season. A handful of people moved in and out of the various establishments, anxious to get out of the cold wind. A young white male bundled in a dark winter parka and wearing a charcoal-coloured woolly hat paced in front of a clothing store, smoking a cigarette and looking thoughtfully down the street, in the direction of Karim's home.

Was he a spotter? Watching for someone to enter the driveway and then calling William Jenner? Fletcher checked all the cars parked in the meter spots along the street. They were mostly upscale models and they all had either New Jersey or New York plates. The vehicles were empty. The man he'd seen smoking tossed his cigarette into the wind and moved inside the store.

Fletcher pulled into a gas-station lot, turned and navigated his way back to the house. He handed the monocular to Karim.

'When I reach the driveway, I want you to look for heat signatures in the surrounding brush before turning your attention to the house.'

Fletcher slowed and turned left. A slight bump and then the car climbed up the steep driveway. From the corner of his eye, he could see Karim's pulse beating in his throat. His own heart rate remained unchanged.

Earlier, Karim had told him about the garage. With both remotes located inside the house, he had given Boyd Paulson a four-digit code to use on the keypad-entry system located on the outside of the garage. Reaching the top, Fletcher found the circular area clear and the garage-bay door hanging open, the black BMW parked inside. The door he'd entered last night – the porch door leading into the kitchen – was closed.

Karim searched the grounds with the monocular.

Fletcher's gaze swept the dunes, on the hunt for movement in the shaking brush and sea grass, the glint of a sniper scope – an unlikely scenario, but one he had to consider.

'There's no one out here,' Karim said, and turned his attention to the house.

The garage, wide and windowless, was painted a dull white. The BMW was parked in the same spot it had been a few short hours ago. Fletcher's roving gaze recorded what he saw now in the daylight, comparing these new images to the ones he had stored in his mind.

'I'm not detecting any heat signatures inside the house,' Karim said. 'This device can see through a single wall but not multiple walls and floors, right?'

'Correct.' Fletcher pulled into the garage bay and looked at the security camera mounted in the right-hand corner, directly above the door leading to the portico that annexed the house. 'The security camera's light is blinking.'

'Because the system's offline,' Karim said. 'If they're in there, they can't watch us from the monitoring station.'

'You mentioned earlier that it contained a hard drive.' Fletcher had his attention on the rearview mirror, watching for movement. Out of the corner of his eye he saw Karim nod.

'The drive is secured by a magnetic lock,' Karim said. 'If you don't remove it with a special key, the drive is erased. I have the key with me.'

Fletcher put the car in park. Karim removed a sidearm – an updated version of John Browning's legendary Colt design, the powerful BUL M-5 10-mm developed in cooperation with the Israeli Special Forces.

'Stay here,' Fletcher said, and withdrew the SIG from his shoulder holster.

He stepped out of the car. No one came running, and no shots were fired. He moved around the car and hit the garage-door button. The bay filled with the roar and clack of gears as the door lowered. He waited until it was halfway shut and then hand-signalled to Karim to kill the engine. Karim did and opened his door.

'I'll talk to you over this,' Fletcher said, and handed over a small Bluetooth headset that clipped around an ear. 'I'll be wearing one as well.'

'You've already found something, haven't you?'

'The garden hose on the side of the house, I used it last night. After I finished, I placed the spray nozzle back on top of the hanging rack. Now it's lying against the ground.'

'Maybe the wind knocked it down.'

Fletcher shook his head. 'Someone used it recently,' he said. 'There are still some damp pockets on the garage floor that haven't evaporated, and the remaining micro-fibre towels I saw last night on the shelves in here are missing, as well as three rolls of kitchen towel.'

Karim stared dumbfounded at the garage shelves.

'I'll contact you when I've secured the house,' Fletcher said. 'Until then, please remain here.'

'Bollocks. Going in alone is –'

'I need to concentrate. I can't do that while guarding you.'

Karim reluctantly waved his hands in surrender.

'Thank you. Now put away your gun before you hurt yourself.'

Silencer in hand, Fletcher locked it in place with a quick snap of the wrist. He approached the door, reminding himself that he couldn't shoot to kill. He needed to keep as many men alive as possible in order to find out where Nathan Santiago had been taken.

Fletcher grabbed the doorknob, turned and stepped back with his weapon raised.

52

The chilly hall of white walls and concrete flooring was empty.

Fletcher stepped inside, closing the door softly behind him. Another door was less than twenty feet ahead; mounted in the corner and watching, a security camera, its single green light blinking.

He raised the SIG as he threw open the door .

The morning's dull light filtered through the gaps between the wooden blinds drawn around all the kitchen and living-room windows. The ceiling fans mounted in the rafters hadn't been shut off. The spinning blades pushed the warm air down him, with its lingering smell of an extinguished fire.

No one came running. Watching and listening for movement, Fletcher crept towards the archway leading into the living room. Then he swung around the corner. The entire living room was empty.

Now he checked the security room. It was empty, the monitoring screen dark. The electrical cord for the security station had been unplugged. He checked the bedroom across the hall, found it empty. Same with the bathroom. The ground floors were empty.

The wind died down and the warm air inside the living room seemed to throb with silence.

Were they waiting upstairs?

Fletcher moved up the carpeted steps, mindful of his shadow dancing across the wall, announcing him.

The first-floor hallway was empty, the air significantly cooler and the three bedroom doors were hanging open. The first bedroom, the one on his left, was empty. The second one was empty. The last one was empty. Everything was in order. Slowly he moved down the hall and when it curved left he walked across the last part and entered the large room where Dr Sin had treated Nathan Santiago.

The hospital bed was still in the centre of the room, the plastic liner covering the pillow and mattress smeared with dried blood. Drops were on the floor, and the rubbish bin was full of bloody gauze.

Fletcher wondered if Karim's surveillance cameras had captured anything useful.

Returning to the security room, Fletcher slid the plug for the console into the wall outlet. As the system turned on, he opened the unit's metal cabinet. The Ethernet cable had been torn from the router, and the system's hard drive was missing, prised from its metal clasps. The person who had performed the work had known exactly where to look. Only someone well acquainted with the design mechanics of security-system stations would be able to locate where the hard drive was housed, as the area was concealed and couldn't be accessed easily. Someone had taken every available action to remove recorded evidence of what had happened inside the house.

The security cameras were back online but not recording. Fletcher spoke into his headset: 'There's no one here.'

'What did you find?'

'The hard drive is gone.' Fletcher moved back to the foot of the stairs. 'Dial Boyd's number.'

No ringing, just the sound of the wind shrieking.

Karim's voice came over his earpiece: 'It's coming from the BMW – the trunk, I think.'

'I'll be right there.' Fletcher did not want the man to pop the trunk and witness Boyd Paulson's manner of execution.

Opening the door for the garage, he found the BMW's trunk already popped open, the small halogen light shining down on Boyd Paulson. A gunshot entry wound the size of a half-dollar had replaced Paulson's left eye.

Dr Sin was not in the trunk. Had she been taken with Santiago?

Karim had a phone mashed up against his ear. Fletcher was moving towards him when Karim yanked the phone away and said, 'FBI and New Jersey SWAT are on their way.'

53

Fletcher looked at the Range Rover.

'Forget that,' Karim said. 'They'll be here any moment. I've got to hide you.'

Karim whisked past him and darted into the hall. Fletcher followed.

'My New Jersey people were monitoring police frequencies,' Karim said over his shoulder. 'They intercepted communications between the Feds and the Jersey cops and state police. They know you're here, Malcolm. I don't know how, but *they know.*'

Racing quickly up the stairs, Fletcher heard the rotor thump of an approaching helicopter over the wind roaring past the house. The sound grew louder when he followed Karim into the treatment room. Fletcher moved to the windows overlooking the back of the house and peered through the blinds.

A half-dozen or so SWAT officers dressed in black tactical gear, faces hidden by helmets and black balaclavas, were crouched in the brush and tall sea grass on the dunes overlooking the water, wind blowing sand and grit across their visors.

Karim had opened the bi-fold doors of a closet. 'You'll be safe in here,' he said, pushing aside the hanging white lab coats. Then he turned to an alarm keypad unit with glowing numbers mounted on the wall.

Karim punched in a four-digit code. Fletcher committed the numeric sequence to memory as he heard a faint click of locks springing free, the sound followed by a soft hiss of escaping air pressure. The closet's left-corner wall opened to a narrow room of dim and flickering light. Fletcher had to duck to enter, and immediately found the light source: a laptop computer on a small table, its fifteen-inch screen holding six camera views of different areas inside and outside the house. No sound, just images.

'The same code opens the door,' Karim said. He handed over his phone, caught Fletcher's puzzled expression. 'Your phone number's listed on it,' he said, speaking rapidly. 'Remove the battery so it can't be traced. Shut off any devices you have that make noise and –'

A booming sound erupted from somewhere downstairs. Fletcher glanced at the computer screen and saw that the front door had been blown open – an explosive had been used on the locks. The order had been given to breach the house.

'Hold the door and it will automatically seal and lock,' Karim said. 'Keep your ass parked in here until I come for you.'

Fletcher pushed the false door shut. The suck of a vacuum seal, and a moment later the locks bolted home. He heard Karim rearrange the clothing and then the closet's bi-fold doors slammed shut.

Quickly he removed the batteries from his phone. Quickly he removed the batteries from Karim's phone, tucking everything inside his trouser pockets. He was standing inside a makeshift panic room. The area, with its three-foot-wide floor, could accommodate several people, if needed. Karim, always the meticulous organizer, had stocked it with every conceivable provision – cases of bottled water and meal-replacement bars; plastic urinals and neatly stacked portable cardboard toilets, the kind used by outdoorsmen. Fletcher found a defibrillator, an emergency first-aid kit and a 'blow-out' kit. Small and portable so that it could easily be stored inside a cargo-pants pocket, backpack or glove box, the blow-out kit contained a number of life-saving emergency items: QuikClot Combat Gauze, a decompression needle, Israeli Bandages and a pair of HALO chest seals.

Karim had installed lead shielding over the walls – a clever touch. Used mostly as a radiation shield, the lead would prevent the government's new thermal-imaging devices from picking up a heat signature. An additional keypad had been installed on the wall near the false door, its numeric keypad glowing.

Muffled shouting on the other side of the wall: '*Stand down! I repeat, stand down!*'

On a top-right-hand corner of the computer screen Fletcher saw a view of the treatment room. The hidden camera had been installed somewhere along the ceiling so its parabolic lens could capture the bedroom's entirety – in a fire alarm, he suspected, given the high angle.

Karim had dropped to his knees, his fingers laced

together and resting on the back of his head as a pair of SWAT officers looked down the target sights of their weapons – HK MP7 submachine guns with extended 40-round magazines, shoulder stocks and collimating sights installed on the top rails. Fletcher knew of only one tactical unit that supplied its men with this new breed of Personal Defence Weapon.

He dropped to one knee in front of the computer. He recognized the brand of surveillance software installed on the system. A quick glance at the screen revealed that recording option for each camera had been turned off.

A tap of a key and the camera view for the bedroom enlarged and filled the entire screen.

Karim was no longer wearing his earpiece; he had tucked it inside the breast pocket of his coat, the tiny microphone end sticking out so it could listen in on the room. Fletcher could hear, over his own earpiece, Karim's erratic breathing.

Now Karim's voice: 'I'm armed. Left shoulder holster.'

One officer stood guard while the other pushed Karim to the floor. Both men wore balaclavas; only their eyes were visible. Fletcher saw a patch on the right-shoulder sleeve of one of the men and zoomed in on it. An eagle patch. Not local or federal SWAT but operators from the FBI's Delta Force-inspired Hostage Rescue Team. To categorize these men as a bunch of steroid-laced elite alpha males itching with buck fever would be both unfair and unwise, as HRT recruited only the brightest tactical minds.

HRT's presence here meant several snipers were now watching the house.

One of the HRT operators had removed Karim's weapon. The other yanked Karim's hands behind his back and bound his wrists together with a FlexiCuff. Now the pair turned their attention to the closet. A slam and rattle as the bi-fold doors swung open, and then Fletcher heard a man's voice just inches from where he stood: '*Clear.*'

The two operators moved to the bedroom's far wall so they could divide their attention between Karim and the door leading into the carpeted hall. Fletcher pressed another key and all six hidden cameras came back on the screen. On each one he saw both HRT operators and New Jersey SWAT officers swarming through the house. They threw open closet doors and overturned mattresses. They crawled through the basement with their tactical lights shining in hidden corners, behind objects and furniture, the video cameras mounted on their weapons capturing everything and sending it to their command post, which had no doubt been set up somewhere close to the house.

The top-left-hand corner of the screen contained a camera view of the driveway. An unmarked Ford Interceptor with flashing grille lights was parked at the top of the driveway, along with a SWAT van and two other unmarked vehicles. Plainclothes officers and SWAT stood armed and ready in a wash of light from blue-and-whites.

The driver's side door for the Interceptor swung open. Fletcher tapped a key. The computer window enlarged and he saw a tall, burly man who hadn't bothered to have his navy-blue suit properly tailored; the jacket had a tent-like effect on his stature. One look at his face and Fletcher knew this man was too young to be the one in charge.

But the gentleman unbuttoning his dark grey overcoat could very well be.

Diminutive in both size and shape, this man had his back turned to the driveway's security camera. He had a folder tucked under his arm and stood a few feet away from the car, speaking to a cluster of law-enforcement officers. Fletcher couldn't hear what was being said, but he had a clear view of the faces staring down at the Napoleonic man, and they all seemed displeased at having him in their presence; a federal agent, perhaps. That would explain the wide berth they had given him. A federal presence in a local investigation was treated with the same distant contempt as a leper at a skincare clinic.

The man brushed past the group and disappeared from the computer screen.

Fletcher found him a moment later, standing inside the living room and slicking back his grizzled, windblown hair with his long and delicate fingers. He wore a pair of aviator-style sunglasses. Fletcher was about to zoom in on the face when the man darted up the stairs.

Fletcher switched to the camera showing a view of

the upstairs hall. The small man had taken off his sunglasses. The folder that had been tucked under his arm was now gripped in a gloved hand. Fletcher saw the federal badge hanging on the man's belt, stared at it as he walked across the hall, on his way to speak to Ali Karim.

54

Fletcher felt as though he were an invisible spectator standing in the back of the treatment room. On the computer screen he watched as the federal agent stepped inside with a companion he'd picked up along the way – another Hostage Rescue operator, this one tall and burly, his face and head covered with a bala-clava and a tactical helmet. Unlike the other operators, he wore a tactical backpack. Clipped to its side was a military-grade gas mask, one equipped with the new voice-amplification system. Fletcher, his senses vibrating like a tuning fork, was set to register any anomaly.

The two operators guarding Karim left the room. The new operator had his HK aimed at Karim, who was still lying face down on the floor. The federal agent conducted a leisurely examination of the room's blood-stained items. When he turned to the bed where Nathan Santiago had been treated, Fletcher got his first solid, clear view of the man's features – the razor-thin lips, weak jawline and pronounced forehead. The man appeared to be somewhere in his late forties to early fifties.

Fletcher had turned up the volume on his earpiece. Still, he had to strain to hear the agent's calm and cultured voice: 'Get Mr Karim a chair.'

The operator rolled a desk chair over and helped Karim into it. Fletcher couldn't see Karim's face, just the back of his head.

The agent said, 'You know why I'm here, Mr Karim.'

'To assist me in finding out what happened to Boyd, I hope.'

'Boyd?'

'One of my employees. Boyd Paulson.' Karim had shelved his grief for the moment; he spoke clearly, and well. 'His car is here – that's his BMW parked in the garage.'

'And the body in trunk?'

'Boyd Paulson. That's what *I'm* doing here, Mr –'

'Alexander Borgia. I'm with the Federal Bureau of Investigation.'

Karim feigned surprise. Then he said, 'I hope you have a warrant.'

Borgia nodded. He removed a piece of paper from the folder and placed it on Karim's lap. Karim, not wearing his bifocals, had to slump forward in order to read it.

Borgia's gaze roved over the shelves packed with supplies. 'Are you opening up some sort of medical office here along the seashore, Mr Karim?'

'A plastic surgeon is.'

'And this plastic surgeon, does he have a name?'

'She does. Dr Dara Sin, from Manhattan.'

'And where can I find this Dr Sin?'

'Good question. She's missing. She called my business partner because she was worried about someone stalking her and he came here to investigate.'

'What happened in this room?'

'I don't know, and I'm done answering your questions. I want to talk to my lawyers.'

Borgia sighed. 'Where is he, Mr Karim?'

'Who?'

'Malcolm Fletcher. We know he came here with you. We've had you under surveillance since you left New York.' Borgia's voice was cordial, but his eyes had taken on the spit-sheen of a rat. 'Where did you hide him?'

'I came here alone. But, please, feel free to take a look around – oh, wait, you're already doing that.'

Fletcher's heart rate hadn't accelerated, but his mouth felt dry. *Colorado*, he thought. *Somehow the* FBI *found out I was at the Herrera home.*

And then Borgia said it: 'Let's talk about Theresa Herrera. I understand you agreed to look into the disappearance of her son, Rico.'

Karim didn't answer.

'And from her phone records,' Borgia said, 'we know you spoke to her twice on the day she died. You told the local police you were planning on meeting her at her home the following afternoon – Saturday. Am I correct?'

Karim didn't answer.

Borgia opened his folder again. 'Right up the road from the Herrera home there's this . . . a retirement community, I guess you could call it. They have security cameras installed at the front gate. The night Theresa Herrera and her husband died, the cameras captured this.' Borgia placed a photograph on Karim's lap. 'This car, an Audi A8, drove right past the cameras roughly ten minutes before the bomb went off. It was the only car spotted in that area that night.

'The car is registered to a New York man named Richard Munchel,' Borgia said. 'The man doesn't exist. The windows are tinted, so you can't see the driver – not yet. Our lab is working on that. Now let me show you this. It's a photograph we took this morning.'

Borgia placed it on Karim's lap. 'What do you think?'

'I don't have my glasses on,' Karim said.

'Then I'll describe it for you. The car is a Jaguar with tinted windows. If you had your glasses on, you would see that it's driving down the ramp leading to the entrance of your home's private garage. *This* car is registered to a man named Robert Pepin. You invited this man into your home, but here's the strange thing, Mr Karim. Robert Pepin doesn't exist either. But I have a feeling you already knew that, didn't you?'

Karim said nothing.

'Of course you did,' Borgia said. 'You can't see it in the picture, but the Jag has Chicago plates. Here's where the story gets interesting, Mr Karim, so please pay attention.'

55

On the computer screen Fletcher saw a slight grin tugging at the corner of Borgia's mouth. The federal agent couldn't keep the satisfaction out of his face. He beamed with the pride of a hunter who had finally ensnared his elusive prey.

'Less than a week ago, early on Monday morning, you boarded your private plane with your assistant, Emma White, and flew out to Chicago. There you picked up a third passenger, a man named Robert Pepin. We know this because your pilot wrote the name down on the passenger manifest. According to the pilot, Robert Pepin bore a rather uncanny resemblance to Malcolm Fletcher.'

Borgia let the words hang in the air for a moment, then continued: 'The pilot told us he flew the three of you to the Dothan Regional Airport in Alabama, where Mr Pepin departed for a number of hours. We know Mr Pepin went to the Hertz counter and rented a burgundy-coloured Ford Escape and drove approximately 126 miles. When he returned to the airport, you flew Mr Pepin back to Chicago.'

Another dramatic pause, and then Borgia added, 'We know all of this because your pilot is one of our informants.'

Fletcher's gaze narrowed in thought, knowing where Borgia was heading.

Borgia leaned forward, close to Karim's shoulder, and said, 'Your connection to Fletcher is no secret. Your son's murder was similar to a number of others at the time; New York homicide thought they had a serial killer lurking in their city and called the Bureau to consult. Guess which profiler we sent?'

Karim didn't answer.

'That's right, Malcolm Fletcher,' Borgia said. 'We sent Fletcher and your son's killer . . . well, no one knows what happened to him as this person was never caught.'

And never will be, Fletcher thought. Three men had killed Jason Karim – three young men whose gang-initiation rite involved the murder of a wealthy Manhattan resident. Fletcher had scattered their remains along the bottom of the Hudson River.

'And then we have Boston,' Borgia said. 'Five years ago you offered your services to a wealthy businessman whose daughter was, in fact, a victim of a serial killer. We know Fletcher was involved because a Boston forensic investigator named Darby McCormick met Fletcher face to face – twice. We couldn't prove your involvement with him then, but I can certainly prove it now, as we know Fletcher came here with you.'

Borgia straightened and resumed his position in front of Karim. 'The penalty for harbouring a fugitive carries a maximum five-year sentence. I'd quote you the six-figure fine involved, but the amount is a drop in the ocean

to a man of your financial means. What's more discon-
certing – what I suspect you're thinking about right now,
Mr Karim – is what will happen if the news gets out that
you, the owner of one of the country's most respected
and highly visible security firms, are not only working with
but hiding the nation's most wanted fugitive.'

'I want to speak to my lawyers,' Karim said.

Borgia went on. 'Fortunately, I'm in a position to
bargain. Tell me where you hid Fletcher and not only
will I guarantee no further damage to your house, I can
guarantee you probation, no more than six months. More
importantly, we'll keep your name out of the papers.'

'I want to talk to my lawyers.'

Borgia, unfazed by Karim's defiance, turned his
attention to the HRT operator and said, 'I understand
Mr Karim was armed.'

The operator nodded. 'We confiscated a 10-mm
sidearm, a BUL M-5.'

'Any other weapons?'

'No, sir.'

'Does Mr Karim have a permit to carry in the state
of New Jersey?'

Karim answered the question: 'The permit's in my
pocket.'

'Untie him,' Borgia said.

'Sir?' the operator asked.

'I think Mr Karim's bindings are cutting off the blood
supply to his head. He might as well be comfortable
while we talk. You won't be any trouble, will you, Mr
Karim?'

Karim didn't answer. The operator didn't wait for one. He clipped the submachine gun to his vest. The video camera mounted to the weapon had been turned off.

Why? Fletcher didn't know but wanted to warn Karim, had no way of warning him. Karim was no longer wearing the headset, had tucked it in his breast jacket pocket.

Fletcher watched as the operator removed the nine from the holster strapped to his leg. Then the man unsheathed a tactical knife, cut Karim's bindings and stepped back with the nine raised.

Slowly Karim reached inside his back pocket. He came back with a thin leather wallet and placed it on Borgia's waiting palm.

'I'm going to go check your gun permit,' Borgia said. 'When I return, Mr Karim, if you don't tell me where you've hidden Fletcher, I'll have tear gas launched inside every room of this house. If for some reason Fletcher doesn't appear, I'm going to have Hostage Rescue, New Jersey SWAT and every other officer I brought here take a sledgehammer to each and every wall – I'll raze the foundations if I have to. We *will* find him, Mr Karim, because we know he's here. You, sir, will go to jail and you'll be all over the news. I already have a press release prepared.'

'I want to speak to my lawyers,' Karim said for the third time.

'This is a limited, one-time offer, Mr Karim. Take a few minutes to think it over.'

Borgia left the bedroom. Karim stared after him, absently rubbing the red circulation marks left on his wrists. The operator was pulling something from underneath his watchband.

It was a folding knife.

Fletcher found himself reacting as though he was actually standing inside the room – as though he could grab the operator's wrist and disarm the man.

On the screen the operator opened the knife and dropped it to the floor. Karim saw it, and was about to stand when an elbow smashed across his jaw.

Fletcher was already on his feet. Over his earpiece he heard a garbled scream from Karim. He punched the code into the glowing keypad, knowing that if he didn't act quickly Karim would surely die.

56

Special Agent Alexander Borgia slipped on his sun-glasses when he reached the living room. The local SWAT agent he'd put in charge of guarding the front door, a former Marine who had seen plenty of combat in his time, hand-signalled to the nearby officers to stand down. Borgia was glad to see the man bark a quick order into his chest mike. At least this one knew what the hell he was doing.

The cold wind blew sand across the driveway packed with FBI and New Jersey police officers. They wore bulletproof vests underneath their winter jackets, each man braced behind the vehicles and holding their weap-ons on car roofs and hoods. FBI snipers were set up on the dunes around the house. Technical Investigative Equipment teams had finished setting up auditory sur-veillance devices mounted to stationary platforms.

As Borgia moved down the driveway, threading his way through the bodies, he caught men glancing away from their gun sights, their high-powered binoculars and thermal-imaging devices, to take the measure of him, to see if they could read something in his body language that would hint at what had happened inside the house. Everyone here knew this wasn't an ordinary fugitive situation.

Borgia wasn't a natural gambler; he hadn't felt entirely comfortable rolling the dice on this. While all the information he collected pointed to Malcolm Fletcher's involvement with Karim (especially the description from Karim's pilot), Borgia still had no visual or auditory confirmation that Fletcher had been inside Karim's home that morning. The agents had tried. Their thermal-imaging devices couldn't penetrate through Karim's garage door or his mansion walls. The laser mikes aimed at the windows had failed to pick so much as a single noise – not entirely surprising, as Karim was in the security business and had access to the same counter-surveillance toys the federal boys played with. The man had remodelled his home to prevent every conceivable surveillance scenario.

But when Karim's Range Rover had pulled out of the garage, agents had picked up not one but *two* heat signatures sitting behind the tinted windows. Karim had brought someone along for the ride, and Borgia's gut told him that that someone was Malcolm Fletcher. Borgia imagined the positive swells he would receive for capturing the elusive fugitive and, gripped with the fever of a man enraptured, had given the go-ahead for Hostage Rescue to breach the house.

Borgia reached the main road. Tactical Operations Command had set up a post within the inner perimeter. He opened the door for the mobile trailer and entered the warm space, grateful to be out of the cold. Agents sitting at the long consoles kept a close eye on their surveillance monitors while listening over their headsets to incoming radio-intelligence information from TOC agents set up in sniper positions.

Special Operation Commander Howard Cronin stood in the room's centre with the thumbs of his meaty hands hooked in the pockets of his Wranglers. Tall with a beer-belly neatly hidden by a generous-fitting khaki field shirt, Cronin took great delight in swinging his dick to let everyone know just who the hell was in charge. Red-faced and wearing a headset, he saw Borgia and yanked the phones away from one ear.

'*What's with this bullshit with the radio and camera silence?*'

A few men flinched. Cronin had been in a foul mood since he'd been informed that Borgia would be speaking to Karim. Alone.

Borgia kept his cool – a task made easier by how much he detested the man. 'Karim's a security expert,' he said. 'He knows everything he says and does is being watched and recorded. I wanted to try a more informal approach first – try to strike a deal with him, so I told Operator Jackman to turn off his radio and camera.'

'I don't give a shit if the man asked for Jesus H. Christ himself, you don't –'

'It was my call, since I'm the one in charge of this operation,' Borgia said. 'If you have any questions about the scope of my role, you can call Director Oberst and ask him –'

'Did Karim give up Fletcher?'

'I gave him a moment to weigh his options while I checked out his gun permit.'

Cronin looked like his head was going to pop off his shoulders.

'I wanted Karim to stew in it for a bit,' Borgia said. 'He's got a lot to lose here – his reputation and his business if this makes the papers and – what's going on?'

Cronin had slid the headphones back over his ear. Two quick steps and he plopped himself down on a chair, his attention swinging to the monitor showing a grouping of windows. Borgia saw shattered glass, the drawn blinds shaking in the wind.

Borgia beckoned with his hand for a pair of headphones. A nearby agent quickly handed his over, stood and moved away.

Over the headphones Borgia heard a clear voice shouting over the wind: 'Repeat, two shots fired from inside the master bedroom.'

Not from Karim, Borgia thought. The man had been searched for weapons. *Has to be Jackman, but why?* The HRT operator had been instructed to drop the concealed knife on the floor – a knife that Karim had had in his possession but was missed during the search. Then Jackman would radio in that Karim had attacked him, and during the confrontation Jackman had had no choice but to defend himself with his own knife.

'Let's flush the son of a bitch out,' Cronin said. 'Alpha Team, move into position. Jackman, report.'

Borgia watched tear-gas canisters being launched and then the sound of shattering glass filled his headphones. A quick glance to another monitor and Borgia saw Alpha Team, wearing gas masks, funnelling through the front door.

Three gunshots rang out over the headsets.

Cronin again: 'Jackman, report.'

Over his headset Borgia heard coughing followed by a Darth Vader-like breathing.

'CP, this is Jackman. I'm hit.' Jackman's painful wheezing voice had a mechanical, robotic tone; he was speaking over the gas mask's voice-amplification system. 'Tango is armed and on the move. Fired three return shots.' A long wheeze and then Jackman said, 'I think he's hit.'

Borgia stirred with excitement. Fletcher *had* been inside the house, but where? Where had he been hiding?

'Stand by, Jackman, help is on the way.' Cronin covered his mike with his hand and, turning over his shoulder, barked at the room: 'Move SWAT paramedics into position.' He released his grip on the mike. 'Snipers, if you have a clean shot, take Tango down. Jackman, keep talking to me, son.'

No answer from Jackman, just that sickly wheeze. Had he been shot? All the operators wore bullet-proof vests. But if Fletcher had used armour-piercing rounds . . .

Borgia prayed to God Jackman had managed to get in at least one critical stab wound. If he had, Karim would die before he reached hospital.

Borgia's stomach climbed with equal measures of hope and fear. *Please, God, let Jackman be dead along with Karim.* Three could keep a secret if two were dead.

Cronin again: 'Talk to me, Jackman.'

On another monitor, grey smoke billowed from the front doorway and scattered in the rough wind. Over the headsets came the sounds of heavy boots crunching over broken glass. No gunshots, not yet.

Elbows on the console top, Borgia rested his chin against his folded hands and stared at the front door, watching and waiting.

HRT operators emerged from the smoke, one of their own slung between them – Operator Jackman, head bowed and bobbing, chest and gas mask smeared bright with blood. Jackman's boots bounced against the steps as he was dragged away. When the trio came into closer view, Borgia caught sight of the bullet holes on Jackman's chest, right above the heart. If Fletcher had used armour-piercing rounds, Jackman was as good as dead.

SWAT paramedics came next, holding a gurney, an unconscious Karim strapped down to it. The man's head swayed back and forth as he was whisked down the steps. Borgia nearly collapsed in relief when he saw the large amount of blood covering the man's clothing, the multiple pressure bandages covering the man's chest and stomach. *No way Karim survived that.*

Borgia thought of Fletcher, felt his heart tripping with pleasure at the thought of standing in front of all those cameras, telling the story of how he'd found and captured the former profiler. His story would hold up, even if Karim survived. It would be Karim's word against the actions of an FBI agent with a pristine record. Karim had hidden a wanted fugitive. He had attacked and, God willing, killed a federal agent. If Karim survived, he would spend his remaining years behind bars.

Karim didn't matter. Fletcher was the prize, and Fletcher was pinned down somewhere, in agony from the tear gas, choking on it. Any second now and they would have him. The monster couldn't ride or hide any more.

A full minute passed with no word.

They're moving slowly through smoke, taking no risks, Borgia thought. Fletcher spooked them – and with good reason. The monster might have the investigative mind of Sherlock Holmes, but he was as cunning and bloodthirsty as a vampire.

Ten minutes passed and the smoke was no longer drifting through the front doorway or shattered windows.

Borgia's eyes narrowed in thought, his insides turning to water even before a new voice spoke over his headset: 'CP, we've found a body hidden inside a closet – hidden inside what looks like some sort of panic room. It has –'

'Is it Fletcher?' Cronin asked.

'No, sir. He's one of ours. Danny Jackman.'

57

The SWAT tactical paramedic kneeling in the back of the swaying ambulance went to work applying new pressure bandages to the comatose stabbing victim strapped down to the gurney. The paramedic had completed two tours in Iraq and one in Afghanistan; he had seen the many ways in which the human body could be torn apart by high-velocity bullets and roadside bombs. This victim was relatively easy compared to those miseries.

Two stab wounds: the lower left quadrant of the abdomen and the other on the chest, just below the left clavicle. The attacker had been aiming for the heart. The vic had worn a bulletproof vest but had opted out of using a steel-plate insert. If he had, the long blade wouldn't have punctured the lung.

The stabbing vic was intubated and had a breathing tube inserted through the trachea to protect the airway. The problem now was blood. The vic had lost a lot, maybe too much. He'd been found lying in at least a litre, and his abdomen was rigid and distended from internal bleeding. Every time he coughed, a fine red mist sprayed the inside of the breathing tube, a sure sign his lungs were filling up.

The paramedic started two large bore IV lines to

replace the lost blood, hoping to God the intravenous fluid would keep the victim's brain and vital organs alive without accelerating the internal bleeding. Then he went to work suctioning blood from the man's endotracheal tube to keep the airway open and oxygenated.

The second victim riding in the ambulance was an HRT operator named Jackman. He had suffered blunt-force trauma from the lead slugs that had struck his chest. The man had been shot three times – once above the heart, the other two dead centre of the chest. His vest had a steel plate, and it had saved his life.

And Agent Jackman had possibly saved this other man's life. Entering the bedroom filled with smoke, the paramedic had found the stabbing vic's vest already cut off, a HALO chest seal on the bleeding wound.

The paramedic had tried to take off the agent's gas mask to rinse away the tear gas, but Jackman had waved him off, saying in a mechanical voice over the mask's speaker that he had on a vest and was fine, just in severe pain. The HRT operator kept pointing to the stabbing vic, who was certainly more in need of help.

The operator was sitting up now. *Christ, he's one big son of a bitch*, the paramedic thought, stripping out of his bloody gloves. He turned to the radio and called the Cape Regional Medical Center. It had an excellent trauma unit, from what he'd been told.

'Cape Trauma, this is Tac Medic One, do you copy?'

'Tac Medic One, this is Dr Notestine, I copy, go ahead.'

'We're en route to your facility, code three with an ETA of ten minutes,' the paramedic said. 'On board we have an older male patient with multiple stab wounds. Wound one is on the left chest, mid-clavicular fourth intercostal space. Wound two is left upper abdominal quadrant. Knife was approximately two-inch-width blade, length of five inches. Patient is unconscious and unresponsive, estimated external blood loss at one litre. Skin is cool and diaphoretic with a delayed capillary refill. Blood pressure 80 over 40, heart rate of 144.' A glance at the monitor and he added, 'He's showing sinus tachycardia.'

Out of the corner of his eye the paramedic saw the HRT agent stripping out of his jacket. 'Patient is intubated with a number eight endotracheal tube,' he said. 'Lung sounds are diminished on the left, right lung fields are clear. There's blood in the tube on expiration. I have two large bore IVs infused with approximately 500cc of normal saline. Patient was found comatose. Medications, last meal and medical history unknown, over.'

'Copy, Tac Medic One, we'll have operating room standing by. Do you know patient's blood type?'

The paramedic couldn't answer. A powerful arm had wrapped around his neck, squeezing the carotid artery and cutting off the much needed blood to his brain.

'My apologies,' Agent Jackman whispered, but it was too late for the paramedic to answer.

Nineteen-year-old Mindy Williams had been driving her boyfriend's pickup when she heard the wailing

283

ambulance. Unlike some of the other vehicles, she pulled over to the far side of the breakdown lane to give the ambulance a wide berth.

After it whisked past her in a wail of sirens and flashing lights, she pulled back on to the two-lane highway, reviewing what she needed to pick up at the mall, when she saw the ambulance's back door fly open. She immediately slammed on her brakes. The seatbelt kept her from smashing against the steering wheel.

A paramedic stood by the opened door; she was close enough to see the bright blue jacket with its reflective bands, the large EMS emblem stitched on the breast. His hands were bloody. *Whoever was riding in the ambulance must've been in one hell of an accident*, she thought.

The paramedic didn't shut the door. Incredibly, he stepped on to the back bumper.

Then he jumped.

Car horns shrieked and tyres skidded, and she watched in fascination and horror as the man hit the fast-moving ground, tumbled and rolled, tumbled and rolled.

What the hell is going —

Her thought was interrupted by a new sound: police sirens. She glanced in her rearview mirror and in the far distance saw a cavalry of flashing blue-and-white lights — police cruisers and undercover vehicles were driving at rocket speed as if trying to outrun an atomic bomb. Mindy Williams looked back at the highway, catching a flash of the paramedic's blue coat before the man disappeared into the woods.

58

Malcolm Fletcher spotted the gated parking lot and stopped running.

His broken ribs had been aggravated by his tumble across the highway, the bones feeling as though they had been turned into shards of glass, the jagged ends shredding his muscles and lungs. His legs fluttered, threatening to give out, and his vision swam with pain. He leaned forward, hands on his knees, and quickly tried to catch his breath.

The gated lot was for people using Cape May's small Woodbine Municipal Airport. The entrance and exit were in the same location, manned by a pair of automated machines that created parking tickets and collected the fees.

The wailing sirens had reached a piercing pitch; the FBI had discovered HRT Operator Jackman's body and realized that it wasn't Jackman riding in the back of the ambulance. Fletcher suspected a small army had been dispatched for him. He ran for the lot, legs shaking and ribs screaming in protest.

His tactical belt, slung across his chest like a bandolier and hidden underneath the bright blue paramedic jacket, did not contain the necessary tools to pop open a steering column. He needed to find a new vehicle with an auto-ignition system and make quick work of it.

This sedan would do – a four-door tan Toyota Camry. He found the Vehicle Identification Number conveniently displayed on the windshield's lower corner, the parking lot's ticket sitting on the dash. The ticket was stamped with that day's date and time.

Smartphone in hand, Fletcher called up the necessary piece of software. Then he entered the Toyota's VIN. A moment later he had the frequencies to unlock and start the car.

Sitting on the passenger's seat was a baseball cap with the words KOREAN WAR VETERAN printed across the front. Even better, he found a pair of sunglasses clipped to the visor, the kind favoured by elderly people plagued with vision problems – wraparounds with big square lenses that fit neatly over a pair of prescription glasses.

Fletcher had slipped the HRT Operator Jackman's roomy tactical trousers over his own. He pushed them down now so he could reach Karim's phone. He removed it, along with the battery. He placed both items on the passenger's seat for the moment.

Cap pulled down across his forehead, Fletcher paid the parking fee in cash and exited the lot. He left the window open, wanting to relieve himself of the atrocious odour baked into the leather's sweat-stained seats: menthol and methyl salicylate, the two primary chemicals used in the pain-relieving ointment Bengay.

Fletcher navigated his way through the quiet back

roads. The paramedic coat he'd taken from the back of the ambulance hid the blood on his T-shirt but not the dried blood on his hands. He kept them on the bottom part of the steering wheel, where they were safely out of view.

Watching the streets and searching for any signs of police, Fletcher replayed the moment when he left the panic room to find Karim lying on the floor and bleeding out from multiple stab wounds. Jackman, considerably taller and heavier, was straddling Karim; the agent's legs were pinning Karim's arms to the floor. The agent was pressing one hand against Karim's mouth, while pinching his nostrils shut with the other, wanting to cut off the airways and ensure Karim's death before any paramedics arrived.

Operator Jackman had pulled out a folding knife and dropped it to the floor to stage the scene. He had turned off his weapon-mounted video camera so there would be no record. Alexander Borgia had brought the man into the treatment room and dismissed the two agents so there would be no witnesses. Borgia had brought Jackman with him so Jackman could kill Karim while Borgia left to check on Karim's gun permit.

Right now Karim was lying on an operating table, clinging to life. If he survived, would Alexander Borgia find another way to strike?

Fletcher needed to speak to Emma White, needed to warn her, but could he risk calling? When Borgia listed the evidence against Karim, he hadn't mentioned a wiretap. That, however, didn't mean the FBI wasn't monitoring Karim's phones and, possibly, those of his personal assistant.

Fletcher had no choice; he had to risk calling before Karim was put in further danger. He slid the battery into Karim's phone.

Emma White's contact information was listed on the BlackBerry. Fletcher dialled the cell number first, as cell signals took time to triangulate.

M's voice came on the line: 'Ali, I just got word –'

'This is Robert Pepin. Are you alone?'

'I am.'

'Is this line secure?'

'On this end it is,' she said. 'What are you doing with Mr Karim's phone?'

'Listen to me very carefully. Don't speak, just listen.

'Karim is being taken to the Cape May Memorial Hospital,' Fletcher said. 'It's imperative that you send people there to guard him. They are *not* to let Karim out of their sight, they are *not* to leave him alone with a federal agent named Alexander Borgia. *Do not allow this man or any other federal agent to be alone with Karim for any reason.*'

'Karim was injured?' She said 'Karim' as though he were an office building, with no emotion or inflection in her voice.

'They'll tell you Karim attacked a federal agent,' Fletcher said. 'It's the other way around. Karim hid me inside a panic room; I witnessed what transpired. Contact Karim's lawyers – and his personal physician. Surround Karim by people you trust.'

'I understand. Now I should –'

288

'*Listen to me*,' Fletcher said, thinking about his Jaguar. There was evidence locked in the trunk and there were traces of blood on the passenger's seat – Nathan Santiago's blood, blood that would become visible under a forensic light or when a chemical such as Luminol was used. 'A black Jaguar is parked inside Karim's home garage. You need to remove it immediately before the FBI impounds it. You'll find a spare key inside a small box located underneath the right-hand side of the front bumper. Have you located Dr Sin's cell signal?'

'No. Her phone is a model that transmits a signal even if it's turned off – provided the battery is installed. I'll keep searching for it.'

'Get back to the house and remove the car. I'll contact you shortly.'

Fletcher hung up and immediately removed the phone's battery to prevent him from being traced.

He did not encounter any roadblocks. He drove on to the highway and entered the smooth-running traffic.

Despite the rush of events, he felt remarkably calm. After breaking Mr Jackman's neck, Fletcher had relieved the man of his clothing and quickly dressed, leaving the agent's tactical vest on the floor. Then, using the man's sidearm, he'd fired three shots against the vest and quickly finished dressing. Lying on the floor, he'd radioed through what had happened.

The scenario had worked out perfectly. With the chaos of an armed federal fugitive on the loose somewhere inside a house full of tear gas, the HRT operators guarding the pair of tactical paramedics did what they were trained to do: remove the injured from the line of fire. Head and face covered by a balaclava, the face shield for the gas mask smeared with Karim's blood, Fletcher had allowed himself to be carried out of the house and into the waiting ambulance.

The only real exposure had come from his escape. Gawking drivers had seen him jump out of the back of the ambulance and run away dressed in a bright blue paramedic's jacket. Blood covered his hands and Jackman's black tactical trousers. He would need a change of clothing – and shoes. Running in the man's ill-fitting combat boots was not at all convenient or comfortable.

It would be foolish to assume the Toyota's owner would be returning sometime later this evening. Any vehicle reported stolen in the Cape May area would immediately be added to the police watch list. He would need to find another car to borrow.

Atlantic City, with its garish hotels and ample shopping choices, was close by.

Fletcher's thoughts turned back to Alexander Borgia. The man wanted Karim dead. Why?

The question hung in his mind, unanswered.

Let's talk about Theresa Herrera, Borgia had told Karim. *I understand you agreed to look into the disappearance of her son, Rico.*

Had Karim stumbled upon something that had triggered the FBI's interest?

The question hung in his mind, unanswered.

Fletcher didn't have his computers. The netbook and

other vital equipment were stored inside the Jaguar's trunk. His whole life was stored inside there.

Her knowledge of computers is frightening.

Karim's words regarding Emma White.

But could Fletcher trust her?

She's my adopted daughter, Karim had said. *She's aggressively loyal – she would fall on a sword to protect me.*

Safe now and driving under the bright sky, Fletcher stared at the highway exits, wondering which one to take. He was reminded of the Greek hero Odysseus, standing on his ship and watching the smoke of family fires visible on the shore of his home, Ithaca. Believing he was safe, Odysseus slept. While he did so, his companions cut open their master's ox-hide sack and, instead of the gold they had sought, found only King Aeolus's adverse winds, which drove Odysseus's ships across the leagues of ocean.

Malcolm Fletcher, forever homeless, contained one navigational rudder, and it directed him back to Baltimore.

59

Borgia stared at the empty gurney inside the back of the ambulance. He felt like he had just been kicked in the stomach.

So close, so goddamn close . . .

Federal agents from the New Jersey office were working in conjunction with local and state police to assist in the manhunt. The New York office had also been alerted and was coordinating efforts with their local law enforcement. Roadblocks were being set up at every tollbooth. Cars were being searched; local buildings were being searched. Any stolen car was being put on the watch list. Borgia had alerted the bureau's Media Office to get the news played on the radio and TV.

Almost an hour had passed since Fletcher's escape and so far nothing had come of it.

Borgia turned away from the ambulance. There was nothing more to do here. He had already been inside the hospital and spoken with the paramedic who had tended to Karim. Fletcher hadn't killed the man, had merely rendered him unconscious by squeezing off the carotid artery. Fletcher, it seemed, had waited to the last moment to do it too; wanting to make sure, Borgia suspected, that Karim had been stabilized.

Karim was still in surgery. According to one of the

ER nurses, he had suffered a lot of internal injuries, and lost a significant amount of blood. Nonetheless, Karim, was in very good hands.

Borgia had a long conversation with FBI Director Oberst on the way back to Karim's home. The man was understandably upset. It had been Oberst who had given the order to take down Ali Karim.

There was one silver lining: there was no recorded evidence of Special Agent Danny Jackman staging the crime scene. And then there was Karim. If he survived, no one would believe that Jackman had attacked him. The man had knowingly hidden a wanted fugitive, one who had then turned around and murdered a federal agent before escaping. The Bureau had Karim bang to rights on those two matters – and there were plenty of additional nails with which to hammer shut Karim's coffin. One of Karim's employees had been shot and killed, dumped in the trunk of a BMW conveniently parked inside the garage. Karim would have to answer for that – and he would have to explain the dried blood on the bed and rubbish bin inside the treatment room. Better for Karim to die on the operating table than face what was waiting for him if he survived.

Emergency Response Technicians from the New York field office were on their way down to process the evidence. A separate team armed with the proper warrants had been dispatched to search every square inch of Karim's Manhattan home.

SOC Cronin would take the hit for Fletcher's escape. Fletcher had slipped through his fingers. Borgia recommended to the Director that Cronin should be served up as bleeding meat for the media. The Director agreed, and Borgia spent the rest of their phone call strategizing the best way to spin the story.

Brandon Arkoff pinned Nathan Santiago's face against the operating table as Marie swivelled the light to the man's bare back. With her fingers she prodded the middle area between the shoulder blades – there it was.

Santiago flinched when he felt the scalpel. He tried to fight it but his wrists had been tied.

Another hit with the Taser settled him.

Marie picked up tweezers, reached inside the fresh incision and removed a glass capsule the size of a Tic Tac. She doubted the people who had abducted Santiago knew about the RFID tag, but she wasn't about to take any chances. She carried the tag to a wall-mounted steel table and smashed it with a hammer. She collected the fragments and washed them down the sink.

Brandon stepped up to her and said, 'The police could be on their way here.'

Marie shook her head as she washed her hands. Santiago moaned from the table.

'They can't find us,' she said.

'Why take the chance?'

'You know why. Santiago has a rare blood type. His first kidney went for two hundred thousand, and now we've got a buyer lined up to pay half a million for the other. The other buyers we have lined up –'

'I know what they're offering.'

'And you're willing to walk away from it?'

'We have more than enough money to survive.'

Marie dried her hands on her coat.

'Get him ready for surgery.'

'She's not going to do it,' Brandon said.

'I'll talk to her. Woman to woman.'

60

Fletcher had exchanged the Camry for a white BMW parked inside an Atlantic City hotel garage free of security cameras. He had also changed his appearance.

After ditching the blood-stained tactical trousers, he entered a hotel and washed up in the lobby's private bathroom. The small lobby shop offered a garish assortment of clothing. He purchased a roomy windbreaker with ATLANTIC CITY embossed on the back to hide his tactical belt and then ditched the jacket after purchasing several new items from a store that specialized in outdoor clothing and gear.

From a drugstore he purchased blond hair dye and a self-tanning lotion. He dyed his hair and eyebrows inside a gas-station bathroom, cleaned up, and was now back on the road, heading for Baltimore.

He dialled M's cell. When she didn't answer, he removed the battery.

Fletcher had tried to call her twice over the past hour and she hadn't answered.

He phoned again just as he was nearing Newark, and she picked up.

'The FBI has locked down Karim's home.' M's voice was cool, almost robotic. 'I couldn't get anywhere near it.'

The Jaguar had his prints all over it, hair and fibres.

The contact lenses stored in the console would contain his DNA. Locked in the trunk were his cases full of tools and equipment; more damning evidence against Karim – if they could get inside the car. Unless they found the hidden key, there was no way they could open the car. The windows were shatterproof.

M said, 'Karim's personal bodyguard, a man named Bar Lev, is at the hospital along with some other trusted people. I don't have an update for you – Karim is still in surgery. Karim's lawyer is there. He insisted on meeting me before he drove down to New Jersey. Karim had given him explicit instructions to hand-deliver a package to me in the event he died or was incapacitated in any way. I have two envelopes here with me, one of which belongs to you.

'Federal investigators are at our main office right now, armed with warrants. They're pulling security tapes, raiding the computer network, everything.'

'Did Karim give the evidence bag holding the drinking glass to the lab?'

'I have it here with me,' she said. 'I can't drop it off. I spotted three men trying to follow me. I think they're federal agents.'

'Where are they now?'

'I ditched their tail. They don't know where I am.'

'Where are you?'

'Someplace where they can't find me,' she said. 'Karim gave me explicit instructions to help you, and that's what I'm doing. He said to trust you implicitly, and that's what I'm doing. I know you removed your phone battery so I couldn't trace you, but I should tell you I've been assisting Karim in researching this . . . project, and I –'

'What about Dr Sin's cell signal?'

'Nothing.'

'Keep searching.' Fletcher hung up and removed the battery.

Marie Clouzot's heels echoed loudly as she walked across the wide, cavernous space of cold concrete inside the old printing press. Fractured sunlight filtered through the building's grated windows, the dank, frigid air smelling of rust and ancient machinery.

The light faded as she moved down a corridor of closed doors. She opened the last one.

The Asian doctor she'd found treating Santiago in New Jersey was sitting in the corner. Brandon had bound the tiny woman's wrists and ankles.

Marie, bending stiffly, removed the strip of duct tape covering the woman's mouth. 'Your driver's licence says your name is Dr Dara Sin.'

The woman didn't answer. She swallowed, shivering in the cold.

'I need you to perform some surgery for me, Dr Sin.'

'I can't help you.'

'Of course you can. You're a doctor. You've performed surgery before.'

'I can't. Look.' The woman turned to one side, and Marie saw the broken fingers.

Brandon hadn't done that. He had been careful

handling her – had made her comfortable before locking her inside the trunk next to Santiago.

'You broke your fingers,' Marie said, more to herself. She blinked at the sight, as though she could wash it away, and then snapped her head to the woman. 'You broke your *fingers.*'

'I can't help you,' Dr Sin said again, and Marie swore she saw the woman grin.

Marie gripped the woman's throat as a high-pitched keening roared past her gritted teeth. The doctor fought back, her bound limbs and wrists kicking and thrashing, but she had no place to go, and she was too small and too old to mount a fight. Marie, considerably taller and heavier, straddled the woman, choking her, slamming her small head against the floor. Marie felt the small crucifix on the thin gold chain bouncing against her chest. She didn't ask God for forgiveness. She had given up on that business a long time ago.

The cheap gold chain and crucifix, a gift from her mother, was a relic from a former life. A reminder of long months locked inside a caged room. Tears burning her eyes, she had prayed to God for help until her knees were callused. He had rejected her because He had decided she was not worthy of His love.

With the rejection had come a revelation: at age fifteen, she had discovered God did not care. The world, made in His divine image, contained no feeling or mercy. Men could rape and pillage and murder without consequence. God and His world didn't pause to grieve for the dead; they continued their deaf forward march.

But you had a choice. You could suffer in silence or you could find a way to cope.

The doctor finally relaxed. Marie kept her grip firm through the death spasms and then it was done.

Marie slumped back against the floor, sitting, her face flushed from the exertion.

Brandon was watching her from the doorway. The dim light coming from the hall behind him highlighted the worry etched on his face.

'Our assistant funeral director has left several messages on my phone,' he said. 'The Baltimore police are at the funeral home, asking questions. It's time to leave.'

'They can't find us here.'

Brandon, she could tell, wanted to fight her on this. But he had no fight left in him.

'You can go if you want,' she said, wrapping her arms around herself. 'I'm staying here.'

Brandon shoved his hands in his pockets, jingling his change and keys as he stared down at her from the doorway. Marie didn't stare back – she didn't want another argument, and she had made up her mind. It wasn't a foolish decision, deciding to stay here. She was safe. She could stay here as long as she wanted, tucked in this womb of concrete half buried beneath the earth. There was no reason to leave, not yet.

Brandon cleared his throat. 'How much longer?' he asked, his question barely above a whisper.

'Until I'm satisfied,' Marie said, wondering if such a thing was possible.

61

Fletcher was closing in on Baltimore, the winter sky beginning its rapid shift into darkness, when he replaced the BlackBerry's battery and called M.

She didn't give him a chance to speak. 'The Feds have accessed Karim's computer network. I need to shut down, and we need to meet so I can show you the videos.'

'What videos?'

'The ones taken inside Karim's New Jersey beach home,' M said. 'I saw what happened to Karim, to Boyd Paulson and Nathan Santiago, all of it.'

Fletcher sat up in his seat. 'The security software on the laptop in the panic room wasn't set to record video,' he said.

'Correct. You set that software to record, and the hard drive fills up quickly.'

'Then how did you come by these videos?'

'I disabled the security software and replaced it with my own – a program that runs in the background. Any time a camera's motion tracker detects movement, the recording starts, and the video images are temporarily stored on the computer's hard drive before this program that I wrote compresses the files and uploads them to an FTP server, where they can be downloaded and viewed. That way we have copies in case a laptop is removed from a panic room, or damaged.'

'Sound?'

'Inside the house, yes, but not outside,' she said. 'I heard the entire conversation between Borgia and Karim. I saw what transpired inside the treatment room. How you intervened and saved Mr Karim's life.'

'What happened to Santiago?'

'A man took him and placed him in the backseat of a Lincoln Town Car – the same man who shot Boyd Paulson inside the garage. The man has some sort of facial disfigurement.'

'And Dr Sin?'

'The man pulled a gun on her inside the treatment room. Then he trussed her and placed her in the trunk of the Lincoln.'

'Alive?'

'Alive. Hold on.'

On the other end of the line Fletcher heard the tap of computer keys. He thought about Santiago and the doctor. They were alive when they were taken, but *where* had they been taken?

Then he thought about the netbook. It contained the information downloaded from Corrigan's phone – addresses and phone numbers, GPS data. The netbook was locked inside the Jaguar's trunk, and he had no way to access it.

M came on the line and said, 'The Feds just found the FTP site, but they won't find the video files. I erased everything.'

'There's always a trace.'

'Not if you know what you're doing.' For the first time Fletcher heard a note of anger in her voice. 'Trust me, they won't find a bloody thing on the laptop *or* the server. I need to shut down and get going. What else do you need me to do?'

'See what you can find out about Alexander Borgia.'

'I've already started,' she said. 'Now, when and where do you want to meet?'

III

The Wages of Fear

62

The bureaucratic powers working overtime at FBI headquarters had been convinced by its Media Office that it would be wise to get in front of the Malcolm Fletcher story before the story got in front of them. A targeted national media campaign would not only be the best way to spin the story, it would also be the most effective way to flush out the fugitive from hiding.

The Bureau's top media experts crafted a succinct press release. The terse paragraphs, along with a handful of accompanying colour photographs of the former profiler they had on file, were released to every major newspaper before press time. Then they went to work on devising commercials that would run in heavy saturation on the daytime shows. They had used this same strategy, to great success, to apprehend another fugitive.

The Bureau focused on the surrounding Tri-State area and then shifted its efforts to New England, an area Malcolm Fletcher seemed to favour, based on reported and confirmed sightings. In the past, such an aggressive campaign would take days; now, thanks to the Internet and its high-speed delivery system, the task took only a few hours.

New York, New Jersey, Boston and Connecticut field

offices personally hand-delivered media packets to all taxi and rental-car companies, stressing the significant reward being offered for information leading to the former profiler's capture.

The Bureau knew Ali Karim had been aiding and abetting a fugitive inside his home in Cape May, New Jersey. Agents had found a lead-shielded panic room hidden behind a false-wall installed inside the closet. At some point Malcolm Fletcher had emerged, broken Daniel Jackman's neck and then, after dressing in the agent's tactical clothing, thrown Jackman inside the closet. Agents had also discovered Fletcher's overcoat, shoes and a suit jacket.

The Bureau decided to keep this information from the public. At the moment, Karim was lying in a coma; if the man woke up, they could use it as a bargaining chip to get him to open up about his connection to Fletcher, as little was known about the former profiler's movements over the past two decades.

The Bureau's public-relations experts argued that the public would want to know why – and how – the former profiler kept eluding capture. To show that the Bureau's interest and determination in apprehending one of their own hadn't lapsed or diminished, it was decided that Alexander Borgia should act as the Bureau's face. He was a natural choice, they said. Borgia had a commanding voice and, despite his short stature, carried a lot of presence. With significant media training already under his belt, he could handle any question thrown at him and spin it effectively.

Borgia was informed of the Bureau's decision shortly before midnight: FBI Director Oberst had telephoned him over an encrypted line. They spent much of the conversation discussing the laptop found inside Karim's well-crafted panic room.

Borgia had examined the computer himself. The security software had not been set to record, and the hard drive contained no video images. Forensic analysis by computer techs from New York's Evidence Response Team revealed, however, that this was not the case.

Karim had installed motion-activated security cameras inside the fire alarms of his New Jersey home. Once a camera was triggered, it started to record; the video images were temporarily stored on the hard drive. Then, a separate program on the laptop uploaded the video files to a secured FTP site on one of Karim's servers before erasing them.

Examination of the laptop's hard drive confirmed that video footage had been captured inside the house during a 48-hour period, uploaded to an FTP site, then downloaded and erased from the server during a single session the previous afternoon, starting at 12.34 p.m. Using sophisticated software, the ERT geeks had discovered the location from which the FTP site had been accessed — a four-unit townhouse in Brooklyn. Malcolm Fletcher hadn't downloaded the files. There was no way he could have reached the townhouse in time.

Agents forced their way inside the townhouse and found the first three units empty of furniture. The unit on the top floor contained computers and illegal equipment that allowed a user to trace a cellular signal. A forensics team was currently working on processing the rooms for prints, DNA, hair and fibres. New York agents were investigating who owned the Brooklyn building while ERT tried to break into the computers. Everything had been password protected with a sophisticated encryption algorithm. The geeks were working methodically to try to break it, afraid of tripping some sort of digital landmine that would permanently erase or destroy the computer's hard drive.

Borgia had already interviewed two of the seven employees who regularly worked out of Karim's Manhattan home. Borgia was more interested in the young woman who had been aboard Karim's private plane: Emma White. Agents watching Karim's Manhattan home had spotted the woman and her shock of white hair entering the house at 6.36 a.m. She left at 8.43 – with a package, a large yellow mailer. The three agents who had tailed her had lost her somewhere in the subway system. The woman hadn't returned to Karim's home, the Brooklyn townhouse or her apartment.

FBI Director Oberst gave Borgia his personal phone numbers. The Director wanted to be updated every two hours on the progress of the investigation. Neither Oberst nor Borgia discussed what would happen if video footage of a Hostage Rescue Team operator planting a knife at a crime scene made its way on to the news or, worse, the Internet.

*

The first stop on Borgia's media blitz was the ABC office building. After his appearance on *Good Morning America*, he would be shuffled off to do an interview for *60 Minutes*. The popular CBS-owned programme agreed to run a profile on Malcolm Fletcher that would air the following Sunday. Borgia's afternoon would be spent at Fox News. The Bureau's media experts were currently locked in a heated debate about which Fox News programme had the better ratings.

At 7 a.m., Borgia sat down for his first interview, conducted by the always affable and courteous host Dan Harris. Manhattanites hustling through the cold streets surrounding Times Square saw the interview being played on the massive LED screens prominently displayed on the front of the ABC building.

Borgia sat down looking sharp and confident. His media escorts had prepped him about the importance of body language, and they had provided him with a new wardrobe. The suit-and-tie combination chosen for this interview had colours that, according to extensive research, projected warmth and trust.

High-definition was not kind to Borgia. The pancake makeup gave his skin an unflattering orange tint; it did a poor job at hiding the dark and puffy circles underneath his tired eyes. Despite his exhaustion, Borgia spoke clearly, and well.

'The task force assigned to find and apprehend Malcolm Fletcher received and acted on a credible tip. I can't get into specifics about what happened or how he escaped – our investigation is still ongoing – but I can tell you that the evidence we've uncovered at this stage suggests that Malcolm Fletcher, in addition to killing one of Ali Karim's employees, a man named Boyd Paulson, attempted to kill Karim himself before fleeing.'

Dan Harris raised an eyebrow, nodding. 'I understand he also killed a member of the Hostage Rescue Team.'

'That's incorrect. We deployed gas into the house. One of our Hostage Team officers rushed up the steps to the first floor, and, because he couldn't see clearly, made a wrong turn and fell over a banister. He landed the wrong way and was killed instantly.' Borgia sighed, then added with real emotion: 'It was an unfortunate accident, and our thoughts and prayers are with the man's family.'

'The victim, Ali Karim, is a well-known security expert and has an office here in New York. Why did Malcolm Fletcher target him?'

'We haven't ascertained why Malcolm Fletcher targeted him or his employees,' Borgia said. 'Our investigation is in the preliminary stages.'

'Tell us about Malcolm Fletcher.'

'He's not an ordinary criminal. Before he became a federal agent, he trained as a Navy SEAL. He has considerable talents, especially in the area of surveillance and counter-surveillance – training which has assisted him in eluding law enforcement. He's also a polyglot – he speaks multiple languages, which has allowed him live abroad and blend in without arousing suspicion.'

'You've called him – and I quote – a rare combination of sociopath and psychopath.'

Borgia nodded. 'Because of his background and training in psychology, he managed to evade detection by our screening process. That gives you an indication of just how highly intelligent he is. People who knew him described him as a loner – and emotionally impenetrable.

'While he worked as a profiler, he was suspected of murdering mass murderers and serial killers – cases he was working on. When the Bureau discovered what he was doing, we sent three agents to his home to question him.'

'And what happened?'

'Fletcher attacked them. One agent is still on life-support.'

'And the other two agents?'

'We don't know what happened to them,' Borgia said. 'They disappeared.'

'And during all these years as a fugitive, what has he been up to, do you know?'

'Fletcher has become, in his own right, a very dangerous serial killer. As long as he's out there, no one is safe. We need the public's help to find him. The federal government is offering a three-million-dollar reward to the person offering information leading to Fletcher's capture and arrest.'

'This picture we're about to show, is it a recent picture?'

'This is the last picture we have of him. Before

313

Fletcher disappeared, he had taken the extraordinary steps of erasing all information about himself from the Bureau – this happened before computers and databases were as prevalent as they are today. Everything existed on paper.

'Malcolm Fletcher has one distinguishing characteristic, as you're about to see,' Borgia said. 'One that's impossible to disguise.'

63

Malcolm Fletcher's face appeared on the LED screens overlooking Times Square. The picture showed him with short black hair and a face composed of chiselled-granite angles. He wasn't wearing contact lenses. His strange, black eyes stared down at the surrounding streets.

Many people stopped to watch. Others shivered and turned away, quickening their pace.

Dan Harris's voice spoke over Malcolm Fletcher's photograph: 'Explain the man's eyes, what happened?'

'We honestly don't know,' Borgia said. 'Unfortunately, there's nothing on file in Bureau records as to the nature of this medical condition. The specialists we spoke with are divided. Some believe it's either ocular melanocytosis or pigment-dispersion syndrome, both congenital diseases which cause an unusual dispersion of dark pigmentation in the eyes. There's also ocular siderosis, caused by iron toxicity. The lack of colour in the eyes could simply be an aberrant genetic mutation.'

'A birth defect, in other words.'

'A rare, one-of-a-kind birth defect.' Borgia paused for emphasis, then continued. 'This defect will allow us to find him.'

'What about contact lenses?'

'It's a possibility. However, when he worked for the Bureau, he made no effort to disguise his condition. Another former profiler told us that Fletcher said he was allergic to contacts. If Fletcher is, in fact, wearing contacts they'll be specially made ones that cover the *entire* eye. We've seen some created by Hollywood prop makers, and even the best ones can't mimic the human eye – the tiny blood vessels, etcetera. If you get close enough, you can see that they're fake.'

'Let's read off that toll-free number.'

A small crowd of scrawny Goth teenagers dressed in black leather jackets and hoodies had gathered across the street from ABC's massive LED screens. Heavily tattooed and pierced, they pounded cans of Red Bull in between chain-smoking cigarettes to counter the downing effects of alcohol and ecstasy. T. J., a reedy man with a blue Mohawk and pierced lips, was the first to speak: 'Jesus, that dude's a freak.'

The man standing near by glanced in his direction. T. J. couldn't see the eyes. Dude was wearing sunglasses.

T. J. looked away, feeling his scrotum tightening. He had noticed the guy coming out of the coffee shop. Something about the dude gave off this, like, primal reaction that made T. J. want to turn and start walking in the opposite direction – quickly.

Maybe it was the guy's size. Dude was built like a brick shithouse – tall and ferociously solid underneath that stylish John Varvatos look he was rocking: scuffed black boots with a grey tie worn against a chambray shirt; a black scarf wrapped loosely around his neck.

He wore black leather gloves and a fedora that gave him that cool and edgy New York artist look.

The only woman in the group stared at the picture of Malcolm Fletcher on the TV screens and said, 'I think he's kind of hot.'

'Hold up,' another man said. 'You think this guy's *good looking*?'

'He's got a sexy face,' she said. 'Strong jaw and nice cheekbones. I'm just saying.'

T. J. saw the big dude with the sunglasses dump his coffee into a bin and start to walk towards them. T. J. waved a hand to shut up his friends.

The stranger stepped up next to them. 'Excuse me,' he said with some sort of accent – British, maybe. 'I was wondering if I might take a quick look at that.' He pointed to the *New York Times* tucked underneath the girl's arm.

'You can have it,' she said. 'I just buy it for the Books section.'

The man thanked her and wished them all a good day. T. J. breathed a sigh of relief when the dude walked away.

Malcolm Fletcher didn't have to hunt for the story. The *New York Times* had printed his headshot above the fold so the news of his escape wouldn't be missed. His picture covered nearly a quarter of the paper. The title read 'American Nightmare'.

The story was long on speculation and short of facts; it reeked of bureaucratic rote. The Bureau's PR executives were working overtime to spin the botched raid.

The last paragraph encapsulated the same lies Alexander Borgia had spouted on that morning's TV programme: 'Malcolm Fletcher defies characterization, at least in any textbook sense. On one hand, he's a very clever and highly intelligent sociopath who lacks any sense of moral responsibility or social conscience. He's also an extremely cunning and manipulative psychopath. He's unable to feel normal human emotions such as love and empathy.'

Fletcher made his way up Seventh Avenue, heading for Central Park. On his way into the city, he had changed into clothing more suited to walking around New York during daylight. The old clothing went inside a department-store bag, which he had tossed into a dumpster. The tactical belt went inside the new backpack. After ditching the white BMW by the side of a busy street, he had wandered for the good part of an hour before finding a suitable vehicle to take him to New York. He had ditched that one inside a parking lot a few blocks away.

Fletcher checked his watch. He had plenty of time.

He found a department store and quickly purchased the clothing he needed. He declined the shopping bag; instead, he neatly folded the clothing inside his backpack.

Inside a drugstore he purchased two disposable, precharged cell phones with sixty minutes of talk time, a mail folder, a marker pen and a copy of *Newsweek*. He found a diner, sat in a quiet corner and activated both phones. He wrote his number on M's phone and sealed it inside the mailer.

After breakfast, Fletcher continued up Seventh Avenue. He turned right on to Central Park South and entered the busy lobby of the New York Athletic Club. The older gentleman standing behind the reception smiled pleasantly, eager to help.

'One of your members, Emma White, asked me to deliver this to the front desk,' Fletcher said, and placed the sealed mailer on the countertop. 'She asked that you place it inside her mail box.'

'Certainly, sir.'

Fletcher left and stood by the lobby windows. Five minutes later, he looked across the street and saw M waiting in the prearranged spot.

64

M sat on the bleached-stone wall surrounding Central Park, her head tucked down as she examined her cell phone. She wore a bulky winter parka with nylon leggings and trainers. A pair of oval sunglasses covered her eyes. The strap of a gym bag was draped across her shoulder, the signal that she hadn't been followed.

Still, Fletcher needed to be sure she was clean. He placed the copy of *Newsweek* flat on top of the folded newspaper and held them in his right hand as he exited the building. He crossed the street, dodging his way around a parked horse and carriage offering a scenic tour of the city, and walked past her. He dropped the newspaper and magazine into a kerbside bin and strode away. He didn't turn to watch her.

He moved to a grouping of pull-cart pavement vendors, their green-and-white carts and umbrellas advertising the same slogan: KEEP OUR PARKS CLEAN. He wandered a few feet away to another group of vendors selling cheaply framed pictures of Manhattan. He perused the selections, tracking time in his head.

When fifteen minutes had passed, Fletcher sat on the wall and pretended to check messages on his smartphone. Behind his sunglasses he watched the entrance to the New York Athletic Club.

At the twenty-minute mark M came through the front doors, dressed in new attire: black yoga pants and a different pair of trainers. A bulky grey hoodie covered her white hair. Another pair of sunglasses concealed her eyes. She moved to the corner to hail a cab.

Fletcher watched the area closely.

It took her five minutes to get a cab. It pulled away and he kept watching.

He waited another ten minutes.

She was clean.

Fletcher stood and then went to hail a cab of his own. He had to wait nearly twenty minutes.

Climbing into the back, he leaned forward and gave the driver an address in the Howard Beach area in Queens. On the passenger's seat he saw stapled pages showing his Most Wanted picture and the three-million-dollar reward for information leading to his capture.

Traffic was mercifully slow; he wouldn't reach his destination for quite some time. He leaned sideways across the backseat, closed his eyes and dozed. He came awake sometime later to the trill of his disposable cell.

Fletcher glanced at his watch as he reached into his pocket. A little over an hour had passed.

'I'm clean,' M said. 'I'm on the Long Island Expressway, driving a black Cadillac Escalade with tinted windows.

I borrowed it from a friend. It has no connection to Karim's company. Now tell me where I'm heading.'

Fletcher gave her the address. 'Call me when you arrive,' he said and hung up.

Forty minutes later, Fletcher arrived at his destination. He paid the driver in cash, along with a generous tip, and exited the cab.

The exterior of the Bayside Motel was still the same drab stucco he'd first seen decades ago, but the interior had been renovated. It had a dimly lit lobby and the owner had tried to brighten it up with silk flowers placed inside wicker baskets.

The motel still catered to budget-conscious clientele, the majority of whom appeared to be foreigners. Even better, a young staff manned the reception desk. In his experience, this wired generation, plugged into their phones, iPods and computers, barely looked beyond their constant texts, emails and phone calls to examine the world around them. They rarely read the newspapers or watched the news – a fact evidenced by the dwindling subscriptions and news ratings that continued their precipitous slide month after month, year after year.

The young woman behind the front desk had long, clean brown hair that carried a lingering trace of coconut. Fletcher spoke in broken English, his accent clearly suggesting he had travelled there from France. He explained he had been mugged during the early-morning hours and had just returned from the hospital.

He didn't have a reservation but enquired about a room, possibly one on the ground floor so he wouldn't have to climb any stairs.

The woman, sympathetic to his plight, checked for vacancies. Fletcher checked the lobby for security cameras. He didn't find any, but behind the front desk he found a colour picture of himself resting on a computer-printer tray.

The woman had a ground-floor room available. She insisted on a licence and credit card. He gave her the passport for Richard Munchel and insisted on paying in cash. She agreed, and gave him a plastic keycard. Fletcher thanked her in his mangled English and courteously declined the porter's offer to assist him to his room.

On the bed he placed the clothing he'd purchased in Manhattan. He took a shower and redressed in the same clothing but exchanged his fedora for a woolly hat. He tucked his sunglasses inside his jacket pocket and put on a pair of glasses with tinted lenses dark enough to hide his eyes.

From his backpack he removed a small digital recorder and placed it underneath the bed. He took the backpack with him and left the hotel.

Cross Bay Boulevard was heavy with fast-moving traffic on both sides. He waited for a break, crossed and then made his way to a diner. He sat at the counter and drank coffee as he read the *New York Post*. His picture had also made their front page, printed under the banner title 'Disgraceful!' The *Post* had decided to focus on the botched raid, citing the FBI's inability to catch fugitives, Malcolm Fletcher being the latest example.

From his seat Fletcher had a clear, unobstructed view of the motel. He had started in on his third cup of coffee when the disposable cell rang.

65

Fletcher brought the phone up to his car as he watched a black Cadillac Escalade with tinted windows pull into the motel parking lot.

'Are you inside the motel?' M asked.

'Ground floor, Room 7.'

She hung up. Fletcher watched her step out of the SUV holding a different gym bag. She had changed her appearance again: a black motorcycle jacket with jeans and black boots. The New York Yankees baseball cap she wore low across her face covered most of her hair, her eyes hidden behind a pair of aviator-style sunglasses.

She disappeared inside the motel. If the FBI had her under surveillance and had managed to follow her here, they would make their move now. They would surround the motel and go in armed. Fletcher left the money for the bill on the counter.

Outside, he moved to the back of the diner and then threaded his way through parked cars and dumpsters until he reached the alley next to a bait-and-tackle shop closed for the winter season. He watched the motel from the alley. If anything happened, he had plenty of avenues of escape.

Minutes passed and no vehicles entered the motel parking lot.

His phone rang and he didn't answer it.

Fletcher's well-honed instincts told him she hadn't been tailed. But the FBI *had* found her townhouse address, and, for all he knew, they had also found her. For all he knew, she had been apprehended and Alexander Borgia had offered her a deal: give him up and Karim would be spared prosecution. For all he knew, she had taken the deal in order to protect the person she loved and trusted the most.

Unlikely, yes, but not outside the realms of possibility. Fletcher had survived all these years by living by one simple law: trust no one. He did not know M, and he did not share Karim's ability to trust. There was too much riding on this next part.

His phone rang again and he answered it.

'Where are you?' she demanded.

'On the bed you'll find clothing that I purchased for you. I had to estimate your sizes, so you'll forgive me if they don't fit properly. After you put them on, I want you to dump your clothing inside the bathtub and turn on the water. Hold the phone up to the water so I can hear it running.'

'You think I'm working with the Feds?' She sounded more confused than angry. 'You think I have some sort of GPS or tracking –'

'A man in my position has to be very careful. I'm sure you understand.'

No answer.

She had hung up.

Fletcher did not call her back. If she didn't call him back, he would have to move on without her.

He'd give her ten minutes.

Six minutes later, his phone rang.

'I changed into the clothes you left,' she said. 'The clothes I wore here are in the tub. Listen.' He heard running water and then she came back on the line. 'What's next?'

'Leave everything inside the room – wallet, car keys, gym bag.'

'There are things I have to give you from Karim's lawyer.'

'Leave everything on the bed. Call a cab and come out wearing nothing but the clothes I purchased for you.'

'Where am I going now?'

'To the Clarion Inn on West Elm Street. Wait for me inside the lobby.'

'How do I know you're coming?'

'You don't,' Fletcher said, and hung up.

He memorized the makes, models and locations of the cars parked in the motel lot and alongside the road. The cab came fifteen minutes later. M stepped out of the motel wearing the clothes he had purchased for her – sandals, bright blue fleece-lined sweatpants and a matching sweatshirt. She couldn't run in sandals.

The cab pulled away. He left the alley and walked around the boulevard, watching the motel. He ducked into several shops. Slowly he made his way through the back streets around the motel and kept watching. Nothing changed, nothing happened.

Finally, after an hour of surveillance, he went back to his room.

M had dumped her clothes inside the bathtub and filled it with water. He sorted through them and went to the bed. She had laid out the items very neatly – her car keys, a leather wallet with a money clip that could easily fit inside a pocket, and a compact SIG SAUER. The package from Karim's lawyer was sealed. Fletcher opened it, found ten thousand dollars in cash and a new pair of contact lenses that matched a passport and Washington licence for Francis Harvey. The handwritten note Karim had included contained all the necessary information to access an account set up at a Cayman Island bank.

Inside the gym bag he found a netbook computer and a CD tucked inside a jewel case.

Fletcher removed a pair of headphones from his backpack and connected the audio jack into an RF Bug Detector. The palm-sized unit used by the government could detect phone taps, hidden cameras, eavesdropping devices, cell-phone bugs and GPS trackers in a range up to 9GHz.

Fletcher scanned the items left on the bed. They were clean.

He placed the car keys inside his pocket. Everything went inside the backpack, except the contacts. He put those on in the bathroom.

Fletcher collected the recorder he had placed underneath the bed. He plugged the audio jack for the headphones into the recorder, turned up the volume and pressed PLAY. He heard Emma White moving through the room and then listened to their phone conversations. He heard her slip out of her clothes and he heard her run the bathwater and call the cab. She didn't call or speak to anyone else.

Fletcher hung the 'Do Not Disturb' sign on the doorknob and left the motel, slipping on his sunglasses. When he reached the Cadillac Escalade, he discreetly checked the outside for a GPS tracker. The bug detector did not go off. Next he checked the interior. The bug detector did not go off. The car was clean.

The hotel where he'd sent M had a parking lot in the back. Fletcher pulled into the nearly empty lot and checked to make sure he had an escape route. There was a road near the dumpster. He parked, left the engine running and loaded the CD into the netbook.

66

Four video files had been burned on to the compact disk. The first one was footage from the treatment room. Fletcher skipped it for the moment, wanting to watch the video taken from the security camera positioned inside the garage.

Boyd Paulson walked across the driveway, heading for the BMW. He popped the trunk. Then a figure appeared from around the outside corner of the garage. Boyd had turned to the sound and was shot in the head.

Fletcher paused the video. Then he clicked through each frame, stopping when he had a good view of the shooter's face – not the woman from Colorado but a man. The woman's partner, Fletcher suspected. The man was roughly the same size as Boyd – five foot ten – but he was wider. Fatter. The left side of the shooter's face . . . something was wrong with it. Fletcher couldn't see anything specific. The man was too far away from the camera, and there wasn't enough light.

Fletcher found out on the third video, the one showing the fat man rushing into the treatment room and apprehending Dr Sin at gunpoint.

The man had been in some sort of accident; what

remained was a face drawn by Picasso – a jagged, scarred mess of severed nerves that resulted in a sagging eyelid and a permanent crooked grin. He bound Dr Sin with zip ties and carried Nathan Santiago out of the room.

The final video showed Santiago being loaded into the backseat of the Lincoln. The disfigured man made a return trip inside the house. He came back with Dr Sin and placed her gently inside the trunk – gently because the man knew the woman was a doctor, and he needed her to remove Nathan Santiago's organs. If that was true – and Fletcher suspected it was – the disfigured man and his partner, the woman in the fur coat, were holed up somewhere.

Fletcher called M.

'Meet me in the hotel parking lot,' he said, and hung up.

Here she came. She did not run, even though she shivered in the cold wind. He found the car controls and turned up the heat.

M slid into the roomy passenger's seat and kept her body pressed close to the door. Her eyes were cold, but not from anger.

He didn't drive away. He turned slightly in his seat and said, 'You left your sidearm on the bed, but not your knife.'

'What knife?'

'The one you carry with you at all times. The one tucked underneath your left-hand sleeve.'

She tilted her head. 'How did you know?'

'The fine scars on your palms and wrists. Give it to me handle-first please.'

'No.'

'Do you want to help Karim?'

'What kind of question is that?'

'Give me the knife and you'll find out.'

M stared at him for a moment before dipping a hand inside her sleeve. She displayed no emotion at being found out.

She came back with a Smith & Wesson Special Operation Bowie knife with a black aluminium handle and a seven-inch black stainless-steel blade. She placed it handle-first against his waiting palm.

'Thank you,' he said. 'How long have you been practising Bowie knife-fighting?'

'Only a few months.'

'Please lean forward and place your hands on the dashboard.'

'I'm not wired.'

'I need to be sure.'

'No.'

'Then you can't help Karim. Goodbye.'

Fletcher opened his door, about to step out, when she said, 'Wait.'

He shut the door. M did not lean forward. She pulled the sweatshirt over her head and dumped it on the floor. Then she slipped out of her sweatpants. Every inch of her body was exposed. No wire, just smooth skin and a slight puckered scar on her left shoulder.

She showed no sense of self-consciousness at being nude. Nor should she. M had worked exceptionally hard on her body.

'Satisfied?'

'Very much so,' Fletcher said. 'My apologies for having put you through this. You'll understand my reasons momentarily.'

67

Fletcher divided his attention between the road and the SUV's rearview and side mirrors. While he felt confident that they were safe, he needed to remain vigilant.

M had finished getting dressed. She sat with her palms flat on her thighs and stared out of the front window with that impenetrable glare that hid her emotions. Her mind, he knew, was very active.

'Where are we going?'

Fletcher didn't answer.

'I don't like surprises,' she said.

Of course you don't, Fletcher thought.

He needed to address it. Now.

'Your rating,' he said. 'What is it?'

She cocked her head towards him.

'During CARS testing, you were given a rating,' he said. 'What is it?'

Her face was a blank mask, but he'd caught the fury building in her eyes at having been found out.

'Childhood Autism Rating Scale,' he said. 'The diagnostic tool measures –'

'I bloody well know what it is. What did Karim tell you?'

'He didn't. He would never betray a confidence.'

That seemed to relax something inside her. 'Then who told you?'

'You did.'

Fletcher didn't elaborate, wanting her to ask the questions so she could control the flow of information, process and store it. The autistic mind demanded order.

'How did – what gave me away?'

'The way you kept your distance on the plane when you shook my hand,' Fletcher said. 'The way you're keeping your distance from me right now by keeping your body pressed up against the car door. Like all autistics, you're aggressively protective of your personal space. And you abhor physical contact – you undressed rather than allowing me to touch you.'

'I don't like being touched by people I don't know.'

'When I called and told you about what happened to Karim, your tone was calm and neutral in the way all autistics discuss emotional matters.'

'I was focused on helping him – on helping you.'

'You have a difficult time maintaining eye contact even though I'm wearing sunglasses. You walked to the car instead of running because you're in a new setting and need time to absorb it so you don't overload your senses. And there's your insistence on knowing our exact destination.'

M was no longer looking at him. She was staring out of the window, her gaze darting over the houses and street signs.

'There's no reason to feel ashamed,' he said.

'I'm not. Are you ashamed of the way your eyes look, Mr Fletcher?'

'I wish they were different. It would make my life much simpler, but there's nothing I can do to change it.'

'I don't wish to change what I am, and I'm certainly not ashamed of *who* I am.'

'I wasn't suggesting you should be. You're quite adept at handling emotional regulation. I suspect people don't know you're autistic.'

'They don't. People think I'm cold. Different. I choose to be private. And, regardless of what my tone says, I do care about Karim.'

'Of that I have no doubt, Miss White.'

'Don't call me that. I'm not anyone's "miss".'

'What's Karim's condition?'

'He's in a coma,' she said. 'His personal physician is there, in New Jersey. He wants to move Karim to Manhattan.'

'When?'

'Sometime later today. Possibly tomorrow. I have no intention of turning you in, if that's what you're wondering.'

'I believe you.'

'I would hope so.'

M kept studying the landscape, memorizing signs and routes. She kept squeezing her knees. *A coping mechanism*, Fletcher thought.

'Forty-six point eight,' she said. 'That's where I fell on the CARS scale.'

Her words carried a sharp edge, as though she'd never been able to dislodge herself completely from the diagnosis.

'The number is complete bollocks,' she said. 'It says I'm incapable of functioning in social situations, incapable of forming or maintaining relationships. I have friends, I've had a number of satisfying sexual relationships, and I don't shy away from social situations. I can hold a conversation. I've learned through reading textbooks and from experience to pick up nuances in speech and body language so I can mirror social situations. And I can speak about myself when I feel it's appropriate, like now.'

But not without great effort, Fletcher thought. Even equipped with all her textbook knowledge and hard-learned experiences, each day she had to fight her way through an alien land plagued with people autistics called neurotypicals. He suspected she lived in a constant state of exhaustion.

Clearly M fell into the high-functioning category on the autism spectrum. Clearly what saved her from a life of complete isolation and loneliness was a high intelligence quotient.

'I've answered your questions, and now I want you to answer mine,' she said. 'Is it true what they're saying about you on the telly and in the papers?'

'Which part?'

'They said you killed three agents sent to arrest you.'

'They weren't federal agents.'

'Who were they?'

'CIA operatives skilled in wet work. They were dispatched to make me disappear.'

M turned in her seat and gave him her full attention. She was watching his face very closely now.

'Tell me,' she said. 'Tell me everything.'

68

The unique psychodynamics and wiring of the autistic brain demanded structure and clarity. Fletcher took a moment to gather his thoughts.

'When the Behavioral Analysis Unit was first established,' he said, 'we were working with a number of psychiatrists who specialized in violent crime. They were assisting us in developing our profiling methods. While interviewing incarcerated serial killers and mass murderers, we learned that, in addition to being overwhelmingly male, they all exhibited certain key traits during childhood.'

'Broken and abusive homes, bedwetting, torturing animals, etcetera.'

Fletcher nodded. 'A good majority also had neurological impairments from past trauma. It changed their brain chemistry. In a few rare cases, their brains had been formed that way in the womb.

'While working as a profiler, I discovered that Behavioral Analysis was engaged in classified research, something called the BMP – the Behavioral Modification Project. Three psychiatric hospitals were involved. They sifted through lists of juvenile offenders in their respective cities and towns and with the help of Behavioral Analysis identified those young males who exhibited traits associated with serial killers and mass murderers. The stated goal was to remove these potential killers from their environment and give them access to therapy and medical resources, education and, later, employment opportunities that were unavailable in their former existence – all of it funded by federal dollars.

'In reality, BMP was using these young men to test a vaccine being developed to eliminate, or at least curb, male violence and aggression.'

'The profiling unit was involved in human medical testing?' M asked.

'Not the entire unit. The director of Behavioral Analysis at the time was involved, along with three other agents. There were also a number of high-ranking agents within the Bureau who were profiting from the testing.'

'Profiting?'

'A vaccine that would curb or eliminate violence would be worth billions of dollars to the drug company that could successfully manufacture it. They paid handsome sums of money to the three hospitals providing the patients.'

'You mean guinea pigs,' she said.

Fletcher nodded. 'The agents involved doctored paperwork so the patients would never be found. They were generously compensated.'

'Were you involved?'

'No. I discovered what was going on by accident.'

'Did this vaccine work?'

'No. All the patients died.'

'How many?'

'Dozens, possibly hundreds,' he said. 'I was never able to find out an exact number.'

M digested this for a moment.

Then she said, 'Go on.'

'The test subjects were carefully selected so their deaths wouldn't raise any questions. The paperwork was doctored in advance, and after a patient died his medical file was transferred from one facility to another. With no one looking out for these young men, these mass murders were washed away in tides of bureaucratic paperwork.'

'And the bodies?'

'We never found them.'

'We? Another agent was helping you?'

'No,' Fletcher said. 'Karim was helping me. I helped him on a . . . private matter a long time ago. He said if I ever needed a favour, I should call him. After the three psychiatric hospitals associated with the BMP shut down, I asked Karim to discreetly search for evidence. Two of the hospitals were set in private, wooded areas. He hired forensic archaeologists to study the topography for burial sites. Nothing came of it.'

'What about the parents? Surely one of them must have —'

'Most of the patients were orphans. Wards of the state. Of those who did have *a* parent, the mother or father wanted nothing more to do with their trouble-some son. No one wanted these young men, and no one came looking for them after they died.'

'That's . . .' She didn't finish the thought.

'Barbaric?' Fletcher prompted.

'I was going to say ghoulish.'

'History gives us examples at every turn,' Fletcher said. 'Let's take your British government – their child-migration scheme. The British wanted to dispose of those members of society who would be a drain on their financial system, so they rounded up thousands of poor and orphaned children and shipped them off to Catholic monasteries in Australia. The Aussies received free slave labour, and the orphans were treated to decades of sexual abuse, beatings and death.'

'That happened in the early 1800s.'

'And continued well into the mid-1800s, when the Children's Friend Society continued to send vagrant children to Australia and Canada,' Fletcher said. 'The truth wasn't made public until 1987, when a British author and social worker took it upon herself to launch an independent investigation. And then we have the esteemed myrmecologist, psychiatrist and eugenicist, Auguste Forel, who, in the thirties, convinced Swiss officials to adopt a racial-hygiene law. Over sixty thousand women were sterilized. Hitler later adopted a similar eugenic law, and we know what occurred there. Here in America we have the Tuskegee syphilis experiment in the thirties, where the United States Public Health Service infected nearly four hundred impoverished black sharecroppers with syphilis. Voltaire said, "History doesn't repeat itself – man does."'

'Voltaire?'

Fletcher sighed. 'Never mind,' he said. 'The British government hid their sins, just as the American government used its vast influence and powers to hide the Behavioral Modification Project. I was in the process of collecting the necessary information to expose what was happening when the three aforementioned CIA operatives were dispatched to my home.'

'And you killed them.'

'I did.'

'And the information you collected?'

'I stored everything inside a safety-deposit box,' Fletcher said. 'The FBI reached it before I could.'

'And then you were on the run.'

Fletcher nodded.

'You're a fugitive because you know about the FBI's involvement in medical testing.'

Fletcher nodded again.

'And the Behavioral Modification Project? What happened to it?'

'Shut down,' Fletcher said. 'All the documentation and evidence was destroyed. It doesn't exist.'

M digested this silently.

'Borgia is calling you a serial killer.'

'I've killed some men,' he said. 'But I'm hardly a serial killer.'

'Did they have it coming?'

We all have it coming, one way or another, Fletcher thought.

'They were guilty of their crimes,' he said. 'I don't regret what I did. Do you have any more questions?'

'Not at the moment.'

'What information have you uncovered on Borgia?'

'Just surface stuff. He's single – he's never been married. Nothing jumps out on his credit-card statements. I downloaded his phone records – that took some doing – but I haven't had a chance to delve through everything. I need more time. I believe you, by the way. What you told me.'

'I'll never lie to you, M.'

'Machine,' she said.

'Pardon?'

'When I was a girl, Karim would periodically check in with the school staff to enquire about my progress. Dr Franklin said, "She never stops moving, that one. Always on the go, like a little machine." That's why Karim calls me M. It's short for "Machine". I want to know where we're going.'

'To get my car. The Jaguar.'

'Why?' she asked in a casual tone.

'Locked inside the trunk is a netbook computer containing information I downloaded from Corrigan's cell phone – call history, contacts, everything.'

'Corrigan as in Dr Gary Corrigan, the former surgeon.'

'Karim told you?'

A curt nod, and she added, 'I told you I was helping him on this project.'

'Corrigan performed the organ removal in another

location. There could be something on his phone that might allow me to find out where Dr Sin and Nathan Santiago were taken.'

'What kind of cell did he have?'

'An iPhone.'

'Then that will make it easier. All iPhones contain a GPS function – the maps icon. The program is always running in the background, recording where the phone travels. We can download that data and analyse it.'

'You said Karim was going to be moved to Manhattan either later today or early tomorrow.'

'That's what I was told.'

'I want you to call the head of his security detail.'

'Bar Lev,' she said.

'Call and tell him to speak to Karim's physician, ask if the transfer can be postponed until tomorrow morning.'

'Why?'

'Let me tell you what I have in mind,' Fletcher said.

69

It was a widely known fact within the Bureau that the FBI's New York field office was considered to be the best in the country. Size was a factor: it boasted the largest office and the greatest number of personnel. Since it was located in the most volatile city in terms of organized crime – and now, because of 9/11, the most volatile in terms of terrorist activities – the Manhattan field office hired only the brightest technical and forensic minds. Their Evidence Response Team was first rate. Consisting of top supervisory special agents, mechanical engineers, computer and program analysts, even forensic K9 specialists, Manhattan ERT could work any major investigation – had, in fact, worked several terrorist cases. Because of the quality of personnel, these terrorist plots had never materialized.

So it came as a complete surprise to 35-year-old Damon Ortega as to why he and the other eighteen Manhattan agents delivered to Ali Karim's historic Park Avenue mansion were being asked to perform what amounted to nothing more than watch patrol.

Bundled into a long overcoat, a scarf wrapped around his neck and a clipboard tucked underneath his arm, Ortega paced the cold garage to keep warm.

A four-man team of evidence technicians had been brought here all the way from the federal lab to search for evidence inside the three luxury vehicles parked against the side of the far wall. Another team was in Cape May, New Jersey, processing Karim's Range Rover.

They refused to touch the Jaguar.

A close examination revealed the car contained armour plating and shatterproof windows. They couldn't unlock it. A tech had tried, using a Slim Jim, and ended up getting shocked – not enough to kill him, but enough to knock the guy flat on his ass. It was the oddest damn thing Ortega had ever seen. Like the others, he kept a safe distance from the car, as though it were a dozing panther that could wake up and pounce at any moment.

One of the evidence guys – or girl, it was impossible to tell which was which with all of them dressed in the same white Tyvek clothing, particle masks and white hoods – saw that Ortega had wandered too close to their work, and waved him away.

Ortega resumed his post near the private elevator. He didn't need any problems here. Some big players from Headquarters had come all the way from Washington to monitor the Malcolm Fletcher manhunt. Like the lab geeks, they looked around to make sure no one was eavesdropping before engaging in hushed conversations.

Why were these Washington suits keeping their cards

so close to their chest? Everyone knew what was going on: they were searching for evidence to tie Fletcher to Manhattan's bigwig security owner, Ali Karim.

When the news broke about what had happened in New Jersey, the Bureau grapevine went into overdrive. Suddenly everyone at the Manhattan field office had some sort of story about the former profiler and his extraordinary – and some said *eerie* – talent for capturing serial killers. Nobody seemed to know the cause of Fletcher's strange ocular condition, and it seemed only to enhance the man's already overpowering sense of menace.

It was maddening to be this close to such a major investigation and yet shut out of the inner circle. He had graduated *summa cum laude* from Yale *and* Harvard Law schools, and here he was acting as a secretary, keeping a log and writing down the time and name of each and every person who entered and exited the garage. His eight-year-old daughter could do this job.

By midnight, Ortega was the only one left inside the garage.

At 1.20 a.m. he called upstairs for a bathroom break. When he came back, along with a fresh cup of coffee, he relieved his temporary replacement. Clipboard in hand, he went back to pacing.

At 1.43 a.m. the big bay garage door started to rise. Ortega heard a revving engine and caught sight of a dark SUV roaring down the ramp before a pair of high beams blinded him.

Ortega moved out of the way. A black Ford

Expedition whisked past him and came to a screeching stop near the stairs leading up to the elevator. The door flew open and an old woman darted out with surprising speed – no, not an old woman, she was young, with shockingly white hair cut short. She didn't so much as glance at him, just dashed around the back of the SUV.

'Stop,' Ortega said, and gave chase. 'Stop *right now*.'

The woman ran up the short set of concrete steps leading up to the platform for the private elevator. Ortega ran after her, reminding himself of what was happening outside, on Madison Avenue, with the news vans and reporters. They had been camped out there ever since the story broke, recording every door that opened, every agent who stepped outside or entered the mansion. And now they had footage of an SUV shooting its way inside the garage.

The woman pressed the elevator button. *Ding* as the doors slid open. Ortega reached the top of the steps, hit the wall control for the garage door and then took two long strides and grabbed the elevator doors before they shut.

'Step out of the elevator,' Ortega said. 'Right now.'

The woman stared at him blankly. Her face was delicate and beautiful, the skin pale, almost translucent; it brought to mind the Japanese kabuki dolls his mother collected. She wore a dark wool jacket over a tight fitting black shirt. She also wore a hearing aid.

Ortega spoke loudly, clearly. 'I said step –'

'I'm Mr Karim's personal assistant.' She had a British accent, very sexy, even though she was shouting at him.

349

'There's an emergency at the Cape May Medical Center, and I need to –'

'No, you need to get out of there and get back inside –'

'*Shut up and listen.* Mr Karim has a history of high blood pressure and heart problems. He's experiencing arrhythmia, and his physician has asked me to make a list of all his medications – yes, yes, I know, the hospital should have all that information on their computer. For whatever reason they *don't*. Now you know why I'm here, so you better bloody well let me upstairs.'

'You aren't allowed –'

'Let me speak to the agent in charge right now.'

'Your name?'

'Emma White. We can go over all of this upstairs.'

'There are procedures –'

'Upstairs. Now.'

'Miss White, calm down. There are procedures in place.' Ortega spoke into his wrist mike and relayed the request to his direct report, Jack Porter.

Porter's reply came over Oretga's earpiece: he had to run the request by his immediate supervisor. He told Emma White.

The young woman paced the small area inside the elevator. Her jaw was set and Ortega could see rising colour in her cheeks.

'What happened to Mr Karim's cars? What's all that powder covering the doors and windows?'

Ortega didn't answer.

'That shit better wash off,' she said.

Porter's voice came over Ortega's earpiece: escort the woman up to the fourth floor. Ortega entered the elevator. Karim's pretty assistant had already pressed the floor number.

'About bloody goddamn time,' Emma White said as the doors slid shut.

In the garage's cold silence, a fibre-optic camera snaked its way from underneath the SUV. It swivelled 180 degrees, paused, and then did a full 360.

The camera disappeared. Then, from underneath the vehicle, a pair of gloved hands touched the garage floor.

70

Ali Karim had stripped one of the ground-level rooms in order to accommodate a large number of monitoring stations that provided a constant, vigilant watch over Park Avenue and the surrounding streets – and over each and every room inside the man's massive home. The technical agent assigned to remove the hard drives from the monitoring stations, a young woman named Miranda Wolfe, thought the abundance of surveillance cameras was overkill; it reeked of Big Brother paranoia. People who deployed such excessive measures were more often than not trying to hide something – in Karim's case, the nation's most wanted fugitive.

She had finished bagging a hard-drive into evidence when she noticed trouble on the four monitoring screens showing the interior of the private garage.

When the Ford Expedition had pulled inside, the screens had flickered from some sort of electromagnetic interference. Now those same four screens had turned into an electromagnetic snowstorm. She couldn't see the garage.

She put down the bagged evidence and turned to the controls.

*

M stood opposite the federal agent as the elevator chugged its way to the fourth floor.

The man was a neurotypical, a term her doctors used to describe what was more commonly known as a 'normal' person. Studying his facial expression, she sorted through the mental list of flashcards, drilled into her head by her teachers, that allowed autistics to understand the emotional dynamics and ranges of neurotypicals.

This man was . . . smug. Like he belonged here inside Karim's home. She wanted to grab him by the neck and smash his face against the elevator panel. She could do it too. Easily. As a child and then later, through her teenage and early-adult years, she had got into numerous fights. She knew which blows could break bones.

The federal agent turned to her and said, 'I can't answer any of your questions.'

M felt the anger building; she diffused it by thinking of Malcolm Fletcher. Like Karim, Fletcher was a neurotypical. Like Karim, Fletcher understood how she was wired and didn't judge her. Like Karim, she sensed Fletcher wasn't trying to manipulate her in any way.

You're going to see federal agents inside your father's home, Fletcher had told her. *Everything you see will be in a state of disarray. They'll be sorting through his things – your things. Your first instinct will be anger. I need to know if you can control it.*

She had told Fletcher she could. Through years of teaching – first in London, and then working with Karim – she had learned to bottle her emotions and

353

store them on a shelf to be dealt with at a later time. Or she could leave them there to collect dust.

Some of these agents may try to touch you, M – not in a sexual way, but they'll pander to you because they'll view you as nothing more than a pretty little girl that Karim hired to be his assistant. Let them. Don't show any anger.

The elevator stopped.

When you feel the anger mounting, think of Karim lying in that hospital bed, Fletcher had told her. *Karim is depending on you to manage your rage.*

The doors slid open. M had started to walk down the hall when the federal agent escorting her put out a hand.

'Please stay right here.'

M looked down the hall. The door to Karim's English library-inspired waiting room was open and blazing with light. She saw people invading the space, their gloved hands taking books off shelves and examining them. Gloved hands rooted through desks and drawers – and her desk. A woman with long brown hair pinned behind her head ran a forensic light over her antique secretarial desk and iMac computer.

Unable to bear the sight of someone touching her things, M forced her attention on to Karim's office. A small group of suited men with badges clipped to their belts had gathered behind her father's desk, their collective gazes fixed on the computer monitors. The man sitting in her father's chair wasn't wearing a suit, just a white shirt. This man was pointing to something on the middle screen.

She couldn't hear what they were saying, but the group of male faces all shared the same expression: frustration. They hadn't found a way to bypass Karim's computer security.

And they won't, she thought. There was no way the FBI could bypass it. *If I could get to his computer I could* –

A short man appeared in the doorway. He had a phone pressed against his ear. He saw her, said something into the phone and hung up.

The man approached her, smiling. This was the same man she'd seen on the video recorded inside Karim's New Jersey home.

He held out a hand. 'Special Agent Alexander Borgia.'

M shook his hand. It took every ounce of willpower not to break the man's arm.

Over his earpiece, Fletcher heard Borgia introduce himself to Emma White. The hearing aid he'd given M not only allowed him to speak to her privately; it was also equipped with a separate, hidden microphone so he could monitor her conversations. They had purchased the hearing aids earlier in the day, at a store that specialized in surveillance gear.

Fletcher was on his back underneath the Expedition, staring up at the padded, hidden compartment. The false bottom, located in the rear of the SUV, was accessed by a square-shaped sliding door. He fitted his gloved fingers inside the grooves for the false bottom's door and slid it up across his chest and face. Now he pushed up and the door for the false bottom locked into place, the sound producing a noticeable echo inside the garage.

The security cameras could neither see nor hear him. After M had parked, Fletcher had used his smartphone to activate a device he'd installed inside one of the Jaguar's panels – an EMP unit that, on a low frequency, sent an electromagnetic pulse strong enough to scramble any nearby circuitry. The Jaguar had been properly shielded so it wouldn't be affected.

M had parked next to the Jaguar, which made his next task much simpler. All he had to do was move himself eight feet to his right and he'd be underneath the Jaguar.

The Jaguar's false bottom wasn't as generous as the Ford's, but his car offered one advantage: the rear seat slid forward, allowing him access to the interior. He would hide inside the false bottom, wait for M to leave, and then make his escape. The spare garage remote M had given him was tucked inside his trouser pocket.

Fletcher pushed the tactical belt and fibre-optic camera across the floor. He kept his phone. He pressed an on-screen button to increase the height of the car's suspension. Now he would have enough room to slide underneath the Jaguar.

Fletcher pushed the phone across the concrete floor and then, lying on his back, began to snake his way out from underneath the SUV.

Special Agent Miranda Wolfe's acting supervisor was a man named Stephen Ratner. She didn't know him personally or professionally. Ratner had been flown in from Washington to oversee the technical aspects of the Malcolm Fletcher operation.

Ratner, his arms crossed over his burly chest, stared at the four monitors showing the garage.

'Could be the cameras,' he said with a sigh. 'Some of the older models when exposed to the cold for long periods of time can –'

'No. Those bullet cameras are top of the line – and they're fairly new. I can see one experiencing a problem, but all four?'

'Then we're looking at a faulty circuit.'

'I think it's some sort of electromagnetic interference.'

'From what?'

'The Ford SUV that pulled in. I've been here for three hours and the garage cameras have been working fine, no problems. Then the Ford pulls in and all four cameras go down.'

'Where's the driver now?'

'An agent escorted her into the elevator.'

'How long ago was this?'

'Five, maybe eight minutes. I want to go take a look at the SUV.'

'You're familiar with the term CYA?'

Wolfe nodded. Cover Your Ass was rule numero uno of every federal investigation.

'Let me call upstairs,' Ratner said, reaching for his radio, 'see what they want us to do.'

71

M stood by the elevator, alongside the agent who had accompanied her upstairs. Alexander Borgia had excused himself to answer a phone call. She was too far away to hear what he was saying, but his gaze was locked on her.

The first part of the plan had worked out perfectly. Entering the garage at this late hour, she had found only one agent inside. Now he was standing next to her on the fourth floor and no one was inside the garage, not as yet. Fletcher was no doubt already underneath the Jaguar. No one could see or hear him. He had told her about the EMP device that would scramble the cameras.

Alexander Borgia may very well be inside your father's home, Fletcher had told her. *If he is, he'll want to question you. You're to fight back verbally — act upset and put out at being detained when you're in a rush to get a list of Karim's medications faxed to the hospital. I doubt they'll waste time trying to track down the doctor by phone to see if such a request was made.*

This afternoon, M had prepared for the possibility that Borgia or another federal agent would try to contact Karim's physician, Dr Segal, who was, in fact, at the Cape May Hospital in New Jersey. Karim's bodyguard,

Bar Lev, had explained the situation to the doctor. Segal had agreed to cooperate to keep Karim safe.

Karim is a powerful man, with a cadre of lawyers at his disposal, Fletcher had told her. *They'll be fearful of a wrongful-death lawsuit and, most likely, allow you to collect Karim's medications under the supervision of an agent. The important thing is to give me enough time to secure myself inside the Jaguar's hidden compartment. It should take no more than ten minutes. I'll contact you once I'm inside.*

Borgia hung up and approached her. He didn't dress in the usual drab colours she associated with federal agents. He wore a pinstriped grey suit with a pale lavender tie and good shoes. Gold cufflinks. The suit, along with his grey hair and the stiff way he walked, gave him the appearance of a private Swiss banker – someone who dealt exclusively with rich clients because he could be trusted to keep their secrets. She saw smudges of TV makeup on his starched collar.

'My apologies for keeping you waiting, Miss White.' He glanced at her hearing aid. 'Am I speaking loud enough for you to hear me?'

'You are. Now may I go to collect Mr Karim's medication?'

'I have someone doing that.'

'I need to do it. Mr Karim is a bit of a slob. This person you assigned won't know where they all are.'

'I think we'll manage just fine.' Borgia pressed the elevator button.

'Where are you going?'

'*We're* going downstairs,' Borgia said. The doors chimed opened and he motioned with a hand for her to enter. 'Mr Ortega, you can remain here. I'll contact you when I'm done.'

Fletcher hadn't contacted her yet; she needed to stall Borgia.

'There's something I need to tell you,' she said. 'Privately.'

'You can tell me downstairs.' When she didn't move, Borgia smiled politely, grabbed her forearm and escorted her into the elevator.

72

Fletcher, lying on his back in the tight space underneath the Jag, had just unlocked the levers for the false bottom when he heard M's conversation with Borgia.

There's something I need to tell you, M had told Borgia. *Privately.*

What was she doing? Fletcher had discussed this with her earlier in the day. Under no circumstances was she to be alone, anywhere, with Borgia – or any other federal agent, given what had happened to Karim.

They were coming down in the elevator. Over his earpiece he heard Borgia say: 'Strangest thing happened when you pulled into the garage. The surveillance cameras? They suddenly stopped working. Nothing but snow on the screens, from what the technical engineers told me.'

Fletcher grabbed the handles disguised as pipes and pulled down. Now he slid the door across him, revealing the false bottom.

'Any idea what may be causing it?' Borgia asked M.

'I'm a secretary, Mr Borgia, not a bloody engineer. I need to get Mr Karim's med –'

'I understand Karim's personal physician is in New Jersey.'

Fletcher picked up his tactical belt and tossed it inside.

'Yes,' M said. 'Dr Segal.'

'Dr Segal doesn't know Karim's medications?' Borgia asked.

Fletcher grabbed the fibre-optic camera and tossed it inside.

M said, 'I was told he couldn't access them from the hospital's computer system.'

'Someone from his office couldn't fax or email Karim's file to the hospital?'

'Dr Segal's office is closed. Do you know what time of the morning it is?'

Fletcher had grabbed the interior handles; he lifted himself into a sitting position, the undercarriage's pipes and metal edges rubbing against his chest, ripping his shirt.

Borgia said, 'He couldn't call someone from his office, ask them to –'

'I was asked, since I live near by,' M said.

'The doctor called you?'

'No. Bar Lev did.'

'Who?'

'Karim's personal bodyguard,' M said.

Fletcher threaded his way inside the cramped compartment, his head, elbows, knees and feet bumping against the walls, creating noise.

Borgia said, 'Why does your employer have a bodyguard posted at his bedside?'

'I suggest you direct these questions to Bar Lev and Karim's doctor. I'm just Mr Karim's assistant.'

Fletcher, wedged inside the hidden compartment's cramped space, was about to slide the false bottom's door shut when he remembered his smartphone. He'd left it on the floor. He couldn't see it, then remembered he had left it lying next to his head.

Quickly he snaked the upper half of his body out, his fingers splayed across the floor as though he were about to perform a push-up. The phone sat near the rear wheel. Slowly he crawled his way to it.

A door slammed open, shoes clicking their way across the garage.

'Bobby,' a woman's voice called out, 'take cameras three and four.'

'It's not the damn cameras, it's the SUV,' Bobby replied. 'You said so yourself.'

'Yeah, well, the boys upstairs want someone else to take a look at it. We're ordered to examine the cameras.'

Fletcher, his weight balanced on his left hand, grabbed the phone. He placed it inside his mouth and, biting down, crawled backwards slowly and carefully.

A pair of shoes whisked past the Jaguar's back bumper.

The elevator doors chimed open.

The man named Bobby said, 'You need help with the ladder?'

The woman answered from the other end of the garage: 'I'm a big girl. I think I can manage.'

Fletcher's arms trembled slightly as he inched his way back, sweat from the exertion and increased adrenalin dripping from his face and leaving small puddles on the floor. From the corner of his eye he caught sight of M's boots and Borgia's polished black loafers heading down the steps.

Borgia said, 'Would you mind if I take a look at your vehicle?'

'As you Americans say, knock yourself out,' M said.

'So I have your permission to examine it?'

'You have my permission. I have nothing to hide, Mr Borgia.'

'You said you wanted to tell me something.'

'I do. But I prefer to have the conversation privately.'

Borgia didn't reply, possibly mulling over the question.

With much effort and concentration, Fletcher had managed to hoist himself back inside the compartment. He couldn't move any further without making noise. He hovered over the opening, muscles straining, sweat pouring freely down his face and splashing against the floor.

A cell trilled inside the garage and then stopped as Borgia said, 'Go ahead.'

Fletcher needed to create a diversion. He grabbed the phone from his mouth.

Borgia said, 'Good news, Miss White. The list of Karim's medications has been faxed to the hospital.'

'Thank you,' M replied. 'I still want a copy. I was told to personally hand-deliver it to the hospital.'

'I had a copy emailed to my phone. We can print it out at the hospital. I'll drive you.'

'I think I can manage, Mr Borgia.'

'I want to speak to Mr Karim's physician, so we might as well go together. We can speak along the way, privately, like you asked.'

No, Fletcher thought. *Don't go with him.*

M's voice inside the garage: 'Where are you parked, Mr Borgia?'

'I'll have a car meet us – where are you going?'

Fletcher didn't hear M's reply; the garage door was rising, the sound loud enough for him to mask his movements.

Clever girl, he thought, and grabbed the door, gently slid it forward and quietly locked it into place. Now he was safely hidden inside the cramped, dark chamber.

His thoughts turned to M. Her safety.

She's quite capable of handling herself, Karim had said.

Phone in hand, Fletcher counted off time in his head. He would wait twenty minutes – that should give M enough distance from the house. Then he would use the phone and turn up the EMP unit's frequency to its maximum setting and escape.

73

Borgia escorted M back into the house. He stopped inside the foyer.

'Please turn and face the wall,' Borgia said. 'Spread your arms and your legs.'

'Am I under arrest?'

'I need to check you for weapons.'

M recalled Fletcher's warning: *Someone may frisk you. I know you detest being touched, but if you don't cage your anger, you'll fail Karim.*

Failing Karim was unacceptable; she wouldn't allow it. She turned and faced the wall.

His hands were rough. She felt as though they were made of fire, leaving burns in the places he touched.

Borgia had arranged for a car to be brought around the back of the house, where there were fewer reporters. Her skin was throbbing as she slid into the passenger's seat of a black Mercury Grand Marquis. The grey interior smelled of fast-food and cigarettes. M cracked open her window to let in some fresh air.

Manhattan, even at this hour, was still a hive of activity. The noise and bright lights did not bother her, as she had acclimatized herself to this environment over the course of many, many years of living here.

'We're all alone now,' Borgia said. He was leaning back in his seat, one hand draped over the steering wheel. 'What did you want to tell me?'

She didn't want to do it here, in the city, with witnesses. She needed to wait until she reached the highway. She needed to draw it out. She needed to act troubled. Concerned and upset.

M had never cried (at least she couldn't remember having ever done so), and when she'd learned what had happened to Boyd Paulson, a hollow space had formed inside her chest. But she hadn't cried. With the exception of anger, she was denied most emotions.

Neurotypicals had a range of facial expressions and gestures to show when they were troubled. She had her mental flashcards ready and consulted them now.

M sighed heavily. Her shoulders slumped and she swallowed.

Borgia concentrated on driving. He kept watching her from the corner of his eye.

Minutes passed.

'Whatever you tell me, I'll keep in confidence,' he said.

M didn't speak. Drew out the silence.

'It has to do with Mr Karim,' she said.

Borgia nodded, waited.

Again she didn't speak. Borgia kept driving, kept shifting in his seat.

'This is . . . difficult,' M said. She ran her fingers through her hair. Then she leaned forward, arms wrapped around her midsection as though experiencing stomach pain, and said, 'Mr Karim has been very good to me.'

'That seems to be the general consensus from the employees I've spoken to so far. Your boss seems to engender a great deal of loyalty.'

'He's been very kind to me. Very generous.'

'I'm sure he is. But, the fact of the matter is, your boss has been aiding and abetting a known fugitive. You know the man I'm referring to.'

M nodded, eyes wide as she stared down at the dirty car mat littered with an empty Dunkin Donuts coffee cup. Borgia was watching her closely.

'Malcolm Fletcher,' she said. 'I thought he was an honest man.'

'Fletcher?'

She looked up sharply. 'No, not Fletcher. Karim. I thought he was a man of integrity.' Her hatred for Borgia made the lying much easier.

'How many times have you seen Fletcher with Karim?'

'Just the one time, aboard Mr Karim's plane. I recently accompanied Mr Karim to Chicago.'

Borgia nodded, urging her along. M leaned back in her seat and stared out of her window, reminding herself to draw out her words, as if speaking them were the cause of her great discomfort.

'Mr Karim left after we touched down,' she said. 'I stayed on board to catch up on some paperwork. When he returned, he'd brought along a passenger – a man he introduced as Robert Pepin.'

'And then you knew.'

'No, not then. Robert Pepin had short grey hair, and he was wearing sunglasses. I didn't realize he was Malcolm Fletcher until this afternoon. I saw Fletcher's picture on the front pages of all the newspapers. On the telly. And then I thought back to Robert Pepin because his face . . . his face was very, very similar to Fletcher's.'

'Why didn't you call the hotline?'

M had anticipated the question. 'I've worked as Mr Karim's personal assistant for the better part of my adult life,' she said. 'I believed he was a man of impeccable integrity. My home phone and my cell haven't stopped ringing over the past forty-eight hours, different people calling to tell me that Karim was stabbed. That he was rushed to a New Jersey hospital and clinging to life. That he's in a coma and is most likely going to die.'

'Is that what the doctors told you?'

'And the nurses. I was in a state of shock – I still am, I think.'

'Understandable,' Borgia said.

'Then I wake today only to find out that Malcolm Fletcher, a man who suspiciously looks like the man who boarded Karim's plane – the papers and the news are saying that this man attacked Karim, and I've been trying to figure out why.'

She waited for Borgia to speak.

When he didn't, she said, 'Is it true? That Fletcher tried to kill Karim?'

'It is, but I'm afraid I can't get into specifics,' Borgia

said. 'You also saw Pepin – Fletcher – inside Karim's house.'

M found the flashcard for confusion. She tilted her head to the side, her gaze narrowing when she said: 'No. I've never once seen him inside the house.'

'You were there when Fletcher arrived in the Jaguar.'

'The one parked in the garage?'

Borgia nodded. 'Fletcher was inside the house for over an hour.'

'I didn't see him.'

'You went to his house that morning. At 6.43 a.m.'

'Mr Karim had some paperwork to give me.'

'And you didn't see Fletcher.'

'No. I took the paperwork and left.'

'Where did you go?'

'To do errands for Mr Karim.'

'Such as?'

'Dry cleaning, post office and what have you.'

'What about the basement?'

'I'm sorry?'

'The in-ground apartment,' Borgia said. 'Have you ever stayed there?'

'No.'

'It's the only locked place inside the house – secured by a steel door that can be only accessed by a code. Odd, don't you think?'

'I'm the man's assistant, not his bloody wife.' M had purposely expressed her anger, wanting to keep Borgia off guard. She let it linger for a moment, then said: 'I apologize for my tone. It's late, I'm tired, and I'm worried about Mr Karim, and I'm confused, as you can imagine.'

'Have you heard him speaking about a man named Nathan Santiago?'

She pretended to think about it. She had seen the video of the room, all that blood. Santiago had left behind his DNA and fingerprints; Borgia had found a match in the federal databases.

'The name doesn't sound familiar,' she said. 'Who is he?'

'It's not important. Is this what you wanted to tell me? That you saw Fletcher on board Karim's plane?'

'There's one other thing,' she said, sliding the Black-Berry from her jacket pocket. 'When Mr Karim left for New Jersey, he asked me to do him a . . . favour.'

'What kind of favour?'

M didn't answer. She read his face and found the corresponding flashcard: discomfort.

They were travelling along the New Jersey Turnpike now, the highway dotted with many lights but only a few cars.

'If you know something, Miss White – if you're in possession of information that can benefit my investigation, I would encourage you to tell me now before this escalates. I would hate to see you go down with your boss.'

'Pull over. I have to show you something.'

'Show me now.'

'You can't watch and drive at the same time.'

'Watch what?'

'This,' M said, and tapped a finger on the screen to play the video.

74

M placed her BlackBerry in Borgia's line of vision. The video played, Borgia's confident voice echoing over the phone's speakers: '*I'm going to go check your gun permit. When I return, Mr Karim, if you don't tell me where you've hidden Fletcher, I'll have tear gas launched inside every room of this house.*'

It was interesting to watch Alexander Borgia's curious physical transformation. He sat up, rigid, a flash of surprise, maybe even fear, on his face. The confidence had vanished. His gaze widened and his jaw dropped, as if a deer had suddenly materialized on the highway directly in front of them. Then he remembered he was driving, righted himself and got control of the wheel.

'Pull into the breakdown lane,' M said. 'Slowly. Try anything stupid and I'll press a button and email this across the country.'

Borgia grew very still. She studied his expression and found the matching flashcard: fear.

He hit the blinker and, checking his mirrors, navigated his way across the lanes. M lowered the BlackBerry. She decreased its volume and then placed the phone on the seat between them. Her eyes never left Borgia.

They had come to a full stop. M unbuckled her seatbelt after Borgia had put the car in park. He left the engine running, and the video played between them, the sound occasionally broken by the *whoosh* of a passing car.

Borgia twisted around in his seat to face her.

'Eyes straight ahead, Mr Borgia.'

He looked out of the front window. 'That video gets out,' he said, draping his arms over the top of the steering wheel, 'you'll condemn your boss. He'll serve time; you know that. You'll destroy his company, his reputation, everything he's built. He'll never recover.'

'Why did you try to kill Karim?'

'Sorry, but that's above my pay grade. And yours.'

'Meaning?'

'What do you think is going to happen next? That you're going to, what, walk away and live your life?'

'Karim's lawyers are in possession of this video,' she said, which was true. She had given a copy of it as well as the others to Karim's legal team. 'If something should happen to me, this video will be posted on Twitter, Facebook and YouTube.'

'That's not going to change your predicament, Miss White.'

'You're going to tell me –' M began, when Borgia reached for her.

Mistake.

M was ready, her fist was ready; she was already out of her seatbelt, and she had enough room to move. She deflected the blow easily with her right arm as her left fist came up. She hit him with a solid blow that broke his nose.

It didn't stop him. Borgia was frenzied, like an animal caught in a snare. He had managed to unlock his seat-belt when she hit him again, and still he went for her. He grabbed the lapels of her jacket, clutching it as though she were the last-remaining life-vest aboard a sinking ship. He was trying to push her down against the floor.

Borgia was smaller than she was, and nowhere near as strong. She grabbed his head and smashed it against the console radio. When he screamed she gripped him by the back of the hair and smashed his face against the edge of the dashboard. She got to her knees and pinned Borgia against the seat and hovered over him the way the HRT operator had hovered over Karim and she hit Borgia again in the face and she hit him in the throat and kept hitting him until he went limp and begged for her to stop, please stop.

75

Special Agent Robert Ortega was back on watch patrol inside Ali Karim's garage, but at least he had something interesting to occupy his attention this time around: a firm, heart-shaped ass. It belonged to Miranda Wolfe, and right now she was bent over the Ford Expedition's engine block, her tight-fitting black trousers hugging every perfect curve. A bald guy with a noticeable beer gut hanging over his belt and – surprise, surprise, no wedding ring on his finger – stood next to her, holding a flashlight.

'Miranda,' the bald guy said, 'do you feel that?'

'Feel what?' she asked.

'The heat. I think it's coming from the Jaguar.'

She moved to the car and pressed her hand against the side.

'What the hell is causing this?' she said, more to herself. She moved her hand away.

'Your hand,' the fat guy said. 'It's covered . . . it looks like black dust.'

The overhead rows of fluorescent lights hanging from the garage ceiling started to flicker.

The fat guy and Miranda Wolfe looked up, wide-eyed. Ortega's attention was locked on the radio clipped to the woman's belt. Smoke was rising from the loudspeaker. He was about to speak when the garage door started to rise.

Ortega flinched at the sound. He was standing near the elevator, only a few feet away from the wall controls for the garage; no one had pressed the button and yet the garage door was rising. He was still staring at it when the fat man said 'Holy *shit*', and Ortega turned to see the guy and the woman backing away from the Ford, plumes of grey smoke drifting up from its engine block.

The overhead lights kept flickering.

Ortega called upstairs on his wrist-mike; didn't get an answer. He grabbed his radio, pressed the push-to-talk button, got nothing but static.

He tried it again. The static grew louder. He looked at his radio, wondering why it –

Plumes of grey and white smoke rose from his radio loudspeaker; the LED panel was dead. He tossed the phone, the smell of burning plastic and fried circuitry filling his nostrils. The fat guy had his radio in hand and it was smoking. Wolfe had tossed hers to the floor; she had her cell in her hand and it was smoking.

A set of overhead fluorescents exploded. The woman screamed, glass shards raining down on her and tinkling across the garage floor. Smoke billowed from the security camera positioned in the corner and scattered in the wind blowing inside the garage.

Another set of overhead lights exploded as the Jaguar's engine roared to life. It backed up, tyres peeling across the garage floor. Ortega pulled his weapon.

He was looking down the target sight, advancing to the car, when the car turned around and faced him.

More lights exploded and he screamed at the driver to stand down. The car's headlights were turned off but eerie green orbs of light glowed and pulsated from the centre of the car's front grille.

The green lights exploded in blinding flashes of light. The colour burned his eyes and he heard the fat guy screaming '*Run, Miranda, get the hell out of the way*' and Ortega couldn't see, oh, God no, he had been blinded by that green light and he couldn't see. He heard tyres squealing and he staggered around aimlessly as the Jaguar raced out of the garage.

76

Fletcher pulled into the destination he had researched earlier in the day – a self-service car wash located on the fringes of Manhattan that operated on coin-and-dollar-fed machinery so people could clean their vehicles any time, day or night. It had four wide bays equipped with sprayers and vacuum hoses, dented kiosks offering Armor All wipes, packages of micro-fibre towels and a wide variety of chemically scented air fresheners. The small shack, where a daytime cashier usually sat behind a bulletproof window to collect money or swipe credit cards for customers who pulled in for gas, was dark and empty.

He would have preferred to wash the Jaguar inside one of the day-operated washes with their enclosed bays and powerful brushes. This would have to do. He fed the final dollar into the machine and the motor's compressor rumbled and roared.

He started with the front hood. The spray of water exploded with a hiss of steam. He moved the spray nozzle closer to the hood and the powerful spray peeled away cracked chips of black paint, sending them flying into the air. It took nearly forty minutes to clean away all the black paint.

Now the Jaguar was white. The police wouldn't

be looking for a white Jaguar, and he didn't have far to travel. Fletcher drove away, watching the streets.

M had made arrangements for the use of another vehicle – a forest-green Jeep Grand Cherokee parked on the fourth level of a private New York garage free of security cameras. Fletcher parked next to it and got out.

He reached underneath the Cherokee's front bumper, found the magnetic box and took out the car key. He opened the hatchback and then returned to the Jaguar to remove a fresh set of clothes from a suitcase.

After he finished changing, he placed his tactical belt on the backseat of the Jeep. He returned to the Jaguar and quickly collected the items he needed. Then he grabbed the final item, the netbook computer, shut the trunk and drove away in the Jeep.

Dawn had broken by the time he reached the back of a strip mall lot in New Brunswick, New Jersey. A silver Ford Mustang was parked by a nearby dumpster. The door opened and M stepped out, bundled up in a heavy coat and wearing sunglasses.

Fletcher parked next to her. He left the Jeep's engine running and, tactical belt in hand, got out and made his way to the hatchback.

M joined him, hands tucked in her jacket pockets, breath steaming in the frigid air.

'I listened to the news on the way here,' Fletcher said.

'I did too.'

'So you know Borgia is missing, and since you were

the last one seen with him, you've become a person of interest.'

'They're also talking about your escape, although they haven't mentioned you by name.' There was no emotion in her voice, just that flat, neutral tone. 'The reporters camped out in front of Karim's house got footage of what happened inside the garage – the smoke and the exploding lights. They're saying an agent has been blinded.'

'I installed a laser dazzler system in the Jaguar's front grille. The blindness is only temporary.'

'Is that the computer?'

'Why?' Fletcher asked. 'Why did you go with him?'

'To talk to him about Karim. Why else?'

Fletcher sighed. 'What did he say?'

'Nothing useful. Maybe you'll have better luck with him.'

'Where is he?'

'Hog-tied in the trunk of my car. I brought him here in case you wanted to speak to him. I relieved him of his clothing in case he was wearing some sort of device that would allow the FBI to track him.'

'And his car?'

'Someplace where they can't find it – unless it has a hidden GPS or tracking unit. I also disconnected the battery from his phone, tossed everything on to the highway. Give me your computer. I want to get to work.'

Fletcher handed it to her, and told her the name of the software program he used to analyse cell-phone data.

'I'm assuming you have a location where you can work safely.'

'I have everything I need.'

'Any news from Karim's Baltimore contact?' Fletcher asked. M had emailed the homicide detective several images of the disfigured man who had killed Boyd Paulson and abducted Nathan Santiago and Dr Sin.

'He left a message,' she said. 'The disfigured man is named Brandon Arkoff. He's the co-owner of the funeral home in West Baltimore, Washington Memorial Park. His partner is a woman named Marie Clouzot. He said he released their images, along with the ones I gave him for Nathan Santiago, to the Baltimore press. He released copies to the newspapers. This morning he's going to hold a press conference asking the public for help. Maybe something will come of it. Karim is awake.'

'When?

'As of an hour ago,' she said. 'I spoke with Karim's bodyguard.'

'Where is he now?'

'Being moved to Manhattan. He'll be heavily guarded. Do you want to speak with Borgia, or do you want me to take care of it?'

'I'll take care of it.'

'The keys are in the ignition. I also left a disposable cell on the seat. I wrote my number on it. I'll get to work on analysing Corrigan's cell-phone data. I'll contact you when I'm finished.'

Fletcher was about to speak when she turned abruptly on her heel and marched around the front of the Jeep.

'M?'

She looked at him from across the Jeep's roof.

'Thank you,' he said.

M seemed genuinely puzzled.

'For what?' she asked.

She didn't wait for an answer. She slipped behind the wheel and drove away.

Fletcher would have preferred someplace private to conduct his questioning. While Karim owned a good amount of both commercial and residential property within the state of New Jersey – some of which, M had told him, was unoccupied – Fletcher did not want any evidence of what he was about to do to be traced back to Karim. There was no need to give the FBI's case against Karim any additional ammunition.

The small town of Monroe, New Jersey, was a fifteen-minute drive from New Brunswick. Named after the fifth President of the United States, James Monroe, the picturesque town offered an abundance of farmland and thickly settled forests.

Fletcher stopped when he spotted an ideal location: an undeveloped field that stretched for miles in every direction, no homes or buildings anywhere in sight. He scouted the edge of the forest and found an area where he could park without being seen from the main road.

He performed a final check and, finding no witnesses or approaching cars, pulled off the road and drove across the field of frozen ground and dead grass. He parked in a spot offering a good amount of tree cover, popped the trunk and got out to speak with Alexander Borgia.

77

Having spent the last hours caged in darkness, Agent Borgia winced in the sudden light. Naked except for a pair of grey boxers, he lay on his side against a bright blue polyurethane tarp, his arms stretched behind him. M had used several zip ties to bind the man's ankles and arms together and then used a final pair to hog-tie him.

She had also worked him over. His face, a swollen, pulpy mess of split skin and drying blood, was almost unrecognizable. Fletcher put his foot up on the back bumper and rolled up his trouser leg, wondering what Borgia had done to provoke her.

Fletcher removed the knife from its sheath. A favorite among scuba divers, this knife had a long blade with a serrated edge that could cut through cartilage and muscle with minimal effort and, if needed, bone.

Borgia groaned as he turned his head, his good eye staring up at the knife. He tried to speak, but his words were muffled by the rag that had been stuffed in his mouth.

'Relax, Mr Borgia. I have no intention of treating you the same way Miss White did. I promise you, I won't be anywhere near as kind.'

Fletcher slit the zip ties binding the man's ankles. He

tucked the knife into his pocket and hoisted Borgia out of the trunk – an easy task, given the man's rather diminutive size.

Fletcher searched the trunk, found the usual assortment of offerings: jumper cables, reusable shopping bags and a plastic container stocked with bungee cords. He selected the jumper cables, shut the trunk, and, with one hand gripping the back of the Borgia's neck, marched the barefoot man across the bumpy mat of dead leaves, twigs and small rocks.

Fletcher didn't speak as he led Borgia deeper and deeper into the woods. The only sounds were Borgia's footsteps and his laboured breathing.

The man's frame held barely any body fat. Without this much-needed insulation, he couldn't stop shivering. He fell several times. Fletcher lifted him to his feet, and he kept stumbling about, disorientated, until he fell again.

Ten minutes had passed; it was enough. Fletcher shoved Borgia face first against a tree. He used the jumper cable to secure the man's neck against the trunk.

Borgia had turned his head so he could watch the forest with his working eye.

'Ralph Waldo Emerson said, "A man must ride alternately on the horses of his private and public nature, as the equestrians in the circus throw themselves nimbly from horse to horse." Emerson was referring to a man's conscience.' Fletcher tapped the blade against Borgia's forehead. 'Now let's see if we can find yours.

'I don't know what you've read or heard about me, Mr Borgia, but know this: I find dishonesty unspeakably ugly. Please bear that in mind before you answer.

'We'll start with the most obvious question: why did you order one of your HRT operators to kill Ali Karim?'

Fletcher pulled the rag from Borgia's mouth. More than one tooth had been knocked loose during his altercation with M.

'You forgot something, Malcolm.'

'Please, enlighten me.'

'I'm not afraid to die.'

'That remains to be seen,' Fletcher said, and grabbed two of Borgia's fingers. A quick turn of the wrist and they broke.

Borgia screamed. Spittle mixed with blood sprayed against the tree bark.

'Why did you try to kill Ali Karim?'

Borgia started to giggle.

'Did that give you an erection?'

Fletcher broke two more fingers.

Borgia gave another scream. When it subsided, the manic giggling returned.

'I know who you *really* are,' Borgia said. 'I know what you did.'

'Which is?'

'Go ahead, Malcolm. Use the knife. Go ahead and cut me and make me bleed. Do what you were born to do – what you *love* to do.'

Fletcher stuffed the rag back inside the man's mouth.

'Goodbye, Mr Borgia.'

The man was still giggling. Fletcher turned and walked back through the woods, heading for the car. He would wait there for fifteen, maybe twenty minutes; any more than that and he would risk losing Borgia to hypothermia. Then he would return, and if Borgia still failed to answer his questions, Fletcher would be forced to take the man to one of Karim's nearby properties.

Fletcher ran down a slope, branches snapping underneath his boots. The car came into view and he caught a blurred shape rising on the other side of the hood. Quickly he turned to his left, his hand already inside his coat and ripping the SIG from his shoulder holster, when the person near the Mustang fired – not a gunshot but a hiss, like compressed air escaping.

Fletcher was moving into the woods, when a man emerged from behind a tree, a man with a disfigured face and holding a handgun. The man who had killed Boyd Paulson and abducted Dr Sin and Nathan Santiago from Karim's New Jersey beachfront home. Brandon Arkoff.

Arkoff fired. A *pop* of compressed air escaping and something shattered against Fletcher's bulletproof vest. Arkoff kept firing and the person near the Mustang – his partner, Marie Clouzot – was firing too.

Fletcher felt something sharp pierce his thigh, like a needle. Warmth trickled through his muscle as Arkoff ducked behind a tree. Fletcher fired off a round, saw the exploding tree bark. He fired again and felt another needle-sting on the back of his head.

He ran, stumbled and quickly righted himself. He pressed ahead until his legs gave out.

Fletcher collapsed against the hard ground. He had dropped the SIG, could see it lying just a few inches away among the brown dried leaves. He went to crawl for it, collapsed. His arms had turned limp, and his vision was fading. He saw a tranquillizer dart sticking in the meat of his thigh.

He heard approaching footsteps and then he saw a rifle. Looking down the gun sight was the pale, almost bloodless face of Arkoff's partner, Marie Clouzot, the woman who had tried to kill him in Colorado.

IV
The Killing House

78

Malcolm Fletcher awoke to warm air and voices.

'Sit still. It will be over before you know it.'

A woman's voice, deep and husky. The kind cured from a lifetime of cigarettes and hard liquor.

'Why can't you give me Novocain?' Alexander Borgia's voice, and it was coming from the same direction as the woman's – someplace straight ahead, only a few feet away. 'Don't you have any of that shit down here?' Borgia asked.

'Just grit your teeth and bear it,' the woman replied. 'You've been through worse – and you're goddamn lucky I installed this thing. Otherwise, I never would've found you, and you'd still be freezing to death out in the woods.'

A great fog filled Fletcher's head, but his senses were working, alert: he was lying on his left side, his cheek pressed against something cold and hard. It had the rough, gritty texture of sandpaper. He didn't feel any bindings on his wrists or ankles. His mouth felt dry, and there was a throbbing in his forehead, a tight band of pressure that had the feeling of a hangover. *The sedative loaded in the darts.* One had hit his thigh and the other had grazed the back of his neck.

New sounds, some near by, some faint: a low, guttural

moan. The rattle of chain link. And everywhere, raspy, sickly breathing. There was a pervasive reek of blood and unwashed skin, and, behind it, the distinct and overpowering stench of human decomposition.

His eyes slit open to a tight cluster of intensely bright lights. A pair of blurry figures stood on either side of what appeared to be a very long and very tall stainless-steel table.

Fletcher didn't move his head or body; he wanted Borgia and the woman to think he was unconscious. He blinked, and kept blinking, until everything came into a sharper focus.

The light came from a portable floor-standing surgery lamp, its wide, twenty-inch elliptical reflector dish positioned over a stainless-steel operating table. Borgia stood behind the table. His face was still grotesquely swollen, but it had been cleaned up. A surgical mask covered his mouth and nose, and he had changed into a grey sweatshirt several sizes too big.

Fletcher glanced over Borgia's shoulder, at the wall and corner shelves packed with sterilized bags of surgical scrubs and towels. He saw boxes of latex gloves, vials and syringes, and a wide assortment of medical equipment.

An operating room.

Back to Borgia: the man's left sleeve had been rolled up and he leaned slightly over the table, his hand splayed across the stainless steel. His skin was covered with a dark liquid that was, most likely, Betadine. Borgia hissed through gritted teeth as Marie Clouzot made a small incision on the webbing between his thumb and index finger. Then she traded the scalpel for a pair of surgical forceps, dipped the ends inside the wound and came back with something small pinched between the prongs. She set the tiny object on the table, not far from Borgia's hand.

Fletcher lost sight of it; Clouzot blocked his view, having turned to a nearby surgical cart. She was much taller than Borgia, stockier. She wore dark jeans, black boots and a pink, V-neck sweater that had the texture of cashmere. She also wore a surgical mask and latex gloves. Her dark hair had been pulled back into a tight bun.

Fletcher's gaze focused on the barrier separating him from the operating theatre: a chain-link door secured by at least one padlock. His head remained absolutely still as he conducted a cursory examination of his immediate surroundings.

The same grey/silver chain-link fencing had been used to erect his walls and ceiling. Eye bolts secured the chain link to a galvanized stainless-steel frame. He had been imprisoned inside what was essentially a custom-made dog kennel: just enough room to lie down. Judging from the ceiling height, he wouldn't be able to stand. To the right of his cage, fifteen to twenty feet away, was an open door leading to a dimly lit passage-way of concrete.

His gaze shifted back to the operating table. Clouzot dabbed gauze on Borgia's hand, then she picked up the needle and went back to stitching his wound. The operating lights were extremely bright but it still took Fletcher a moment to find the small object she had removed from the incision: a glass tube, the size of a grain of rice. Something was contained inside the glass. He was too far away to make out what this was, but his mind was working.

Slightly larger than a grain of rice, Karim had told him.

Then the information came to him: he had been riding with Karim to New Jersey, they had been discussing how Nathan Santiago could have been found, and Karim offered up a theory – radio-frequency identification.

A glass-encapsulated RFID *chip slightly larger than a grain of rice can be tucked inside a pocket or sewn into clothing – or, in the case of biometric security, surgically inserted beneath the skin,* Karim had said. *The Mexican attorney general did that to his senior staff, had a chip implanted in that web of skin between your thumb and index finger. You notice anything like that on Santiago?*

Fletcher hadn't. But Clouzot, he suspected, had just removed an RFID chip from Borgia's hand – Special Agent Alexander Borgia's hand.

'When do you think he'll wake up?' Borgia asked.

'Hard to say,' Clouzot replied, pulling the surgical thread. 'One dart hit him in the thigh. The one that grazed his neck delivered maybe a quarter of the sedative. He's a big man.'

'So, what, another hour? Maybe two?'

The woman laughed, a deep, throaty sound. 'You're not going to let it go, are you?'

'I have to try,' Borgia said.

'You can't reason with a monster, Alexander.'

Borgia made no reply. The conversation ended, and was replaced by moaning, dry and plaintive whispers asking for mercy and forgiveness. Fletcher couldn't see Clouzot's face, but Borgia gave no indication that he'd heard the inhuman cries. Either he had inured himself to this suffering, viewing it as nothing more than a necessary by-product of his cause (whatever it was); or, like most psychopaths, his limbic system was defective, rendering him incapable of feeling empathy, fear, guilt and remorse.

Clouzot finished stitching Borgia's wound and straightened. Fletcher, his eyes nearly closed, could see her boots as they whisked past him. He watched them until they disappeared through the passageway. He was listening to her footfalls when Borgia approached his cage.

79

Fletcher lay still, waiting, his eyes shut. The footsteps stopped in front of the kennel door. He heard Borgia's laboured breathing.

'*Wake up*,' Borgia screamed, and kicked the cage door.

Fletcher didn't flinch at the sounds; he remained motionless.

Another kick.

'*Wake up, you son of a bitch.*' Borgia kicked again.

Again. '*Wake up.*'

Clearly Borgia wanted a confrontation, but what would happen if the target of his rage failed to awaken? Would the man have the nerve to remove the padlock and enter the cage? Fletcher hoped the man had a key. *Unlock the padlock and come inside, Mr Borgia . . . No, he's decided against it.* Fletcher heard the man's footsteps storm away.

Fletcher rolled on to his back. The stench in the room was overpowering; he breathed deeply through his mouth to clear the fog from his head. Eyes opening wide, he stared past the cage's chain-link ceiling, at the hanging water pipe. It contained sprinkler heads. Was this how they showered the prisoners? He thought about Nathan Santiago, wondering how a seventeen-year-old had wrapped his mind around living inside a chain-link kennel minute after minute, day after day, year after year. How had Santiago and the others kept from going mad?

No, don't think about that now, Fletcher told himself. A final deep breath and he sat up, groggy, head swimming.

They had removed his overcoat and tactical belt. All he had left was his shirt and trousers, his leather dress belt and boots. They had emptied his pockets. The tranquillizer dart that had hit his thigh had left a small hole and a crust of drying blood on the trouser fabric. He appeared to be uninjured. He swivelled around to examine the rest of the room.

Fletcher had seen many things over the long course of his professional life. He had seen hidden torture chambers used by serial killers, had viewed corpses dumped by roadsides – he had witnessed first hand the ways dark and sinister urges found expression on human skin and bone. But what lay inside this rectangular concrete room of dim light momentarily overloaded his senses: human eyes peeking out from behind chain-link kennels bolted to the walls and floor. The prisoners were young and old, male and female. Some wore threadbare clothing or no clothing at all. Some were slumped against the bars or curled into foetal positions. Some of the victims were missing hands or feet or both. He wondered if they had been surgically hobbled to prevent them from escaping.

They all had IV needles hooked into their arms or necks. Tubes ran out of the crates to plasma bags

397

hanging from the water pipes. An industrial-grade padlock secured each door. He counted eight kennels and all eight were occupied.

A pair of corpses had been dumped in the far corner. Dr Dara Sin had started to bloat.

But not Nathan Santiago. The young man had been stripped of his clothing, and his chest cavity had been cut open to harvest his organs.

The sight crawled through Fletcher's flesh and shot its way into his bones. He recalled his final words to Nathan: *No one will hurt you, I promise.*

'Help me.'

The dry, whispery voice came from the adjoining kennel – a sickly woman dressed in dirty jeans and a roomy dark cotton T-shirt. She sat crossed-legged and was slumped against her chain-link wall, her mouth hanging open, the paper-thin lips cracked and crusted with sores. All of her teeth had fallen out.

Fletcher inched closer to her. 'Are there others down here? Are there any rooms?'

The woman didn't answer. Stringy blonde wisps of hair barely clung to her balding scalp.

Fletcher inched closer and said, 'What's your name? How long have you been down here?'

No answer. Fletcher pressed his back against the concrete wall. He sat with his legs tented and his forearms resting on his knees. Adrenalin was coursing through his system now; he needed to manage it, needed to focus and concentrate on the task at hand: escaping.

He was looking around the ceiling, searching for cameras, when he heard footsteps approaching from the passageway – marching, not walking.

Alexander Borgia's slight frame filled the doorway. In addition to the roomy grey sweatshirt, he wore dark nylon running pants that were too long; the cuffs had been rolled up several times. No shoes or socks, just a pair of flip-flops that were too big for his small feet. The clothes on his short frame gave him the appearance of a boy who had dressed up in his father's clothing.

Borgia gripped a Glock in one hand. In the other he gripped a cattle prod.

'Good,' Borgia said, his voice trembling with rage. 'You're awake.'

Fletcher had a hand on his belt buckle, watching as Borgia placed the cattle prod on the operating table.

Borgia approached the cage, the Glock held by his side. It appeared to be a .45 calibre. Fletcher suspected the clip was loaded with hollow-tipped rounds.

'Was it worth it? All that money?'

Fletcher straightened his legs. Put his hands on either side of him and lay his palms flat against the floor.

'My head is rather foggy, Mr Borgia, so I'm afraid I'm at a loss to answer your question.'

Borgia fumbled for something inside his trouser pocket. His hand came back and then he bent forward and rolled something underneath the kennel door.

Fletcher didn't track the object; his eyes never left Borgia's face.

'*Pick it up!*'

The occupant in the next cell flinched. A cry of anguish came from another cage and died, replaced by a chorus of low moaning.

Borgia didn't register their presence. Looking only at Fletcher, he raised the Glock. '*I said pick it up.*'

Fletcher found a vial lying on the floor. It was half full of a clear liquid. Taped to its side was an aged, peeling label stamped with faded red lettering: *Namoxin*.

Fletcher went cold. Namoxin was the name of the experimental medication used to treat psychotic male patients who had been in the Behavioral Modification Project.

The question jumped out of him. 'Where did you obtain this?'

'You failed to destroy *all* the evidence, Malcolm.' Borgia grinned in sour triumph. 'As part of the new task force assigned to find you, I was given access to all sorts of classified files and evidence. I know how you and the other agents from Behavioral Analysis who started the Behavioral Modification Project worked –'

'I had *nothing* to do with that,' Fletcher said, surprised by the heat in his voice. 'I was trying to expose it.'

Borgia wasn't listening. 'I read the files,' he said. 'Your war crimes are all laid out in black and white, everything you and the others did.' He spoke with great fervour, working himself into a near-religious mania. 'I know how you all got rich by working in collusion with select pharmaceutical companies developing this miracle vaccine to eliminate male violence. How you picked the test subjects. I know you helped bury the bodies – the ones you didn't cremate at the psychiatric hospitals – and I even know how you and the others doctored the paperwork.'

'I tried to *expose* the project,' Fletcher said again.

'Next you'll try to convince me you didn't kill the three agents who came to arrest you.'

'They were CIA operatives, not federal agents. They had been sent to my home to kill me. The FBI retrieved the evidence I collected on the BMP, all the –'

'Lie to me all you want, Malcolm. I know the truth.'

'You mean *your* truth.' Fletcher tilted his head to one side, his gaze narrowing. 'Have you read any patient files? Seen any documentation on the Behavioral Modi-fication Project?'

Borgia didn't answer.

'I didn't think so,' Fletcher said. 'You haven't been able to put your finger on any patient files or any docu-mentation regarding the project because *they don't exist*. The FBI destroyed every last shred of documentation to keep the *truth* from seeing the light of day – and, it appears, conveniently used me as their scapegoat.'

'If you tell me, I'll show you mercy.'

'Tell you what?'

'Where you buried my brothers and sisters,' Borgia said.

80

'You're a patient,' Fletcher said, more curious than surprised. 'A former patient of the Behavioral Modification Project.'

Borgia's head craned back. He stared up at the ceiling as though there were a hole up there through which someone was speaking to him.

'Which hospital?'

'You tried to save Ali Karim,' Borgia said. 'You risked your life and your freedom to keep Ali Karim from dying.' His head snapped forward, and he looked back through the chain link. 'You're capable of empathy.'

'Unlike you.' Fletcher motioned with a sweeping hand to the others in the room. 'How many people have you tortured and killed, Special Agent Borgia? How many children?'

The man blinked, confused. 'I didn't kill anyone,' he said. 'All I did was find them.'

'Them?'

'The doctors and nurses from the hospital, the ones who helped engineer a private mass murder,' Borgia said. 'All those patients who died, and what happened to the doctors and nurses who killed them? They were placed inside witness protection. They were given new identities and new lives and allowed to go back to work in psychiatric facilities all over the country. The Bureau couldn't let their sins – or yours – become public knowledge, so they did what they did best – sweep everything under the rug.'

Fletcher thought back to Theresa Herrera's missing medical records. WitSec had expunged them along with any other traces of her former identity when they placed her into witness protection. And the other families he had found – their medical records too had been obliterated.

'And you found their new identities,' Fletcher said. 'And you gave them to Marie Clouzot and Brandon Arkoff.'

A thin, knowing smile and then Borgia added, 'You did provide me with one piece of inspiration, Malcolm.'

'Do tell.'

'You taught me the importance of taking justice into one's own hands. It's the only way to mete out a punishment that properly fits the crime.'

'One difference.'

'What's that?'

'I didn't dissect innocent children and sell their organs.'

'I have nothing to do with that. My job was to find out their new identities and make sure they were properly punished.'

'You mean tortured. I'm assuming your two companions are patients like yourself.'

'I didn't kill anyone,' Borgia said again.

'Spoken like a true psychopath.'

Borgia pressed himself up against the kennel door. His eyes were hot. Wet.

Was he crying?

He *was* crying.

'Don't you want to clear your conscience?' Borgia asked. There was no real emotion in his voice, but the manufactured tears continued to spill down his cheeks. 'Or are you really the soulless psychopath they say you are?'

'Your name – your *real* name. We'll start there.'

Borgia swallowed, his jaw set. 'Terence Davidson,' he said. 'I entered the project when I turned fifteen – the Spaulding Psychiatric Center in Philadelphia.'

'Why? What happened to you?'

'A neighbour's dog kept shitting in our backyard, so I decided to take care of the problem. The neighbour's daughter caught me with the dog before I could do anything, and when she threatened to tell everyone, I . . . made sure she wouldn't be able to talk.' Borgia voice's contained no shred of shame, regret or guilt. 'Instead of juvenile detention, the judge said I could undergo psychiatric help at Spaulding, and you know what happened there. You know what you did.'

'And your two companions, Marie Clouzot and Brandon Arkoff?'

'They were at Spaulding.'

'I want their names. Their *real* names.'

'Marie Clouzot and Brandon Arkoff. Now tell me –'

'No,' Fletcher said. 'When were you released from Spaulding?'

'I wasn't *released*, I *escaped*.'

'How?'

Borgia grinned. 'Marie freed us – all of us. Brandon, Marie and I – we fled together. She took care of us. We stayed together, we lived together – we survived. Together.'

'How heartwarming,' Fletcher said. 'Why did you try to kill Ali Karim?'

Borgia recoiled as if slapped. 'I didn't kill him,' he said.

Fletcher sighed. 'Why did you give the *order* to have him killed?'

'That came from above. The Director himself. You've made a lot of enemies, Malcolm. We can't afford to have you or anyone associated with you running around the country – who knows how many people know your dirty little secret.'

'I'll say it again. I had no involvement with the Behavioral Modification Project. I was trying to expose it. Ali Karim spent a small fortune hiring forensic archaeologists to try to find out where the hospitals buried the bodies.'

Borgia's eyes widened, surprised and possibly offended. 'Karim,' he said, his voice rising, 'was helping that murdering whore the world knew as Theresa Herrera find her *precious* little boy. Karim was helping to hide you all these years – you, a murdering psychopath who had helped to orchestrate a secret mass murder. Karim protected you, the Bureau protected their murderers – gave them new identities, relocated them, paid for *everything* – and who helped me and the others? Who protected us? Nobody. Nobody helped us and nobody was looking out for us. Karim deserves to die, you deserve to die – the whole goddamn murdering lot of you needs to be punished for what you did. And you're going to tell me, right now, where you buried the bodies.'

Fletcher said nothing, mesmerized by Borgia's psychotic breakdown.

Borgia kicked the kennel door. '*Where did you bury the bodies?*'

Fletcher said nothing.

'*TELL ME!*' Another kick, another roar: '*TELL ME WHERE YOU BURIED THE FUCKING BODIES!*'

Beats of silence, and then Fletcher said, 'Do you want the truth or your version of it?'

'The truth,' Borgia said, panting. 'This has always been about the truth.'

'Then I'll tell you.' Fletcher waited a moment before continuing. 'Contrary to what you've been told, I had no involvement with the Behavioral Modification Project.'

Borgia backed away from the kennel door.

'I didn't bury any bodies,' Fletcher said. 'After the Bureau closed down the project, well after they shredded all the documentation and destroyed every last bit of evidence, I –'

Fletcher cut himself off when Borgia turned, raised the Glock and fired randomly into one of the kennels.

Fletcher jumped to his feet, the ceiling's web of chain link preventing him from standing upright, and he yelled as Borgia fired again.

'*Look at me.*'

Borgia swung his attention back to him. 'You made me do that,' he said. 'You killed them. Their deaths are on your hands because you keep lying.'

'I'm telling you the truth.' Fletcher's ears were ringing from the gunshots. 'I can't tell you where the bodies are buried because I don't know. The Bureau took measures to make sure the bodies would never be found – that no evidence or documentation regarding the project would ever be found.'

Borgia's eyes were vacant, his grin vicious. 'Marie was right. You are a monster. A liar and a monster, just like the rest of them.'

Fletcher was about to speak again when he heard a faint scream, the sound coming from the passageway. The scream was followed by a clear voice crying for help.

Borgia backed away from the cage and grabbed the cattle prod from the operating table.

'I'm telling you the truth,' Fletcher said.

'The world will know soon enough what you did,' Borgia said. He pointed the cattle prod at him and added, 'And so help me God, you *will* tell me where you buried the bodies.'

Borgia stormed through the passageway. Fletcher sat back against the floor and grabbed his right boot.

81

Fletcher gave the heel of his boot a sharp twist. The seal broke. Quickly he unscrewed the heel. Now it was in his hands and he slid the compartment open, revealing the false bottom. Inside and set in the hardened, contoured plastic were lock picks and a small, five-inch folding knife.

The knife went into his mouth. Lock picks in hand, he threaded his fingers through the chain link, grabbed the padlock and went to work.

Jimmy Weeks had jumped to his feet when he heard the gunshots.

The police had found him. They had come in with guns ablazing and they were searching for him and they didn't know where he was because he was locked alone inside this dark room. He sucked in a deep breath and screamed at the top of his lungs, screamed '*HERE! HELP ME, I'M IN HERE!*'

He stopped when he heard the deadlock for the big, heavy door snap back.

Jimmy swallowed, his throat raw, throbbing, and nearly collapsed in relief. He was alive, he had survived; he was going home to see his parents.

The lights for his room went on; the sudden

brightness, as always, felt like needles flying into his eyes. He gripped the cage's chain link as the big, heavy door swung open, and with his eyes slammed shut he screamed in relief and fear and, now, anger: '*That crazy woman locked me inside here — there are other people in here, I heard them, they're —*'

Jimmy cut himself off when he heard an electric crackle. His eyes flew open but he couldn't see much of anything. Something sharp and cold hit his neck and then a blast of lightning flew through his body like millions of tiny electrified bolts. His legs gave out and he collapsed against the floor. His muscles twitched in painful, uncontrollable spasms. He heard keys jingling and then the crackling sound came again and more bolts of lightning slammed into the back of his head and through his limbs and the scream died on his lips.

Marie Clouzot stood in one of the printing press's ground-floor offices, undressing in the submarine glow of Brandon's computer screen. She'd heard the gunshots; they were faint, coming from the basement. She knew what Alexander was trying to accomplish (and that was his name, Alexander Borgia, not Terence Davidson; they didn't use their old names any more). Alexander believed he could convince the monster to tell him where he'd buried the other patients.

During the drive to Baltimore, she had reminded Alexander of the many doctors and nurses who had been caged inside the basement's chain-link kennels over the years. True, some of them confessed to knowing full well that Namoxin was an experimental medication with many side effects. And, yes, two of the doctors had admitted to working in the secret Behavioral Modification Project. But *none* of them — not *one* single doctor or nurse, she reminded Alexander, would say where the bodies had been buried. They kept professing their ignorance of such matters before *and* after a hand or foot had been amputated. When they watched their sons and daughters being led to the operating table.

Alexander's response was always the same: *I have to try.* Alexander could shoot the doctors and nurses rotting in their cages, he could march Jimmy Weeks into the operating room and torture the teenager in front of Malcolm Fletcher and nothing would come of it because Malcolm Fletcher was a psychopath — a devious and cunning psychopath who would rather die a horrible death than share his secrets. The man was without a conscience.

Alexander refused to let the matter go, and, finally, she threw up her hands in surrender. *Do whatever you want*, she'd told him. *Just get me the hair.* The company who crafted the beautiful diamonds on her necklace could, if cremated remains weren't available, create any size jewel using human hair. Alexander promised to grab a sample from Jimmy Weeks — and Malcolm Fletcher.

Marie slipped out of her trousers. She was going to change into the only piece of clothing she'd taken from the funeral home—a coveted black Chanel suit. Brandon had bought it for her, and, as much as she loved it (and she truly did), she had put the ensemble aside, wanting to preserve the delicate fabric for the day of her own funeral. No one would come, of course, except Brandon – provided he survived her.

Brandon was hunched over his laptop. Its screen held multiple windows, each one offering a different camera view of the basement. He was busy downloading the final set of videos. Years ago, as a surprise, he had purchased a commercial security-camera kit, complete with night vision and microphones. Every night before bed he'd hooked up the computer to the television, and together they would watch the wonderful movies. Sometimes she closed her eyes and listened only to the moaning, the pleas and cries for help. The unanswered prayers to God.

The movies were wonderful: the video quality was superb. When they had first started, Brandon recorded everything on videotapes and audiocassettes. During the day, she would listen to the audiocassettes on her Walkman while she was out and about, doing errands, while at work. At home, she would play them on the portable radio/cassette player. At night, she would fall asleep to the lovely voices. Sometimes she played the cassettes or videotapes while they made love.

Marie felt a sense of finality grip her. It was over – at least here in Baltimore. There were still other doctors and nurses living out their lives under new identities. Alexander wouldn't be able to find them, however. He would disappear with her and Brandon, and Alexander

Borgia would become just another one of Malcolm Fletcher's many victims.

'What the hell is he doing?' Brandon nearly whispered the words.

Before she could ask, he had grabbed the wireless mouse. A click and he enlarged one of the camera windows. On the screen she saw Malcolm Fletcher pressed up against his cage door, his fingers threaded past the chain link and gripping the padlock.

Marie didn't have to tell Brandon what to do. He had already turned back to the keyboard.

Fletcher felt the padlock spring free. He threaded it out of its clasp and it dropped against the floor. He took the knife out of his mouth.

'Help me.'

The dry croak came from the sickly woman dressed in dirty jeans and a dark cotton T-shirt. The remaining fingers of her right hand gripped the chain link.

'Help me,' she croaked again. 'Please.'

'I'll have you out of there momentarily,' Fletcher whispered. He was standing outside his cage. 'I need to secure the area –'

The sprinklers turned on, water raining down on him, on everything.

Not water.

Gasoline.

82

Fletcher's eyes clamped shut. His mouth clamped shut and he heard the woman's low scream as he turned and ran blindly through the spraying downpour of gasoline, heading towards the open door leading into the concrete hall.

The gasoline was no longer raining down on him. He stopped, gagging and gasping for air. Gasoline slid down his face and hair. He whisked it away. Some sort of gritty substance covered his fingers. He opened his eyes. They burned and everything in his field of vision was blurry – the bare bulbs hanging from the corridor's ceiling, the doorway leading back into the operating theatre. Some of the people trapped in there were screaming, some were rattling the chain links.

Pop and *hiss* as a bright blue flame ignited on one of the pipes and clouds of flame exploded through the room in a series of white flashes and sparks. A loud rumble followed, and then a thick sheet of steel dropped from the top of the doorway and crashed against the floor, sealing off the room.

Screams erupted from behind the door and another scream erupted behind him. Fletcher turned, coughing on the gasoline fumes rising from his skin and clothing, the piercing, agonizing howls of the trapped victims trailing him as he staggered down the hall. He wiped at his face again. His vision had cleared slightly but his eyes continued to burn and tear. He brought the hand closer to his face and saw tiny rough particles the colour of dark chocolate covering his skin. Not sand. Sand wouldn't be added to gasoline.

Fletcher heard the electric crackle of the cattle prod followed by another scream.

'Stop fighting me, you little shit,' Borgia hissed.

Marie had turned away from the computer screen, about to run, when Brandon clutched the meat of her arm and pulled her back.

'*Let me go*,' she screamed. '*I've got to warn Alexander.*'

Brandon was on his feet. 'You're not even dressed.' He held on to her as he reached inside her handbag and came back with the 9-mm. 'I'll get Alexander. Go to the car.'

The hallway ended, turned to Fletcher's left. Through his watery vision he could make out another doorway and, past it, another room containing the same dog kennels. Borgia was dragging a blond-haired man out of an open cage. Borgia clutched the back of the man's hair and the man – a teenager – was fighting back.

Borgia hit the teenager with the cattle prod, tucking his Glock inside his pocket to keep his hands free.

Fletcher moved inside the room. Borgia, too focused on the teenager, didn't see him until it was too late.

Fletcher didn't use the knife; he landed a solid blow

against the small man's ear. Borgia dropped the cattle prod as he staggered. A kick and Fletcher sent him flying across the floor.

Borgia turned on to his side and reached inside his pocket for the Glock. Fletcher kicked the man in the face. The blow knocked him to the floor. Fletcher raised his foot and brought all of his weight down on Borgia's neck and snapped it and Borgia lay still.

Fletcher grabbed the Glock and ejected the magazine clip. It contained eight hollow-tipped rounds. The teenager was curled up against the floor, whimpering, his shaking arms covering his head. Like Borgia, he wore mismatched clothing. No shoes, just woollen socks. There were no pipes hanging from the ceiling.

Fletcher moved to the teenager. 'I'm going to bring you out of here,' he whispered. 'Take my hand. Stay behind me and stay quiet.'

Marie didn't get dressed and she didn't head to the car. She was sitting in Brandon's chair, staring in disbelief at the computer screen. Malcolm Fletcher had escaped from his cage and now Alexander lay dead and the monster was talking to Jimmy Weeks.

Brandon. Marie jumped to her feet and reached for her handbag, almost knocking the laptop off the table. Brandon was heading down there to help Alexander and she had to warn him. She grabbed her cell and dialled his number, hoping to God he had it with him.

The phone rang. She looked back at the laptop and saw the monster hunched near the doorway leading into the hall. The phone rang a second time and she looked at another computer window, this one showing the hall. Brandon was creeping across the floor, heading towards Fletcher. She realized her mistake and hung up.

It was too late. Brandon's phone was ringing. She couldn't hear it but she saw Brandon reach inside his pocket to shut it off. Fletcher had heard the ringing and she watched in horror as the monster turned the corner and shot Brandon dead. Brandon was dead. She screamed but couldn't tear her eyes away from the computer screen. The monster picked up Brandon's gun and removed Brandon's phone and car keys. Brandon was dead, Alexander was dead, and the monster was creeping down the hall with Jimmy Weeks. If she stayed here she would die. The drums of explosives packed inside the basement would blow this building to smithereens. She couldn't stop it; the timer had started as soon as Brandon typed the keys to start the fire to incinerate the bodies. Brandon had told her she had fifteen minutes.

Marie didn't have time to finish dressing. She quickly slid into her coat and grabbed the computer, the wires coming undone as she fled the room. Brandon was dead and oh dear God did it hurt, but if she could beat the monster to the garage she could release the videos stored on Brandon's computer and then the whole world would know.

83

As Fletcher crept up the stairwell of dimming light, listening for sounds and watching for shadows, his mind kept replaying the odd white flashes and sparks he'd seen before the fire had started. The answer drifted away, came back: a thermite reaction. The sand-like particles covering his hands, his hair and clothing, were either iron oxide or copper oxide.

When he saw the heavy steel door crashing down and sealing off the room, he knew: the basement chamber had been turned into a crematorium. Gasoline alone couldn't turn human bones into dry fragments: it could reach a maximum temperature of only 560?°F. Destroying human bones required a temperature of between 1,400?°F and 1,800?°F. Gasoline mixed with a metal powder and a metal oxide, like the one covering his clothing and skin, created extremely high temperatures upwards of 2,500?°F. Such a temperature would also melt most of the medical equipment.

At the moment it was contained – had to be, in order to effectively destroy evidence. Someone intelligent and clever enough to create a home-made crematorium would know that large bones like the femur and thick, dense joints supporting the hip wouldn't burn away. *All* the bones needed to be pulverized into ash or they would be discovered. Someone this intelligent would have installed the proper mechanism to ensure no evidence of what had occurred here would ever be found.

Alexander Borgia and the disfigured man, Brandon Arkoff, were dead. That left Marie Clouzot. She had blown up Theresa Herrera's Colorado home in order to destroy evidence; it stood to reason the same measures had been taken here.

The stairs ended. The teenager bumped up against his back. Fletcher could feel the boy trembling.

Tall windows bordered a large, rectangular-shaped room, and they were dimly lit from the outside streetlights. The windows were cracked and broken and each one was barred with heavy steel grilles. There was enough light for him to make out his surroundings.

To his right, a long, cavernous space that had once been the site for some sort of manufacturing; ancient machinery shrouded in shadows and covered haphazardly with cloth tarps was scattered among waist-high work stations made of wood. Plastic crates were stacked in corners, strewn across the floor. Everywhere he looked Fletcher saw steel drums and wooden pallets used for shipping.

To his left was a half-opened door. There was light beyond it. He opened the door and saw a small passageway leading to a landing that overlooked a garage wide enough to accommodate delivery trucks. Fletcher was moving down the passageway, the teenager clutching his hand, when the garage door started to open.

He reached the landing. Two vehicles were parked in

the bay – a vintage black Mercedes and a dark Lincoln Town Car, the one that he had tailed in Baltimore.

Marie Clouzot was running for the Mercedes. She wore the same fur coat he'd seen in Colorado. She was barefoot and clutching a laptop computer.

Fletcher fired.

The first shot hit her high in the shoulder. She dropped the laptop and her car keys as he fired again, a double-tap into the centre of the woman's back. Marie collapsed face down against the garage floor.

The teenager was shaking violently; he had trouble standing, and he had gone into shock. Fletcher helped him down the steps, reassuring the young man that he was safe. A cold wind inside the garage, and there was still light in the sky.

Fletcher placed the teenager in the back of the Mercedes. He shut the door as Marie Clouzot rolled on to her back. She hadn't buttoned her coat and, oddly, wore nothing except a pair of white panties. Her long fingers with their dark-painted nails traced the visible scars along her chest and ribs, the tight skin over her breast implants. The scars were thick and wormy, all shapes, sizes and lengths. He knew they had been caused by knives, and by fire. He saw the marred areas where she had been branded with something hot, like a fireplace poker.

The fingers didn't touch the network of scars along the belly above her penis.

Her eyes were huge and white. 'They pulled me into alleys and beat me, men like you,' she croaked. 'When

419

I fought back, when I kicked them to the ground and made them bleed, men like you arrested me. Men like you judged me.'

Fletcher scooped up the car keys from the floor.

'Men like you sent me to a psychiatric hospital and injected me with poison because I was different. They tried to kill me and they raped me and I survived it. No matter what men like you did, I *survived*.'

Fletcher grabbed the laptop and moved to the car.

'I watched them suffer, every last one,' she said. 'I regret nothing. *Nothing*.'

As Fletcher backed out of the garage, he saw Marie Clouzot pulling something out of her jacket pocket – an ornate gold necklace adorned with jewels of various sizes and colours.

84

Fletcher took out Brandon Arkoff's cell phone as he raced around the side of the brick-faced building. It was three-storeys high, weathered and desolate, all the windows covered with security grilles.

The alleyway dumped him into a street of similar brick buildings. They were covered in graffiti, and the windows were broken. He turned left, the tyres spinning, and as he tore across the road he saw a weathered sign hanging from the front of the building: DECKLER & SONS PRINTING. He also found a street sign.

He called 911. A police dispatcher for the city of Baltimore picked up. He told the woman on the other end of the line about the bomb and gave her the address and the name of the building. Told her it had been set off by Brandon Arkoff and Marie Clouzot. Told her the bomb was planted most likely somewhere in the basement, told her she should evacuate the area, repeated the address and hung up. There was nothing more he could do. He took solace in the fact that the printing press was located in a desolate area of other vacant buildings. Collateral damage would be minimal, perhaps non-existent. Every street he passed was empty.

Fletcher glanced at his rearview mirror. The teenager

was exhibiting the outward physical signs of shock: sweating, rapid breathing and blank stares.

'I need to contact your parents,' Fletcher said. 'What's your name?'

The teenager's face was bloodless. He shook violently in shock and fear at what he'd just endured, at the pair of strange, black eyes staring at him from the rear-view mirror.

'Jimmy Weeks. That's my name. I'm from Petersburg, Pennsylvania.'

Fletcher asked for the boy's home number. Weeks gave it to him.

Fletcher's next call was to M. She answered her disposable cell. He told her he couldn't stay on long, then quickly explained that he'd used this phone to call 911. M didn't ask questions. She knew any 911 call placed to a police dispatcher anywhere in the country was automatically traced. He figured he had no more than five minutes until Baltimore dispatch triangulated his cell signal.

He gave her Weeks's name and phone number, told her where the teenager was from and followed it up with a concise summary of what had happened. M told Fletcher where to bring Jimmy Weeks. She gave him an address and directions, and they spent the remaining minutes discussing strategy and tactics.

When Fletcher hung up, he tossed the phone out of his window. The teenager watched from the backseat. Fletcher told him the truth.

'I don't want the police to trace it. My reasons have

to do with the man who attacked you. That man was a federal agent. The police and the FBI are looking for him. I need to make sure you arrive safely.

'The person I just spoke with works for a security company – one that specializes in finding missing people,' Fletcher said. 'Her company is going to contact your parents and let them know you're safe. When you meet her, she's going to give you a phone so you can call your parents. The important thing to remember is that you're safe.'

Jimmy Weeks gave a small nod and then retreated behind his blank gaze.

'If you want to talk, I'll listen. If you have any questions, I'll answer them. If you prefer to be left alone, I understand. Again, the important thing to remember is that you're safe.'

Weeks was no longer listening. He had buried his face in his hands, sobbing.

85

Fletcher reached Cherry Hill, New Jersey, in two hours. It took him another twenty minutes to locate the name of the street M had given him.

The road, long and wide, snaked its way through a quiet suburban neighbourhood of pleasant and well-kept middle-class homes. He took a right and saw, far ahead and parked against the kerb, the same Jeep he'd driven to meet M earlier in the day.

Fletcher parked a good distance away. He killed the lights and engine. M stepped out of the Jeep and headed towards him, a phone pressed up against her ear.

Fletcher turned around in his seat to speak to Jimmy Weeks. 'This is the woman I told you about, the one who works for the security company. Her name is M, like the letter. She's going to take you to a house, the white Colonial at the end of the cul-de-sac. The house belongs to a friend of hers – a friend who also works at the same security company.

'I need to speak to this woman in private for a moment. Please stay inside the car. When I'm finished, she'll take you to the house to call your parents.'

'Before you go,' Weeks said. 'I just . . . you know.'

'You're welcome.'

Fletcher lingered near the front bumper as M finished her conversation.

She hung up and said, 'People from our Philadelphia office are at the Weeks home right now. The police are there, and the FBI. They've been handling the phone traces in case James Weeks calls.'

'Have you spoken with Karim's lawyers?'

'Several times. They're in heated negotiations with federal prosecutors.'

'What kind of negotiations?'

'The FBI is willing to drop the charges against Karim in exchange for the surveillance videos from the New Jersey house, and all information he has regarding you. Karim told them to go to hell.'

I'm sure he did, Fletcher thought. 'And what have Karim's lawyers advised you to do?'

'To keep my head low for the time being.'

Fletcher unbuckled his leather belt.

M eyed him curiously.

'There's a micro-camera installed inside the buckle,' he said. 'Open it and you'll find a micro-SD card. I started recording the moment I woke up in my cage.'

'What's on it?'

'Borgia's confession, Marie Clouzot, all of it. The video will show me killing Borgia. You can tell your lawyers that I coerced you into helping me. They'll help you concoct a proper story. It doesn't matter what you say, really, because once federal prosecutors see the video stored on that micro-SD card, they'll do anything to prevent the truth from coming to light.'

'Karim won't stand for that,' she said. 'Neither will I.'

'Marie Clouzot was carrying a laptop. It's in the Mercedes, on the front seat.'

'What's on it?'

'I don't know, but I'm sure you'll find out.' Fletcher handed over his belt. 'We've spoken long enough. Get Mr Weeks to the house so he can speak to his parents.'

'You're leaving, aren't you?'

'I have to.'

'Why? You just told me this video contains Borgia's confession.'

'The government will never stop hunting me,' Fletcher said. 'They'll never admit to framing me for a crime I never committed.'

'Which is all the more reason why you need to fight this.'

'If I want to stay alive, I need to keep moving.'

M said nothing.

'Did you manage to find me a coat?' he asked.

'In the backseat of the Jeep. There's money in the pockets.'

'Thank you.'

'I will . . . I hope to see you again.'

M darted behind the wheel of the Mercedes and shut the door before he could reply.

Fletcher approached the Jeep. M had brought him a black winter parka. It was stuffed with down. The size was perfect: an XXL. She had also purchased a hat and gloves for him.

The Mercedes whisked past him as he slid inside the jacket. He settled himself in the front seat and watched M help the teenager out of the backseat.

There was no reason to linger. James Weeks was now in safe and reliable hands.

Fletcher started the Jeep. He needed to go to New York to retrieve his Jaguar. Then he needed to find a place to hide. He mulled over several possible destinations as he drove away.

86

Celine Strauss had celebrated the arrival of spring in Boston with a weekly ritual. Every Friday after work she stopped by the Oak Bar and ordered the same drink: a pomegranate and cucumber mojito. At nearly twenty bucks a pop, she drank no more than two. Money wasn't the issue. At thirty-three, she was about to become a partner at Banks & King, one of Boston's hottest public-relations firms. Any more than two mojitos, and someone would have to carry her to a cab. She was well past the age where she went out on Friday and Saturday evenings and got sloppy drunk – especially at an establishment like the Oak Bar.

The Oak Bar was part of the Oak Room, the city's premier steakhouse. Located inside the Tony Fairmont Hotel at Copley Plaza, the restaurant and bar resembled an old-fashioned cigar room decorated with Victorian flair – a small, intimate space crammed with tables and furniture, surrounded by rich, dark wood, chandeliers and heavy maroon brocade curtains with gold stitching. The place was a magnet for professional men. While she had never been in the market for a husband – she had no desire to have children or to settle down just because all her friends had – she did enjoy men, and the Oak Room offered an abundance of intelligent and successful candidates.

Celine went in looking sharp. She wore a dark charcoal pencil skirt and a matching jacket cut so it seemed stylish without being flamboyant. The shoes were tasteful open-toe pumps, and her jewellery was plain but elegant: diamond stud earrings and a Cartier watch. As she walked across the small dining room to the bar, she caught the stares of several men, most of them old enough to be her grandfather.

It was half past seven and there were no available chairs at the bar. She moved to the far-left corner, sidled up to the edge of the polished wood and waited for the bartender. The man to her right was nursing a scotch while he scrolled through his BlackBerry. The man to her left was reading a newspaper – that morning's edition of the *Boston Globe*.

He stood, and Celine was taken aback by how incredibly tall he was. His black suit jacket had been tailored to accommodate his broad shoulders and long arms. He motioned to his chair.

'That's not necessary,' she said. 'I can wait for one to open up.'

'Or you could simply take this one.' The man graciously held out the chair for her. 'Please.'

'Well, if you insist. Thank you.'

'My pleasure.'

The bartender came over. Celine ordered her drink and then turned slightly in her seat to the man who had just offered up his chair. She thought he was going to come on to her. She hoped he would. He was classically handsome, with chiselled features and a pair of deep green eyes – and his British accent was lovely.

Instead, he pushed the bridge of his black-framed glasses up his nose and went back to reading. His hair, thick and black, fell over the back collar of his shirt and nearly covered his ears. Normally she preferred a man with a more conservative haircut, but he carried the style well. He radiated confidence.

Celine wasn't the only woman who had noticed the tall, muscular Englishman. She saw several gazes around the bar stealing glances at him.

She was wondering how old he was when the bartender returned with her mojito.

The man was still reading the newspaper.

She had finished half her drink when she turned to him and said, 'What do you think?'

'Pardon?'

She leaned closer and tapped the *Globe*'s headline banner: 'Hospital Grounds Searched for Remains of Former Patients'. The accompanying colour picture showed police and forensic archaeologists searching a dense and heavily wooded area in Harvard, Massachusetts – the site of a former hospital called the Graves Rehabilitation Center. The Gothic brick building, tall and intimidating, had caught fire sometime in the mid-eighties and subsequently closed.

'Do you think it's true?' she asked. 'That the FBI was

involved in this clandestine research project that used patients for medical testing and buried their bodies?'

'The federal agent, Borgia, admitted he was a patient in the Behavioral Modification Project, along with his two partners, Marie Clouzot and Brandon Arkoff. The Baltimore police found evidence connecting them to the abductions.'

'The first two hospitals they searched, Texas and the other one.'

'Philadelphia,' he said. 'The Spaulding Psychiatric Center.'

'They didn't find any buried remains on the hospital grounds. And now they're searching this Graves place. They've been at it for nearly a week and haven't found anything remotely sinister.'

'No,' he said. 'Not yet.'

He looked sad when he said it.

'I take it you've seen the video.'

The man nodded.

'Unfortunately,' he added.

Celine knew what he meant. The video had gone viral two months ago. Like everyone else she had watched it. Once. She couldn't stomach a second viewing. Seeing all those starving and near-dead people locked in dog cages and trapped inside that abandoned printing press in Baltimore, the shootings . . . it had given her nightmares.

'Those poor children and their parents,' Celine said, shuddering at the thought. 'Still, there's no concrete piece of evidence linking the victims to the FBI and that BMP thing. Even if it's true, the FBI will squirm their way out of it. They always do.'

'You think so?'

'Absolutely. I'm in public relations. The Bureau is a PR machine. No one can beat them when it comes to spinning a story.'

The man smiled. He had nice teeth.

'I think you may be right.'

'Unfortunately,' she added with a smile of her own.

'Yes,' he said. 'Unfortunately.'

'I don't place much trust in the government either. But unless solid evidence comes forward concerning this research project, I think the story will die out.' Celine drank some of her mojito. 'What about Malcolm Fletcher? Do you think he's innocent?'

'The video seems to suggest he is.'

'True,' she conceded. 'He did rescue that boy, what's his name.'

'James Weeks.'

'That's it. But you know the saying, where there's smoke, there's fire.'

The man laughed quietly and picked up his glass. He was drinking bourbon. He polished it off and glanced at his watch.

'Can I buy you another drink?'

'No,' he replied. 'But I'll buy you one.'

'Thank you.' She offered a hand. 'Celine Strauss.'

'Francis Harvey. A pleasure to meet you.'

'Likewise.' She stood and touched his forearm as

she leaned in and said, 'Would you excuse me for a moment? I'll be right back.'

Celine went to the ladies' room to freshen up. When she returned, she found a fresh mojito waiting for her, but Francis Harvey was gone.

87

Malcolm Fletcher drove his new vehicle, a used but sound Volvo, out of Boston. He was heading to the western part of the state, the Berkshires, where he had rented a secluded home under the name Francis Harvey.

He had grown up during a time when payphones dominated nearly every city corner, restaurant and hospital. Cellular phones had slowly killed off the market, and, while payphones still existed, he had to use the Internet to find one.

The payphone he used to speak with Karim was located several miles from his rental home, at a gas station, which was conveniently closed for renovations. Fletcher parked his car and walked through the cool evening, the surrounding woods throbbing with crickets.

It was now mid-April and Karim was still inside Manhattan's Sloan-Kettering Hospital, undergoing rehabilitation. Three evenings a week, at quarter past nine, his bodyguard would wheel him into a different hospital room to use a different phone. The FBI was still monitoring Karim's home and business phone lines but had failed to secure a wiretap for the hospital switchboard.

His lawyers were still in negotiations with federal prosecutors, who were working feverishly to prevent him or one of his people from leaking the surveillance video of Hostage Rescue Team Operator Daniel Jackman's attempted murder of Ali Karim. Karim was using the video as a bargaining chip to force the FBI to go public with the names of the patients and doctors involved in the Behavioral Modification Project.

Fletcher used his smartphone to check his email. M had sent him an encrypted message telling him the number of the room where Karim would be this evening. Fletcher fed the quarters into the payphone.

'Always.'

'I don't have any news for you, I'm afraid. The drinking glass from the closet had fingerprints on it –'

'And since the FBI owns and operates the fingerprint database, they won't release Marie Clouzot's real identity.'

'Exactly,' Karim said. 'The Bureau is maintaining its stance that the Behavioral Modification Project, along with its doctors and nurses, never existed. As for the parents of James Weeks, they're under federal protection. My lawyers can't get access to them. I don't know which one was involved with the project, but haven't given up hope. My people are still working on it. We're using the video as leverage to get either the mother or the father to come forward and admit their role in this and –'

'You need to stop this.'

Karim laughed and started to cough.

'I live for this.'

'The FBI will never stop searching for me, even if you clear my name. You know that.'

'What do you suggest I do?' Karim asked. 'Roll over?'

'"There are truths which are not for all men, nor for all times."'

'Voltaire would think differently if he had to deal with the US government.'

'Use the remaining videos to protect yourself – and M. As long as you have those videos, the FBI will leave you alone. You'll be safe.'

Karim was silent for a moment.

'Until our next adventure, then.'

Fletcher softly replaced the phone on the cradle. He was examining the night sky when he heard a woman's scream.

The sound came from the dark woods directly in front of him.

Fisher cats and foxes, he knew, produced shrieks that mimicked a woman's. The fox was especially prone to do so if it discovered its mate dead.

He waited, listened for another scream. Seconds passed, and the only sound he heard came from the leaves rustling in the spring breeze.

Malcolm Fletcher walked through the darkness to investigate.

Acknowledgements

Each book is a challenge, and *The Killing House* proved to be especially difficult. Fortunately, I had several guides: Mari Evans, my amazing (and amazingly patient) editor; and my agent, Darley Anderson, and his talented staff – Clare Wallace, Madeleine Buston, Camilla Bolton and Zoe King.

Thanks to the people at Penguin UK: Louise Moore, Stefanie Bierwerth, Nick Lowndes, Donna Poppy. Patrick Tom Notestine, author of *Paramedic to the Prince: An American Paramedic's Account of Life Inside the Mysterious World of the Kingdom of Saudi Arabia*, was generous with his medical advice. All mistakes are mine.

And thanks to the people who keep me sane: my wife, Jen; Mark Alves, Randy Scott, Neal Sonnenberg, Gregg Hurwitz, John Connolly, Ted and Lynne Castonguay, Donna Bagdasarian and Maggie Griffin.

CHRIS MOONEY

THE SECRET FRIEND

Two dead girls in the river
Two tiny statues of the Virgin Mary concealed in their clothing
One CSI on the hunt for their killer

When Judith Chen is found floating in Boston's harbour, links are made with the murder of Emma Hale, a student who vanished without trace, only for her body to wash up months later.

CSI Darby McCormick is assigned to the case and uncovers a piece of overlooked evidence from the Hale investigation – which brings her into contact with Malcolm Fletcher, a former FBI agent now on the Most Wanted list after a string of bloody murders. And when a third student goes missing, Darby is led into a dangerous game of cat-and-mouse with deadly links to the past – and a man who speaks to the Blessed Virgin. A man who wants to be a secret friend to the girls he abducts …

'Masterful … dark and disturbing' Linda Fairstein

'Chris Mooney is a wonderful writer' Michael Connelly

CHRIS MOONEY

THE MISSING

The woman missing for five years.

The Crime Scene Investigator who finds her.

And the serial killer who wants them both dead …

When Boston CSI Darby McCormick finds a raving and emaciated woman hiding at the scene of a violent kidnap, she runs a DNA search to identify the Jane Doe. The result confirms she was abducted five years earlier and has somehow managed to escape from the dungeon in which she's been caged.

With a teenage couple also missing and Jane Doe seriously ill, the clock is ticking for Darby as she hunts for the dungeon before anyone else disappears or dies. And when the FBI takes over the investigation, it becomes clear that a sadistic serial killer has been on the prowl for decades – and is poised to strike again at any moment. A killer with links to horrors that Darby has desperately tried to bury in her past …

'The season's most unrelenting thriller … will keep readers enthralled'
George Pelecanos

He just wanted a decent book to read ...

Not too much to ask, is it? It was in 1935 when Allen Lane, Managing Director of Bodley Head Publishers, stood on a platform at Exeter railway station looking for something good to read on his journey back to London. His choice was limited to popular magazines and poor-quality paperbacks – the same choice faced every day by the vast majority of readers, few of whom could afford hardbacks. Lane's disappointment and subsequent anger at the range of books generally available led him to found a company – and change the world.

'We believed in the existence in this country of a vast reading public for intelligent books at a low price, and staked everything on it'
Sir Allen Lane, 1902–1970, founder of Penguin Books

The quality paperback had arrived – and not just in bookshops. Lane was adamant that his Penguins should appear in chain stores and tobacconists, and should cost no more than a packet of cigarettes.

Reading habits (and cigarette prices) have changed since 1935, but Penguin still believes in publishing the best books for everybody to enjoy. We still believe that good design costs no more than bad design, and we still believe that quality books published passionately and responsibly make the world a better place.

So wherever you see the little bird – whether it's on a piece of prize-winning literary fiction or a celebrity autobiography, political tour de force or historical masterpiece, a serial-killer thriller, reference book, world classic or a piece of pure escapism – you can bet that it represents the very best that the genre has to offer.

Whatever you like to read – trust Penguin.